TWO RIVERS

MICHAEL W. HENRY

TWO RIVERS

REDEMPTION PRESS

Front cover art work by David Wright (www.davidwrightart.com).

Published by Redemption Press, PO Box 427, Enumclaw, WA 98022.

Toll-Free (844) 2REDEEM (273-3336)

Redemption Press is honored to present this title in partnership with the author. The views expressed or implied in this work are those of the author. Redemption Press provides our imprint seal representing design excellence, creative content, and high-quality production.

Scripture quotations marked KJV are taken from the Holy Bible, King James Version, © 1979, 1980, 1982 by Thomas Nelson, Inc., Publishers. Used by permission.

This is a work of fiction. All of the characters, names, incidents, organizations, and dialogue in this novel are either the products of the author's imagination or are used fictitiously.

ISBN: 978-1-64645-081-7 (Paperback)
978-1-64645-082-4 (ePub)
978-1-64645-083-1 (Mobi)

Library of Congress Catalog Card Number: 2020903673

Dedicated to my parents,

Myron and Ruby Henry,

who set me on the path of adventurous faith.

CHAPTER ONE

On the night of the spring equinox 1840, three rituals took place.

THE FULL MOON CALLED FORTH shadows from the earth. They arose and danced like demons. Their images distorted and wavered in the bonfire's competing light. The shadows were fixed to the feet of twelve painted warriors wearing animal masks and fetishes. Though just past midnight, the drums would pound relentlessly until dawn. The ritual's swelling frenzy intoxicated the dancers and drummers. The intensity surged in anticipation of the climactic song, the cry of terror, and the sacrifice: an invocation of powerful spirits.

The spring equinox meant the celebration of new life for most Arapaho, but not for this renegade band. They sought the power to kill and curse their enemies—the tribe that had expelled them and the white men who had invaded their land.

In the invisible realm of the spirits, tension grew in the form of hatred, violence, and control.

Dark Wolf stepped forward. The restless drums halted. Wiry and bony, shrouded with a wolfskin, he lifted a buffalo horn high above his head and turned to the four winds. He shouted words, his sharp voice piercing the night. He turned and flipped the contents of the horn into the fire. It flared, shooting flames and sparks.

The dancers shouted and yipped. The drums throbbed again. Dark Wolf, the witch doctor, deftly coerced the fire at just the right moments to increase the ceremony's drama. He summoned a host of demons that would fill his men with the power to steal, kill, and destroy.

"It is time," he said.

Kicking Lion, a chieftain, dragged a girl into the circle. She had been kidnapped for this very occasion. It did not matter that she was from his village. She was an unspoiled sacrifice. Terrorized into silent submission, she awaited her doom at the hands of the wicked men. The sudden flash of a dagger ended her torment. The wound rendered its dark wine, which they guzzled and grabbed from each other. The fire became her transport to a peaceful world as the warriors resumed their intense dancing and received the infilling of evil spirits.

It had been a good dance. Two Rivers, the village holy man, was satisfied with the order and unity. Of the many spring dances, this was among the best. His heart assured him it had been honorable to the spirits. The Arapaho village had celebrated the circle of life in a dance that included women and children. The traditional ceremony to honor the end of winter and the coming of spring had for generations appeased the Giving Spirits. It would bring forth the fruit of the land for the tribe.

Dozens of men wore buffalo hides on their backs and horns on their heads. They crouched low, dancing and weaving around the circle formed by hundreds of spectators. Other men—the hunters—wore breechcloths and feathered headdresses, carried lances decorated with feathers and strips of fur, and held gourd rattles.

White and vermillion striped their faces and chests. They filed around the circle in search of buffalo. Pounding drums encouraged them as the song made a plea to the spirits to send the herds.

The spellbound children watched and moved their feet in rhythm. Old women hummed the familiar song and prayed for a plentiful year. Even in the reverence given to tradition, the villagers made room for laughter and pride. The costumed dances depicted the heroic exploits of braves and the interaction of the ancient ones with the spirit world. Men, women, and children humbly offered the symbols of their families through gifts of beadwork, pottery, and food to stay in harmony with Earth.

While the village celebrated, part of Two Rivers's heart grieved for the many losses the tribe had suffered in the past few months. Children had disappeared, women had been violated, and hunting parties had been attacked. Somehow, like a deer alert to a predator, he sensed that evil would be perpetuated that very night. While most tribes danced according to the custom, his rival, Dark Wolf, would be offending the Giving Spirits and seeking power from the destructive ones.

Two Rivers closed his eyes, and the disturbance in his soul created images in his mind—spirits clashing, maneuvering, and setting traps. The visions revealed mounting turmoil for the Blue Cloud People, the Arapaho, and all other tribes. The spirits told of a coming flood that would change their way of life. Two Rivers sensed that Dark Wolf saw it also, but instead of preparing the People, he devised schemes to feed his insatiable greed for power and revenge.

Under moonlight, Two Rivers hiked over a few hills, away from the pounding rhythms of the village. He needed to be alone to seek the wisdom of the wind and would continue moving until he received a sign. Then he might understand the gray cloud that covered his heart.

What was to be done about the increasing power that left fear and destruction in its wake? Dark Wolf had recruited many rebels who responded to his every command to inflict damage on innocent families and travelers. Two Rivers worried that his own power would weaken against the spreading poison. He was withdrawing now to protect his tribe and to seek the wisdom to fight.

Deep down, though, he perceived the answer had already been given to him in previous visions. He recalled the vision of a white seed planted in the earth, which sprouted and grew into a great tree that protected many birds and animals. But what did it all mean?

Two Rivers raised his hands to the full moon. "My fathers, I will fast and sing until you give understanding to your son. What is your wisdom?"

Bearded men in black suits and women in long black or gray skirts filled the sanctuary even after the service had begun. The rented pews were full, as were the common pews in the back, and many people stood against the walls.

The Methodist Church of Buffalo, New York, was hosting a congregation that had gathered from throughout the Genesee Conference to witness the commissioning of Reverend Bannister's missionary band.

After the glorious hymns and the inspirational sermon, twelve men and women moved forward to kneel at the altar. There the superintendent, the mission secretary, and Pastor Gilbert read scriptures from the *Book of Discipline*, laid hands on each missionary, and commissioned them in the name of Jesus Christ.

By the time they reached Allen Hartman, the repeated words had become monotonous. But as the mission secretary laid hands on Allen's head and said, "Take authority to preach the gospel," vibrating energy surged through Allen's body. Another wave rushed through him at the words "I commission you to live and minister among the Indians, in Jesus's name."

An image flashed into Allen's mind: the Lord Jesus towered above a mountain range, holding a shepherd's staff and watching over his people. Warmth coursed through Allen's heaving chest like an ember fanned to flame.

Following the service and reception, Allen strolled out of the brick church onto the cobblestone street with his parents, Reverend Arthur and Ruth Hartman.

"It looks like it's going to clear up," his mother said. "Those clouds have been so gloomy."

"I hope so." Allen's father slipped on his black flat-brimmed hat and settled it into position. "It would be nice to have a few days of sunshine."

Allen gazed up at the western sky and spotted the full moon through a break in the clouds. *I wonder if the Indians are looking at the same moon.*

CHAPTER TWO

THE CURTAINS DRIFTED UP AND flapped like the white falcon Allen had just seen in his dream. He shifted the pillow against the oak headboard and leaned back on it. Allen breathed deeply, willing his heartbeat to slow to a reasonable pace.

When he closed his eyes, the image invaded his mind, of a wolf so black it seemed to be silhouetted against the night shadows. So instead he kept his eyes open and watched the curtains flutter in the cool breeze that slipped in under the partly open window.

In the dream, Allen had ridden across a grassy plain until he came to where two rivers joined, forming a single, mighty flow. His horse stamped the ground, and before Allen could nudge the steed, it leaped into the water as if spurred by a shared thought. Together they flowed in the strong current until it swept them onto a bank.

Not far from where he emerged from the river, a group of people dressed like Indians laughed and danced. Allen dismounted and ran to them. He was acquainted with them. They turned toward him, their faces transfigured into the horrifying decay of death. The sun dropped rapidly, and in the hazy darkness, a wolf howled.

Allen panicked and rushed back to his horse and the safety of the river, but the wolf, snarling and snapping, charged him and lunged for his throat. In the moment before he felt the hot breath and the fangs about to snap, a white falcon flew above them. As it soared, Allen looked down on the wolf below, as if peering over the bird's wing, as if he were one with the falcon.

He now took a deep breath. "What does it mean, Lord?"

But no answer came. God had been clear in calling Allen to missionary service and confirming it with many signs. Why would God be silent about this frightening image that Allen felt sure was related to his upcoming venture? He would be leaving in a few days for the Oregon Territory wilderness. Was this dream a warning? An indication he would die? Or was it a message of intimidation by an evil spirit to pressure Allen into disobedience?

"Lord, I am going because I know it is your will. I will be a minister to the Indians even if it means dying for you." Speaking the words out loud might have been unnecessary, but it convinced his mind to relax and forget about the wolf.

His thoughts drifted to packing, to collecting the last of his financial support, and finally to Violet. She could not have looked prettier than she had earlier that night at the commissioning service. She radiated beauty and pride in him. Her blue velvet dress accentuated her sky-blue eyes, making them sparkle even more than normal. Blond springy curls framed her pretty face, and she moved gracefully among the people. Allen felt himself beam when she took his arm as she charmed the reception attendees. Everybody told them what a fine couple they made. She would be the perfect pastor's wife. She played the piano and sang beautifully. And she loved to teach children Bible lessons. Images of Violet calmed Allen's mind.

In the morning, Allen sipped at a cup of coffee at the breakfast table.

"What an awful dream," his mother said as she refilled his cup.

Allen caught his father's eye. "Do you think it means anything?"

"Probably. But I'll have to ponder it for a while. There is no doubt in my mind God called you as a missionary. So it comes as no surprise that the devil will try many schemes to keep you from fulfilling that call, including fear and intimidation." His father's twenty years as a pastor had produced a great supply of wisdom for his parishioners and his family.

Allen swallowed hard. "Do you think it means I will die?"

"I'm not sure, Allen. You don't appear to die in the dream, but the threat of death comes very close. I tend to believe it has a prophetic message that you are helping Indians who are facing death, but you are spared."

"I was wondering if the white bird was perhaps carrying me to heaven after I died." He watched his mother's reaction from the corner of his eye, hoping he hadn't worried her.

"If it were a dove, I might believe that. But a falcon makes me think you are involved in a spiritual battle. I'm not sure what the two rivers indicate either." He peered into Allen's eyes. "In any case, I want to assure you we will be praying for you every day."

His mother joined them at the table and covered Allen's hand with hers. "When you were a baby, we dedicated you to the Lord, knowing that it might mean sending you to the uttermost parts of the earth. We also knew it could be dangerous. It's just hard to face it as reality and not just a promise." Tears welled. "But we are holding to our part of the promise, Allen. And we will pray for you daily."

"It gives me great security knowing that you two are praying. More than anyone else, I trust you." Allen squeezed his mother's hand. "I'm convinced I can face anything. My greatest fear is to be unfaithful to this calling to serve in Oregon. I never want to be distracted or discouraged from it."

Days later Allen rode his black mare across the edge of Buffalo to the hill where Violet's home stood like a castle with a grand view of the lake. He hitched the horse to a rail, strode up the long stairway, and tapped the shiny brass knocker.

Mrs. Chamberlain opened the door and offered him a warm smile. "Hello, Allen. Won't you come in? We've been expecting you." She swept aside to make room for him to enter. "I trust you had a decent ride into town."

"Yes, ma'am, thank you."

"Mr. Chamberlain is in his study. Why don't you join him there while I check on the progress of your lunch? Violet will be down in a minute, I'm sure."

"Thank you."

Allen cleared his throat at the doorway to the study. Violet's father, John Chamberlain, was a financier and heavily invested in building the city of Buffalo. He had provided the bulk of funds to build the Methodist church, where he faithfully attended and served as a board member.

"Allen. Come in. It's always good to see you. And I must say that Violet is excited that you're coming." Mr. Chamberlain gestured toward a tall-backed leather chair.

Allen sat and tried to get comfortable.

"Well, you'll be leaving in just a few days. You must be very excited."

"Yes, sir." Allen slid to the edge of his seat and clasped his hands in front of him. "I am excited. I have a few details to take care of, but otherwise I am ready to leave on the fourth."

"That's wonderful. And how is your funding coming along?" Chamberlain avoided Allen's eyes.

"Of the thousand dollars necessary, I have raised about four hundred in cash offerings from several churches. And with the seven hundred and fifty dollars that you and your associates have promised, that will put me in good standing for several years. I hope to build a nice house so that Violet can join me and live in comfort." Allen glanced around the well-adorned room. A log cabin would be no match for this grand house.

Chamberlain frowned. "Allen, I'm afraid I have some bad news. The past couple of years have been very hard on the economy in Buffalo—all over the region, for that matter. Many businesses are in trouble. They haven't been able to make payments on their loans. My associates have had to back out on their promise to you. It is difficult for me as well, but because you'll likely become my son-in-law, I have put together all I can give—five hundred dollars. I wish I could meet the full pledge myself, but it's just impossible right now." Chamberlain pursed his lips.

Allen huffed. He felt like he'd just been punched. *No, no, no.* "Five hundred. That's very generous of you. And please tell the others that I understand about hardships. I'm sure the Lord will provide by some other means."

"There you are!" Violet flowed into the room, her yellow dress sweeping the floor.

Her father's eyes lit up, and he stood to greet her. "My lovely daughter. You certainly bring the sunshine with you." He leaned down and kissed her cheek. "I'd better leave you two alone for a moment."

Allen breathed in the fresh air her presence offered. Violet's smile chased away the drizzly clouds of frustration and brought rays of hope and encouragement.

"You look handsome in that black suit. It makes your blue eyes look bolder." She reached up to touch his wavy brown hair. "You're as strong as a farmer and yet so passionate to serve people." She sank against his chest.

"You are going to make a lovely missionary's wife."

"I can just picture you in the pulpit of the First Methodist Church in New York City. And then as a denominational leader." She gently bit the tip of her index finger.

"I can't imagine that ever happening," Allen said.

"Come along. I have a picnic lunch for us." She led him by the hand outside the house and to a blanket on the grass, where a basket waited. Under the bright-blue sky, they chatted and munched on bread, cheese, and fried chicken.

"Allen, here we are, alone on a beautiful day, yet you seem distracted."

"I'm sorry." He forced a smile. "Your father just told me that his group is not going to give the offering they pledged. So I don't have all the funds I need. I'm disappointed. Sorry that it's spoiling our time together."

"It's not Father's fault. The others are going through hard times." Her face tightened.

"Please don't take me wrong." Allen lifted her hand. "I'm not blaming anyone. I just don't know how I'm going to get the last hundred dollars. I'm supposed to give it to Reverend Bannister tomorrow. If I don't have it all, he might not let me go."

"Maybe it's the Lord's way of saying you're not supposed to go. Maybe it's just a test, like Abraham sacrificing Isaac." The corners of her mouth lifted slightly, but her eyes stayed focused on the grass. "You have shown yourself willing, but quite possibly the Lord has another plan for you."

"No, that can't be it. I am sure of this calling, and it's been confirmed in so many ways. I think this is more of a last-minute test of my faith. Also, I had that wolf dream again."

"Oh, that terrible wolf." She grimaced. "Do you really think God would call you into such a dangerous place? I think you'd be more valuable to him here."

"I think the dream is a prophetic message that I am supposed to go and help people who are in desperate need. The wolf tries to stop me, but he can't. My father thinks this too. Yes, it's making more sense to me now as I speak it."

"Well then, if that's the case, God will provide the money for you. Maybe you'll just have to sell something—something you love or think you can't live without."

Allen gazed across the long yard, his sight landing on his horse.

"That's it! I can sell my horse." He jumped up. "I can sell the mare for a hundred dollars easily. I'll bet Mr. Harper will buy her. Yes! That's brilliant. It answers so many questions." He took her by the hands, pulled her up, and held her close. "You. Violet. My encourager."

She gasped.

"Violet, this is just another reassurance for me. We are meant to be together. We've been sweethearts for a long time. I want to wait until the proper time for a formal proposal, but right now I want to renew my intentions to you. I want you to be my wife. After I build a house for us, I will come back and propose to you on my knee. We'll have a splendid wedding, and you'll join me at the mission.

"I promise you, Violet"—he cupped her face—"I will cross rivers and streams and push through blizzards if I have to. I will fight off wild Indians, fierce beasts, even wolves, because I love you and want to spend my life with you serving God. You make me feel confident and bold, like I can do anything. I need you in my life so I can be the man that God wants me to be."

"But, Allen . . . do you really have to go?"

"Shhh, don't say anything." He pressed a finger to her lips. "Just let me tell you how lovely you are. You're prettier than any woman I've ever seen. But it's your beautiful spirit that makes me soar. You have a heart of gold for me and for the ministry. I've seen it when you teach little ones. Those Indian children don't know what a wonderful blessing that's coming to them. With you by my side, we will have the greatest church in the wilderness of the Oregon Territory."

Allen hugged Violet. "I feel magnificent!" He released her and spread his arms. "Hallelujah!"

Violet stooped and packed up the basket. "I'd rather have the greatest church in New York City."

Her pouty voice stopped Allen cold. He dropped his arms to his sides. He'd been insensitive to her feelings. Of course Violet didn't want to be apart from him. That was why she was acting this way. But she'd soon embrace the same passion he had for missionary work. There could be no other way.

CHAPTER THREE

THE LITTLE MAN DROPPED CHUNKS of buffalo meat into the stew-pot that hung on a tripod over a small fire. He held a few scraps out to a dog whose every rib could be counted through its short tan fur. It gazed through droopy eyes. The animal flinched constantly, as if expecting to be kicked at any moment. But Dark Wolf scratched behind the dog's ear and fed him another piece of meat.

The witch doctor wore a buffalo-hide shoulder wrap, a breech-cloth, and buffalo leggings that sagged around his ankles, exposing skinny legs. Warriors used to ridicule him. Now they feared him.

Sensing someone's approach, Dark Wolf stood and snatched his lance in one swift move. He closed his eyes, listening and waiting. Intuition told him that the intruder was not dangerous. He leaned the lance against the tree and returned to his stew. In a moment, a warrior rode into view and tied his black-and-white pinto to a tree. He stood at the edge of camp.

"You bring something worth my time?" Dark Wolf placed more sticks on the fire.

The warrior swallowed hard and lifted a doeskin bag full of seeds and roots.

"You do the work of a woman?" Dark Wolf spat.

"No. I stole it from a woman."

Dark Wolf glared at the warrior. "Why did you not bring me the woman?"

"I had her . . ."

"You were going to rape her, but she got away." Dark Wolf gestured toward the warrior's groin. "Do you still feel the pain where she kicked you?"

"I have this." He held up black locks. "The hair of Yellow Flower, the niece of Two Rivers, the daughter of his sister."

Dark Wolf accepted the homage. A kidnapped woman had many uses, but the hair of his enemy's family had a special value. With it he could demonstrate his greater power from a distance. He would strike fear and pain in Two Rivers and his village by killing his niece. Yes, he would inflict a strategic wound on his rival.

"Next time do not let a woman run from you. Perhaps your manhood will not suffer." Dark Wolf dismissed the warrior with a wave of his hand.

Squatting by the cook fire, the witch doctor stroked the dog, clearly longing for another piece of meat. He stirred the stew, scheming with grim satisfaction. "This will be a good night."

Long past midnight, Dark Wolf sat in front of a small fire in his tipi. Positioned before him were snake, raven, wolverine, and wolf skulls. He massaged the black strands of Yellow Flower's hair and rubbed into them a pasty substance made from rattlesnake venom. He chanted softly but with an intensity that produced sweat, which dripped from his beak-like nose.

"Uncle! Uncle! Yellow Flower needs you." A young boy stood outside the medicine man's lodge and called to him.

Two Rivers groaned as he arose from the buffalo blankets. He gathered his medicine bag and pipe and stepped into the cool night air. Earlier he had given his niece sage tea and sung over her when he had learned of the assault. He assumed that the tormentor might attempt to use her hair to curse the young woman.

But as Two Rivers knelt beside Yellow Flower, he suspected a more serious sorcery. Gray and clammy, she had the look and smell of someone bitten by a rattlesnake. Since the spirits had taught him the cure-song for snake venom, he would start there. Yellow Flower's medicine came from the deer spirit and would usually be strong enough to fight off such attacks, but this sickness was not usual.

Two Rivers smoked his pipe, sang, waved his ancient turtle rattle over her, rubbed her with grass and herbs, and sang again. In the blackest hour, between midnight and dawn, her fever broke, but the delirium persisted, and she grew more agitated. In the deep concentration of his song, he saw images of the wolverine and the wolf and knew immediately he was fighting Dark Wolf, whose power was strong. But the evil witch doctor usually made the mistake of pouring it all out in a direct assault. This time, though, he'd connived, adding secondary curses. Two Rivers did not worry, for his songs were more powerful than Dark Wolf's curses. Two Rivers would endure the struggle until his niece was set free.

He cleansed her with song and rattle until the afternoon. Yellow Flower awoke, ate some food, and left her bed, eventually returning to her chores.

Weary of soul, the medicine man shuffled to the river. He sagged into the water and let it run over his body. The coolness refreshed him. He scrubbed his body with sand, then waded out to a rock, on which he sat and sang a prayer of peace and restoration.

Later in the night, he dreamed of a white falcon coming into his tipi and smoking the flat pipe with him.

Two Rivers rose in the morning to greet the sun. "Oh Great Father, you provide for all things. Will you provide wisdom? Why do you send the vision of the white falcon and no understanding? When will this come to pass?"

CHAPTER FOUR

ALLEN ARRIVED HOME AFTER DARK. The soft glowing light from the windows comforted him, but sadness tugged on his heart. The familiar sight soon would be a memory of what he'd left behind—maybe forever. He loved the small farm. He loved the village of Tonawanda and the congregation. He loved riding the preaching circuit with his father.

Through the window he watched his parents sipping tea at the dining room table and, no doubt, praying.

"Thank you, Lord, for this home. I will miss it greatly."

Allen stabled the mare and brushed her down. "I'll miss you too, Glory." He patted her muzzle. "You have been faithful and strong, and I'm sorry I have to sell you. Somehow it doesn't seem like a fitting end to our friendship."

Walking into the house, Allen greeted his parents with a weak smile. He slumped into a chair at the table. "I'm really going to miss this sweet home."

"I can only imagine. It's the only home you've known since you were born upstairs twenty-three years ago." Mother held up a cup. "Would you like some tea?"

"No thanks. I'll be going to bed right away."

"You don't look like the day has ended victoriously," Father said.

"Of all the times in which I'd expect a rudder to steer my course, this would seem the one. But I've felt tossed about by the wind all day long." Allen paused. "I went to the Chamberlains' to receive the pledge of seven hundred and fifty dollars, but I received only five hundred.

"Then I was having lunch with Violet, feeling discouraged, when she suggested I sell Glory to get the final amount. I tried the rest of the day, but no one can give me a hundred dollars for her. The economic depression has everyone worried. Later, I met up with Reverend Bannister to give him nine hundred, but he insisted on having the full amount. He said if I don't have the final hundred dollars by tomorrow, I won't be able to go."

"Oh my." His mother shook her head. "I can't believe he would be that rigid. After all you've been through, and the commissioning."

"He made it clear that each member of the missionary band would raise a thousand dollars for the cause. I agreed to that as well." Allen rubbed his temples. "All the money was pledged—even more—but now it's not coming through. He said the money is the final confirmation from the Lord."

"Allen, don't worry." His father stood and placed his hand on Allen's shoulder. "We should get some sleep. We'll pray together in the morning. I believe the Lord will provide the money somehow."

By noon the next day, their carriage rolled to a stop by the stables in the Canal District. His mother remained seated while Allen and his father climbed down. It was not the part of town they were used to visiting. The men from the church had come before to preach to the dock and canal workers on the street corners, but this was no place for a lady.

The livery man stepped out. "What do you want?"

"Good day, sir. I'm selling the mare, and I wanted you to take a look." Allen smiled, but he hated to part with his fine horse.

"Yeah. What's wrong with her?" The unshaven man studied the animal.

"There is nothing wrong with her. She is healthy and a fine brood mare."

The livery man rubbed the back of his neck. "I'll give you forty."

"Forty!" Allen gasped. "She's easily worth a hundred and twenty dollars or more. Anyone can see that."

"Forty is my offer. Take it or leave it."

"I need at least a hundred for her." Allen needed the money, but he didn't want to give his beloved mount away.

"She ain't worth that to me."

"I'll come down to seventy-five, but that's it." Just saying the words made Allen's stomach churn.

"Maybe I can do something with her. I'll go fifty."

Oh, Lord, there must be some other way. He looked at his father, who only shrugged. The decision was wholly Allen's. His two trunks and canvas bundle with all his possessions were in the carriage.

Another wagon pulled up to the livery. Two men, a father and teenage son, who appeared to be canal workers, demanded attention.

"Throw on two sacks of feed," the father said.

"Can't you see I'm busy here?" the livery man barked.

The canal men took in the scene with narrowed eyes, like predators sensing weakness in the clean, honest folk.

"Arthur?" Allen's mother called softly, and her husband climbed onto the seat next to her. He clasped her hand, and they bowed their heads together.

Something didn't feel right. Allen needed to get his parents out of there. "I think I'll pass. I'm going to look for a better offer. Thanks just the same."

"Hold on," the livery man said. "I can see you're under some pressure. I'll give you sixty dollars for the mare, but that's as generous as I can be."

Against his better judgment, Allen agreed. It wasn't $100, but it was closer.

"I'll be right back," said the livery man, disappearing into the shadowy stables.

"Glory, I'm so sorry. I just pray he won't mistreat you." Allen held the mare's muzzle and patted her neck one last time.

The man returned, handed Allen sixty dollars, and led Glory away.

"Got anything else to sell, mister?" The canal man, smelling of alcohol, peered into the back of the carriage. "What about that musket?"

Allen looked down and saw the butt of his Pennsylvania long rifle sticking out of the canvas. "Sorry. I can't sell that. It belonged to my grandfather, and it was passed down to me when he died. It's special to me." His maternal grandfather had used the rifle in the War of 1812. Allen used it hunting for deer, black bear, and turkeys and had become a proficient hunter with it.

The canal man reached in and pulled out the musket before Allen could stop him.

"Now, that's a fine-looking gun." He stroked the long black-walnut stock with scrolls of brass inlays. "I'll give you twenty-five for her."

"It's not for sale." Allen glanced around and scratched his head. It would bring him closer to the goal . . . but it was such a good rifle. His time was running out. He shook his head. "Unless you'll give me forty."

"Forty. That's a might steep for this old musket." The stranger sighted down the barrel, aiming at a woman down the street. He stepped around Allen again and tossed the long rifle up to his son. "What do you think, Jackson?"

Allen held his breath and watched the dirty hands caressing his inheritance. He moved forward with his left hand reaching out. "Be careful . . ."

"It ain't worth no forty dollars," said the youth as he leaned forward to hand it back to his father. But the gun dropped from his hand, scraped against the wagon wheel, and clattered on the cobblestones.

Allen gasped and grabbed the rifle before the man could reach it. The son laughed. A foot-long gouge running down the side of the stock had knocked out some brass. In an instant, the heirloom had been transformed into heartache. Allen's face burned. *Why is this happening?*

"It sure ain't worth forty now," the man said, chuckling.

Allen turned and walked away. He climbed onto the carriage behind his parents and held the gun on his lap with the good side up.

"Let's go please."

After a long silence, they arrived at the guest house where Bannister and the missionary band were staying until their departure the next day.

"Allen, leave the gun with me." His father shifted in the front seat and faced him. "It didn't seem right selling it anyway. I'll take it to the gunsmith and have it refinished." He offered a kind smile. "You'll get it back someday."

"Thank you, Father. It's heartbreaking, but I think that's best."

"Very well." Father nodded. "Let's go find Reverend Bannister."

The Hartmans entered the Tudor-style inn across the street from the lakefront. Bannister and his wife, Olive, welcomed them. But Bannister's forehead creased upon hearing that Allen was forty dollars short.

"Allen, this is very disappointing. I've been hoping that you would be along with us. But you understand that this is the final confirmation that you are to be part of my missionary band. Everyone else has paid the full amount. You're the last one, and you've fallen short. I'm sorry." His eyes were cold and held no grace.

That is it then. God must have some other design for him. Violet was right after all. It had been a terrible day, and now it was sealed.

Numb, Allen turned and strode past the parlor where his parents were talking with another couple—he didn't care to see who. He hurried across the street and gazed at the horizon of Lake Erie. A steamboat docked a short distance away. Allen reached down and picked up a few loose stones from a pothole in the cobblestone street. He threw one into the water; it made an insignificant splash in the great lake.

"Allen!" his mother called. "Allen, dear, come over here please."

He crossed the street to join her.

"Come. I want you to see someone," she said. "You remember Martha Jolifer and her husband, Virgil? They are also part of the band."

Martha wore a black skirt and gray peplum jacket with a double row of buttons and high collar. She'd pulled her black hair into a tight bun at the back of her head. She was as tall as Virgil, who slouched in a wrinkled gray suit. His bald head reflected the sun.

"Happy to see you again, Allen," Martha said. Her husband stood quietly behind her. "Your parents tell me that your funding fell short."

Allen nodded.

"I think I can be of some help. You see, the Lord provided abundant offerings for me . . . um, for us. I would be delighted to turn over forty dollars to your account."

"You don't have to do that," Allen said.

"Oh, pish-posh. I won't hear any of that. The Lord has provided, and it must be for this purpose. Let's go find Bannister, um, Reverend Bannister, and settle it right now."

Startled by the sudden change of prospects, Allen was speechless.

Martha took his arm and led him past her husband and into the room where Bannister sat looking over his ledger. "Besides," she added, "I'd hate to see such a handsome young man be disappointed."

"I don't know what to say," Allen said, "but thank you."

"Not to worry. Not to worry. I'm sure we'll find some way for you to pay me back."

Martha, though an attractive woman fifteen years Allen's senior, possessed a certain sternness around her eyes and mouth.

"This is an interesting turn of events. May the Lord be praised," Bannister said. He shook hands with Allen and welcomed him to the band. "We will all gather tomorrow one hour before the ship sails."

Allen found his parents and hugged them. "What a day this has been."

"I'm grateful our prayers have been answered," Mother said.

"Praise the Lord." His father's eyes glistened with tears. "Well, I'll be. Tomorrow you're off."

"Yes. Tomorrow the journey begins."

CHAPTER FIVE

ALLEN JOINED BANNISTER'S MISSIONARY BAND in the conference room of the hotel located across the street from the wharf. Everyone had delivered their belongings to be loaded onto the steamship and now waited for their departure. Allen studied the faces of his new comrades.

The Reverend Samuel Bannister, a tall, barrel-chested man with large features, made a striking and formidable figure. He'd gained renown by preaching with a booming voice through which the Holy Ghost broke the hearts of stubborn men. He was credited with igniting revivals in Buffalo, Rochester, Syracuse, and as far away as Philadelphia and Baltimore. When people claimed that Samuel Bannister walked in the footsteps of John Wesley, he denied it but beamed with satisfaction.

"I am glad that we are all together and on time," Bannister said. "Everything is in order, just the way I like it. I am honored to have been asked by the bishop to take on the challenge of expanding the Methodist church in the mission field of the Oregon Territory.

"I am also honored that you have all responded to the call. Allow me to make introductions. This is my wife, Olive."

A portly woman with a friendly face gave a welcoming smile. She wore her brown hair parted in the middle with matching buns behind each ear.

"I am also pleased to present my right-hand man, Reverend Reginald Foster, who organizes my evangelistic crusades, and his lovely wife, Beulah."

The couple nodded. Foster, a short man with the pasted-on grin of a politician, seemed to assess those around him. His tailored black suit bore precise creases. Beulah was the same height and nodded in agreement with everything her husband said.

"And next we have Reverend Phineas and Eva Mills."

They wore matching spectacles and nervously darted their eyes about.

"Then Jacob and Rachel Herbert," Bannister said. "And what are your boys' names?"

"This is Joseph and Benjamin," Jacob said as he pointed to each one.

The boys shifted from one foot to the other.

"And you can tell by the family's red hair that they have Irish heritage," Bannister said and laughed. "That brings us to Virgil and Martha Jolifer."

"Thank you, Reverend," Martha said. "I believe we are the only ones on this team with missionary experience. I would also mention that even though Virgil is not ordained, he does possess many gifts."

Virgil scratched his bald head and looked down.

"Yes, thank you, Martha," Bannister said. "And next is Gloria Shannon, our only single woman, and next to her, Allen Hartman, our only single man." Again Bannister laughed, but when no one else did, he continued. "Well, I suppose it is time for us to be going. We will have plenty of time to become better acquainted on our journey. Also, keep in mind that I will join you in Portsmouth, Ohio, after I address the General Conference in Baltimore. Reginald Foster will take charge until then."

Allen stood next to his parents while scanning the crowd for Violet. He wanted to see her smile one last time. He wanted to kiss her goodbye and reassure her with words he had rehearsed for days. Once he came back for her, they would never again be apart.

"Have you seen Violet, or any of the Chamberlains?" he asked his parents again.

His father shook his head. "They must have been held up."

"I'm sure Violet is heartbroken, Allen." His mother linked her arm around his. "No doubt she'll write you a long letter soon."

The captain's mate hollered the final boarding call.

"Time to say goodbye," Father said.

"I'm going to miss you so much." Allen embraced his mother.

"The Lord be with you." Tears streamed down her cheeks.

His father put his hand on Allen's shoulder. "We'll be praying every day for you, son."

Allen's eyes welled. He tried hard to swallow the lump in his throat. Finally, Allen hugged his father firmly. When they released, Father nodded.

"I'll pray for you as well." Allen took several steps up the gangplank, then turned back. "Please tell Violet goodbye and that I'll write to her."

The big wheel paddles began to churn, creating a cascade of foaming swells. The ship slid away from the dock and headed out to open water. Allen stood amidst the crowd of passengers at the stern, hoping to catch a glimpse of Violet. She did not appear. Why hadn't she come?

His parents waved.

When he could no longer recognize the people on the shore, Allen strolled to the bow. He gazed at the western horizon, took a deep breath, and spoke into the wind. "Lord, I'm ready to go with you into the wilderness."

"May I join you?" Gloria stepped to his side and leaned on the railing. "I don't want to interrupt if you prefer to be alone."

"Feel free to stay. I was just thanking the Lord for a beautiful day and a marvelous creation."

"It is a glorious day to begin our journey."

Gloria wore a blue-gray dress with a black collar. Her sandy-blond hair was pulled back into a bun. Her hazel eyes sparkled like the lake. Allen was acquainted with Gloria from working at evangelism meetings.

Allen shifted his weight against the railing and faced her. "Do you feel nervous about moving to the wilderness?"

"No, I'm thrilled with anticipation. A year ago I prayed, 'Lord, I'm twenty-seven years old. If you're not going to give me a husband, give me an adventure.' And here I am."

Upon arriving in Cleveland, the band reloaded their belongings onto a barge. Allen watched as the hoggy adjusted straps on one of the towing mules.

"I only go as far as Akron," the grizzled man said. "Other crews will get you through all one hundred forty locks down to Portsmouth."

"Are there any points of interest along the way?" Allen patted the mule.

The hoggy looked over the missionary band. "Doubt it."

The oak, elm, and willow trees along the banks of the Ohio and Erie Canal stretched from one end of the state to the other. The three-hundred-mile trip from Cleveland to Portsmouth took eighty hours.

Allen found a space to sit and observe the view and the interactions of his new friends.

Reginald Foster seemed to take his leadership role seriously by reviewing his plan for building a mission. Then he would ask someone to share his or her life story.

On the fourth day, Martha Jolifer fidgeted and huffed. "I can't believe we're paying a dollar and seventy cents per person to be dragged along so sluggishly through this foul-smelling, insect-infested canal."

"I should think you encountered similar discomforts in Argentina," Allen said.

She and Virgil had spent two years establishing the Methodist mission school in Argentina with Reverend Dempster. But their school closed, and facing other hardships, the Jolifers had been forced to return to the United States.

Martha swatted at a fly on her forehead. "Yes, of course we did, and far worse than this. I guess I shouldn't complain. Virgil and I are delighted to have another opportunity to serve God among the lost. We knew immediately upon Reverend Bannister's invitation that it was our open door to join the band."

"Let me say again, Mrs. Jolifer, how grateful I am for your generosity. Without it I would not be on this ship with you," Allen said.

"Young man, you are quite welcome. It just didn't seem right to leave you behind for lack of forty dollars."

The next day they reached the end of the canal. Men barked orders to secure the barge and release the mules. Allen and the band members stepped off the barge and looked around at more trees, dirt riverbanks, and a few brick houses.

Foster hired wagons to haul the band's considerable belongings to a warehouse on the Ohio River. They kept the luggage and trunks that held their clothing and sundries while they awaited Bannister's arrival.

Because they were not sure when Bannister would arrive, they found lodgings. They separated into smaller groups for their accommodations. The Fosters, Mills, and Olive stayed at the Philip Moore House. Martha insisted on staying there as well but sent Virgil with Allen. The two men were hosted in a farmhouse a half mile away. The local pastor's wife invited Gloria to stay in the parsonage of the Methodist church. The Herberts, with their boys, Benny and Joseph, went to the home of a church family

On the third day, a message arrived from Bannister saying he'd take a steamboat from Pittsburgh to Portsmouth and arrive on May 7, three days from then.

Feeling the need to explore, Allen followed the river road to the west. The warm sun on his face felt good. He'd hiked quite a distance before coming over a low hill. The narrow road led between a farmhouse and a run-down white church with a bell tower. Over the door a sign hung: Methodist Church, All Welcome.

Allen stopped and took in the poor section of town. Several ramshackle cabins were randomly situated along the road beyond the church.

The ring of laughter caught his attention. He looked to his left and spotted three children playing leapfrog near a shack where a man sharpened an axe on a grindstone. The church was in need of repair and paint. Instead of asking for the pastor, Allen walked on to the riverbank.

The Ohio seemed expansive after spending the last several days on the narrow canal. He closed his eyes and listened to the water lapping against the shore. The birds whistled their spring salutations. A musty odor rose from the ground. The Kentucky side, about 250 yards away, mirrored the Ohio countryside, with oak, walnut, hickory, maple, and elm trees.

Allen sat on the grassy bank to enjoy the scenery. A Scripture passage from Ezekiel that told of a river streaming from the altar in the temple came to mind. As it flowed, the river grew in depth, it teemed with life, and abundant fruit trees lined its shores. The prophet described walking into the river until it reached his ankles, then until the water reached his knees, and eventually to where he had to swim. Allen figured he was already at swimming depth, since he had committed himself to a missionary venture. He was being swept along in the flow toward the West, in hopes of starting new works.

Allen startled when he saw a little boy watching him. The lad wore no shoes, and his homemade britches were dirty and tattered. His shirt lacked buttons. Allen couldn't tell if brown was its original color or if it was dark from grime and stains.

"Good afternoon, young man. What brings you down to the river on this fine day?"

The boy didn't answer, but only watched him.

"Do you live in one of those houses?" Allen pointed toward the shanties. "I have traveled a long way from my house. It's in New York."

Still quiet, the boy stared at him with big dark-brown eyes.

Allen glanced around and scratched his head. "Is it good fishing here? I bet you could catch some nice ones if you had a pole and worm. Do you ever fish here?"

"No, sir," the boy finally said. "Don't fish here. Too many picker bushes. You got to go over there in them trees. It ain't good now. You gots to fish in the morning."

"I suppose you're right. Fishing is usually better in the morning. It sounds as though you have a lot of experience for an eight-year-old boy. Are you eight years old?"

The boy looked puzzled and shrugged. "I don't know."

"I guess it doesn't really matter, does it? The important thing is that you know how to catch fish."

The boy stared, expressionless.

"My name is Allen." He extended his hand. "What is your name?"

"Daniel, you come here right now!" A large woman called from the yard with the white house back up the slope.

"Is that your mother?"

The boy didn't answer. He just turned and ran to the woman. She led him into the house.

Allen turned back to the river. "Lord, is there anything you are going to have me learn while I'm here in Portsmouth? I am willing to serve you in any way possible." His thoughts returned to the biblical river and the life it produced.

Whistling interrupted Allen's meditation. A slender black man with a burlap bag slung over one shoulder strode toward him along the river road. Allen recognized the tune the man was whistling—Allen's favorite hymn by Charles Wesley.

"Good afternoon, sir," Allen said. "It's a lovely day, isn't it?"

"Yes, sir." The man smiled, revealing white teeth. "The Lord has given us a fine day."

Allen walked up the gentle slope alongside the man. "If I'm not mistaken, I'd say the song you were whistling was 'And Can It Be.'"

"That be the one, sir. Are you a Christian man?"

"Yes, I am a Christian and a minister in the Methodist Episcopal Church."

"Well, praise the Lord, brother. I'm Deacon Abraham, pastor of this here Methodist church." He pointed to the church up the hill.

"I'm Allen Hartman. It is a pleasure to make the acquaintance of a fellow Methodist pastor and one with a good ear for hymns of praise."

"And can it be, that I should gain,'" Deacon Abraham sang, "an interest in my Savior's blood? Died he for me who caused his pain? For me, who him to death pursued?"

Allen joined in. "Amazing love! How can it be that thou, my God, shouldst die for me?"

The two pastors sang the second verse as they walked to the

little church. Allen sensed a kindred spirit with Deacon Abraham. Something in his voice made the words come alive: "That thou, my God, shouldst die for me."

As they started the third verse, Deacon Abraham swung the burlap sack from his back and set it down by the door. The sleeves of his white shirt slid up, exposing scars on both wrists. Allen wondered if the scars were from shackles.

"Long my imprisoned spirit lay fast bound in sin and nature's night. Thine eye diffused a quickening ray; I woke—the dungeon flamed with light! My chains fell off, my heart was free . . .'"

Allen swallowed the lump in his throat, finding it hard to keep up as Deacon Abraham turned and raised his hands toward heaven. "I rose, went forth, and followed thee. Amazing love! How can it be . . ."

Allen listened. He'd heard the hymn sung by some of the best-trained voices in New York and by large choirs, but none had stirred his soul as this humble man near the shore of the Ohio River.

"Bold I approach the eternal throne, and claim the crown through Christ my own. Amazing love! How can it be that thou, my God, shouldst die for me?" Abraham's callused hands were still raised as he slipped into prayer. "Thank you, Lord, for dying for me. Thank you for setting me free from the chains of sin. Thank you, Lord, for sending Brother Allen to visit. Thank you, Lord Jesus."

Abraham's eyes sparkled with joy, even though Allen assumed by the scars on the man's wrists they had seen a world of suffering and hostility. Taken in by the black man's smile and warmth, Allen wanted to stay and get to know this pastor and his flock. But it was time for him to get back to his host's home for supper.

"It has been a real pleasure to meet you, Brother Abraham. I hope I can see you again sometime." Allen offered his hand.

"Surely we'll be seeing you." Abraham shook Allen's hand with a firm grip. "If you want, you can come for preaching services. We meet every night."

"You're having a service tonight?" Excitement sparked within Allen's heart. "What time will you begin?"

"Folks start gathering after supper, and we commence about seven o'clock."

"I'll try to come and bring some friends along," Allen said, turning to leave.

Arriving at the farmhouse in time for supper, Allen washed and took his seat. At an appropriate lull in the conversation, he asked the host couple if they knew Deacon Abraham or had any contact with the church.

"That's a Negro church. They keep to themselves. We tend to our own," the husband said.

Allen tried not to flinch. From his understanding, God not only wanted but expected his people to care for one another. "Has the Portsmouth Methodist Church ever considered sending a crew over to paint the church as a local missions project?"

"No. We sent an offering to help missionaries in Africa, I think." The farmer glanced at his wife.

She nodded but kept her head down.

Allen wondered how a well-to-do church could overlook a need so close by, especially for a sister church. Obviously the farmer and his wife didn't care to discuss the topic.

Allen shared his experience and the invitation with the missionary band at the Morris House.

"Brother Mills and I will be going over the inventory, and we'll have group vespers here this evening," Foster said.

"I'd like to go with you, Allen, but I've offered to lead the singing here," Martha said.

Virgil appeared interested but remained silent when his wife glared at him.

"Oh, I don't want to take Benny and Joseph out so late," Rachel said.

Olive chimed in. "That's so good of you to invite us all, but I have things to do here to prepare for my husband's arrival. I'm sure you understand."

Allen looked at Gloria.

She twisted her hankie. "Um, well, I've never been to a Negro service before. I-I guess it's okay to go with you."

"Oh good. I'm sure you won't regret it," Allen said.

CHAPTER SIX

THAT EVENING ALLEN AND GLORIA arrived at Deacon Abraham's service after the singing had started. The small church was full, with about seventy people all standing, singing, and clapping in unison. The large woman who led them hesitated when she saw the two walk in, but she continued singing. The congregation, absorbed in their worship, didn't seem to notice.

Allen recognized the words to the next hymn, but the tune and rhythm were altered. He looked over at Gloria, who clapped and seemed to enjoy herself as she sang along.

After the singing, Deacon Abraham stepped up and told everyone to take a seat. Those who could sat on plank benches, while others stood along the walls. Some people on the back bench shifted to make room for the two visitors.

"Thank you, Sister Lydia. Thank you, everybody. That was some fine singing. Bless the Lord." His enthusiasm filled the room. "I believe the Lord Jesus is sitting proud in heaven for the way we sang praises tonight. Bless the Lord."

"Amen! Hallelujah!" the congregation agreed, clapping their hands.

"Now, brothers and sisters, I want to make a special introduction. Just today I was walking along the river when I seen a man standing there. The Holy Ghost told me he was a man of prayer."

Several people said "amen" and "glory."

"He was friendly to me, and we shared a hymn together. He is a Methodist preacher all the way from New York. The testimony of the Holy Ghost was with him, so I invited him to join with us. Brother Allen, why don't you come on up here and bring the Word of the Lord." The deacon held out his arms and smiled.

Allen went forward amidst the amens and hallelujahs. Being introduced was fine, but he had not come prepared with a sermon. Did "bring the Word of the Lord" mean bring greetings and a testimony, or preach? He'd introduce himself and Gloria and share briefly about their missionary venture. That should be interesting to the people, who probably had never met missionaries to the Indians.

Allen tugged on his suddenly too-tight collar. He glanced out over the congregation. That was when he noticed the little boy Daniel, whom he'd met by the river, sitting by Sister Lydia. He assumed she was his mother. Allen cleared his throat and smiled.

"God bless all of you."

Amens interrupted him.

"I want to thank your pastor, Deacon Abraham, for the invitation to join you tonight."

More amens.

"I would also like to introduce my colleague, Miss Gloria Shannon." He paused while she stood up, smiled, then took her seat again.

"We are part of a missionary band under the leadership of Reverend Samuel Bannister."

No reaction. They must not have heard of Bannister's reputation as an evangelist.

"We are beginning our journey west to the Oregon Territory, where we will establish a mission to the Indians."

He described the rest of the missionaries, their particular contributions to the team, and the vision Bannister had for expanding the church throughout the West.

Thinking he had shared long enough, Allen glanced at Deacon Abraham, who nodded, as if expecting more. Spontaneous preaching was not Allen's gift, so he desperately prayed for a spark of inspiration. Then wonderfully, the verses of the Great Commission in the gospel of Matthew came to mind.

"These were some of the Lord's last words to his disciples, the imperative for us, all of his disciples, to go to all nations, all peoples, to preach the gospel. Our missionary band has responded to this call to take the Good News to the Indians, who have no preachers of their own. They have no song leaders of their own. They do not yet know the joy of praising Almighty God with hymns and spiritual songs as we have done tonight."

With a burning rush in his heart, he preached with fervency like he never had before, but the amens dwindled. Upon finishing, he turned the pulpit back over to Deacon Abraham, expecting him to make an altar call.

Allen took his seat next to Gloria.

She patted him on the hand. "My goodness, that was bold."

Picking up where Allen left off, Deacon Abraham preached from the Great Commission reference in Mark. He emphasized Holy Ghost power by which Jesus's disciples were to heal the sick and cast out demons. He went on for more than a half hour, exhorting with such fire, it made Allen's sermon seem like a candle. The glory shouting increased. People responded with genuine conviction.

"Brothers and sisters, God has put the call on this young preacher. God is sending Brother Allen out into the wilderness, just like he sent the Lord Jesus. God is sending Brother Allen to the wilderness to be tempted by the devil. Brother Allen is obeying the Lord. He is going to the wilderness to meet the devil. He did not say no to Jesus. He did not choose to be the pastor of a fancy church in the big city. No, brothers and sisters! Our brother says yes to Jesus. Brother Allen is going to the wilderness to wrestle with the devil. And he's going to get the fire of the Holy Ghost on him. Yes, he's going to get the fire of the Holy Ghost on him and heal the sick and cast out the demons. He's going to preach the Good News of Jesus to those lost in the darkness."

The glory shouting shook the walls. People looked at Allen and nodded. Those close by touched him on the shoulder.

"You know what I'm talking about," Deacon Abraham shouted as he wiped dripping sweat from his brow. "Some of you have been to the witches. You've been obeying the devil. Some of you live in the darkness, and Jesus is calling you into the light. You got to say yes to Jesus. You can't deny the Lord when He's talking to your heart. Say yes! Come up here now and say yes to Jesus. Brother Allen will come up and pray with you. He's got the anointing on him. If a demon is tormenting you, he will cast it out in Jesus's name. If you are sick, he will pray for you. If you need to repent of sin, he'll lead you to forgiveness."

A lump lodged in Allen's throat. He didn't mind praying with people or helping them to invite Christ into their hearts, but casting out demons? It must be a figure of speech. Making his way to the front, Allen had to sidestep several people who were lost in their prayers. Many had their hands in the air. Others cried out as if in agony. A number of people went forward, some standing and some kneeling.

Allen's favorite parts of ministry were meeting people at the altar, praying, and giving counsel. But when he helped them, it was usually quiet. He'd experienced camp meetings where people had cried out and fallen to the ground or shaken handkerchiefs, but this was loud and confusing.

Allen knelt beside a young man on his hands and knees crying out to God in repentance. He tried to ask how he might pray, but the young man couldn't hear him. Deacon Abraham shouted his prayers and moved from one person to the next. Allen took the cue and prayed a blessing over the young man as loudly as he could and moved on.

A piercing shriek filled the room, and a woman crumpled to the floor. She lay there screaming and shaking.

Sister Lydia stepped forward. Pointing her finger at the woman, then toward the wall, she commanded, "Go out in Jesus's name. Go out in Jesus's name."

The woman screamed again then lay still. Sister Lydia placed her hand on the fallen woman's forehead.

Allen turned back to the man standing before him. He prayed, trying to listen to the Holy Spirit. Allen put his hand on the man's forehead, and with an unexpected infusion of authority, declared, "Lord, set this man free from wickedness. Set him free from the chains of sin. Forgive him, Lord, for stealing, and lead him into your holy light."

He didn't know if this man was a thief. The words just came out. The man shuddered, and he fell backward into the arms of two men standing behind him. They gently laid him on the floor and returned to worship.

Allen moved to the next person on his left, a skinny girl of maybe thirteen or fourteen. He reached to put his hand on her forehead, but before he touched her, she screamed "No!" and fell to the floor.

The girl lay on her back, writhing like a snake. Not just wiggling, her movements simulated those of a serpent. She hissed and snarled, her face contorted as if trying to become a snake. Allen squatted beside her and reached again to put his hand on her forehead. Just before he made contact, Sister Lydia grabbed his wrist.

"She got a voodoo demon," she shouted in Allen's ear. "Don't lay hands on her until it's out."

"Listen to Sister Lydia," Allen heard Deacon Abraham say from across the room.

Allen paused, expecting her to take over, but she didn't.

"Go ahead, Brother. Send this one on its way."

Others gathered around, watching and praying, undisturbed by the scene.

He gulped and prayed quietly. "Lord Jesus, this young girl has come to be set free. Release her from the grip of Satan so she can serve you and know your joy."

"No, I won't go." Her voice was not that of a young girl. It was like a raspy old woman.

Allen shivered. The hairs on his neck stood up. "Lord Jesus, release this girl from the Enemy's grip. She is a precious child of God."

"I am the child of Satan," she growled. Her black eyes glared like daggers.

It unnerved Allen that the demon reacted to his prayers. Some people held down her arms and legs to keep her from scratching and kicking. Her hands formed into claws. She growled again.

"Just command it to go out," Sister Lydia said. "You got the authority, just like you was preaching about."

"In the name of Jesus Christ, I command you to go out of her now." Allen spoke low but firm. No change. He raised his voice and tried sounding authoritative. "In the name of Jesus Christ, I command you to go out of her now!" Still nothing. Allen looked at Sister Lydia and sent a silent plea to her.

Kneeling beside him, she shifted her large body and got close to the girl's face. Allen leaned in so he could hear what she said.

"I cover this young girl with the holy blood of Calvary. I bind you, demon, and remove your claws from her in Jesus's name. Almighty God is calling her name, and you may not interfere. Your work here is done. She came here repenting, and you will not stop her. Go out now, in the name of the Lord Jesus Christ."

She spoke with notable authority and sternness.

Sister Lydia knelt upright and raised her hands high. "Lord Jesus, send this one away to the pit or wherever you want it to go. O Lord, come and hold this child so's her soul can be healed."

The girl's body went rigid. An angry grunt escaped from deep within her throat. Her head, neck, and back arched. Her whole body heaved and strained. Her throat bulged. With one sharp gasp, she went limp.

Sister Lydia scooped up the girl and hugged her like a rag doll. "Thank you, Lord Jesus. Thank you, Lord. Your power won the victory. Only you, only you, Lord Jesus."

Deacon Abraham still blessed and laid hands on others. Gloria stood with a hand over her mouth, shaking her head as though she couldn't believe what her eyes beheld.

Allen smiled to reassure her.

A man took the girl from Sister Lydia and sat her on a bench next to her mother, who held the sobbing girl and watched as a glow of innocence returned to her face.

Deacon Abraham shook hands and moved throughout the people, hugging his flock. Sister Lydia spoke in another woman's ear, and together they broke out in song. Soon, the whole group fell into singing and clapping. Allen didn't recognize the words, but he clapped in rhythm and gave thanks to God.

A mighty thing had happened. A captive had been released from a terrible bondage. How could such a young girl be possessed like that? At least she was set free. Allen closed his eyes, raised his hands, and praised God.

Someone touched his arm. He turned to a smiling Deacon Abraham, and they embraced. Allen suddenly broke out weeping, as if a wineskin had burst, and warmth washed over his soul. The sensation was new and difficult to comprehend, but he recognized the presence of the Holy Spirit. With his eyes closed, he imagined Jesus holding him and smiling as if to say, Well done. Deacon Abraham moved on to hug Gloria and others.

After a couple more hymns of praise, the group was dismissed.

People shook hands with Allen and Gloria as they left. He opened his silver pocket watch and showed it to Gloria. The time showed eleven o'clock. Even with arriving late, they'd been there for more than three hours.

Gloria laughed. "I've never been to a service like this before."

Allen saw Sister Lydia speaking to the woman with the young girl. The mother nodded, and Sister Lydia hugged her. The mother thanked Allen as she passed him on her way out. Allen approached Sister Lydia, who hugged him first, then Gloria.

"Praise the Lord!" Sister Lydia said.

"Praise the Lord! And thanks for your help. That was my first experience with a possessed person."

"The Lord Jesus did some mighty work tonight," Deacon Abraham said, joining them. "I'm happy He sent you to visit us, Brother Allen."

"Yes, the Lord is good. I've learned many new things tonight, and I thank you." Allen scratched his head. "I was just telling Sister Lydia that this is the first time I've encountered a person possessed by a demon. I wasn't quite sure what to do."

"The Lord is always faithful to lead us in every situation," Deacon Abraham said. "You have to trust in his power for preaching, healing, and casting out demons."

Allen turned to Lydia. "You said she had a voodoo spirit?"

"Yes." She passed her hand over her forehead. "I seen it on her before, but it wasn't until tonight that she was healed. I guess she finally let Jesus do some cleaning."

"You mean to let Jesus come into her heart?" Allen wanted to fully understand.

Sister Lydia shook her head. "She asked Jesus into her heart about a month ago. Shortly after they crossed the river."

"I'm sorry, but I don't know what you mean."

"The girl and her mother are runaway slaves." Deacon Abraham's eyes saddened, as if remembering his own journey. "They're on their way north but stopped here for help. They came to church, and both of them got saved. Not all folks stay so long, but they was real poor, nothing but skin and bones when they got here."

Allen knew that the preacher risked a lot to confide in him about runaway slaves. Their location on the north shore of the Ohio River provided a safe haven for runaways. Most of the former slaves wouldn't deny those who came for help.

Questions swirled in Allen's mind. "Why didn't the demon go out when the girl invited Christ into her heart?"

"The devil don't like to give up on the things he's stolen." Abraham made a pulling motion with both hands. "He'll put up a fight to see if you get scared off, or maybe just hide away like a snake and come out later. Jesus comes into someone's heart, but he only gets as much as they surrender to him.

"That demon can stay there because he deceived the person into an agreement, a deal. So the demon gets part of the soul, and the person thinks they're getting power or pleasure. They end up sinning against the Lord, and the devil puts a chain on him. He'll keep telling lies until that soul is all wrapped up in chains, and they can't hear a word Jesus is saying. Some people get saved, and they give up liquor and chasing women that same day. But others have to fight with temptations until they can surrender everything to Jesus."

"That girl's mama probably took her to a voodoo witch doctor down there in Louisiana to get her healed," Sister Lydia said. "They might have done a blood sacrifice or something, but the evil spirits went in and chained up her soul. And tonight you saw her get loosed from some of those chains. Thank you, Jesus."

Allen furrowed his brow. "You think there are more chains? More demons?"

"Oh yes, there are plenty more demons," she said. "The girl and her mama are coming to my house tomorrow afternoon, after they get some rest, and we are going to pray some more."

That made sense to Allen, based on what he'd just experienced, but his years at seminary had not prepared him for this. Wasn't a

Christian cleansed from "all unrighteousness"? But then, maybe it was a matter of the "sin which easily besets us," like entangling vines, which might as well be chains.

"Why didn't the demon go out when I commanded it to go?" Allen tapped his chest.

"Son, you believe in the authority Jesus gave you to be a missionary, but you don't believe in your authority to cast out demons or heal the sick," Deacon Abraham said. He quoted Mark 6:13, which spoke of Jesus giving such authority to his disciples and how the apostles trusted that authority in ministry.

"A demon won't listen to you. But when you speak as the ambassador whom Jesus sent, it sure will listen and do what you say. But you got to believe that Jesus sent you to do this for him. Then the demon sees that Jesus is standing right behind you, and it won't mess with you, 'cause the Holy One is there. You'll see."

Sister Lydia squeezed Allen's hand and smiled. "You come back tomorrow afternoon and help us pray for that girl."

They closed the church, and Allen drove Gloria back to the parsonage in the borrowed carriage, hoping the pastor and his wife were not waiting up. It would be hard enough to explain why the two single people were out until midnight, let alone what they had seen.

When the missionary band gathered for their morning meeting the next day, Allen shared with cautious excitement. He described his invitation to preach as humorously as possible to lighten their mood. But when he described the girl writhing on the floor, he was met with silence. No one knew what to make of it. Gloria confirmed all that he had relayed and that he had not exaggerated.

"There must be some reasonable explanation other than demons," Foster said. "I hear of this from African missionaries, but not here in our civilized country."

Mills nodded. "Not here, not here."

"When we were in seminary, we never studied this aspect of Scripture. I just do not see this as essential doctrine," Foster said.

Allen paced. "In seminary we debated between Wesleyan and Calvinist theology. We studied how to reach educated people with doctrinal principles. That girl didn't need to hear about doctrine. She needed the power of Jesus's name."

"In the Bible, Jesus told the demons to leave, and they left—immediately. He didn't take hours to do it," Mills said.

"Yes, but the disciples failed to cast out the demon of a boy, and Jesus told them it required much prayer and fasting," Allen said.

The discussion posed a dilemma for the team of ministers, but it also opened a door for Allen. "I'd like to go back this afternoon for another prayer session with the girl. Perhaps I'll learn more and be able to give a clearer explanation."

"You might as well go. There is nothing else to do until Reverend Bannister arrives," Foster said. "Try teaching them from Romans where it says, 'For with the heart man believeth unto righteousness.' Just make sure you keep your head in the right place."

CHAPTER SEVEN

ALLEN KNOCKED ON THE DOOR of Sister Lydia's house. A girl opened it and let him in.

"Thank you, Esther," Sister Lydia said. "Come in, Brother Allen."

Esther joined her little brother, Daniel, playing on the floor in a corner. The kitchen table, rustic and long, consumed the center of the room. A bench and a couple of chairs had been moved into a seating arrangement.

Deacon Abraham, relaxing in a rocking chair, smiled and invited Allen to sit in a small wooden chair beside him. The runaway-slave mother shifted on the bench, clasping and unclasping her hands. Sister Lydia took the mother's hands in hers, as though to comfort her. The girl who had been set free from the demon sat quietly looking at the floor.

Deacon Abraham introduced Allen to the mother, Louella, and the thirteen-year-old girl, Mabel. He then began praying, so Allen bowed his head. Sister Lydia tapped him on the leg and silently indicated he should keep his eyes open. He'd always considered it disrespectful, but he complied as he noted that the deacon's eyes were open and watchful.

Then Allen understood why. Mabel squirmed in her seat. She became increasingly restless, even agitated, as Abraham prayed. With forceful and direct words, he claimed authority of the Lord Jesus Christ. Praise and honor to the Lord flowed from his lips. He declared the power of the blood and then began binding the strong-man demon by quoting Scripture.

Mabel's face twitched, and her eyes darted about. Louella whimpered and squeezed Lydia's hand.

Abraham stopped.

The girl swayed on the bench.

Abraham leaned forward in his chair and focused on her alone. "Mabel. Mabel, can you hear me?"

"You can't have her. We won't let her go." It was Mabel's voice, but with an edge. It clearly was not the girl speaking.

Louella cried, and Allen's skin crawled upon seeing that some other being controlled the girl's body.

Sister Lydia called to her daughter. "Esther, take Louella outside for some fresh air."

"I demand that you release her now in the name of the Lord Jesus Christ!" Abraham commanded.

"No!" cried a demon.

Mabel's body jerked, and she fell to the floor. Abraham and Allen knelt beside her and held her arms and legs.

"Release her now."

No response.

"Allen, you command the demons to go out."

"In the name and authority of Jesus Christ, I command you to releaser her," Allen said.

Mabel struggled and squirmed.

Abraham leaned close to Allen's ear. "Now command the demons to give their names."

"I command you in Jesus's name, identify yourself."

"No!"

"Tell me! Now!"

"Ignacious." Mabel groaned.

"Who else?" A feeling of confidence was flowing into Allen.

"Ugh! Marie." Mabel choked and coughed.

At Abraham's prompting, Allen asked, "Who else is there?"

"La Marque." Mabel spat and twisted again.

Allen then ordered the three demons to go out in the name of Jesus. The girl struggled, tossing her body first one way, then the other, then immediately stilled. Her face grew tight, and she squeezed her eyes and lips shut. She did not move or respond.

Allen looked at Abraham.

He stood, poured himself a drink of water, and offered one to Allen.

The little boy, Daniel, politely asked his mother if he could play outside. He'd been there the whole time but seemed bored. Lydia sent him out but told him not to go to the river. They all acted as if nothing out of the ordinary was happening.

Allen accepted the drink, sat in his chair, and sipped the water. The demon-possessed girl lay at his feet. How could this be boring to a small boy?

Abraham slipped back into the rocking chair. "Is the Lord showing you anything, Sister?"

"The three demons have closed up her mouth, her eyes, and her ears," Lydia said. "She can't hear us or speak. The demons have some claim to be there and won't leave."

"What do the names mean?" Allen leaned forward, resting his elbows on his knees. "They're all common."

"Let's ask her mother," Lydia said. She called for Louella, who came in and watched her daughter, clearly not knowing whether to hug her or run from her.

"Do the names Ignacious, Marie, or La Marque mean anything to you?" Abraham spoke calmly. He offered no explanation.

Louella gasped. "Yes, they are the three healers I went to back home."

"Healers?"

Lydia sighed. "Was they voodoo witches?"

"Oh." Louella whimpered. "We always went to them for healings, but we knew they did the black power. My mama took me and Mabel whenever we was sick."

"Did you go on your own?" Abraham's voice carried no judgment. "Did you pay them money?"

"Yes." She began crying.

Lydia reached for her hand. "You need to repent for trusting the black magic. Will you ask Jesus to forgive you?"

"Oh yes. Yes. I am so sorry. I done wrong." Louella knelt at the bench and poured out her heart to Jesus, repenting and begging forgiveness for her dealing with the dark powers through the three witches.

Mabel remained on the floor, her face tense, her lips pursed.

Lydia guided Louella to renounce the practice of witchcraft.

"I renounce the witchcraft of Ignacious. I renounce the witchcraft of Marie. I renounce the witchcraft of La Marque in Jesus's precious name. Oh, forgive me, Jesus."

"Aagh! Ohhhhh!" Mabel heaved and bucked forward, then dropped back. She lay still again and breathed deeply for a moment. She turned her head to her mother. Great sobs tore from her.

"Them evil spirits come in when they pays the witch-man for healing or to put a curse on someone." Abraham sipped his water. "Sometimes the spirit of the witch-man comes into the person if they have that much power. When Louella asked Jesus into her heart, them demons left her and went into her offspring, the next generation."

"Mabel, honey," Sister Lydia said, "did you ever go to the healers by yourself? Did you ever pay them to do some magic for you?"

The girl was quiet.

"Answer her, Mabel," her mother said.

"Yes." She squirmed. "I went so's they'd put a curse on a man. He done bad to me. He hurt me, so I told them to fix a curse on him."

Sister Lydia touched the girl's knee. "Who did you pay, Mabel?"

"La Marque."

"Child, what man are you talking about?" Louella squeezed Mabel's elbow.

"You know, Mama." Tears spilled down the girl's cheek. "That man at the store."

Louella's shoulders sagged, but her eyes flashed. She explained that near the farm where they'd worked as slaves, a storeowner took advantage of women who could not pay with cash. He allowed credit in order to pressure and control people. Farmers, white and slaves, were indebted to the cruel man. He had abused both Louella and Mabel.

"Mabel, in order to be free from the evil spirits, you got to forgive that man and repent to Jesus for having ordered the curse," Deacon Abraham said.

Mabel responded without hesitation. "Lord Jesus, forgive me for going to the witch-man and sending that curse. I promise I won't do that no more."

"That's good, Mabel," Abraham said. "Now you got to forgive the store man for hurting you."

Mabel closed the dark-brown eyes that betrayed her distress. Her chest heaved. "I can't. I just can't forgive him. He hurt me bad," she cried.

Louella clenched her jaw and breathed heavily through her nose. Her angry eyes gazed at the wall, as if watching her own painful history.

"Mabel, child." Sister Lydia wrapped her arm around the girl. "You got to forgive the man, or else you keep the chain of hate around your heart. You can't let your heart be a slave to hate."

Mabel closed her eyes. Her right hand gripped her left forearm. She shook her head.

Allen breathed deeply. What vile things had they suffered? He put his right hand to his chest, as if to lighten the burden.

Lord, I have never raped a woman or even been tempted in such a way. Why do I feel so heavy hearted . . . so guilty? He had looked upon women with lustful thoughts before, but his sense of propriety and conviction had overcome the temptation.

The burden in his heart intensified. But distinguishing a subtle difference in his spirit, he realized it was not his own guilt but the guilt of men. Lord, forgive me and other men for lustful thoughts and actions toward women.

Allen fell to his knees before the two runaway slaves—the wounded victims of witchcraft and terrible abuses.

"I take the place of the store owner and any other men who have mistreated you. And I ask you to forgive me."

Louella and Mabel stared at Allen. After a moment they both burst into tears.

"Can you forgive that man now?" Sister Lydia seemed to be able to read their faces.

Holding each other and sobbing, Mabel and her mother nodded their heads.

Allen bowed low and prayed in repentance for sinful and lustful men. He repented for greed and control and slavery. His heart rent in two before the Lord.

Deacon Abraham rallied a chorus of prayer and praise. The presence of the Holy Ghost filled the room like a swirling breeze.

Louella and Mabel danced like soaring birds. Deacon Abraham pumped his arms in the air and marched with high steps, shouting, "Glory! I'm free of the chains."

"Thank you, Jesus. Thank you, Jesus," Sister Lydia said, holding herself in a tender embrace, swaying gently.

The rejoicing finally faded.

A large grin spread across Sister Lydia's face. She flung her arms out wide. "We ought to have ourselves a victory feast."

Louella and Mabel helped prepare food as Sister Lydia instructed them about guarding their faith and womanhood.

Allen stayed for dinner. Daniel and Esther taught him a hand-clapping game.

The time for church arrived. "Daniel, you take my new boy, Allen, to wash up and get over to the church," Sister Lydia said. "Go on now, both of you."

So stuffed with pork and potatoes, Allen didn't think he could walk to the church. He had never felt so accepted and peaceful except in his parents' home.

Deacon Abraham preached with energy and fire. Allen clapped and sang and raised his hands because he had seen the mighty power of God free a poor little slave girl that day. He recalled the line from the hymn Deacon Abraham had sung the day they'd met. My chains fell off, my heart was free, I rose, went forth, and followed thee.

After noting how Allen had helped with the healing, Deacon Abraham called him before the congregation. "I want you to gather 'round Brother Allen so's we can bless him before he goes to preach to the Indians."

The congregants gathered around and laid their hands on his shoulders and back. Tears streamed down Allen's cheeks. Abraham shouted a prayer for the heavens to be opened and the Holy Ghost to come down. He touched the missionary's forehead. Allen dropped back into waiting arms. He lay on the floor, unable to move, not wanting to move. He just wanted to rest in the presence of the Lord Jesus Christ.

Allen finally opened his eyes, took a deep breath, and rose. Deacon Abraham and Sister Lydia were shaking hands as people left the little church. Allen looked at the wooden benches, the peeling paint, and the humble people, happy and edified.

As the last one left, his new friends turned to him.

"How long was I on the floor?" Allen said, brushing himself off. "Your hand felt hot when you touched me."

Lydia laughed. "Bless the Lord! Hallelujah! You got touched by the Spirit."

He surely had—and like nothing he'd ever experienced before. After all he'd witnessed over the past several days, Allen knew he'd been changed forever. He'd never read the Bible the same or pray the same as before. He felt a new light of understanding had come to his spiritual eyes.

But how in the world was he ever going to explain it to Reverend Foster and the others? And what would Reverend Bannister think?

CHAPTER EIGHT

IN THE MORNING, ALLEN DIDN'T have a chance to share his experience with the missionary band, because Reverend Samuel Bannister arrived on the steamboat. The missionaries had little time to load their belongings onto the side-wheeler, named the Pegasus, that would carry them down the Ohio River and on to Saint Louis.

On the second day, Allen leaned on the rail, watching the corridor of trees open to the west. A deckhand stopped at his side, pulled a flask from his hip pocket, and took a long swig. He offered it to Allen. "Care for a hit of whiskey?"

"No thanks."

"You sure? Nothing happens along here until we get to Cave-In-Rock. Then we got to watch for pirates."

"Pirates? You can't be serious."

"As sure as I'm standing here." He took another swig. "Pirate gangs rob riverboats and barges. We'll pass by before dark when we can keep the speed up. I seen it happen. It's been a while, but you never know. They're crafty." Before he could say more, he was called back to work.

Allen prayed and shook his head, wondering what his future

held. "Pirates. Lord, protect us. Protect us as we travel into the wildlands. May this danger pass us by and other dangers as well."

The next day around noon, the Pegasus merged into an open space along with twenty other riverboats on the levee.

The Saint Louis waterfront swarmed with dockworkers and traders of every color and class. He gawked at everything. Men in buckskin outfits unloaded wagons full of buffalo hides. Businessmen dressed in fine suits and tall hats watched cargo going one way or the other. French voyageurs from Canada with sun-leathered faces added bright splashes of colors with their vibrant shirts and scarves.

Brick buildings stacked against each other lined the narrow city streets. Wood-plank buildings competed for attention with high false fronts, and a good deal of new construction expanded the edges of town.

The missionary ladies held handkerchiefs to their noses and complained of the smell of mud and decaying fish. Bannister ordered Allen and Virgil Jolifer to watch everyone's belongings while he guided the rest of the group to find a hotel.

Allen and Virgil sat on trunks, their elbows resting on their knees, and watched the people at their various activities.

"This reminds me of Buenos Aires," Virgil said.

Allen stared at Virgil, who seldom initiated a conversation.

"Buenos Aires, Argentina." Virgil gazed about. "We went there as missionaries for a short time. When we got off the ship, I sat by the luggage, as we are now, until Martha found a hotel. The smell of the river made me think of it."

Allen stretched his legs out to relieve a small cramp. "May I ask why you went that far for just a short time?"

"We intended to live there for the rest of our lives. I guess it was not what the good Lord intended for us. We did manage to build a mission school for Reverend Dempster, and things were going along smoothly until . . . until the incident."

"Incident?"

Virgil hesitated. He took a deep breath and blew it out. "One night three girls showed up on our porch. They were poorly dressed, hungry, and filthy. Martha cleaned them and fed them. They didn't speak Spanish, so I went for the cook, an Indian lady who had converted. We hoped she could speak their language.

"The girls said very little. Only that they were lost. Martha had the cook tell them the gospel story, but they refused to speak. They stayed through the second night. But just before sunset on the third day, a strange man appeared in the middle of the compound and shouted something. The girls ran out to him. Martha grabbed one of the girls to hold her back, but she scratched Martha's arm and ran off through the trees. The man pointed his finger at Martha and cursed her. At least that's what the cook said. She said the man was some kind of brujo, a witch doctor."

"What did you do?" Allen recalled the witchcraft demons he'd recently encountered.

"We didn't know what to do. We cleaned the scratch on Martha's arm and tried to forget about the whole affair. A few days later Martha started complaining of bad headaches. Many of the girls in the boarding school complained of nightmares and frightening mysteries of all sorts. Then one day the cook's husband dropped dead while hoeing in the garden.

"After that the students were so fearful of a curse, they began leaving. Parents withdrew support, and we were forced to close the school. We tried to turn the matter around, but there was just too much superstition. Martha's headaches persisted to the point of keeping her bedridden for days at a time. Reverend Dempster finally ordered us to return to New York for medical attention and recovery."

"Does she still have the headaches?" Allen stroked the back of his neck.

"No. They faded away as we sailed north. That was a few years ago, and they have not bothered her since."

"Do you really believe it was a curse?"

"I suppose it was." Virgil sat up and rubbed his knees. "I don't know how else to explain what happened."

Bannister approached, stepping over horse droppings. "This city has more gambling houses than stores, hotels, or churches combined. The three decent hotels are too full to handle the whole group." He sighed heavily. "And I insist that we stay together. We'll have to look farther out."

When a hired wagon finally came, Allen helped load the luggage. He was ready to see more of the city than the wharf.

They finally found a hostel run by a plump German woman whose husband worked as a carpenter. Her strongly accented English might have been charming, but she spoke loudly and cussed frequently. The accommodations were meager, the men in one dormitory and the women in the other, but they were together.

Bannister called for a meeting, but the only place to gather was in the hallway between dormitories. Each member of the band stood uncomfortably against the walls.

"You all understand that our circumstances are far from ideal, yet they could be much worse. When one takes into consideration all that we have seen in this city, we must be thankful for our blessings, though meager.

"We will all share one lavatory outside in the alley. At least the hostess is providing plenty of clean wash water. I believe our best course of action is to take care of business as quickly as possible, then be on our way."

Everyone agreed, and after vespers, they turned in.

The following day, the men went into the city to arrange their next phase of travel. Allen learned that the predominant French influence in Saint Louis also meant a predominant Roman Catholic presence. That, along with a motivated temperance organization, kept public drinking to a minimum, for which Allen was grateful.

Bannister and Foster found an association of Protestant ministers, who proved helpful in directing them toward a good travel agent, someone who would outfit their wagons with equipment and livestock as well as locate a guide.

They reconvened at the boardinghouse for lunch. The band divided into committees. Virgil and Jacob were sent to locate wagons, one for each married couple. Gloria and Allen would include their belongings among the other wagons.

Olive and the Mills would purchase equipment for the journey: tents, canvases, rope, tools, barrels, and such. Later they would purchase food, kitchen supplies, and medicines. Rachel stayed at the hostel to mind her boys and help Beulah write letters to supporters.

Allen joined Reverend Bannister, Reverend Foster, Martha Jolifer, and Gloria to secure a trail guide.

The American Fur Company frequently sent caravans to the West, but the officers were too busy with an incoming train of wagons overflowing with buffalo hides to discuss arrangements with the group just then. Bannister decided to return later. The committee entered a mercantile store, and Allen pulled Gloria aside to look at the items on a table.

"These must be Indian trade goods." Allen picked up a pair of leather moccasins with elaborate beadwork.

Like children in a toy store, they pointed out to each other buckskin pouches and bags, beadwork belts, knife sheaths, and powder horns. Allen held a knife with an obsidian blade and a deer-horn handle wrapped with rawhide. Fascinated by the crafting of the black, glassy stone, he was about to run his fingers across the blade, when a deep voice interrupted.

"Careful. That'll cut you quicker than steel," said a bald man with a southern accent. "I'd just as soon not have blood on the merchandise."

"How much are you asking for it?" Allen would be willing to pay three or four dollars for such a curio.

"Fifteen dollars."

Allen's brows shot up and his eyes went wide.

The man chuckled. "Surprised? That knife alone will fetch me forty dollars back East to some banker or senator to decorate his office. Come over here." He motioned for the two missionaries to follow him to a glass case behind the counter table.

"I bought this off of Joe Meek himself." He pointed to a stone tomahawk with an eighteen-inch handle wrapped in rawhide and elk tendon. "See those dark spots there? Bloodstains. A Blackfoot Indian attacked Old Joe and tried to smash his head in, but Joe ended up killing the warrior with his own tomahawk."

Allen found this intriguing, but seeing bloodstains put a bitter taste in his mouth.

Gloria gulped, turned, and walked away.

They lingered in the store for a few more minutes until Bannister called them to look at livestock. He had located a supplier of horses, mules, and oxen and was about to interview a potential guide.

The owner of the livestock company recommended Jean Lebeau and his two comrades.

"They been free trappers for ten years," he said. "Early on they worked for the Hudson Bay Company, but left to do business for themselves. They know the lay of the land and how to deal with Indians."

Bannister nodded at Foster. "They sound competent, even though they are Catholic."

Martha grilled him about their personal behaviors. "I won't tolerate whiskey in the camp or drunkenness at any time."

Upon meeting Lebeau, she immediately gave her approval. Bannister negotiated a salary—clearly too high for his comfort—but probably worth the expense, especially if Lebeau could get them all the way to the Oregon Territory.

Jean Lebeau appeared to be a straightforward businessman. His eyes always seemed to be hunting. Allen hadn't seen the man smile, so he figured him to be the serious type. A tanned complexion, dark hair and beard, he was not tall and had a muscular build. One of his colleagues had a similar build, only slimmer. The third man, taller and barrel chested, had dark-red hair and bushy muttonchop whiskers that rivaled Bannister's.

While they discussed a list of supplies, Allen wandered over to look at the horses. The corrals extended for a ways and divided into smaller sections with runways between them to control the flow of animals. He looked over some long-legged thoroughbreds and spotted a black mare with a white diamond on her forehead that reminded him of Glory. He moved on to the next corral, where a number of mixed-breed horses milled around. Allen stepped past a small weathered man who wore a leather hat with a wide floppy brim and leaned on a stack of crates, smoking a pipe.

A buckskin with a keen look in its eyes caught Allen's attention. A bay packhorse strolled over and muzzled his hand. He stroked her neck, but his eye was on the buckskin gelding across the dusty corral.

"You be heading west soon, pilgrim?" The man with the floppy hat rested his foot on the lower rail next to Allen.

"Yes, as a matter of fact." Allen took his eyes off the buckskin and smiled at the stranger. "We'll be leaving in a few days."

"You got a keen eye for the cayuses, if you like that mustang. He's a good mountain horse. If you're a heading into the mountains, he'll do you a sight better than those big 'uns." He nodded toward the thoroughbreds.

"Well, they are tall and strong. I'm sure they'd be very fast."

"Paugh! They might be fast enough on the prairie, but they run outta steam in the rough country. Besides, they're just for folks to look pretty here in the city. They're too tall for packing, too tall for the brush and branches, and they make a bigger target for them Indians. Did you-uns think of that?" He puffed his pipe. "You'd be better off with that mountain-bred mustang, if you can stay on him."

"No, I guess I hadn't thought of that." Allen kicked a dirt clod. "Have you been in the Rocky Mountains? Trapping, maybe?"

"Oh yeah, I been across the Rockies many a time. Trapping and hauling. Mostly hauling freight wagons for the Company."

"Have you done any guiding for travelers?" Allen watched the mustang. "We're looking for a guide now. We're a group of missionaries on our way to the Oregon Territory."

"Yeah, I've guided some too." He mentioned names that didn't mean anything to Allen.

"Are you available for hire? I'd like to tell Reverend Bannister about you." Allen scanned the area for his group.

"Well, slow down a mite. I ain't sure I want to be hauling a passel of pilgrims across the prairie. No offense."

"Wait right here." Allen started off to find Bannister, then wheeled around. "Oh. Excuse me. I'm Allen Hartman." He held out his hand and smiled.

"Name's Ferguson Ragsdale, but most folk call me Old Rag." He shook Allen's hand. "Good to know you."

Allen found Bannister and told him about the weathered little man who seemed quite knowledgeable about the business. The horse broker said he knew Ragsdale. He had a good reputation for hauling but probably was a lesser choice for guiding than Lebeau.

"Old Rag!" Martha pursed her lips. "Not much of a moniker. Personally, I prefer Lebeau. It sounds much more competent."

They viewed Old Rag leaning on the crates again, smoking his pipe, and watching the street activity. His gray shirt and tattered pants, along with the floppy hat and slight frame, didn't make a striking impression.

"Allen, I have already agreed to hire Mr. Lebeau and his men. They are very competent and come highly recommended," Bannister said. "That's one of his men over there—the big one with red hair. Le Moyn, I think is his name. I'd say he's twice the size of Old Rag."

Allen studied Le Moyn as the Frenchman talked with three other men across the street.

Allen walked back over to Ragsdale. "I'm sorry, but it looks as though Reverend Bannister has already hired a guide and two helpers. A man named Lebeau."

"Don't worry, son. Lebeau can find his way across the Great Plains, I reckon. He overcharges though."

Just then a woman's gasp and men's laughter drew their attention. As Gloria walked by the men with Le Moyn, one of them pulled her into the midst of their group. They made rude comments and passed her between them. Le Moyn leaned down and tried to kiss her.

Gloria struggled but couldn't escape their hold on her.

Allen rushed to the scene. "Let her go!"

One of the men squared off with Allen. His black eyes bored into Allen's. "Be off with you, pup. We're just charming the lady."

Allen held the man's stare. Le Moyn and a third man joined the first. They stood shoulder to shoulder, forming a wall between Allen and Gloria.

Fighting, even killing, was likely a part of life for these frontier men. If they wanted to sport with a woman on the street, they acted like it was their right. If they wanted to provoke a fight, Allen figured they wouldn't hesitate.

Allen remained calm and unmoved. Fear, fighting, or negotiating were not options. Out of the corner of his eye, Allen saw Bannister step into the street, then stop and watch.

Allen sensed someone coming up behind him. He shifted his gaze and saw Old Rag standing just behind him and to his right.

"Let her go." Allen spread his feet, preparing for a blow.

"When we're ready," the first troublemaker said.

"I ain't got my kiss yet," Le Moyn said. He grinned as if it were a joke, but his hostile eyes told something different. The guide wrapped his hand around the handle of his knife in his belt, but held it there.

"It's finished now. Let her go."

The center man tensed; the muscles in his arms flexed. He worked his jaw. He blinked, and then with a huff he turned away.

Le Moyn slammed his fist into Allen's stomach, knocking him to the ground. He clenched Allen's shirt collar, pressed his right knee into Allen's chest, drew his knife, and held it under Allen's nose. "Maybe I'll still take my kiss . . . and more."

Allen gasped to catch his breath. With unyielding resolve he held Le Moyn's glare. "You're fired."

Le Moyn's brow furrowed. He lowered the knife and stood up slowly.

Allen rose and repeated the command to the man who held Gloria. The ruffian released Gloria and backed away.

As she stepped over behind Allen, Bannister and Lebeau approached.

"What are you doing, you fool?" Lebeau's eyes flamed at Le Moyn.

Bannister wiped his apple-red face. "Lebeau, if this is the company you keep, then I will not do business with you. Our agreement is off!"

"I'm sor—" Lebeau must have known it was pointless to apologize. He glared at Le Moyn, who cowered and shuffled off. Lebeau spun on his heel and stomped off after his companion.

"Thank you, Allen." Gloria clutched his arm.

"Yes, good work, Allen." Bannister patted Allen's shoulder. "That could have become nasty, very nasty, if you hadn't stood up for Gloria that way. Well done."

"Thank you, sir." Allen took a deep breath to calm his nerves. Thank you, Lord.

"Yes, you handled that intimidating situation very well," the reverend said. "I'm glad we learned the truth about their character before we started our journey. Now, we must find a new guide, and I'm not sure I want to trust this livestock agent."

Allen glanced at Ferguson Ragsdale, who nodded his approval while taking a drag on his pipe. "I been out West for a long time, and I ain't never seen those sort of men back off like that. I thought for sure I'd see pilgrim blood."

"Reverend, this is Mr. Ragsdale, the one I told you about. He's a prairie guide, familiar with the Rocky Mountains. Mr. Ragsdale, this is Reverend Bannister, our leader," Allen said.

"Pleased to meet you, Mr. Ragsdale." Bannister gave a quick nod. "It appears that God has directed our paths to cross today. If you are available, we are looking to employ a guide to take us to Oregon. We'd like to leave just as soon as we can complete the outfitting."

"God, eh?" Old Rag tugged up his trousers. "Well, I reckon I can guide for you. But I'll take you as far as Fort Laramie. I don't believe I'd care to cross the Rockies one more time. They'll be plenty of mountain scouts to help you get into Oregon."

They shook hands to complete the agreement.

Allen leaned against the wall of the hotel room looking over the circle of seated and tired missionaries. He watched intently as Old Rag stood before the easterners, and swallowed hard.

"Crossing the prairie ain't no picnic. A storm might stop us, broken axle, not to mention the Sioux, the Pawnee, or the Cheyenne. We'll be in Indian country, and we ain't been invited . . ."

"But what about our cooking supplies?" Eva interrupted.

"Yes. And how often will we be able to wash our laundry?" Rachel asked.

"Now, folks, you'll need to be knowing about the risks . . ."

"We need to know our place in the wagon order," Martha directed. "I'd like to suggest that being the experienced missionaries, we be at the front."

Finally, the evening ended, and Old Rag walked out, his shoulders sagging.

Allen noted that in due time Old Rag obtained all the supplies and gear the band needed. He negotiated a low price for livestock and even bought the buckskin gelding for Allen. By the end of the second day, they were ready to travel, at least on to Independence, where they would pick their final essentials and two hired hands.

Allen followed the guide out of the hotel. "Thank you, Mr. Ragsdale," Allen said. "You've assembled everything we need far more quickly than we could have done. And at a better price too! I am convinced that God brought you to us at just the right time."

"Well, I don't know about that God part. I'm just doin' my job."

"We are eager to begin our journey and appreciate your making it happen."

Early the next morning, the band looked on as workers maneuvered six loaded wagons onto a river barge, along with mules, oxen, and horses.

For three days, as they rode the barge, Allen quizzed Old Rag about life on the river and the prairie.

"I can't believe we're actually leaving civilization and heading into the wild frontier." Allen absorbed the scenery. "What's it like out on the prairies?"

"If you go to missing people, it feels mighty empty." Old Rag puffed on his pipe. "But if you take it for what it is, you just feel small."

Once they arrived in Independence, the missionary band set up a camp on the western edge of town. Old Rag found his two partners, Obadiah and Thomas, and introduced them to the group.

"Obadiah can lift a wagon wheel in place without any help. He never shirks a task and will kill whatever he shoots at," Old Rag said.

Obadiah, scowling at the attention, stood over six feet and had strong, broad shoulders.

"Now, Thomas is shy but as loyal as a hound dog. Been with me for years. He don't drink whiskey, and he can cook good. He cooked coyote meat for us once . . . when that was all we killed for a week." Old Rag rubbed his belly. "It tasted fair enough."

The women's faces soured.

"Of course, with so many women along, there won't be much opportunity for Thomas to put his skills to use," Foster said, putting an end to the conversation.

Bannister led the band in a special worship service that evening. They sang hymns of praise and glory, thanking God for blessing their journey and calling them to save the savages of the western wilderness. Bannister preached a heated sermon from the gospel of Mark and added brimstone to the verses about casting out demons.

Since Allen had witnessed such a deliverance the week before in Portsmouth, he nodded knowingly at Gloria. He still hadn't mentioned the matter to Bannister.

"Mark 3:27! 'No man can enter into a strong man's house, and spoil his goods, except he will first bind the strong man; and then he will spoil his house.'" Bannister punched the air with his fist. "We are heading into the strong man's house, and we will bind him and plunder his house, in the name of the Lord Jesus.

"'The Spirit of the Lord is upon me. He hath anointed me to preach the gospel to the poor. He hath sent me to heal the brokenhearted, to preach deliverance to the captives, and recover sight to the blind. He hath called me to set at liberty them that are bruised and to preach the acceptable year of the Lord.'" Bannister shouted and waved his arms.

"We go now into the wilderness to preach deliverance to the captives of the strong man whom we now bind in Jesus's name. We go now into the wilderness to bring sight to those blind to the glory of salvation. We go now to preach to them the good news, and they will hear and be saved."

The camp was as quiet as a church on Monday morning. Bannister closed his Bible. "We can turn in for the night. We begin our wonderful journey bright and early."

Allen wondered if everyone felt the nervous tension mixed with the spirit of adventure and challenge of the call of God.

Old Rag, resting his head on a saddle, tapped out his pipe and made ready to sleep. "Well, I expect he's done for the evening," he said to his comrades, who laid out their bedrolls outside the circled wagons. "Wonder if he's going to preach like that every night."

"I don't mind the singing," Thomas said.

Obadiah grunted and rolled over. Rumbling snoring began within minutes.

Old Rag gazed at the stars. *God, I believe you created the earth and the sky, the animals and such, but it's the strangeness of people I ain't getting. And I ain't so sure this group of people are cut out for the hard journey ahead. That Allen's got the makings, maybe Gloria. I just don't know about the rest. And that old crow Mrs. Jolifer . . . I bet she don't make it. Someone's going to kill her.*

CHAPTER NINE

A COLD MOUNTAIN WIND BLEW DOWN the valley, rattling the spring cottonwood leaves and clacking branches together. The full moon, dimmed by intermittent clouds, cast inconsistent light on an Arapaho camp on the upper Laramie River. The watchman examined the trees and dancing shadows.

Expecting an attack, the chiefs had sent their best men out to guard the herd. One of them, Six Kills, a skilled horse thief, had counted many coups against the Pawnee and the Sioux. With the advantage on the side of the raiders, Six Kills slipped from shadow to shadow, sweeping around the herd grazing nervously at the clearing. He stayed well inside the line of trees, moving and scheming like a thief. He scanned likely lines of approach and listened for a sound outside the wind's dissonant rhythm.

Slithering to a concealed vantage point, he checked the horses' behavior. The swirling wind kept the mustangs on edge as they alternated grazing and sniffing the air.

Someone was out there. Straining to grasp some indication of the presence he felt, Six Kills turned his head to the right and to the left. His left hand stroked the medicine bag hanging around his neck. *Spirits, sharpen my eyes and my ears. Help me protect my people.* Nothing but the wind stirred.

Six Kills flinched at a sharp scratch on the back of his neck.

His body fell dead, but his thoughts remained with his people as his spirit drifted up through the trees and into the light of the moon.

Kicking Lion hissed as he sliced into the scalp of the fallen man at his feet and yanked up the patch of hair. He could not respect a foe who did not fight or even sing a death song. This one had died like a yearling doe—pathetic for his weak medicine, easily hunted, easily killed.

As Dark Wolf's primary lieutenant, Kicking Lion relied on the power of his medicine to become a silent stalker for hunting, horse stealing, kidnapping, and murder. As a young man full of fire to prove himself in war, Kicking Lion proudly followed the older shaman, who recognized his potential.

Dark Wolf promised him special power in battle in turn for allegiance in serving him. Kicking Lion had the athletic ability, keen eye, and sharp wits to become a warrior chief. But the shaman looked for other characteristics as well: ambition, deep-rooted anger, and rebelliousness, which he used to mold the young brave into a skillful tactician of death and intimidation.

Other chiefs and elders counseled Kicking Lion against this alliance with the witch doctor, who had been banished from the camp by Black Bear, the greatest of Arapaho chiefs. But Kicking Lion refused their advice and even mocked them as he left to join Dark Wolf.

Those old fools. They would never respect him, as they did not respect his father, who had died in battle before vowing into the sacred Crazy Lodge, leaving the family without honor. Kicking

Lion had considered this a grave injustice due to politics, and he refused to impress those he had grown to hate. He completed the Star Dance but was denied training to the Tomahawk Lodge, an honor coveted by all young men. He then leaped at the chance to gain power and reputation as a warrior from Dark Wolf.

"I will make you a warrior chief. Together we will make the Arapaho Nation the greatest of the plains. We will take back the Black Hills from the Sioux. We will push the Ute out of our mountains," Dark Wolf had promised. "We will kill the white man, and he will be no more."

Dark Wolf offered him the opportunity to rise to the level of greatness he could never achieve on his own. To do so would require a power so strong that the ordinary measures of the tribe's spiritual beliefs could not gain. Kicking Lion would have to enter into realms of the spiritual world that other warriors feared.

"You must follow me into the cave," Dark Wolf had said.

"I will follow." Kicking Lion had swallowed hard. He'd committed his life to the dark power. He'd vowed that he would claim vengeance on those who dishonored him. His hatred conquered his fear.

After many years of building a reputation, hearing the name Kicking Lion shot spikes of fear through mothers and children. He kept the scalps and bones of his victims, whether killed in battle or on his murderous raids. Medicine men throughout the region feared him for his bloodthirst. Kicking Lion stalked and killed men for spirit power, not for lust of blood.

As a disciple of Dark Wolf, he learned to gain power from vision quests and trances, through rituals and intoxication. Kicking Lion surrendered himself to the shadow spirits that guided him silently and invisibly to his quarries. The spirits of power and guile instructed him in the art of camouflage and silent killing. He painted his face in the bands and colors of a wolverine and wore a wolverine skin cape.

Dark Wolf taught Kicking Lion to kill with a wolverine claw. He'd bound a set of claws, spread and sharpened, with rawhide on the end of an elk-horn handle. When dipped in a poison mixture, he merely needed to break the skin of a victim to bring instant paralysis or even death. It became his preferred weapon when close contact and stealth were necessary.

On that dangerous night, Kicking Lion's purpose went beyond just killing a night guard and stealing horses. His men would kill any other guards or dogs and slip away with the horses. And a couple of them would remain behind, hidden and ready to help him get away with his primary prey, the village medicine man.

The chieftain had purchased the services of a spy in the village. For a jar of whiskey and a small bag of vision mushrooms, a lazy man agreed to tell Kicking Lion which lodge belonged to the medicine man. The spy told him on which bedroll to find the shaman and who else slept around the fire. Kicking Lion also learned where the shaman hung his medicine bag, as he would need to capture that as well.

Moving under the cover of shadow and wind, Kicking Lion crept to the edge of the camp. He stopped to listen for hint of anyone moving about the village. His confidence rested in the slumber spell that Dark Wolf had cast over the village. For several days before, he'd beckoned a power to lull the camp into lethargy and fatigue. Dark Wolf had carefully selected a time after a successful buffalo hunt and celebration dances. With full bellies and contented hearts, the innocent tribe believed they could rest in the capable skill of the night watchmen.

Kicking Lion rose and stalked through the camp until he reached the medicine man's lodge. He stepped silently through the doorway and crouched low, blending with shadows on the floor. He allowed a moment for his eyes to adjust to the darkness. No movement. In the center of the lodge, the fire's coals glowed dimly red, like demons' eyes. If the spy's information was correct, and it appeared to be, the medicine man slept across the fire and to the right with one of his wives. The other wife and three children lay to the left.

The chieftain poured white powder out of his leather pouch into the palm of his left hand. Staying low to the floor, he crawled toward the sleeping shaman. He blew the fine powder so that it drifted over and fell onto the heads and faces of the man and his wife. Kicking Lion turned and blew more on the others. He shrank into the shadows and waited for the bone dust to sink the unsuspecting victims into deeper sleep.

Kicking Lion opened his bag again and withdrew his wolverine claw. He dipped it lightly into a deer-horn vial, covering the tips with enough poison to paralyze the medicine man. Certain the sleeping powder had taken effect, Kicking Lion dropped a handful of tinder onto the coals. In seconds the fire brightened the tipi. He then reached over and pulled the buffalo blanket off the medicine man and raked the claw across his chest.

The medicine man's eyes flashed open. In panic he raised his arm to strike out, but the drug overtook him. He moaned, then his eyelids faded closed. The bone dust might not have been enough to keep the fat woman unaware of the kidnapping taking place at her side, so Kicking Lion scratched the wife with the wolverine claws to ensure she wouldn't awaken and cry out.

Kicking Lion untied the medicine pouch that hung over the shaman. He reached across and poked through some bundles until he found the shaman's medicine pipe. With these items, he held the medicine man's spiritual power and identity.

Grabbing the medicine man by the feet, Kicking Lion dragged him out the doorway of the lodge. Hoisting the man up over his shoulders as if he were a dead deer, the chieftain latched the door flap and silently moved out of camp.

The brave who held Kicking Lion's horse tied the medicine man over a third horse. They rode away from the camp into the night unnoticed. Other men met him at a designated place to act as rearguards, but for Kicking Lion, it was an unnecessary precaution.

They traveled north for many miles before turning west. Anyone attempting to follow their tracks would not have a difficult time, but Kicking Lion didn't set up an ambush. Once they headed west toward the big mountain, the one white men called Laramie's Peak, any pursuers would give up and turn away. No other would ride into Dark Wolf's lair and into the depths of the underworld.

For many generations, the elders of the Arapaho and other tribes told their children of the cave where spirit beings came from and went into the underworld like bats. Anyone who went into the cave never returned, and those who saw the spirits at the cave entrance would lose their souls. A forbidden place, no one hunted or camped in the valley of the cave, lest they endangered themselves, their families, and the tribe. They were not to drink from, or even step into, the water that flowed through that valley. So great the fear and horror of the cave, even the bravest warriors refused to step foot there.

That terror led Dark Wolf to the cave—to live in it, to practice sorcery, and to be where he could invoke the demons to do his bidding. The people's fear fed his power. Kicking Lion and the other warriors lived in another hidden cave nearby. Because they purchased power, or in some other way surrendered to Dark Wolf, they were allowed to enter the forbidden area, but they could never disobey their master, for it would be their final deed in this life.

Dark Wolf claimed a large territory. Along with Kicking Lion and the other men, he prowled the range from the eastern point at Scott's Bluff to Independence Rock in the west, to the headwaters of the Laramie River, and into the mountains as far as he wanted. Dark Wolf captured or killed as many rival medicine men as possible. He desired to be the sole spiritual leader and power over the Northern Arapaho and to force the chiefs to bow before him.

I will capture that good-seeking fool, Two Rivers. I will not kill the one called Medicine Man of Chiefs. But I will torture him and steal his power.

Sensing Kicking Lion's return, Dark Wolf came out of his trance. He grabbed a coup stick and waited in the shadows at the entrance of the cave. "Bring him," he snapped.

The paralyzing drug had worn off, but hours of hanging across the horse had weakened the medicine man's body. Kicking Lion and the brave dragged him to the cave and dropped him before Dark Wolf. He screamed and floundered. Dark Wolf whacked him across the face with the coup stick. Horror filled the shaman's eyes when Kicking Lion handed the pipe and medicine pouch to Dark Wolf, who now possessed his medicine, his soul.

At Dark Wolf's orders, the two men bound the captive, dragged him deep into the cave, and tossed him onto six other enslaved medicine men. One slave grabbed at the brave, who jumped back. Kicking Lion kicked the slave in the ribs.

The brave staggered away from the emaciated slaves and swallowed his revulsion.

The firelight flared. The three men turned. Out of the darkness a small figure emerged. As the witch neared the men, the brave pressed his back against the wall, as if he could sink into the rock and hide. Even in the low light, her ugly, bony features were evident, her white hair matted around patches of baldness.

The witch bent over the new captive and uttered strange words before slicing his arm with one swift movement.

The shaman cried out.

Ignoring his pain, she collected the flowing blood into a bone vial. She sliced off a piece of skin from his chest, adding more agony to the man's suffering. Leaving the wound open, she cackled as she shuffled past the fire and back to the black depths of the cave.

Kicking Lion knelt by the shaman and gave him a drink of water from a deer bladder. The medicine man quenched his parched throat but had to know it was no act of kindness. The captors would only feed him enough to keep him alive. Kicking Lion tied a rawhide strap across his mouth.

Dark Wolf held the brave and Kicking Lion with a piercing glare. "You will never speak of what you saw here. Or I will make you one of them." He tipped his head to indicate the bound medicine men. He dismissed the two men with a gesture.

Dark Wolf returned to the new captive. He spit on him. "I have your medicine." The cruel slave master bounced the small leather pouch in his hand. "You know what I can do, don't you. I will use your totems and your blood to bind your weak spirits, and they will serve me. Then the witch will send infections on your wives."

The new slave shook his head and whimpered.

"I'm not going to kill you. But if you die along the way, I will let them eat you." He nodded toward the slaves.

Dark Wolf despised the medicine men and holy men who taught the dances and ceremonies to honor the spirits of the tribe. They were weak dogs who gave children animal totems and songs and healing herbs. Dark Wolf held real power. What they thought was evil, he controlled. He journeyed through the underworld they feared. He grew stronger. His spells broke the power of all who challenged him.

He sat on his heels by the fire ring and mixed together plants and animal parts. The concoction would bind the soul of the man he'd just captured. Dark Wolf opened the stolen pouch, revealing secrets of the medicine man's power. He sneered as he began the cursing ritual.

He breathed deeply. In and out. Slowly. In and out. He opened his mind, chanted a song, and released his soul to venture into the spirit world. Holding the contents of his victim's medicine pouch, he brought the medicine man's spirit guides, an owl and an antelope, under the dominion of his own demons.

Dark Wolf projected his soul into the shape of a rattlesnake and slithered through the passageways of the underworld. Knowing the demons would attack a human spirit for interfering in their matters, he watched through the eyes of the snake hidden between two low rocks. When the demons of his alliance had received the spirits of the captive shaman, he slithered back out of the underworld.

He shape-shifted back to his human form. Dark Wolf meditated, waiting for his spirit guide, Wolf Spirit.

A large gray wolf with fierce yellow eyes materialized before him. "A white falcon will fly in from the east, with the great power of a legion of blazing spirit warriors following him. If you do not stop him, he will destroy you.

"The white falcon comes with other men, but his greatness is hidden from them. The only way to thwart the victory of the falcon is through intimidation and creating great fear that will force him to turn back."

Wolf Spirit vanished like a wisp of smoke on the breeze.

Dark Wolf came out of the trance, his body slick with sweat and shaking like an old woman. He clutched the medicine pouch hanging from his neck. He breathed deeply. "This is my territory."

He did not sleep or rest that night. In the morning he ordered Kicking Lion and the men to make ready for battle.

"Prepare now. We leave to the east, to the trail of the white man."

By the time news reached his camp that another shaman had been kidnapped, Two Rivers was already gone. That very night he had slept fitfully. A couple of hours before the sun came up, he arose, prepared his medicine bag with the sacred pipe, carried his sacred lance, and left camp on foot, heading seven miles east to a small butte. Most other men would climb spirit mountains, like Cedar Top Butte or the long rimrock ridge of Horse Tooth Mountain, on their vision quests. But Two Rivers would not risk being disturbed by other humans.

He would meet his spirit guides and learn of what was happening in the region. They would teach him to help his people vanquish the evil rising like a flooding river. He would learn a new song with power to restore peace to his people. Perhaps.

Assuring himself no one had followed, Two Rivers stopped at the small stream at the base of the butte. Here he would bathe in preparation to meet his spirit guide. Careful to follow the sacred ritual, the old man would construct a sweat lodge six feet long, five feet wide, and four feet high, in the shape of a dome with the opening facing east.

For Two Rivers, every part of the ritual had meaning that brought him into a harmony with the earth and sky. The Great Spirit would not honor any lack of integrity, no casual disregard of any of the elements or materials of worship.

He used willow branches to frame the dome because the leaves of the willow died in the winter and came back in the spring, just as men died on earth and then lived again in the world of the Great Spirit. Before raising the willow frame, Two Rivers drew a cross in the ground to create four sections, the four quarters of the universe. Four, being a sacred number, occurred in many parts of the ritual: four cardinal points of the compass, north, east, south, and west; and the four elements, earth, water, fire, and air. He laid the willow branch frame along the cross to represent the four winds.

He secured the frame to stakes he'd pounded into the ground and covered it with overlapping elk hides he had brought with him. Two Rivers took ten steps from the front of the sweat lodge toward the east and mounded dirt that had been dug out from the center of the dome.

Just beyond the mound, he built a fire pit on which he would heat rocks for steaming. This short trail became the sacred path by which heaven and earth were connected. Walking along the path represented crying out for mercy. The rocks symbolized the life connection with Mother Earth, and the hole in the center of the dome floor symbolized the presence of the Great Spirit, who dwelled at the center of the universe. With all this meaning and relationship, Two Rivers would humble himself and seek wisdom and insight.

Continuing the ritual, the holy man heated the rocks until they were red hot. He placed them in the center hole of the sweat lodge and poured four cups of water on the rocks to produce steam. He sat there in silence and darkness. Before long, sweat flowed from his body.

He opened the door to let in light and fresh air, representing wisdom, then closed the flap and poured seven cups of water on the rocks. Two Rivers once again, as he had a hundred times in his life, opened the door for more wisdom, then tipped ten cups of water onto the rocks. He did this one more time before leaving the lodge to wash in the creek, cleansing his body, even scrubbing his fingernails. He then cleansed his soul by rubbing a smudge of burned pine needles on his body, burning sage incense on the fire, and covering his body with white clay.

His prayers drifted heavenward with the smoke and steam. Two Rivers had stepped out of the ignorance and darkness of the sweat lodge and walked into the light of wisdom, now ceremonially pure to climb the mountain and present himself worthy of attention from the spirits.

Two Rivers found a place where he could see across the plain. He lit his pipe and raised it to the sky, the earth, and the four winds, then sat down and smoked and prayed until the pipe was empty. He sang his prayer songs, which he had been taught years ago in visions and quests.

By the third day, after having no food or water, and having seen no vision, Two Rivers sang out louder. He would have to draw blood. Sacrificial mutilation, which he believed hurried the response of the spirit guides, had already claimed the tips of four fingers. In desperation, he grabbed a small obsidian knife to cut three slashes into his left arm. But just before he made the initial slice into his arm, a small voice inside him said, *No.* This was not a voice he recognized as one of the familiar spirits.

Then it spoke again. You must wait. Be still.

Anticipation blossomed in his soul. But Two Rivers waited many more hours, late into the night and dark hours of the morning. He lingered until he began to doubt he had heard a spirit voice. Had they been his own thoughts? He shook himself, stood, and raised his arms to heaven. Two Rivers cried out in desperation to the Great Spirit. "Father, what do I do?"

When no answer came, he bowed his head, slumped his shoulders, and fell to the ground. Great sobs surged from deep within. The spirits must think him unworthy, or perhaps they were punishing him.

When he had no more tears to shed and defeat overwhelmed him, Two Rivers rolled to his back and pleaded with the sky. "How can I return to my village with no answer, with no help to offer? Oh, Great Father, I need you now."

But there was no answer. Two Rivers fell asleep on the ground, on the bosom of Mother Earth, with his soul laid bare before the heavens.

He lay in troubled sleep for a couple hours. Just as the eastern horizon released its first rays of the new day, Two Rivers snapped awake at the sound of the same strange voice.

He sat up and gazed out on a dark valley with a great tree in the middle. How had he missed seeing such a tall and full tree where birds and animals lived? Then he saw a river flowing at the base of the tree that fed the roots year round. A brilliantly shining cloud formed in the east and drifted toward the tree, chasing the darkness out of the valley. A white falcon flew out from within the cloud and landed on top of the great tree. The bird was crying, its tears falling onto the tree. Then the white falcon flew up, and circling the great tree shouted, "Honor to the Great Spirit! The mountain peaks belong to him!"

Two Rivers opened his eyes. The sun was clearing the horizon. He had seen a vision. A mysterious one, but one that gave him hope, as if a mighty peace would soon come over the land. He sang a song of thanksgiving.

He hiked back down the mountain to the sweat lodge camp and drank deeply from the creek. Two Rivers ate some pemmican and then slept. When his strength returned the next day, he carefully took apart the sweat lodge, packed his belongings, and left the site without a trace that he had been there.

From a ridge, Two Rivers could look down upon his village a half mile away. It was the scene of everyday activity—women working, children playing, horses grazing, and smoke rising from cook fires.

An inner sense made Two Rivers look to his left. Scanning the rimrock escarpment, he spotted two men who also watched the camp. They must have felt his stare, because they rose and hustled around the edge of the rimrock to where he assumed their horses waited. Two Rivers suspected they were Dark Wolf's spies.

Two Rivers looked to the sky. "When will you come, White Falcon?"

CHAPTER TEN

SAMUEL BANNISTER JUMPED DOWN FROM his wagon and took a deep chestful of air. The early morning smelled fresh and clean. Sunlight sparkled on the North Platte River. The prairie came alive with birds and wildlife the missionary had never seen before. Traveling the bumpy trail seemed lighter simply because the new day was smiling at him.

Morning devotions awakened everyone's spirits with a hymn of praise. Reverend Bannister was happy because things were going well. They were now in their fourth week of travel into the prairie, about three hundred miles from Independence and more than half-way to Fort Laramie.

The band members were getting along well with one another, in spite of Martha's occasional complaints. In fact, she even appeared happy on this beautiful morning. That in itself was worth praising heaven. Supplies were holding out better than expected, game was plentiful, no wagon wheels squeaked, and they had not encountered any savage Indians. The Lord was blessing them for their obedience and faithfulness. Even the guides, Ragsdale, Thomas, and Obadiah, had to admit that things were going uncommonly well.

"Well, Mr. Ragsdale," the reverend said, "it's a fine morning, wouldn't you say?"

Ragsdale scanned the horizon. "It is a fine morning. I reckon we'll have us another good day of traveling. But I remind you—you'll run into your share of troubles along the way sometime."

Bannister chuckled. "Oh, you do not have to play the pessimist with me."

"I'm not playing at all, Reverend. We've had us a row of easy days. More than our fair share. I'm thinking we're about due for a passel of trouble. I truly hope not, but that's how it always comes about."

"Well, perhaps you have not traveled with a band of the faithful such as ours. We are in the blessed hand of Almighty God, Mr. Ragsdale. It is he, the Faithful One, who is seeing us through, because he has seen fit to call us to this noble undertaking."

Thomas trotted up alongside Ragsdale. "Who needs an undertaker?"

"No one needs an undertaker, you stump!" Ragsdale said. He turned back to Bannister. "I'll admit that this has been a good trip. Maybe the Almighty is looking out for you special. All my years on the plains have taught me that good luck and bad luck go together. It's better to have a little of both, 'cause when you have a heap of good luck, there's always a heap a bad luck sneaking up on you."

"I can assure you that luck, whether good or bad, has nothing to do with this journey. It is the blessing of obedience. You, Mr. Ragsdale, and of course you also, Thomas, are benefactors of that blessing. I believe the Lord is demonstrating His kindness to you, to draw you unto him." Bannister smiled at his spontaneous homily.

"Might be, sir, but the Holy Book does say that the proud will always fall. Even Moses had his share of bad luck, I'm thinking."

"Yes," the reverend said. "You have a point, but our circumstances are much different from Moses's. I suppose we are more like the apostle Paul at this point of our missionary journey, traveling to preach to the Gentiles. Perhaps we will be like Moses when we lead the Indian nation into the promised land of salvation." Bannister beamed with the conversation and his witty analogy.

"As I recall, they stoned Paul and left him for dead a time or two, or am I mistaken, Reverend?" Not giving Bannister a chance to respond, Ragsdale continued. "All I'm saying is that it ain't in the best interest of the group's safety to have such hopeful notions." He mounted his horse and wiped his forehead with his sleeve. "I'd best ride on ahead and scout out the trail for a piece." Nodding to the reverend, then to Mrs. Bannister, he trotted off.

Thomas shrugged and drifted back to the livestock.

Bannister stewed. What Ragsdale said made sense, but it robbed him of the euphoria in which he delighted himself. It was hard to believe that the old trail scout quoted Scripture to a seminary-trained minister.

"Well, Ragsdale is wrong about this. The band rests in the shadow of the Almighty, our safe refuge. The blessings will surely continue," the reverend said under his breath.

"What's that, dear?" Olive said.

"Nothing. I think I shall walk for a while, Olive, and get my morning exercise. It's such a beautiful day, I would regret not having taken the opportunity to fill my lungs with this fresh air." He handed the reins to his wife and stepped to the ground.

Olive slapped the oxen's backsides to get them moving.

The reverend took a deep breath and began outpacing the oxen. He would praise the doubts away by quoting Scripture and singing hymns.

"Lord, save Mr. Ragsdale. Have mercy on his sin-stained heart." Bannister smiled to himself, imagining the day when Ragsdale would kneel down and ask Christ into his heart and know the joy of salvation. "Oh, what a great day that will be! Then Ragsdale will understand about living in the blessing. Then he will understand that I know what I'm talking about."

He lost track of time as he prayed and imagined the many people he would lead into the kingdom. He lifted his eyes to the sky and stretched out both arms. "Lord, I will save many in your name, as I am your humble servant." He stumbled over a clump of grass. Regaining his balance, he looked back to see if anyone had seen his clumsiness.

How far had he ventured ahead of the wagon train? He turned a full circle. Nothing but the rolling prairie and horizon stretched out in the distance.

"Oh goodness!" He ran toward a knoll. "No, wait." He ran back down.

Bannister's chest heaved. Panic filled his gut. He forced it away and cleared his mind so that sensibility overcame fear. The brush line of the river lay off to his left, so he would simply walk straight back and meet the wagons.

A few minutes later, relief swelled within Bannister when he spotted his wagon breaking the horizon. The white canvas gleamed like the sail of a ship on a sea of grass. Soon the rest of the party came into view. His wife waved at him, and he returned the gesture.

"Bless her sweet heart." He smiled.

Olive stood with the reins in her hands, waved her bonnet, and pointed toward him. Probably signaling to someone that she'd spotted her husband.

Ragsdale came over the rise, galloping toward the wagons. Evidently seeing Olive's gestures, he veered off in Bannister's direction. Maybe Olive was worried and had sent Ragsdale after her husband.

Ragsdale raced up to him and yanked back on the reins. His mustang skidded to halt. "You dern fool! What are you doing away from the wagons without your musket?"

"I beg your pardon, sir! I was just spending some time in devotion. I may have ventured out farther than usual, and I apologize. But I will not have you—"

"Get back to the wagons, now! There are Indians about! I just seen a whole string of 'em not more than two miles from here. I reckon they're Cheyenne. Now, let's get the wagons circled up."

"Indians! Are you sure?" Bannister scanned the slopes.

"Course I'm sure. 'Twernt no church picnic."

Allen heard shouting and slapped his horse to catch up to Old Rag as he passed each wagon, yelling orders to circle up and load all weapons. They ran over to inform Thomas and Obadiah so they would hustle the livestock into the circle while keeping their eyes open.

When Old Rag turned back, he groaned. Allen could see the wagons were in total disarray. They'd broken formation, and some people were standing around gawking.

"What are you doing?" Old Rag shouted. "Get these wagons around. You, Mills, pull forward and get out of the way, then circle back to the left. For crying out loud, folks, this is an emergency! Now—"

"Mr. Ragsdale," Martha interrupted, "will you please stop bellowing and explain to us about the Indians. Where are they? We want to see them."

"Oh yes! Let's do!" Gloria sounded as excited as a girl about to see a parade.

Foster stepped up. "If we are in no immediate threat, Ragsdale, I see no harm in observing the Indians from a distance. It would be of great interest to us all."

The others nodded in agreement.

"Confound it! A war party could be watching us right now. Them warriors have scouts out all the time. They know we're here for shore. They'll attack if they think we're getting close to their women and children. No! We need to circle up and let them go off in peace, like we never seen 'em."

Bannister joined the group. "Mr. Ragsdale, I see no Indians. It seems that you are getting everyone excited for no reason."

Old Rag sighed. "You folks don't understand that those are Cheyenne. They own this prairie, and we're trespassing. They don't take kindly to strangers passing through, especially white strangers. And we're no match for even five or six of their warriors that might drop down on us in a matter of minutes."

Thomas and Obadiah searched in all directions while keeping the small herd of horses and milk cows together.

"Rag, suppose we drive the wagons over to the rise just to see them from a distance? At the first sign of danger, we'll circle and follow your orders for defense," Allen said.

"That sounds reasonable, doesn't it, Ragsdale?" Bannister raised his eyebrows. "If they are already two miles away, we won't be much of a threat to them. But we would be interested to see them."

Shaking his head, mumbling something about the lack of good judgment, the old scout consented. "Maybe you'll just have to learn the hard way."

The missionaries rushed back to their wagons and horses. Old Rag got them moving and angled off toward a point about a quarter mile away where the rise would allow them a view.

"We're heading toward that lone tree yonder, but keep your guns in easy reach, and make sure they're loaded!"

They stopped the wagons about fifty yards from the tree. At a higher place, Allen pointed to the long line of three hundred or more Northern Cheyenne.

"I hope they don't look back this way." Old Rag fidgeted in his saddle.

The travelers climbed down from the wagons and walked to the top of the rise. Foster and Bannister both dug out brass binoculars from their handy trunks. Foster viewed first, then handed his binoculars to Allen. From two miles away, he didn't get a good look at the Cheyenne, but he was impressed to see them on foot, single file, and seemingly disciplined.

"Do you suppose that is how the Israelites traveled through the wilderness?" Rachel held her face with both hands.

Old Rag scanned the horizon as the missionary band watched for a few more minutes, passing the binoculars between them. The Herbert boys took a turn but then wandered off toward the front of the wagons.

"Boys, come on now. Stay by my side," Rachel said as she strolled toward them.

"Aw, Ma." Joseph sighed and pointed his finger. "These Indians are closer."

"Oh my!"

A hundred yards ahead of the lead oxen, three Indian braves on horses watched the band.

"Magnificent!" Foster said.

Two were dressed in beaded buckskins, and one had several feathers tied into his long braids. The third wore a vest that revealed bronzed muscular arms. A bow and quiver hung on his back.

Old Rag glared at Bannister and then pulled three trade knives out of a canvas bag in the supply wagon. He slipped them in his belt underneath his buckskin overshirt. Long rifle in the crook of his left arm, he strode toward the Indians with his right hand raised and said a few greeting words in Cheyenne. Using sign language, he indicated that the band was traveling west along the river. They saw the tribe and stopped to look, but clearly meant no harm.

One of the braves responded. Then Old Rag turned and walked away from them, but not straight toward the missionaries. He pulled out a knife and stuck it into the ground. A few more paces and he stuck the second, and then the third knife. He rejoined the bewildered Americans.

"You are a lucky bunch of people," he said for all to hear. "Just stand still until they leave."

Allen stepped up beside Old Rag, rifle in hand. Old Rag noted the weapon but slightly shook his head.

"Watch."

One at a time, the braves bolted forward on their horses. In an instant, the first one swung down and grabbed a knife out of the ground and rode off. The second also swooped down, a leg wrapped around the horse's neck, and snatched the knife. In an easy motion, he righted himself and rode away, not stopping to watch his comrade. The third rider, the one in the vest, rode forward with bow in hand. He suddenly slid over to the far side of the horse, and from beneath its neck, shot an arrow that stuck in the ground three feet in front of Bannister. He swung back up and raced over the rise with a loud cry. The knife was gone.

The message was clear to Old Rag.

"Marvelous riding! Outstanding!" Bannister applauded. "That is the most impressive riding I have ever seen."

Some of the women clapped.

"How did the last one pick up the knife? I never even saw it." Eva looked at Old Rag. "How did he do that?"

"Yes, Ragsdale, how did he accomplish such a feat?" Foster stepped closer. "Since you set the knives out, you must have seen this kind of thing before."

"Did you know this was going to happen, Ragsdale?" Bannister stood with his hands on his hips. "What did you talk about with them? Why did they leave us alone? Are they the ones you suspected would attack us? Come on, man. Let's hear it!"

"I recognized the first one. He was in a party I traded with last year. Swapped 'em for some buffalo hides. Luckily, he remembered me. I think that's why they left with only the knives instead of taking off with our horses. That last one was Buffalo Tail. He has a reputation as a fearsome warrior. I judge by the way he was looking us over, he was fixing to count coup. Wouldn't a been a problem for him neither. That's why I warned you back there. These braves can sneak up on a coyote. We're shore lucky they thought you-uns were too helpless to attack."

"Once again, Mr. Ragsdale, luck has nothing to do with it. The Lord Almighty was protecting us, and he gave us an impressionable look at these Indians," Bannister said. "It was in his providence that you recognized one of them. Then we were blessed with that stunt-riding spectacle. Now, what did he tell you over there?"

Allen surmised that Old Rag's message of caution would not sink in to these stubborn pilgrim heads.

"He said the tribe is moving south to Bent's Fort on the Arkansas. They're going to some big powwow, meeting up with the Arapaho, Kiowa, and the Comanches. I reckon they're choosing up new territory lines or trying to decide what to do about all of us white folk moving in. But who knows for shore."

"How far is it to Bent's Fort? I long to know more about the Indians," Allen said.

"A good two hundred miles."

"We might as well be moving along ourselves, don't you think?" Bannister said.

Old Rag sighed and gave the order to mount up.

CHAPTER ELEVEN

ALLEN DROVE THE SUPPLY WAGON, with Gloria next to him. They followed the other wagons in silence until they were back on the trail alongside the river.

"Can you imagine the Indians traveling on foot with women and children for over two hundred miles?" Allen shook his head in disbelief.

"We're doing it." She shrugged.

"But we're making a onetime journey. It's their way of life. They're nomads. It must be like Abraham and Sarah, living in tents and moving families and livestock. And how did those braves get so close without our being aware? Just seeing them for a few minutes awakens awareness of their culture and adaptation to the prairie. Old Rag was right—they own this territory. And we don't belong here. At least not until we earn the right."

"I guess I hadn't thought of it like that," Gloria said.

"I'm so impressed with their confidence and pride. You could see it in the way they looked at us. It's different from the Indians I encountered in New York, who seemed lost." Allen gazed at the trudging rhythm of the mules.

"We travel with a wagonload of material possessions, and they have just essentials. We live such a complicated life. I can't see them as savages anymore." Gloria sat tall in the seat.

"I feel like I have just received a second great awakening on this journey," Allen said. "The first was seeing the power of the Holy Spirit in a tiny Negro church. The second is right now, to realize that I have a yearning to know these people. What they believe and why. How they raise their children, and to know their language and culture, and to communicate the gospel in a way they can understand." Allen fidgeted. "How can we expect them to understand what our culture has developed over centuries? We have to walk in their shoes, not make them walk in ours. The commissioning makes sense to me now."

"Just imagine what we will know a year from now. What we saw today will seem like nothing." Gloria retied the ribbons beneath her chin and readjusted her bonnet. "Seeing those three Indians was frightful."

"It was remarkable."

Gloria studied Allen, as if deciding whether to say more. "I'm not sure if you will understand this, Allen, but seeing those men made me feel threatened."

"What do you mean?"

She paused a few beats. "It was exhilarating to observe their riding skill, but I realized at the same time how dangerous they are." Gloria drew her shawl tight around her. "I'm used to being among respectful Christian men. When those men accosted me in Saint Louis, I felt vulnerable, but out here . . . there might not be someone to help me like you did." She patted Allen's knee.

"We need to depend more on God, don't we?" Allen spoke with conviction. "I mean, back home we took everything for granted. Those Indians could have attacked us and left us all for dead. But they just watched us, studying us as if we were the strange ones. God was protecting us and at the same time reassuring us of his faithfulness to our mission. Knowing that makes me feel secure in his grace."

"Oh, Allen, you're right. I'm blessed by your true heart." Gloria sounded relieved. "You inspire me by your trust in the Lord and by your adventurous spirit. You won't be shaken from your purpose, will you?"

"I feel so humbled by this, all of this." Allen swept his hand to encompass the wide stretch of land. "I get on my knees every morning and thank God for letting me be a part of it. Then I get on my knees at night and praise him for all the glory he's shown me. All day I wonder what could be more awesome than this vast prairie. Then I see the sunset. I wonder what could be more glorious than that, and I see the stars. Then I wonder what else could there be, and I wake up to a glorious sunrise.

"And now those Indians. I'm just speechless as to God's greatness. He made them just as he made us. Yet we are completely different in how we live our lives. They may not know of the Savior, and that's the most amazing of all. The Lord called me, and you, to tell them about salvation. 'How beautiful on the mountains are the feet of those who bring good news.' Gloria, it is such an honor to be here, to be called to this. Do you know what I mean?"

Gloria smiled, her eyes damp with unshed tears. "Yes, Allen, yes."

Allen, his heart overwhelmed, passed the reins to Gloria. He stood up in the wagon and shouted at the top of lungs, "Hallelujah!"

The sudden shout startled the mules. They bolted, knocking Allen back onto his seat.

Gloria pulled on the reins. "Easy, there."

She laughed at Allen. "That humility always gets in the way, doesn't it?"

Allen chuckled.

Shouts of "whoa!" came back through the short wagon train. All wagons stopped.

Allen heard Martha's voice above the clinking of harnesses and reins. "For goodness' sake, what are those young people doing back there? They should be separated. A single woman needs to be more discreet. Just listen to them laughing."

Old Rag trotted his horse back to their wagon, flinching as he passed Martha. He stopped next to Allen's wagon. "Everything all right back here?"

"Yes, sir." Allen looked Old Rag straight in the eyes. "Everything is fine."

"What happened? Did that pretty lady give you a kiss?"

Allen blushed. "No, sir, nothing like that happened."

"We're more likely to avoid us an accident if you-uns save the glory shouting for Sunday morning." Old Rag hollered the forward-ho command and rode off toward Obadiah and the livestock before Allen could explain.

For the next few miles, Allen and Gloria fell into silence. The only sounds they heard were the wagons creaking, the mules plodding, and the occasional call of another driver to his animals. Once in a while, they sighted a deer or a grouse, but mostly they saw the same old grass and the same old river. Allen refused to let boredom into his thinking. If he wasn't pondering the marvels he'd seen, he was planning how to build a cabin and a chapel in their new mission settlement, wherever that might be.

That evening after making camp and eating supper, the band members attended to their assigned chores before gathering around the campfire. Thomas and Obadiah were dutifully on watch. Allen would spell one of them in a couple of hours, but for the moment, he enjoyed the conversation, for which he had been waiting much of the day.

"How do Indians get their names?" Rachel asked Old Rag.

"My, yes!" Martha sat at attention. "What kind of a mother would name her child Buffalo Tail?"

"A Cheyenne mother leaves that duty to the father or an uncle." Old Rag sharpened his knife on a whetstone. "The infants are given a name for one of several reasons. The child might be named after a relative or for some omen or vision."

"Oh, that's superstitious nonsense." Martha waved her hand like she was swatting a fly.

Ignoring the comment, Old Rag continued. "An omen might be that the father, mother, or medicine man would have seen an animal in a dream. This is what they favor 'cause they know the child will have special strength or ability. What you may call superstition is their religion. It's how they make all their choices and how they get their wisdom. Like all the other Indian tribes, they have their proverbs and such. The older folks teach the young'uns. It's part of their schooling so's they grow up to be a responsible part of the tribe. Like good citizens, you might say."

Martha interrupted. "They also teach their young men to steal horses. That does not sound like good citizenship to me."

"To a Cheyenne, stealing a horse is a way a man gets rich. They don't think of it as no sin. Having a herd of horses is like having cash in the bank. A man can trade for things he needs. Teaching young men to fight, hunt, or steal horses is what's important to show strength and courage."

"It's no wonder why God has called us out here, with these people in such desperate need of civilizing. To imagine stealing horses as a good thing—that is absurd." Martha's comments soured the once-pleasant mood.

Allen sighed. The guide seemed caught between a rock and a wagon wheel about to run over it. Couldn't Mrs. Jolifer see that Rag wasn't defending the Cheyennes' way of life? He was just explaining what he knew of it. "Rag, how do you suppose he got the name Buffalo Tail, anyway?"

"It ain't for shore, but I was told that one day a buffalo heifer was running toward a cluster of women. The brave jumped onto his horse and galloped right up next to the buffalo. He grabbed the tail and swung its backside, forcing the buffalo to tumble before it charged into the women. After that he was a hero of sorts, and they named him Buffalo Tail. He's known as a tough fighter, always eager to get into a scrap."

"He certainly was a stout fellow," the reverend said.

"It would be quite the challenge to tumble a bull by the tail," Foster said. "A rather incredible stunt."

"Well, that's what I been told. Maybe someday you-uns will get a chance to ask him yourself." Old Rag rose from his place at the fire. "I best go spell Obadiah, let him get some rest. Allen, you do the same for Thomas, will you?"

"Yes, sir." Allen picked up his long rifle and followed Old Rag away from the fire. Once far enough away from the group around the campfire, Allen said, "Sorry about Mrs. Jolifer."

Old Rag glanced at Allen and then kept walking. "That woman could rile a rabbit into biting her. I weren't about to mention that a man could trade a horse or two for a wife. Lord knows what kind of a fuss that would raise."

"Oh my, yes. You were wise to be silent on that point."

Old Rag stopped. He studied Allen for a moment, as if he were going to say something. Instead, he nodded and walked away.

Finding Thomas, Allen relieved him and bid him good night. Allen dropped to the ground, leaned against a rock, and found the Big Dipper among thousands of brilliant stars. He thanked the Lord for a memorable day.

Over the next three days, Martha's discontent baffled Allen. She grew more critical and condescending of Old Rag, Thomas, and Obadiah, and even of the reverend. Her unending complaints about Allen and Gloria's traveling together forced Bannister to order the young people to travel separately and to keep private conversations at a minimum.

By midafternoon of the fourth day, a cloud formed low on the horizon to the southwest. Allen noted that it was not an ordinary cloud. No one paid particular attention except Old Rag, who studied it every so often.

Old Rag and Thomas rode ahead of the wagons to scout the trail and pick a campsite for the evening. Allen could see them about a half mile ahead on a rise overlooking the distance beyond. In an instant, Thomas turned his horse and galloped back to the train. "Buffalo," was all he said as he flew by each wagon.

Judging by the size of the dust cloud, Allen surmised it was a substantial herd. He wanted to whip the mules into a trot, but he held back, keeping his supply wagon in line behind the other wagons. Soon enough the command to halt was given. Allen locked the wheel brake and tied off the reins. He hopped off the wagon, ran up the rise, and stood by Old Rag's side. The rest of the group gathered. Now that the wagons were silent, they could hear a rumble, like constant thunder.

Old Rag swept his arm across the scenery. "We're going to see a big herd of buffalo come right up this valley, moving north."

"Won't they stop at the river?" Jacob said.

"River don't mean nothing to them. They'll cross it without slowing down. I'll send Obadiah down there to shoot us a calf, and we'll have some steaks for supper. Nothing like fresh buffalo steaks and liver, unless, of course, it's the tongue. Now that's mighty fine eating."

"There they are!" Mills pointed to the animals.

First a few buffalo entered the valley, then many, then a broad black line that spread across the depression. The buffalo dipped and came over another prairie swell. The thunder increased. Allen felt the trembling in his feet, knees, and chest. The rush of exhilaration made him want to run away, but he stood frozen in place. He could not will himself to move. The massive migration poured over the rises like a flood.

CHAPTER TWELVE

RACHEL CLUTCHED HER HUSBAND'S ARM. "Are we in danger?" She had to yell to be heard over the rumble of the buffalo herd.

"We're fine right here," Old Rag shouted back. "The closest animals are a quarter mile away." He waved to Obadiah, who walked down the slope, carrying his Hawkins rifle.

The herd was more than two hundred yards wide and stretched for a half mile.

"My goodness." Eva held her hand over her heart. She reached for the ground to sit; Rachel settled beside her.

The buffalo ran through the river and pressed northward. A half hour passed before the last of the roaring stream of hide and hooves was abreast of the onlookers. Obadiah finally rose and aimed. Smoke puffed out of his gun, and he reloaded. A second later, a fat calf, about a hundred yards from the hunter, staggered and fell.

Allen pleaded with the women to take a break and let Thomas do the cooking, and he did wonders with the loins and a few wild onions. The meat sizzled over the campfire. The smoke wafted amidst the wagons, carrying with it the scent of fresh meat. Standing with their plates in hand and mouths watering, the easterners waited to be served.

"That herd of buffalo was astounding," Gloria said.

"The power and energy reminded me of Niagara Falls." Phineas made a sweeping gesture with his arms.

Gloria faced Old Rag. "Mr. Ragsdale, why do the Indians worship the buffalo?"

"The prairie Indians make a god of the buffalo because it's their source of food, clothing, shelter, weapons, and tools. The buffalo provide about everything they need."

"That's no reason to worship it." Martha looked like she was about to go on, but Thomas dropped a large steak on her plate.

He served the others, Bannister led grace, and they fell silent as they ate. It had been several days since they'd had fresh meat.

Allen watched as Old Rag savored his first bite with his eyes closed. Then Allen took his first bite and understood the feeling. The warm meat juice filled his senses with a delicious connection to prairie life. It was primitive and wild, and now he was a part of it.

"Mr. Ragsdale, you were telling us about the Indians' beliefs," Gloria said.

"The Indians believe that the herd is moved by the Buffalo Spirit," he said. "That's why they sing and dance—to make the Buffalo Spirit pleased enough to send the herds. The people grow stronger by hunting the buffalo. The spirit is honored by a thanksgiving dance."

"That's very interesting," Gloria said. "We sing hymns of thanksgiving . . ."

"That's all superstitious nonsense." Martha wrinkled her nose. "No wonder they live in such primitive conditions."

"Like I said, it's what they believe. You-uns sing and pray to your Provider. They sing and pray to theirs," Rag said.

"Thomas, thank you for an excellent meal," Olive said.

Thomas smiled shyly as the others showered him with compliments on the excellent meal.

After the clean-up chores were finished, the band rested their full bellies by the campfire. The only one to complain was Martha.

"I see nothing of virtue in an uncouth prairie vagabond like Thomas Thomas or that mule-of-a-man Obadiah. Something is wrong with a man who has the same first and last name. And the other has no last name or no first name. Whatever the case may be, they are both lacking in manners, education, and obviously proper parenting."

"Martha, don't you think you're being hard on him? After all, he did just prepare us a wonderful meal," Eva said.

"No. He smells foul, and he wears greasy clothing. I have no sympathy for any of them whatsoever." Martha brushed her hands, as though shaking off dirt.

The three scouts sat at their own fire but close enough they could hear the conversation. Allen barely caught Old Rag's words to his companions.

"It'd be easier to teach a grizzly to fetch a stick than to make that woman happy."

Allen spent as much time as possible on his horse hunting for sage grouse or turkey. The wagon seemed confining, and he longed to see over every hill.

One day a brief late-afternoon rain shower rinsed the earth and released her fragrance of rich soil and wild grass. Rows of clouds lined the sky in all directions. With every passing moment, the declining sun painted the sky with the increasing intensity of colors from yellow to orange, and pink to red, each one contrasted by thin streaks of blue, as if making pews for the angels.

"I suppose only people who live on the prairie would see such dazzling beauty." Beulah hugged herself as she gazed upward.

Eva sighed. "I feel like I'm seeing through a window into heaven."

Each member of the band stopped what they were doing to watch the sky.

Gloria moved closer to Allen. "Isn't this overwhelming? I just want to embrace it." She extended her arms.

Allen looked from the glorious sunset to her tanned face, sparkling blue eyes, and hair that shined in the sunset glow. Her beauty surprised him, for he hadn't taken note of it before. In that moment he felt closer to her than he ever had to Violet. He shook away those unbidden feelings. She was more like a sister to him than someone he would consider courting.

"Rider coming!" Jacob announced and pointed.

Several men grabbed their rifles. Silhouetted by the western horizon, Allen saw that the lone rider was not an Indian. The way he sat on his horse, his build, and, of course, the hat distinguished him immediately.

He reined his horse. In a voice that seemed to rumble across the prairie, he said, "Permission to come into camp?"

"Come on in," Bannister said. "Are you alone?"

"I ride alone." He dismounted and tied his horse to one of the wagons. He stepped into the circle and scanned the group.

Bannister approached him with a smile and extended his hand. "Greetings. I'm Reverend Samuel Bannister. You are welcome in our camp."

"Pleased to make your acquaintance." He shook Bannister's hand. "I am Reverend Maxwell Covington." His blue eyes were sharp, piercing, taking in everything and everyone. He was equally as large as Bannister and perhaps broader in the shoulders. A commanding presence, he dominated Bannister's close-knit band.

Olive stepped forward, and her husband introduced her. "Would you care to join us for supper, Reverend Covington? You must be hungry."

"Yes, I would be most grateful to join you."

"Come, and I will introduce you to the rest." Bannister extended his arm, allowing the guest to pass closer to the awaiting missionaries. He presented Reginald Foster and his wife first, then the rest of the group, mentioning Old Rag and Thomas last.

"It certainly is a welcome surprise to host a guest such as yourself out here on the lone prairie. We are delighted that you are an American, and a fellow minister at that," Bannister said. "May I ask what brings you out here alone?"

"I prefer traveling alone," Covington said.

Eva shuddered. "Aren't you afraid of Indians?"

Her husband elbowed her and furrowed his eyebrows at her.

Covington turned his attention to the woman. "No, ma'am. I do not fear the Indians or wild beasts. I am traveling for the purpose of my Lord and trust entirely in his protection."

Old Rag kicked a stick deeper into the fire and muttered, "I've heard this before."

"You must travel with a firearm," Bannister said.

"I keep a set of pistols in my saddlebags and a fowling piece in a scabbard."

"That's rather lightly armed, considering the territory you're traveling," Bannister said.

Allen caught Old Rag's smirk. He leaned toward him and whispered, "What are your thoughts on this fellow, Rag?"

"I don't know. Something about him seems different from the rest of you pilgrims," Old Rag said under his breath.

"No, sir. As I said, I travel on the Lord's business and under his protection. I am on my return trip, and so far have had no call for concern about my safety." Covington stood with his fists on his hips. He looked over the camp like an inspector and smirked.

"Well then, might I ask the nature of the business for which the Lord has brought you here to the frontier and now across our path?" Bannister swallowed hard.

"I am a minister of the Methodist Episcopal Church, South Carolina Conference. I was asked by Bishop Seyborn to accept the call to serve as a missionary to the Indians in the Oregon Country. Rather than blindly committing myself, I requested a leave of absence from my parish in Greenville in order to see the potential for ministry success."

Bannister shifted his feet and rubbed his hands together. "We also are ordained and commissioned by the Methodist Episcopal Church from the New York and Genesee Conferences. I made an address at General Conference in Baltimore just a few weeks ago." He folded his arms and planted his feet firmly. "The Secretary of the Missionary Board introduced me to the assembly. We each accepted the call and commissioning without hesitation."

Covington made no reply. Accepting a plate of food, he sat at the head of the table and waited for the other men to be served. Then he said grace.

Bannister huffed and sat next to Benny. Martha poured the guest a cup of coffee and sat beside him.

"Reverend Covington, you said you were assessing the possibility of ministry among the Indians. What did you determine?" Foster unfolded his napkin.

Covington held Foster's glare. "It would be striving after wind, sir."

"You mean a vain endeavor?"

"Yes. I see no point in attempting to make faithful converts of these heathens. I do not believe that the good Lord would appropriate the resources of the church in the effort of changing the unchangeable. They desire neither change nor our presence. The Indians are content in their animistic beliefs and savage behavior. They are typically adulterous and inclined to blood vengeance. The best way to handle them is to send in the army to cleanse the land of their presence and defilement."

"By that, do you mean to kill them off?" Bannister's face grew red.

"Yes, sir. Just the way God directed the Israelites as they entered the land of Canaan. They need to be destroyed—man, woman, and child—and their religious high places torn down." Covington declared this atrocious idea as calmly as if planning a church potluck.

"That is the only way to purge this land of their idols and superstitions. Once the army has done its job, the land can be settled by civilized Americans who will make this an even greater nation, the true promised land. We will succeed where the Israelites failed."

Allen looked on the faces of the others. They looked as stunned as he felt. He'd never heard such notions before. Yet here was a stranger, a fellow Methodist preacher, making bold statements contrary to Allen's thinking. He couldn't fathom the man's convictions.

Foster cleared his throat. His voice was tight, as though trying to hold back fury. "Reverend Covington, you're saying that you see no reason to preach the gospel to the Indians?"

"Exactly."

"How could it be that God would lead you to such a conclusion when we are being led by God to do that very thing? We have responded to his missionary call to do what you claim to be a worthless undertaking."

"So you say." Covington forked food into his mouth.

Bannister straightened. "We, sir, have no doubt as to our calling by the Lord Almighty and by his church. We in no way would doubt nor contradict that call. And I certainly would not be so presumptuous as to challenge the bishop's word in order to satisfy my own curiosity."

"Bishop Seyborn has never been west of the Mississippi River." Covington remained unflappable. "He relies on reports of others who would say what they believe he wants to hear. Jason Lee, for example, describes Oregon as a place of great potential for the expansion of the church. Yet after three years he has little to show for his labor other than a meager settlement. He has been reduced to carpentry and farming, not preaching the Word of God. He now requests help of blacksmiths and cartwrights to continue developing a settlement. That does not sound like the high calling of the gospel to me."

Covington wiped his mouth with his handkerchief. "I chose to see for myself because I respond first to God, then the church. No, gentlemen, do not elevate the bishop to a place reserved for the divine. He is a mere man, and as such is prone to make mistakes. He, too, can be tempted by ambition and success. Therefore, I base my judgment on what I have seen for myself. And I will report this to Bishop Seyborn upon returning to the States. I must say, he will be appreciative of my evaluation of the matter. It is likely to save a great deal of human and financial resources."

"But what of the missionary movement that is reaching the uttermost parts of the earth?" Foster asked. "We have Methodist missionaries in Africa, China, and South America, not to mention the work among Indians in most states. There are even missionaries working among the Negroes in your own conference."

Bannister interrupted. "Our founder, John Wesley himself, was sent to work among the Indians in Georgia. You must see that our tradition is to take seriously the Great Commission of Jesus Christ!"

"John Wesley's mission to the Indians was a failure. He returned to England defeated, without having converted a single savage." Covington continued to eat, seeming to care little for any opinion but his own. "The Methodist Missionary Society is pursuing expansion in any and all directions because it is infatuated with reports of increased numbers and apparent success."

Allen feared Bannister might have a heart attack. His face went from red to almost purple. "Are you insinuating that we are on this journey merely to enhance the report of the Missionary Society?"

Covington set his fork beside the plate. "I am not insinuating anything. I simply have observed that many people are confused as to God's calling to purposeful ministry."

"Confused? Purposeful ministry?" Bannister rose to his feet.

His wife clutched his arm and tried to get him to sit down.

Allen leaned forward. "Reverend Covington, do you not believe that all people, whether Chinese, Indian, or Negro, have the right to hear the gospel and know the salvation of Jesus Christ?"

"No, of course not." Covington scowled. "Is it not obvious to you that those people are not predestined for the kingdom of God?"

Allen stared at the fellow pastor.

"Now you sound like a Calvinist," Bannister said.

"No, sir, I am no Calvinist. And you do John Calvin's theology a disservice with such a statement. I am a pragmatist. I merely point out the practical reality that those people are not capable of understanding the meaning of the Holy Bible. Therefore, they should not be expected to bear the responsibility of living the Christian life."

"But we have ordained Negro ministers within our denomination. You are in agreement with our church in that matter, aren't you?" Allen lifted his hands, palms out.

"Our denomination is a fallible human institution. I do not take personal responsibility for decisions I did not make."

"I have met some Negro preachers who are among the godliest people I know. They demonstrate a depth of understanding of Scripture that I did not observe even in seminary," Allen said.

"I have lived around Negroes my entire life," Covington said. "And I have yet to meet one to whom I would trust my knowledge of God's saving grace."

Allen kept his voice calm, but indignation rose in his belly. "But there are educated Negroes—"

"Educating Negroes is a precarious undertaking. We have taught ciphering among some of our slaves, but when you teach them to read, they become flippant and conceited."

Foster leaned forward. "Excuse me, did you say 'slaves'?"

"Yes, sir, my family has owned slaves for generations. I myself own three."

"I don't believe I have actually met a slave owner before. How do you go about acquiring a slave?" Olive asked, seemingly sincere.

"They can be purchased at auctions but are usually handled through agents or brokers," Covington said.

"How can you justify owning another human being?" Foster worked his jaw, his agitation evident.

"Justify? I have every legal right to own slaves."

Foster's brows knit. He ran his hand through his hair. "Of course it's legal, but as a minister, how do you explain the morality of slavery? Certainly you cannot believe that God would honor such an institution?"

"Morality is not the question, sir," Covington said. "Slavery is legal, and I treat the Negroes very well. In fact, if you were to offer my slaves their freedom, they would refuse because they know they are better off than if they had to fend for themselves in society."

"But shouldn't they have the right to choose to fend for themselves?"

"You sound as if you have been misguided by those Yankee abolitionists. Slavery is legal. Slaves in general are better off now than they were living wild in Africa."

"I must disagree," Foster said. "I have known many Negroes who progress rapidly when given the choice to do so and take the opportunities available."

"How many of those Negroes are doctors, lawyers, or community leaders? How many are capable of teaching school, even at the elementary levels? I would venture to say that the Negroes in the North are working at menial labor, and they live in poverty at best," Covington said. "They probably have children out of wedlock, and some children may not know who their fathers are. Isn't that the case?"

"I know many capable Negroes who own businesses and are striving to improve their condition," Foster said.

"Are you speaking of the general population of Negroes, or a mere few? Are there not poor neighborhoods dominated by Negroes? How many attend your church or live in your neighborhood?"

"I admit the majority live in their own part of town, which is not as well developed, but they are making a go of it." Foster stood and stepped to the opposite end of the table.

"I would challenge the well-being of my slaves against your 'free Negroes.' My slaves are content, they are taught the Bible and to cipher, and they wear clean clothing and live in clean housing. They eat fresh food every day and have not suffered any illness of significant severity. The children are cared for, and the families are kept together."

Allen's stomach twisted. He recalled the story Deacon Abraham had told him about being beaten and chained. Allen had never encountered a slave owner whose convictions were so strong and so different from his as those of Covington's.

Foster entered the argument again. "It is hard for me to imagine that God condones slavery. John Wesley himself wrote a treatise against owning slaves. If you do not see it as a moral issue because it is legal, or because they are treated well, certainly you must see it as opposition to God's will."

"Slavery is an institution recognized by God. I am following God's will by owning slaves and by treating them well."

"Following God's will?" Bannister glared at the reverend.

"Of course. Look at the Old Testament. Abraham owned slaves, as did Isaac and Jacob. His son Joseph was sold into slavery to the ultimate glory of God. Jesus taught that slaves should honor their masters. And the apostle Paul had a similar admonition in Ephesians chapter six. The Bible is definitely on my side here. In fact, I do not believe you have a biblical argument at all."

"Those passages do not command us to own slaves. Our society is growing beyond the maltreatment of all human beings. All men are created equal. This issue was discussed at length in the General Conference. I believe as a denomination, we will be prohibiting slavery very soon," Bannister said.

"As I said, owning slaves is legal and honorable. To release the slaves would be immoral. They could not decently provide for themselves, as you seem reluctant to recognize. It is our God-given duty to care for them.

"Division has been created in our nation and denomination by the misguided perceptions of those who do not understand slavery and have been influenced by the abolitionists." Covington's voice deepened. He wagged his finger at Bannister. "I guarantee you, within the next twenty years, there will be a split in both country and church over the issue of slavery and who has the right to decide about them."

"I do not foresee any divisions as long as the truth of God is understood. It's all the more reason for us to evangelize this nation and let the Holy Ghost lead us into all truth." Bannister clutched the lapels of his coat and rocked back on his heels.

Covington finished the last few bites of food and guzzled his coffee. "Thank you very much for the meal and conversation. I believe I will resume my travel and leave you folks to your camp duties."

"Certainly you will stay the night here in camp, where it is safe," Olive said.

"No, I will add several more miles before I retire for the night. As to safety, I do not believe that I would find protection here should a war party decide to attack. My goal is to return to Greenville as soon as possible. Therefore, I must add as many miles as I can each day. Again, I thank you for your hospitality." Covington mounted his tall roan thoroughbred and rode into the night.

"That was a disturbing conversation, I must say." Foster shook his head. "He has some nerve dismissing the work among the Indians like that."

"Let's clean up and get to bed," Bannister said as he watched the lone figure disappear into the blackness.

Allen felt drained and unsettled by the minister's disconcerting argument. His words had devalued the dear friends he'd made in the little Negro church, even though they had purchased their freedom, releasing them from dehumanizing treatment. What if the issue of slavery did lead to a split in the denomination?

From a rise about two hundred paces from the white man's camp, Kicking Lion and two scouts watched. They were downwind of the animals and the rifleman who guarded them.

"Let's kill them and take the horses. They are weak," a scout said.

"Dark Wolf did not say to kill them," Kicking Lion said. "We watch."

"The big one leaves. The angry one now is quiet. Soon they will sleep."

Kicking Lion assessed the scene. Which one was the White Falcon? Finally, he unleashed the predators on his left.

"Go. The big one is yours."

CHAPTER THIRTEEN

ALLEN RESIGNED HIMSELF TO DUTY on the supply wagon. He scanned the horizon, expecting to see rain clouds to warrant his dull feeling.

"Good morning, Allen," Old Rag said after he'd eaten a hearty breakfast. "We'll put on some miles today. Chimney Rock is behind us, and that up yonder is Scott's Bluff. Means we only got about two weeks to Fort Laramie."

He turned to the others, cleaning up from breakfast. "Let's get a moving, folks," Old Rag shouted. "I want to move up the trail a fair piece before siesta time." They were already an hour behind their usual schedule, but no one worked any faster. Old Rag rode up to Bannister and Foster, who leaned on his wagon.

"How can a Methodist minister believe that Indians are beyond saving?" Bannister shook his head and kicked at a stone. "How could he challenge the missionary call?"

Foster shrugged.

"Reverend, they ain't no point smoldering like a moist buffalo chip on the campfire," Old Rag said. "Let's move on and let last night go."

Allen slumped on the supply wagon bench. "Rag, we can't

shake last night's discussion about slavery. What do you think? Should people own slaves?"

"I don't need no slaves. Can't afford one," he said. "Besides, I got Thomas." Old Rag chortled, but seeing Allen's downcast face, he changed his tone. "Listen, people back East have slaves. Some Indians keep slaves. It's just the way life is. I came out West to live free, and I ain't never been a slave. But I don't want to live by another man's say-so neither. I believe all men should be free, but who am I to change the way of things?"

"Thanks, Rag." The insights seemed to lighten Allen's mood. "I have some friends who bought their freedom, and I was thinking of them."

"Well, if they're friends of yours, then the good Lord is watching over them." Old Rag nodded at Allen. "It's time for us to be moving."

"Yes, sir."

"Let's roll!" Old Rag commanded.

Whips cracked and commands shouted; mules and oxen strained against their now-familiar loads.

They stopped midday at a bend in the river west of Scott's Bluff. "We won't be stopping long folks," Old Rag announced. "We got a fair piece to cover yet."

Old Rag ate heartily. Allen took a few bites but was distracted by the group's discussion.

"I think what he had to say was very valuable," Martha said. "Perhaps he's right. Bishop Seyborn knows no more than what he is told by ambitious men who are trying to get on his good side. Perhaps you are 'chasing after wind.'"

"We are not chasing after wind, Mrs. Jolifer," Bannister said. "We were called by God and the church to this missionary service. We had reports about the need for the gospel out here in the wilderness. We have seen that for ourselves. And please do not forget, we each made a commitment to establish a mission in the Oregon country."

"He certainly is brave to be riding alone, all the way across the country and back. He is a man of sure faith and solid understanding of his purpose in life," Martha said.

"He is foolish to be out here alone. He didn't even keep a rifle at hand. I would not be surprised to learn that he never makes it back to South Carolina and his slaves. What a shameful thing for a minister of the gospel." Bannister still fumed over the encounter.

Instead of arguing further, Martha focused on storing kitchen utensils in the wagon's side-box. "Are we ready to go?"

By the end of the day, they had covered thirteen miles. Old Rag's trail sense was more valuable to the band than they understood.

Old Rag had disclosed to Allen that he hoped to encounter Indians again in order to put a little fear in the missionaries of the potential for trouble. They worked well enough around camp and were good with the animals, he said, but they were anything but sharp when it came to watching for possible dangers.

Allen had observed that Old Rag and his men had to pull extra watch duty. Several times Mills, Herbert, and Foster had been caught asleep at their posts. Allen stayed awake, but he watched the stars more than the shadows.

Allen helped Beulah lift a utensil box onto a wagon. He looked for a place by the fire to sit and whittle. Relaxing by the fire was a peaceful time of a weary day.

Thomas brought an armload of firewood to camp. As he stepped around one of the wagons, a crooked branch caught on the canvas and fell out of his arms. He set the load by the fire and returned to get the dropped piece. Right then Martha came around the same wagon, holding a pot of water. The toe of her shoe caught under the stick's curve as her other foot stepped on the branch. She screamed as she tripped forward, spilling the water and falling into the wet dirt. Thomas rushed to her and reached to help her up.

Martha slapped his hand. "Don't touch me."

Thomas jumped back as if a snake had bit him. He clearly hadn't left the stick there intentionally. The other ladies rushed to help but stopped short, as if bumping into a wall.

"You did that on purpose, you malicious, cowardly fool." Martha picked up the stick and swung at Thomas's head.

He lifted his arms to ward off the blows while backing out of her reach. Virgil Jolifer came up behind his wife and grabbed the branch out of her hand. He didn't say a word, just walked over and dropped the stick on the pile of firewood. Bannister and Old Rag came near as Martha began her verbal lashing.

"You filthy, vulgar, little man! You're a clumsy, good-for-nothing idiot! You can't even carry firewood into camp without causing a problem. No wonder your mother abandoned you. If you even knew who your father was, he would have abandoned you too—"

"That's enough!" Old Rag stepped between Thomas and the woman.

Any frontier woman would likely have gotten a beating for such an outburst, Allen thought. But then again, most frontier women would understand that a man's past was his past. You measured him by what he did now. Thomas didn't have the privilege of a proper family upbringing, but he was a solid worker.

Allen put his hand on Thomas's shoulder. "Mrs. Jolifer, that is not fair. I've gotten to spend time talking with Thomas. You need to know that Thomas's mother did what she could to survive. Like many women in Saint Louis, her husband never returned from a trip out West. Hard to say if they were killed by Indians, the rivers, sickness, or if they just ran off.

"After his mother died of pneumonia, Thomas survived by doing odd jobs for several tradesmen and sleeping in a hay shed. Then five years ago, Old Rag needed help with a freight wagon and took him on."

"I don't care about any of that." Martha glared first at Thomas, then at Bannister, her face twisted and red and her fists clenched. "I don't know why you tolerate these uncouth, foul-mouthed heathens in our camp. I think we would do just fine without them, and it would certainly be less dangerous to do chores." Martha grabbed her pot, spun on her heels, and stomped off.

"Let's all get back to business now," the reverend said. He patted Thomas on the shoulder. "I don't know what set her off."

Allen followed as Thomas sulked away and found Obadiah. "I tried real hard to get on her good side, but it ain't no use."

"I'm ready to pull out and head back to Saint Louis." Obadiah slapped his hat on his thigh. "The money ain't worth it. I can't abide by that woman."

During the night, Allen awoke. He saw Thomas bringing in an armload of firewood and setting it down gently, making almost no noise. It must have been 3:30 in the morning, judging by the stars. Then a few minutes later, he brought in a bucket of water.

At daylight, Martha called everyone for morning prayer. She was about to begin with a song when Bannister interrupted. "I think it is important that we keep our focus on the Lord and his gracious kindness to us all. Let us be mindful of this throughout the day, and certainly now as we begin with this meditation and song." He nodded at Martha to begin the song.

She glared back with a tight smile and began singing "Love Divine, All Loves Excelling."

Bannister read the Scripture verses from the liturgy. He then concluded with prayer and was careful to mention their three prairie guides. Within an hour, the wagon train rolled on its way.

During the day, Allen rode up alongside Gloria. "How are you doing?"

"Hi, Allen. I'm fine for the most part. I have a little bit of a headache, but otherwise I'm just fine."

"You're not getting a cold, are you?"

"No, it's different. It feels more like a band is being pressed around my head. I don't know what to think about it." Gloria frowned.

"Have you seen Thomas around?"

"No, the poor man. I was surprised at how angry Mrs. Jolifer became last night. It was much more than was called for."

"Yes, that was quite an outburst. I thought maybe I'd ride with Thomas for a while and see if I could take his mind off it. He brought in more firewood and water during the night, but he hasn't been anywhere near the camp since then."

"I haven't seen him at all today." Gloria massaged her forehead. "But I wonder if that has something to do with my headache? For the past couple of days I've been feeling something strange, and it seems to be growing."

"You're sure it's not a cold or the flu? I'd hate to see an illness spread through the camp." Allen knit his brows together.

"No, I . . . I know this will sound odd, but I think it's a spiritual matter. I've had trouble praying. I get the feeling that we're about to experience something strange. It frightens me." She wrapped her arms around herself and shivered, as though suddenly cold.

"Now that you mention it, I've been distracted while praying too. I guess we'll have to make a concerted effort to get back on track."

Gloria nodded.

"I'll go look for Thomas." Allen rode back and asked Obadiah.

"Ain't seen him," Obadiah grunted.

Allen scanned the hills as he rode away. Where could he be?

As he built a small fire, Dark Wolf considered the information Kicking Lion had shared. He dropped an ember out of the clam shell, blew gently, then added sticks as the flame grew. Sitting cross-legged on a black wolf hide, he set a bunch of sage in the fire to smolder. Dark Wolf sang to the Rattlesnake Spirit as he wafted smoke over his head and body. He rubbed sage ash on his face and chest.

Next, he lifted a white feather from a prairie falcon into the rising smoke. Chanting intently, he bobbed his head as if he were a striking snake. The smoke shifted, and he released the feather to drift counter to the wind, in the direction of the white man's camp.

CHAPTER FOURTEEN

ALLEN STRETCHED HIS BACK AND shook his legs. This had been their longest day yet. Old Rag hadn't spoken for hours except to give the command to stop. Every movement in camp was deliberate. The polite tension eased when Olive announced dinner was ready.

"Riders coming," Jacob hollered as he rushed in with firewood.

"Oh my, are they Indians?" Eva set down the dishes and looked for a place to hide.

Allen looked back toward the east, seeing two riders wearing buckskins, each leading two packhorses as they trotted toward the camp.

The missionary men grabbed their rifles, and the women moved behind a wagon for protection.

"Hello, the camp! May we come in?" the first rider called.

"Jack, Joaquin? Glad to have you!" Old Rag stepped forward with a smile on his face and shook hands with the strangers. "Where you heading?"

"On our way to Bridger's Post to finish up some trading. Looks like you've up and got religious." He moved to greet Bannister.

"Hello, sir, and welcome to our camp. I'm the Reverend Samuel Bannister, leader of this missionary band. Allow me to present you to Reverend Foster."

The visitor shook hands with each of the men, as did his partner. Outgoing and polite, they were instantly welcomed by the missionaries.

"I am pleased to make your acquaintance, one and all. And look at these lovely ladies." He bowed toward the women, who blushed. "I am Jacques Burkett—most call me Jack. And this is my partner, Joaquin Del Castillo."

Both men were tall, with shoulder-length dark hair, tanned skin, and bright smiles. Their simple movements were smooth and confident, Allen thought, tucking in his shirt, but these men were strikingly handsome. They wore buckskin jackets over calico shirts, and they would have been equally as dashing in business suits back in New York. They would no doubt catch the admiring eyes of the most important and beautiful women of the city. Which made Allen think of Violet.

"This is my wife, Olive Bannister." The reverend held her elbow and nudged her forward.

Jack took her hand and bowed low. "Madame. I assure you that over the vast Great Plains there is not a field of wildflowers that compares to your loveliness."

She blushed. "Would . . . would you like—"

"Gentlemen, we were just about to sit down to supper. We would be honored if you would accompany us," Bannister said.

"Thank you very much. We would be delighted." Jack smiled.

Joaquin nodded in agreement.

"Very good then. Ladies, please set two more places for our guests." The reverend directed them to a hand-washing basin and invited the guests to take seats at the middle of the table. Bannister led a brief blessing for the meal.

Old Rag passed the plate of cornbread to Jack. "So you're on your way to Bridger's Post?"

"Yes. We will make a brief stop at Fort William, then deliver this load to Bridger's place on the Green River." Jack took a piece of cornbread.

"Fort William? Do you mean Fort Laramie?" Bannister seemed confused.

"Yes, they are calling it Fort Laramie now. We are to deliver the post and some documents to Milton Sublette there. He runs the trading company."

"How much farther is it to Fort Laramie?"

"We should make it by the end of the fourth day from now, I expect. Of course, it will take you folks twelve days or so if the weather treats you right. I do want to recommend that you cross—" Jack was interrupted by a barrage of questions.

"Twelve days? That's good. What is Fort Laramie like?"

"Have you been to Oregon, Mr. Burkett?"

"What can you tell us about the Indians?"

Martha stood, and without a word she went to the far side of her wagon.

"Let's let Mr. Burkett speak, shall we?" Bannister said.

"We are Methodist missionaries from New York, and we are bound for the Oregon Territory to establish a work among the Indians. Have your travels taken you to Oregon?"

Jack flashed an easy smile. "As a matter of fact, I was among the party that led your colleague Jason Lee and his group to the Willamette Valley. I rode along with Joe Meek."

"You know Joe Meek?" Mills leaned forward.

Allen's ears perked up. Meek's reputation as an Indian fighter and explorer was known from stories that circulated throughout the East.

"Yes, sir. I crossed paths with Joe back in thirty-four. We got into a scrape with some Blackfeet after the rendezvous. I was working for Jim Bridger, hauling some pelts—"

"You know Jim Bridger personally?" Mills leaned closer to hear, causing his wife and Gloria to move down.

"Mr. Ragsdale, have you been holding out on these folks?" Jack rubbed his hands together. "Well, folks, it appears your guide, Mr. Ragsdale, is a virtuous soul. A man of great exploits. Yet his humility has overcome his opportunity for boasting."

Allen looked at Old Rag squirm as if ants were crawling up his legs.

"Mr. Ragsdale knows these men we speak of—Jim Bridger, Joe Meek, Kit Carson, and even Jedediah Smith. Old Rag has ridden and fought with the best of the plainsmen. Isn't that right, Rag?"

"Well." Old Rag bolstered himself. "I guess I seen a thing or two."

"I'd say us pilgrims owe you more respect than we've been giving," Allen said.

Martha returned and refilled the visitors' coffee cups. She then inserted herself between them, forcing everyone to shift on the bench. She had combed out her hair and put on a clean apron.

Jack sipped the coffee. "Mr. Ragsdale and I met during that same year. After that fight with the Blackfeet I mentioned, I rode down to Fort Hall with ol' Jim, packing a passel of prime beaver plews. These were ones we cached for the winter but didn't collect in time for the rendezvous trading.

"Mr. Ragsdale hauled that load clear back to Saint Louis and was returning with a freight load of supplies for the fort when they were attacked and robbed. It seems some trappers that Bridger wouldn't do business with got together with some renegade Indians and attacked Mr. Ragsdale's freight train. Obadiah was with you then, too, wasn't he?"

Old Rag nodded. "That's right. Them yellow-backed bandits came at us—" He stopped, glancing at the ladies.

Jack smiled. "They fought them off, but not before some men were killed and most of the supplies were taken. Your guides, folks, made it to Fort Hall two days later with only two wagons out of eight and not even half of the men who'd started out. Mr. Ragsdale was shot twice, and Obadiah was nearly dead.

"Once we heard what happened, we set out to recover what we could. Bridger, Joaquin, a few other trappers, and me. Old Rag wanted to go along, but Bridger wouldn't have it. He was just too shot up to be of much use."

"Then what happened?" Mills couldn't seem to sit still.

Everyone's attention remained riveted on Jack. "A couple days later we caught up to the thieving scoundrels, only to find that they had burned the wagons and destroyed much of the supplies. They took the horses and mules, some guns, and the things that were easy to carry. We figured they were going to take the freight somewhere to sell, but when they found that the country was too rugged, they lost their ambition.

"We got into a fight with them, but they were so drunk they couldn't shoot straight. Some of them ran off, but we served justice to the leaders. We got back what was left of the goods and the horses. Ol' Bridger was grateful to Mr. Ragsdale for being loyal to their agreement, even though it nearly cost his life. You folks are fortunate to have him as your guide."

Allen caught Old Rag's eye and nodded.

Rachel jumped up. "Oh my, you boys should have been put to bed an hour ago."

"Tomorrow we can play Rescue the Supply Wagon," Benny said.

"For sure." Joseph's eyes were wide with excitement.

"Well done, Ragsdale," the reverend said, thumping the table with his fist. "I had no idea of your heroic and colorful past."

"We could tell you plenty more stories about Mr. Ragsdale if we had the time." Jack sipped his coffee.

Martha sat between the two gallant travelers as if she belonged with them. She smiled at Jack.

Joaquin sat quietly. He smiled at Gloria. "Thank you for the food. I enjoyed it."

She blushed and looked down at her clasped hands.

"And what of you, Joaquin?" Bannister turned to the mostly silent visitor. "Are you a Spaniard?"

"Yes, sir." Joaquin nodded and grinned. "My grandfather was from Spain and served as a Mexican officer in Nuevo Mexico, in Santa Fe." His English was fluent and without accent.

"I see. And what brings you up to the north country?"

"As Jack has mentioned, we are on our way to see Jim Bridger to finish a trading deal."

Old Rag whispered to Allen, "Joaquin don't ever say much. Lets Jack do the talking."

"Joaquin, like your Mr. Ragsdale, is not one to boast on himself." Jack put his hand on his friend's shoulder. "His grandfather was from Spain and became a wealthy landowner in Santa Fe. He married a beautiful girl whose mother was Mexican and father was a powerful Apache chieftain. Because of her Indian blood, the Apache didn't make war against him, so his ranch and herds thrived.

"But a corrupt Mexican governor was so jealous of him, his beautiful wife, and his wealth that he began to steal the land by changing decrees. Of course, that turned into a fight, which led to the deaths of the grandparents, Joaquin's father and mother, and all of his uncles.

"The Apaches later killed the governor in revenge. They took Joaquin to live among them for a few years, as it was the only safe place for him."

As Jack spoke, Joaquin stared into his coffee cup.

"Now, the land is in the possession of some other corrupt official, and so Joaquin is left without his home, land, or family."

The missionary band was quiet. Allen had only read of such things in novels, and now they were eating supper with a person about whom such romantic stories were written.

Jack told how he and Joaquin had met at Bent's Fort on the Arkansas River. Both young men were hired by a team of buffalo hunters to do skinning and packing. They became good friends and had ridden together ever since.

"We saw some Indians last week, hundreds of them," Mills said.

"Oh, is that so?" Jack said. "They didn't cause trouble, I hope."

"No, no trouble. There were a couple hundred Cheyenne on their way to Bent's Fort. Isn't that right, Mr. Ragsdale?" Mills described how the three young braves demonstrated horsemanship like they had never seen before.

Old Rag groaned. "Why did Mills have to mention that?" he muttered to Allen.

"Buffalo Tail?" Jack looked at Old Rag. "If you came across Buffalo Tail and still have all your horses, then I would say the good Lord is watching over you carefully."

"Yes, that is what I told Mr. Ragsdale," Bannister said. "It is true then—the Cheyenne Indians are walking all the way to the Arkansas River?"

"Yes, it's true." Jack frowned. "Joaquin and I were at Bent's Fort before we went to Saint Louis. There's to be a large gathering of Cheyenne, Arapaho, Kiowa, and Comanches. They are no doubt talking about territorial rights. You see, the Cheyenne and Arapaho used to live up near the Great Lakes but were pushed out by the other tribes of the east. They keep moving west ahead of us white folk. Now these tribes are trying to decide how to share hunting grounds and whether or not they'll tolerate more white people coming through."

"So those hundreds we saw walking were on their way down there?" Mills still leaned against his wife.

"No doubt. From what I hear, there will be thousands of Indians at that gathering," Jack said.

"I was impressed to see so many families traveling in order," Allen said.

"Well, of course, it's obvious they are an organized people." Martha rolled her eyes at Allen.

"That's right," Jack said, looking at Allen. "The Cheyenne are nomadic and can move hundreds of people on short notice. They move camps frequently to follow the herds or for other religious reasons. They're a disciplined people in their own way."

Jack swallowed his coffee, then turned to Joaquin. "¿Pues, Compadre, debemos irnos, que no?"

"Cuando quieres," Joaquin said.

"What are you two saying?" Gloria said.

Jack laughed. "I said, 'Well, partner, we had better be leaving.' Then Joaquin answered, 'Whenever you want.'"

"Oh, por favor, quedense con nosotros esta noche."

Everyone stared at Martha, clearly surprised by her obvious fluent Spanish. She clutched Jack's arm. He removed her hand when he stood.

He looked at Bannister and nodded. "Thank you for the fine meal, warm hospitality, and"—he turned to Martha—"the invitation to stay the night, but we'll be moving on a few more miles before we stop for the night."

"If you feel you must, but you are most welcome to stay the night here in the safety of our camp," Bannister said.

"Much obliged, I really am, Reverend and Mrs. Bannister, but we need to tend to our business, which is to get to the Green River as soon as possible."

"Oh, please stay, Jacques. We'll make sure you're comfortable." Martha tilted her head and smiled.

Ignoring her, Jack turned to Old Rag but spoke to the group. "You folks are in good hands with Mr. Ragsdale. He'll see you safely through any trouble you may encounter. He's a good man." Jack and Joaquin shook hands with several people and moved toward their horses.

Eva frowned. "How come no one wants to stay in our camp?"

As Jack adjusted the saddle on his bay gelding, Allen offered to fill Jack's and Joaquin's canteens with fresh water.

Old Rag stepped up next to him. "Nice to see you again, Jack. Glad you stopped by. This has been an interesting trip, I must say."

"No doubt, Rag," Jack said, keeping his voice low, and Allen remained riveted to his spot. "Most of them look like good people, but it's hard to say how they'll fare in the wilds. I reckon Allen here will do. But I'll tell you this—keep an eye on that Jezebel woman, Mrs. Jolifer. She'll be trouble for sure."

"You don't know the half of it, Jack. But I'll accept your sympathy."

Jack swung up into the saddle. "I also suggest you move across to the north side of the river for the next few days. You're heading into Dark Wolf's territory, and he won't take trespassers lightly. He and his men have been stirring up things lately. It'd be best to steer clear of him."

"That bloodthirsty Arapaho?" Old Rag spit. "Yeah, I hear you. Trouble is getting these folks to cooperate with things they don't understand. But I'll get them across tomorrow. Thanks."

"You watch your topknot, Old Rag."

"You watch your'n." He patted Jack's horse on the rump. "Adios, Joaquin."

Jack leaned over and shook hands with Allen. "Be seeing you."

"Hope you folks have a good journey," Jack said as he and Joaquin rode off into the darkness.

Allen was reaching into a supply wagon to grab his bedroll when he heard the women's voices.

While clearing the table, Eva said, "Have you ever seen such dashing men?"

"Eva! I'm surprised at you." Beulah perched her hands on her hips. "But I have to admit, Joaquin's smile was enough to sweep you off your feet." They giggled.

"What did you think, Gloria? I noticed him looking at you. Didn't he take your breath away?" Eva beamed like a schoolgirl.

"No. I didn't think . . . well, I . . . yes," Gloria said. "Yes, I guess he did take my breath away. Joaquin is very handsome, and so steady and confident. Both of them are. And can you believe his life story?"

Mrs. Mills sighed. "Oh my, that was so romant—"

Martha approached. "Now, ladies, let's not lose our composure over a couple of guests."

Upon hearing Martha's voice, Allen looked up to see Old Rag duck behind a wagon, and Allen chuckled. He finished setting up his bedroll and leaned against the supply wagon, looking at the stars.

Old Rag cleared his throat.

Allen shifted. "Oh, Rag, I'm sorry. I didn't see you come up."

"That's fine. I seen you was thinking."

"I find myself wishing I could have ridden off with those two men. I've met businessmen and politicians in New York City, even bishops and denominational leaders, but none impressed me as much as Jack and Joaquin."

Late into the night, Old Rag entertained Allen with adventures he'd lived with the two mountain men and Indians.

"I apologize for taking you for granted, Rag," Allen said. "I had the wrong idea about what life was like out here. You and Thomas appear so ordinary. I meet Jack and Joaquin, and they lived the stories I've heard about. Then I find out you lived as exciting a life as them."

"Aw, I wouldn't go saying that. Those two are tops among all mountain men. I'm just a freighter who got into trouble and happened to live through it. I couldn't keep up with them even in my younger days. Jack and Joaquin are mountain savvy. Some might think they rush into danger like fools, but they know what they're doing every step of the way. You saw how friendly they were and charming to the ladies, but I tell you, if we'd been attacked, they would have turned into ruthless warriors to protect the lot of you-uns. They might have some education, but they are mountain men, born and bred."

"I feel so small out here." Allen looked to the stars. "Like I don't know a thing. I don't belong here, but I want to. I feel like a . . . like—"

"Like a prairie scout in a church meeting?" Old Rag grinned. "You don't fret on it, now, Allen. You got a good head and you learn quick. That's important. The good Lord's watching out for you. Even I can see that." He patted the young preacher on the shoulder. "You'd best get some sleep now."

"Thanks for talking to me, Rag. I'm very glad I've gotten to know you." Allen shook Old Rag's hand.

The scout nodded his head but did not look Allen in the eye.

Driving the supply wagon, Allen was the last to cross the North Platte River. Old Rag made a quick check of the wagon's condition and scanned the far side of the river.

Allen looked back. "You look nervous, Rag. Is there a problem?"

"Not certain. Something's got my belly in a knot. I ain't sure what's worse, fighting Indians or arguing about my choices." He nodded at Bannister, who was on foot, with his fists on his hips.

"I don't understand why we should cross the river when the main trail is over there." Bannister pointed over his shoulder. "And you know we are here to show God's love to the Indians."

"Reverend, I know your intentions. But my job is to get you folks to Fort Laramie safe and sound. This side will be safer." Old Rag dismounted. "Let's say that you have a church full of nice folks, and you learn that a new man in town is a murdering thief. Would you put all those families in danger just to try to save his soul?"

Bannister stiffened. "Mr. Ragsdale, you don't understand the power of Jesus Christ to transform a man's life."

"Food's ready!" Olive called from the wagons.

"Well, I'm good and hungry." Taking full advantage of the angelic interruption, Rag rushed to the table.

"You will not eat until you wash properly," Martha said.

Old Rag's shoulders sagged as he turned to find the wash bucket.

Allen handed Rag the bar of soap and wiped his hands on a towel.

Just then Thomas came around the corner of a wagon. The toe of his boot kicked a straw broom he didn't see leaning against the side by the wheel. The falling broom poked Martha in the behind, startling her. She bumped the wash bucket, which splashed back on her. She stepped back and lost her balance, falling against the wagon. She caught herself but tore her skirt on the wagon brake.

Had it happened to any of the other ladies, it might have been humorous. But when she saw the guilty look on Thomas's face, Martha fully believed he was the source of her humiliation. Her faced turned red, she narrowed her eyes, and she pursed her lips.

"You imbecile! You did that on purpose." She grabbed the broom and started whacking Thomas. "You demon-possessed, filthy, son of a whore—"

"That's enough!" Old Rag tried to snatch the broom.

"Don't you touch me!" She turned her rage on Old Rag and began beating him.

The rest of the missionary band seemed paralyzed. Finally Virgil Jolifer moved behind his wife, trapped her arms, and forced the broom out of her desperate grip. Allen flinched as she spewed angry wrath on Thomas, Old Rag, and Bannister.

Once her husband had removed Martha, Thomas faced his boss. "I won't take that no more, Rag. She's crazy. I never seen that broom. It was an accident. She got no right saying those things and calling me names. It ain't right." He dabbed at his torn and bleeding ear.

Old Rag took a close look at the damaged ear. "Better it was you than Obadiah. He would have struck back and killed her."

Old Rag turned to Bannister. "That's it. I quit as your guide. We're pulling out. You folks are on your own. Just follow the river." He spun and marched off, pushing Thomas ahead.

Bannister hurried after the guide. "Mr. Ragsdale, I'm terribly sorry for this. It won't happen again. Please reconsider." His pleas fell on deaf ears.

Old Rag, Thomas, and Obadiah loaded two packhorses with their gear and provisions. They rode off to the north without looking back.

CHAPTER FIFTEEN

"JUST HOLD ON A FEW more days," Bannister said. "We can't turn around now."

Allen was just as weary as the rest. After three days, the missionary band still missed their guides. The wagons worked their way over another rise. The prairie taunted them with their elusive goal and tempted them to cave in to hopelessness. The relentless sunrises and sunsets, no longer glorious, mixed together like a stew of impatience.

Such sensible wisdom did nothing to inspire fresh hope. Someone in a less fatigued state of mind might have said something more creative to break the tension. But even creativity was an annoyance when the end was not in sight. It was out there somewhere, just not over this rise.

Allen caught a horned toad and gave it to the Herbert boys, hoping to keep them amused.

"Let's fill the wagon with horned toads," Joseph said.

"Why sure," Benny said. "We can trade them to the Indians for tomahawks."

Allen laughed as Benny straightened to his full height. Every Sunday the boys measured their growth by standing next to a stack of buffalo chips.

Joseph counted. "You're twenty-five chips tall this week, Benny."

"Now let's count you." Benny added more chips to the stack.

"Stop that, boys. There's no dignity in measuring yourselves that way." Rachel always interrupted their fun.

The boys did the same thing every week, never once minding their mother's admonition. It seemed as though she could not allow herself to stow dignity in the wagon as if it were a trunk, only to be pulled out when a mission was established. Propriety was apparently so ingrained that it was as much a part of her life as eating. Every day she pulled back her hair into a tight bun and brushed down her dress. Cleanliness, modesty, and manners were clearly her pillars of Christian witness, even on the trail.

Bannister stood with his hands on his hips, looking westward across the prairie. He bit his lower lip. "How much longer?"

"Why don't we send someone on ahead to determine just how far we are from Fort Laramie?" Martha said. "We need to know precisely what lies before us. After all, Mr. Ragsdale said we would be there in less than twelve days, and we are already into the fifteenth. I never did trust him. I am indeed grateful that the Lord took him away from us."

Bannister had already considered the notion, but decided it was wiser to keep the group together, since they were without a guide. Patience would prove the greatest virtue. If they didn't arrive tomorrow, they would arrive the next day. What difference did that really make?

"Thank you for your concern, Mrs. Jolifer. Now that he is no longer with us, we do not make the same distance every day," Bannister said.

"Are you insinuating that it is my fault Mr. Ragsdale and his helpers left us? I will not accept responsibility for his poor judgment." Martha's lips tightened.

"No, ma'am. I am not insinuating anything. I am merely pointing out why we have not yet reached Fort Laramie. The simple truth is that we averaged almost fifteen miles a day when Mr. Ragsdale was with us. On a good traveling day now, we cover only nine or ten miles. Naturally, our arrival time will be set back."

Silently, Bannister did blame her. She had ridden poor Ragsdale and his men so hard it was surprising they stayed as long as they did. Bannister regretted having taken Ragsdale for granted. He was a textbook of information about Indians and life on the frontier, and he was skilled in finding the smoother course. It would be worth doubling his wages to have him back. Bannister would gladly pay that much out of his pocket, not just to share the load of leadership but to bear the burden of this woman's piercing glare.

The next morning Allen worked with Jacob as they cleaned up the camp and packed the wagons.

"If Jack Burkett's estimate was sound and at the miles we're covering each day, we have seven more days on this trail." Jacob settled a box of kitchen supplies. "It would cheer my soul to know that for certain."

Allen considered Jacob's estimation. "I believe all of us would be cheered by that information."

"My wife is growing weary of this prairie." He looked around at the same hills they had been seeing for days.

"Today is a new day to find a reason to rejoice." Allen placed the last box in the wagon. "The Lord is bound to show us something good soon."

Bannister gave the first call to move out. He circulated among the wagons, stopping when he came to Allen and Jacob. "Jacob, I'd like for you to ride ahead and scout out the trail to Fort Laramie. You are a reliable man, and I believe I can trust you to bring back some good news." He leaned his hand on the supply wagon. "I calculate you will require a day or two to locate the fort and then return promptly."

Jacob's face lit up. "You can trust me. I'll find the best way to Fort Laramie and get the group there in short order." He grinned at Allen as Bannister left.

Rachel stepped next to her husband. "I have a bad feeling about your going off."

"Aw, darling, what could go wrong? We've been following this river for weeks now. All I have to do is ride up ahead a little to find the fort. It will help the group's morale."

Her eyebrows furrowed. "I know why you want to do it, Jacob. I am fearful that somehow you will be hurt. It's just a bad feeling. Can't somebody else go?"

"No. I need to do this, and Reverend Bannister is waiting for me." Jacob tried to hug his wife, but she turned away. "Pray for me, will you, honey? I know I'll be fine." Mounting his horse, he repeated, "I'll be fine."

Allen grabbed the horse's bridle. "We'll all be praying for you, Jacob."

Bannister stopped his horse next to Jacob. "Mr. Herbert, are you ready?"

"Yes, Reverend, I am all ready to go."

"Very good then. I will accompany you the first two miles and see to the morning's path." Bannister looked down at Mrs. Herbert. "Jacob should be back by tomorrow's supper or by midday of the next at the latest."

Rachel wrapped her arms around herself and stared at the ground.

Allen thought she looked like a lost little girl. He watched the two riders drop into a draw, then found Gloria. "Could you try to encourage Mrs. Herbert throughout the day?"

"I'll see what I can do, but I feel disturbed by her fear. It is not like her to look so grim. To be honest, I wish we would just stay together. I'm not able to pray for very long. My thoughts get tossed about like leaves in a whirlwind."

"I know what you mean. It's a troubling feeling, as if a heavy weight is upon us."

Within an hour the reverend met the group at the top of a rise. Everyone seemed subdued. Only Martha seemed cheerful that morning. They pushed on, Allen with the supply wagon while he rode his horse.

"Allen!" Bannister waved Allen over to his wagon. "I believe we'll stay on this course for today. However, the other side looks better to me. I want you to look for a good place to cross the river."

"Yes, sir, but shouldn't we wait until Jacob returns with his report? I believe Mrs. Herbert will be uncomfortable with such a change. She's very worried."

"Her worry is in vain. Mrs. Herbert must decide for herself not to fret when we're in the Lord's protective care. Besides, Jacob will be able to see us from here."

Bannister took out a white handkerchief and wiped his forehead. "We should cross later this afternoon. You will see what I mean about easier ground across the river once you are ahead a few miles."

"Okay, I'll find a place for us to cross." Allen trotted away.

After locating two or three possible fording places, Allen sat by the side of the river to eat some biscuits. "Lord, the clouds are drifting by. The flowing water is singing a peaceful song, but I do not feel any peace. Please protect the band. Please. Why do I feel so uneasy?" He forced down the biscuits, took a drink of water, and mounted his horse.

Where is Old Rag when you need him? And that was when the idea hit him. Allen broke into a lope.

The reverend pulled up on his reins. "Allen, what is your report?"

"The first good ford is about three miles up. There's a better place about two miles beyond that."

"Very good news, young man, very good!" Bannister said. "We will head for the better ford, since we are making good progress." The other men nodded their agreement.

"Reverend . . . there's something else," Allen said.

"Go ahead." Bannister rolled his hand, as if to pull to the words out.

"I recalled advice Old Rag gave us before he left." Allen paused, not sure what the reverend would think of his idea. "He said that the Indians don't always cross a river when it's convenient. Sometimes they'll go miles out of their way to avoid the river spirits."

"They believe there are evil spirits living in the water?" Bannister rolled his eyes.

"Yes, sir, that's what Old Rag explained to me. He also said that the Indians believe spirits dwell in trees and mountains and caves. That Dark Wolf you heard about lives in a cave that no one will go near. They say brave warriors have gone in but never come out."

"What does that have to do with us crossing the river?" Foster creased his eyebrows.

"Well, he said that we should always stay on the north side of the river because of the Indian curse on the other side," Allen said.

Bannister stared at Allen and then chuckled softly. "We don't need to be concerned about any curse. Besides, the ground is much better on the other side."

Martha startled the men by elbowing her way into their cluster. "When are we going to cross the river, and what is this nonsense about curses? Heathen curses have no effect on the children of God. I thought we were done with that when Mr. Ragsdale left us, the old fool."

Allen took a deep breath. "Mr. Ragsdale warned us to stay on the north side of the river. Perhaps it's advice we should heed. At least until Mr. Herbert returns—"

Martha erupted like kerosene splashing on a campfire that quickly ignited the prairie grass and rushes into a wildfire. "Forget Ragsdale. He left us. And if Jacob Herbert can't find us, then he deserves to die out there."

"Mrs. Jolifer, you must stop—" Bannister said.

"Stop. I will not stop. Someone must direct this operation."

She effectively tore the reins of authority from Bannister's hands and began giving orders. "Mr. Foster, you will see to your wagon and Mrs. Herbert's. And for goodness' sake, keep those boys out of trouble." She turned abruptly, her fists clenched. "Reverend Bannister, attend to your wagon and increase the pace of your oxen. Allen, you help as needed. Mr. Jolifer, you return to my wagon immediately. I will walk for a time."

Allen exchanged worried looks with the men, who said nothing. Bannister slumped in his wagon seat.

They crossed the river that afternoon. Every few minutes, Rachel peered behind the wagons, and seeing no sign of Jacob, whimpered. Allen hoped the other women could console her.

Virgil appeared next to Allen's wagon.

"You look disturbed," Allen said.

"I'm not wanting to cause a problem, but I don't think we should have crossed without Jacob," Virgil said.

"I agree, so we'll have to keep watching for him." Allen waited a few beats. "Your wife appears determined . . . and quite angry."

"She's agitated, for sure." Virgil shook his head. "She's been having bad headaches. They get worse every day."

"Headaches?"

"Yes. It's like the headaches she had in Argentina. I'm convinced there's a witch doctor curse here. But she won't admit it."

The south side of the river looked like a flat plain that once, probably many generations ago, was the riverbed itself. Now covered with dirt and grass, it made for the most comfortable wagon travel they'd experienced in weeks.

By the end of the next day and another fourteen miles upriver, Rachel was a nervous wreck. Benny and Joseph were sullen. Jacob still hadn't come in by suppertime, and Rachel went to bed early.

Allen spotted Gloria staying up late, obviously praying for Jacob's safety.

When Jacob didn't appear the next morning either, the men gathered to decide what to do.

"Allen, you and Foster ride out and see if you can catch sight of him," Bannister said.

The two men untied their horses from the back of the wagons and rode out of camp. When Allen looked back at the group, he saw that every member, even the boys, wore a grim expression.

They rode to one high point after another searching for Jacob. Foster focused his binoculars. "Where could he be?"

Allen and Foster returned a few hours later and reported that they'd seen no sign of Jacob.

"Let's stop for a short break," Bannister said. "The horses could use the rest."

Allen sensed that it wasn't the horses that needed a break, but he kept quiet and helped haul water for the horses.

"There's Pa! I see him coming," young Joseph shouted while watering horses.

Everyone stopped what they were doing and looked in the direction Joseph pointed.

Jacob, on foot and leading his limping horse, was coming in from the northeast. Rachel fainted. Gloria rushed to her aid and leaned her against a wagon wheel.

Olive put a wet towel on Rachel's forehead. "The poor dear. How terrible this has been for her."

"Thank God he's back," Gloria said. "Our prayers have been answered."

Allen and Foster rode out to offer assistance.

The band gathered around as Jacob patted his wife's hand. She came to but couldn't stop crying. Allen, though relieved to see Jacob, had knots in his stomach. Something did not feel right.

"Well, Mr. Herbert," Martha said, "how far is Fort Laramie from here?"

"Please be patient, Martha," Virgil said, his eyes beseeching. "You can see that he needs food and rest."

Martha scowled. "Patient? He was supposed to have been back two days ago. How patient do we have to be, for mercy's sake?"

"We will give him a chance to rest." Bannister allowed an extra hour for their midday break, and he led a brief thanksgiving prayer service.

Allen helped Jacob form a bed in the wagon for Rachel to rest on. "Jacob, I'll help in any way I can. Watching the boys or anything."

He nodded his appreciation, and they rejoined the group. Olive handed him a cup of coffee. "I never made it to Fort Laramie." He didn't look anyone in the eyes, but focused on the ground instead. "So I can't say how long it will take to get there from here."

Martha's eyes widened and her jaw dropped. "You what?"

The reverend held up his palm. "Hold on. Let him continue!"

"I do not know what happened exactly." Jacob shook his head. "I left you and rode until sunset. I figure I made forty miles and stopped for the night. As I was setting up camp, a wolf came close and stared at me with yellow eyes. I shot at him, but he didn't flinch. I shouldn't have missed him at that close range, but I did. I quickly saddled my horse and rode north a mile to get around him before I tried again to make camp." He sipped his coffee.

"But there he was again. I rode into the night, but I could hear that wolf following me. I turned back to the river, but I never found it. I held the North Star over my right shoulder and in the morning kept south. I have never been so bewildered in all my life.

"That wolf followed me the whole time. The mare stumbled, and I fell off. I was so tired, and I couldn't get up off the ground. By then I didn't care if the wolf ate both me and the horse. I fell asleep where I lay. When I woke up, I continued heading south and didn't see the river until just when Joseph caught sight of me. I sure am glad to be back." He held his sons close.

"You must be exhausted," Beulah said.

"I'm sorry I failed. I honestly don't know what happened." Jacob shook his head.

"Never mind that," Bannister said. "We thank God that you are back safely and can tend to your family. We will reach Fort Laramie soon, and as a group. Let's be on our way."

Allen checked the hitch on the supply wagon, when Gloria approached him.

"I truly praise God that Jacob is back safely," she said. "I can't shake this odd feeling in my stomach about this area."

"Do you think it has something to do with that curse?" Allen patted his stomach.

"I don't know, but I'd like to ask Jacob some questions."

"I'll go with you."

They found him rubbing down his horse. He admitted fighting panic for three days and nights. "When did you cross the river?"

"The same day you left," Allen said.

"There were times when I had given up hope, but something kept me going." Jacob held his hands palms up.

"I believe our prayers sustained you, Jacob," Gloria said.

Allen nodded. "We prayed diligently while you were gone."

He needed to come right out and say what had been on his mind. "There's an oppressive feeling around here. Do you remember hearing Old Rag talk about an Indian curse? I wonder if your experience had something to do with that."

"Before, I would have thought that was ridiculous, but now I am not so sure. I suppose it could be a curse of some kind. I can't explain any other way how I couldn't find the river." Jacob stared ahead at the Mills' wagon, as though deep in thought.

The band trudged on a few more miles before making camp for the night.

Allen stretched out on his bedroll near the fire and thanked God for bringing Jacob back safely.

The quarter moon slid across the night sky. No coyotes yipped; no wolves howled.

At about halfway between midnight and sunrise, Allen bolted from sleep, gripping his rifle. His heart pounding, he breathed deeply to clear his mind. He scanned the camp. He felt his senses sharpen. He visually probed underneath and beyond the wagons. He tuned out the familiar snores and soft camp sounds and strained to hear movement or commotion among the horses. Nothing. He rose quietly and walked around the wagons. The livestock seemed fine, yet they were awake, and the horses' ears were pricked forward, as if hearing something that Allen couldn't discern.

Gloria emerged from her lean-to and joined Allen. "What is it? Did you see something?"

Foster climbed quietly out of his wagon and moved toward the young people. "Something woke up my wife, and she sent me out here to check on things."

"Something woke me also," Gloria whispered. "Not a sound, but a heavy feeling. Perhaps we should pray together."

"A heavy feeling? Don't tell me you're still harping on that so-called witch doctor curse?" Foster said. "God is big enough to handle a witch doctor. I refuse to let superstition ruin my slumber. I will see you in the morning."

Allen prayed. "Almighty Father in heaven, we beseech thee to grant us peace and security in this wilderness land." He stopped. It sounded like a liturgy.

Deacon Abraham's words came back to him. You go into the throne room of glory with boldness because you're the son of God. That host of heavenly angels will stand aside so's you can get to your Father's throne. And you tell him what it is you want. You tell your Father what your heart is saying.

Allen pleaded for wisdom and revelation about the heaviness in their hearts. But peace never came.

CHAPTER SIXTEEN

"IF IT IS NOT ANY trouble, Allen, we'd like to use the fire to fix breakfast." Bannister and Foster stood looking down at Allen, who moaned and pulled the gray wool blanket tight around his neck.

Foster nudged Allen's foot. "I was up in the middle of the night and found him and Gloria looking about for a disturbance. They started talking about a curse, so I went back to bed."

"A curse?" Bannister smirked. "Well, it looks more like Brother Allen has been put under a sleeping spell." They both chuckled at the remark, and then Bannister nudged Allen with his boot.

Allen forced his eyes open. Bannister and Foster stared at him. Allen jumped up. "Sorry, sir. Sorry, everybody. I guess I had a rough night." Allen set his bedroll aside and helped set the breakfast table.

Gloria smiled at him. Martha scowled. Rachel acted more like her usual self.

Allen was glad that Rachel appeared to have gotten some much-needed rest. He hoped that whatever had happened to disturb him and Gloria last night would someday be revealed.

Bannister held morning devotions and read Psalm 23. "Let us

trust to the Lord's shepherding care today as we do every day. And we give thanks for Jacob's safe return." He nodded and smiled at Rachel.

An hour later, the Conestoga caravan gained the next bend in the river. "It looks like another good day for traveling," Bannister said. "We ought to make another fourteen miles. I am glad we crossed the river."

Foster suggested another scouting foray. "Allen's not married. We should send him."

"Allen, I want you to be discreet about this," Bannister said. "Ride upriver to see if you can get sight of Fort Laramie. When you leave, head off in another direction, as if you are going out to hunt game, then get back on the river and stay there."

"Yes, sir." Allen said. "I don't think anyone is going to believe I'm going hunting. We have plenty of fresh venison."

"That doesn't matter. I don't want to worry people, especially the Herberts. So we will keep your scouting quiet. Is that understood?" Bannister glanced over his shoulder.

Allen nodded. He quietly picked up some hardtack biscuits and jerky and filled his canteen. His horse was fresh. If he rode hard, he could explore ahead about fifteen miles, maybe twenty, and be back before supper.

As he trotted past the Jolifers' wagon, Martha demanded to know where he was going.

"Just out to do some hunting." Allen kicked the horse into an easy lope and turned toward the river.

"Why don't you hunt upriver and try to catch sight of Fort Laramie for us!" Martha shouted after him.

Allen faced south toward Table Mountain, a landmark that announced the end of the prairie. He let the buckskin, whom he'd named Caleb, have the reins. Seeing the ground blur past his horse's hooves usually gave him a thrill, but this time he felt no sense of freedom. His heart weighed heavy in his chest. He wanted to bring hope back to the group, but he couldn't shake his apprehension.

A couple of hours later, Allen spotted a cabin overlooking the river. He rode up carefully, calling out.

No response.

The cabin, more of a ten-by-ten shack, looked like it had been built from the boards of a dismantled wagon. The wall showed gaps, and a window space was cut out of one wall, but it had no glass or shutters. The door leaned outward at an awkward angle. As Allen rode closer, he saw that the top leather hinge had torn loose.

He dismounted. "Hello? Anyone home? I'm Allen Hartman." He pulled open the door and stuck his head inside the dark interior. Nothing, just a dirt floor. No furniture. It obviously had not been used for a while. Allen turned and walked out.

As rickety as the cabin was, the view out the front door of the river and distant hills was spectacular.

He leaned against the front wall and ate a quick lunch of biscuits and jerky. Allen's interrupted night, the long ride, warm sun, and full belly added up to a nap. He allowed himself the luxury of sleeping a half hour. Then he mounted up, studied the horizon for another moment, and loped back toward the wagon train.

Bannister halted the wagons as they reached a creek that flowed from the distant mountains and poured into the North Platte about a hundred yards to the right. The creek was nameless to them, just one more of dozens they had crossed. It was rocky and had a low bank on the other side. At least it would not require any engineering or earth moving to get across.

"We'll get everyone across, then eat," he bellowed. He turned to speak to his wife.

"What's that you say, dear?"

Bannister huffed. "I said we cross now and then eat. How could you not hear me?"

"Don't speak to me like that, Samuel Bannister! I'm not a child."

Martha pulled her wagon out of line and up to the creek edge. Bannister glared at her. "What are you doing out of line, Mrs. Jolifer?"

"Are we going to cross the creek, or do we have to wait for you two to stop quarreling?"

"Get back in line, Mrs. Jolifer. You are out of order!" Bannister struggled to keep his temper. "And we were not quarreling."

She raised her mule whip and glared at the reverend. "Don't you use that tone of voice with me." She snapped at the mules and barked, "Get on up!"

Her mules lunged into the water and stumbled dangerously on the pumpkin-sized rocks in the creek bottom. The two-and-a-half-foot bank posed an obstacle for the mules and added to their difficulty as they stumbled and fought the fast-moving water. Martha barked again and snapped the whip above their ears. The men rushed into the water to help, pushing on the wheels and slapping the mules. With great effort, the wagon bucked up onto the opposite bank. The men were soaked and muddy.

Bannister fumed. "That was a foolish thing to do, Mrs. Jolifer. You endangered the mules and us."

She stared at him. "I am on this side of the creek, and you are not."

He tried to ignore her impudence and turned his attention to assisting the other wagons. It was hard to remember her as the dutiful, respectful girls' schoolteacher she once was.

The other wagons crossed without mishap.

The group ate their midday meal in silence. The men rechecked the rigs and harnesses. As they climbed onto their wagons, they turned at a sharp cry.

"Wolf!" Jacob pointed at the empty hills to the southwest. "Did you see it? It was a big black wolf. It ran into the next draw." He looked from one person to the next.

All eyes scanned the landscape. No one indicated that they saw any animals, much less a wolf.

"Maybe you just think you saw a wolf, Jacob," Bannister said.

"I know what I saw. It was a black wolf."

Bannister mounted his horse. "Well, whatever it was, it's gone. Everyone, let's get moving."

Before reins could be slapped against rumps, Olive shouted, "Indians!"

Twelve warriors raced at full speed out of the draw Jacob said he'd seen the wolf run into. The bare-chested Indians came screaming and whooping. Bannister tried to admonish the band to stay calm, but no words came out, as terror seized him.

The Indians skidded to a halt about twenty yards from the wagon train. They continued their shrieking. Their faces were hideously painted with black and red markings. The horses they rode stomped and snorted, as if ready to attack.

Without warning, the warriors silenced. Even the ponies stilled. As though a secret signal had been given, the line parted, and a thirteenth rider moved through to the front of the pack. He was smaller than the other warriors and appeared older. His horse was slightly larger than a pony. The younger Indians seemed to esteem him. They stood still and glared at the group. Though their voices were silent, their demeanor shouted their hatred.

Bannister swallowed hard. He held his hand up and attempted to smile, to demonstrate friendship. "W-we c-come in peace." And not really knowing what to say, he uttered the first thing that came to mind. "We will trade you for food." Hoping they might understand English, he added, "W-we have come far and w-wish to pass through this land. We are s-s-servants of God and will work among Indians in the West."

The old Indian glared at Bannister, yet he did not move or speak. He wore a head covering with black feathers protruding from the head of a wolverine. The animal's teeth were open, its lips pulled back in a snarl, as if ready to kill. A rattlesnake skin hung around the Indian's neck and chest. Dried snakeheads dangled from it, their mouths and fangs ready to strike. He didn't sit upon a saddle or blanket but on a black wolf hide. The head was held in place by leather thongs, and the legs, with claws intact, hung down the side of the war pony. The macabre effect made it look as if the wolf were running.

The leader spoke to his men, pointing over the heads of the missionaries toward the river. The braves' horses shifted and pawed the ground.

Martha stomped forward. "You have some nerve threatening us when we offer you friendship." She chastised them as if they were New York hooligans. "I refuse to be intimidated by your shouting and these filthy animal skins." She marched right up to the old man and returned his stare. "If you want to know the salvation of Almighty God, you're going to have to start by humbling yourself before us."

As she shouted her demands at him, another warrior shifted his horse behind her, yanked out a cluster of her hair, and handed it to the old man.

Martha screamed and grabbed her head. "Ow! You keep your hands off of me."

The leader silenced her by shouting. He held up her hair, shook his fist over her, and then at the group. Though Bannister had no idea what the man said, the action horrified him.

The Indian stopped abruptly, again looking beyond the band. Then he turned and whipped his horse. The warriors rode away as quickly as they had come.

Allen rode across the North Platte River and caught up to the petrified group. "Where did the Indians go? Did you get to talk to them?" Then alarmed by a different possibility, he asked, "Is everyone all right?" He counted his immobile companions.

Gloria broke the silence. "Martha, are you all right?" She went over to hold Martha and look at her head. "He grabbed out a clump of hair," she said, looking at the red spot where the skin had been torn.

It had been a hostile encounter, and Allen thanked God no one was seriously hurt. Each person tried their best to make sense of what they had just seen.

Martha pushed Gloria away, her face contorting into an ugly mask. "How dare you let him rip hair off my head?" she screamed at Bannister. "You stood there watching him and did nothing about it. You coward! You make a woman do your work, and then you did nothing to defend me! Now, I guess you expect me to ride after them myself to take revenge!"

Bannister gave crisp orders. "No one is going to take revenge. Everyone get to your wagons. We are moving out immediately. Keep your guns ready! Allen, I want to hear your report."

Martha was left alone in her flaming rage.

CHAPTER SEVENTEEN

ALLEN RECOUNTED WHAT HE HAD seen up to finding the cabin, mentioning that there were wagon tracks on the other side of the river. Perhaps another day, or day and a half, past the cabin they would find protection at the fort. Allen asked what had happened with the Indians, since he had been too far off to see.

The reverend was slow to answer, so Mrs. Bannister spoke up. "We had just come across that creek back there"—she pointed in the direction of their crossing—"when Jacob said he saw a wolf. Nobody else saw it, but just then those Indians careened toward us, screaming and brandishing their spears. I thought for sure they were going to kill us all. Lord have mercy! He grabbed a handful of Martha's hair and shook it at us while shouting some gibberish. I think it was a curse. Then they turned and rode off when you came up."

"Yes, they rode off like the cavalry was chasing them. That was strange," Bannister said. "I do not understand why they didn't attack us, but I thank the good Lord for protecting us. We are going to have to push hard and keep extra guards out at night."

Allen felt disappointment at not being on hand to observe the incident. He wondered when he'd ever be close to these wild men. Allen shivered. A curse? Could the leader possibly have been a witch doctor?

That night Bannister forbade lighting a campfire. Though the consensus was that the Indians knew where they were, Bannister said it would be prudent not to have one. They camped close to the river to make a line of defense on one side. The men took turns in two outposts fifty yards from the wagons. They moved the livestock within the circle of wagons. Bannister gathered the group for a time of prayer for protection from the Indians. Before he prayed, the group revisited their earlier discussion.

"It was strange that the Indians rode off so suddenly," Gloria said.

"The black wolf hide that the old man sat on looked like the one I saw running," Jacob said.

No one responded.

"Whatever the reason, we can thank God for his protection. Let us pray," the reverend said.

The missionaries bowed their heads, but Allen refused to close his eyes.

"Oh, merciful Father, we are in a time of need. We take refuge in thee, our Rock and our Fortress. Protect us, Lord, from the hand of thine enemies. We have come to teach them thy ways. We come that they might walk in thy paths, oh Lord. The Evil One has a grip on them, and so we rebuke him in Jesus's holy name. Bless us, Lord, in safety. Quicken the journey to Fort Laramie. Guide us into thy peace. Amen."

The group divided into their sleeping areas. Allen and Phineas Mills stood watch together.

"I feel an oppressive cloud around us," Allen said. "It's as if some tragedy will befall us."

"Maybe the worst is past us. It's like the reverend says—we're in the protection of the Almighty," Mills said.

Allen didn't say any more, but in his heart he travailed for God's mercy and protection. His eyes strained at the dark shadows all about him.

At about three o'clock in the morning, Allen, along with the rest of the camp, woke up to Martha, Evan, and Rachel screaming simultaneously.

Allen ran to the Jolifer wagon, while Phineas ran to his wife. It took some time to sort through what had happened.

All three had been startled awake from fitful sleep by dreams of snakes. "I dreamed I was bit by rattlesnakes," Martha said. "My head feels like it's on fire."

Bannister checked the sky. "If we had moonlight to guide us, I'd say let's move out. But it's too dark, which poses too great a risk to the animals. There are still a couple of hours before daylight. Try to get some sleep. We'll start rolling with the first streaks of sunrise."

No one slept well after that. A couple of hours later, as soon as the eastern sky became gray with the coming sunrise, the group rigged up and pulled out.

It wasn't long before they came to the little cabin Allen had found when scouting.

"Circle up the wagons," the reverend ordered. "We will rest here for a short time. Keep the teams harnessed, and bring them water in buckets. Keep your eyes open." Bannister carried his rifle while he hauled water for the animals.

Allen kept watch over the group as they tended the horses and mules. His eyes flicked from the horizon to the faces of his fellow travelers. He noted the wariness as they went about their duties, stopping every few minutes and looking over their shoulders. The constant vigilance brought its own fatigue. They had no choice but to keep their guard up, and he would do his part in keeping them safe.

Martha caught his attention because of the way she glared at Gloria.

Gloria had just finished watering the horses, when Martha asked if she would bring water to their mules.

"I'll get to your mules in just a moment."

Her arms akimbo, Martha nearly spat her response. "Oh, never mind. I'll take care of it myself."

"I only stopped to pick up your husband's tool," Gloria said. "He was checking the shoes on his mules and dropped the cleaning pick out of his reach. I just wanted to watch."

"He does not need your help. And he certainly does not need a flirtatious girl hanging around at a time like this." Martha's body seemed as pinched as her face.

Gloria gasped. "I-I-I just stopped to hand him the pick. And I did not flirt with your husband. I resent that accusation."

"I saw you leaning into him. You don't think I know what a single woman desires? You would take advantage of me, after all I have done for you. You are pitiful, Miss Shannon, pitiful."

Gloria's eyes filled with tears at Martha's venomous rebuke.

Allen stared in disbelief. Martha had reached the bottom of wretched behavior. Her accusation of Gloria was absurd, if not downright hateful. After all these months together, there had never been even a hint of impropriety, let alone flirting. The idea seemed preposterous in the midst of a possible Indian attack. Not even a Saint Louis saloon girl would flaunt herself at a time like this.

Gloria walked away behind a wagon with her arms folded before Allen could offer a comforting word.

Allen watched the draws and ravines, knowing that the Indians could gallop down on them in a matter of seconds. *Oh, Lord, protect us.* Allen studied the southern horizon. He noted its peculiar haze, like smoke. He checked the western horizon. It looked normal. He looked back to the south. The sky was clear.

The men gathered to study the creek bed facing them. Directly ahead, the way was flat. The creek itself was slightly more than a trickle compared with what they had already been through that day. A few yards upstream, the abrupt bank stood about four feet above the water level, with several deep pools.

Gloria filled the bucket with water at one of these pools, to carry back to the livestock. Martha was on her way to fill a bucket, when she halted abruptly, staring straight ahead. She raised her hand to shade her eyes, and her body stiffened.

"The wolf!" Jacob shouted, pointing across the creek.

The men turned, reaching for their guns, but saw only low grass. Jacob bolted for his rifle, which was leaning on his wagon. Rachel turned pale and collapsed.

Allen readied his rifle.

"Indian!" Martha shouted at the same instant. She rushed forward to the creek. "You infernal heathen, I'll teach you to yank out my hair." She threw a rock at something across the creek. She turned. "Shoot him. Somebody shoot him!"

"Where?" Foster said. He looked at the other men, but they shook their heads.

Gloria scanned the area and shrugged.

"Shoot him! It's that Indian chief!" Martha bent over to grab another rock. She bolted up, screaming.

Allen could scarcely believe his eyes. A rattlesnake hung on her arm, its fangs buried deep in her flesh. She tried shaking it off, screaming while twisting and turning, but to no avail.

Allen ran toward her. Before he could reach her, another rattlesnake, as thick as a man's arm, leaped off the bank and struck her in the neck. Martha writhed and fell onto the rocks of the creek bed.

Thirty yards seemed like a mile as the men ran to help. Allen and Mills were the first to reach her, just in time to see three snakes slithering under rocks.

Allen scrambled up the embankment and ran to the highest point, his rifle stock tucked into his shoulder, ready to fire. He searched the grass for any sign of the Indian or wolf. He found nothing. He stayed on guard while others assisted the fallen woman, keeping one eye on the scene to his left.

Mills flipped over a few rocks to kill the snakes, but he found no trace of them.

Martha's neck and arm were swelling. Virgil knelt beside her. She convulsed and sucked in a deep breath. Her face tightened, and she glared at Bannister. "Why didn't you shoot the old Indian? It's your fault." Her voice was strained and raspy. She arched her back, and with eyes wide in terror, her last breath hissed from her lungs.

Martha Jolifer died on the rocks beside a nameless creek. Allen estimated they had to be within twenty-five miles of Fort Laramie.

The women who prepared Martha's body reported they'd found four more sets of fang marks on her arm and left leg. One bite alone could have killed her, but she had no hope of surviving six.

They wrapped her body in a blanket and laid it in the wagon. Virgil wanted to bury her in a proper cemetery, if possible, at the fort.

The reverend granted that favor, considering the present danger they were under. They would have taken the time to dig a grave right there, but the group made no complaints about leaving that awful place and seeking safety at the fort as soon as possible.

Before they pulled out, Allen, Bannister, and Mills searched for but found no tracks of Indian or wolf.

"I don't understand it," Jacob said. He ran his fingers through his already tousled hair.

"Where did you see it?" Allen said.

Jacob searched the distance with his eyes. He shook his head. "I'm not sure now. I'm so upset. But Martha's rock almost hit it."

"Well, let's not stand around trying to figure out what's past," Bannister said. "Let's move out."

Allen mounted his horse. He scanned the missionary band, now minus one member. Rachel had crawled into the back of her family's wagon and now lay there whimpering. Benny and Joseph were, likely for the first time since leaving home, quiet.

Allen couldn't help but recall the group's enthusiasm when

they'd boarded the ship at the beginning of their journey. They'd been full of dreams and hope. Their confidence in what the Lord was sure to do through them had known no bounds. They'd been on the Lord's work, and nothing could discourage them.

But that was then and this was now. Their guides had deserted them, they seemed to be lost, a fellow preacher of the gospel had derided them, they'd experienced a hostile run-in with some Indians, and now they would soon put one of their own in a grave.

Even praying had become difficult. He knew God hadn't abandoned them, because he promised never to leave or forsake his people, yet if Allen went strictly by feelings, he surely felt alone.

By nightfall the caravan had added nine more miles on the trail. Even though the tension had subsided, the shock of death had not worn off. In fact it seemed to have settled deeper within them. Some were still unable to talk about what had happened. Others attempted to explain the apparition of the Indian and the wolf.

"How come Jacob saw a wolf when she saw an Indian, and no one else saw anything?" Mills said.

"It was the curse the Indian made with her hair," Olive said.

"I agree," Gloria said. "But I can't explain why. It's something I discern in my heart."

"The notion that a curse is behind this is ridiculous," Foster said.

"Then what's your explanation for Mrs. Jolifer's odd behavior?" Gloria said.

Foster shrugged and poked the fire with a stick, sending up a spray of sparks.

Vespers were awkward that night and ended quickly. Bannister organized the night watch. Allen would take the second watch, and Virgil, even though he was in mourning, would take the last watch.

While Allen took his turn, he paced around the camp. Keeping a watchful eye, his mind wandered to the strange events. "Lord, how can I ever teach Indians about you if I can't understand the way they think or why they act as they do?" Receiving no answer, he continued to pray for protection over the band. He sensed they were out of danger.

Allen approached the Jolifer wagon to wake Virgil for his turn at guard duty. Allen noted the unmistakable odor of the decaying body wrapped up in the back.

He woke Virgil, who stood up quickly.

"Thanks, Allen," he said. "Where was your post?"

"I was out there a ways, but it doesn't really matter. It's very quiet tonight."

"Very well," Jolifer said, cradling his long rifle in his arm.

"Listen, Virgil, it disturbs me to say this, but Mrs. Jolifer's body smells quite badly. Maybe we should bury her out here in the morning before we pull out. It's only going to get worse. We don't know exactly when we'll arrive at the fort."

Virgil leaned over the tailgate and lifted the blanket. Allen turned his head.

"I reckon you're right. It must be the snake poison and the heat that's making her swell up so much. I guess I'll go dig a grave. We can bury her after breakfast."

"I'll give you a hand." Allen pulled a shovel off the side of the Conestoga. They took turns digging and standing watch.

At daybreak the missionaries prepared for the funeral. Virgil carried the body to the grave and placed it gently into the waiting earth. He grabbed the shovel, filled in the dirt, then covered it with rocks. Phineas and Eva made a cross and inscribed it with Martha Jolifer and the date. The reverend read the graveside ritual from the *Book of Discipline*. They sang a hymn, and Bannister recited a prayer. It was all simple and short.

Before anyone could share any words, Virgil thanked them and walked away. Allen thought Virgil looked relieved. Without another word, Bannister's tiny congregation returned to their wagons.

They waited while Virgil picked out clean clothes and a bar of soap from one of his trunks, trotted down to the river, and bathed.

When he finally climbed up in his wagon seat, he nodded to Bannister, indicating he was ready to roll.

Two Rivers lifted a four-pound cutthroat trout out of the trap. He added it to a stringer that already held five large fish. Hoisting it, he dangled three fish on one side of his horse and three on the other side. He then knelt at the river, scooped water in his cupped hands, and turned to the four winds, giving thanks for the provision of food.

Hours later, after eating and smoking his pipe, Two Rivers lay down to sleep. It had been a good day. His people were enjoying a time of peace. But he wondered how long it would last.

While he slept, he dreamed again of the white falcon. This time his dream included a group of people who were traveling slowly because they were heavily burdened with many possessions. They spoke of great accomplishments, but they were weak and fearful. Then wolves came to attack, but the white falcon chased them away. The wolves feared the white falcon. A rattlesnake bit one of the women of the group. Bitterness had made her old and haggard. She died in her bitterness. Two Rivers saw himself smoking the pipe with friends, in peace, when suddenly the white falcon walked into his lodge.

He awoke with a start.

The white falcon had come into Two Rivers's lodge. He felt no fear but great strength. "Great Father, what does this dream mean?" he pleaded in the dark.

CHAPTER EIGHTEEN

BANNISTER'S MISSIONARY BAND ARRIVED AT Fort Laramie in the middle of the afternoon of the next day, July 4, Independence Day, and they celebrated that evening with other Americans: trappers, traders, buffalo hunters, and adventurers. Even some French Canadians and a broad assortment of Indians joined the celebration. In the wilderness, no one needed a reason—a party was a party.

Allen reflected on some ironic coincidences. They'd left three months ago, on April 4, with a goodbye party, and now they'd arrived to another celebration. Not really in their honor, but a celebration nonetheless. They'd departed from Buffalo, New York, and were now eating buffalo. They'd first crossed the expansive Lake Erie, and they had crossed the Great Plains, a virtual sea of grass.

The mere thought of having conquered both geographical obstacles made Allen's head spin. And perhaps more significant, he had left a community where the Christians were many and the heathens few to come to a land where the heathens were many and the Christians few. Yet God was still with him. Allen walked out from the camp enveloped by the night sky. Feeling small and powerless, he knelt and worshiped in the hand of the Almighty.

July 5 was their first day in months to wake up and not think about traveling. The band organized their camp and set up a rope corral for the livestock.

After morning prayers, Bannister presented their plans. "We'll stay at Fort Laramie for a week before continuing on to Oregon. Our tasks include refreshing food supplies and water, repairing the wagons and equipment, and plenty of rest. I will make it a priority to secure a new guide. It is regrettable that Ragsdale is not here to help us find a replacement, but we will just have to trust the Lord for the right man."

They'd set their camp in the trees along the Laramie River, about three hundred yards from its confluence with the North Platte and a couple hundred yards from the fort.

Fort Laramie stuck out as a bastion of civilization in a field over a mile wide to the south. The walls of hewn timbers formed a great rectangle with blockhouses on diagonal corners. Another block-house, perched over the entry gate, housed a cannon.

Outside the fort proper sat clusters of tipis, canvas tents, stick lean-tos, and wagons. Several times a year there might be up to two thousand Indians gathered for trading. On this particular day, just a few hundred passed through the fort gate. Horse trading took place outside the fort. Supply wagons were loaded and unloaded.

Bannister took Allen to the fort to meet Mr. Sublette, the trade master, to seek out the best source of supplies and to find a new trail guide. As they entered the main gate, Allen stared wide eyed at the buzz of activity.

The courtyard, approximately 150 feet square, contained offices and quarters built against the fifteen-foot-high walls. The site was rustic and dusty but much busier than the band members anticipated.

Inside the fort was a makeshift market. Trappers, Indians, and traders from the East gathered to make deals for furs, blankets, beads, guns, traps, knives, cookware, and anything one might need to make a life in the wilderness. Others passed time being sociable before heading back into the lonesome high county.

They found Milton Sublette in his office. He had an air of authority about him, answering questions for three freighters. When the two missionaries walked into his office, Sublette glanced at them briefly while listening to one of the frontiersmen explain about the load he was hauling to Saint Louis.

Beams only a few inches above Allen's head supported the low ceiling. Trade goods hung on the walls. Crates sat stacked in corners. Furs and blankets lay across a long table that served as both desk and counter.

Once the men left the office, Bannister stepped forward. "Mr. Sublette, I'm Reverend Samuel Bannister, and this is Reverend Allen Hartman. We are from New York State and have been called by God and the Methodist Episcopal Church to establish a mission among the Indians in Oregon."

"They's already missionaries in Oregon," Sublette said. "And more on the way. As a matter of fact, a group of Presbyterian missionaries came through here just a few days ago on their way to join the Whitmans. God willing, they'll make it."

"Presbyterians, eh?" Bannister stroked his chin at the news. "What do you mean, 'God willing, they'll make it'?"

"I've been out here a good many years." Sublette leaned forward, both hands on the table. "I can tell when a man is cut out for life in the wilds. Most of the easterners I've seen come through here don't make it too long. It's a hard and dangerous life. You have to be determined to pay the price. That last group of missionaries wasn't prepared for the hardships they'll be facing. Even if they make it to Walla Walla, they're going to have a tough time living with the Indians, let alone converting them to Christianity."

"Sir, with all due respect to your experience, I believe you may be underestimating the determination of one called by God to fulfill the Great Commission. I assure you that we are willing to face any hardship, unto martyrdom, to proclaim the gospel of the Lord Jesus Christ," Bannister said.

"That's my concern, Reverend Bannister. I'd rather not see any more martyrs. I've seen many good, experienced mountain men die unpredictably. In a given moment, an accident or a wrong choice can end in death."

"We're not innocent lambs, Mr. Sublette." Bannister folded his arms across his chest and stood with his feet shoulder width apart.

Allen listened, recalling the Indian encounter, Martha's mysterious death, and Jacob Herbert getting lost. Sublette was right. One wrong move could prove fatal. God had called the band to service but not to be ignorant of the new rules for staying alive. Allen determined to learn all he could from these mountain men about survival, living with the Indians, and even fighting. He realized he was no longer pastoring a congregation in a white church with a tall steeple. He had been unprepared to cast out demons, barely survived a street fight in Saint Louis, was awestruck by Jack and Joaquin, and now danger was part of his parish. Standing in a dark, dusty room that smelled of beaver plews and freshly tanned leather, Allen knew he had to change.

"What can I do for you, other than give free advice?" Sublette said.

"Well, sir, we are in search of a guide to take us on to Oregon. Perhaps you could recommend someone trustworthy."

"Trustworthy? Hmm. There are a lot of men who can get you there, but I'm not sure I could vouch for their honor. You missed two of the finest possible guides, Burkett and Del Castillo, by a week."

Bannister's face brightened. "Jacques Burkett?"

"Yes. Do you know Jack?"

"We met on the trail about two weeks ago."

"You should have hired him on the spot. A couple of the finest mountain men ever to cross the crick," Sublette said. "They had some business with Bridger, but if you're lucky, they'll be back this way soon."

Allen flinched at the word lucky. He knew Bannister enough to know that a sermon was coming.

"The word luck," Bannister said, "has the same root as Lucifer, a name for Satan. I never rely on luck, and I won't associate myself with the devil in any remote way. I trust only God."

Wanting to get back to the original topic, Allen stepped forward. "Are there any other guides you might know of who'd be available?"

"There's Daniel Carter—he's around. Or Whistling Pete. I believe I saw the Limms here yesterday. They'd be good for you. They'd likely be willing to take you all the way to Whitman's Mission or the Willamette. I'm sure you'll find them if you ask around."

"The Limms? Are they brothers?" Bannister rubbed his chin.

"No, a married couple. They work as a team. Did quite well for themselves trapping beaver. They know their way around the mountain, and they're honest folk." Sublette's recommendation seemed straightforward.

"Humphrey and Gwendolyn Limm. They ride a pair of red mules. Don't be put off by their gentle manner. He's quiet but solid as a rock. She can hunt and ride as well as any good man out here. I think you ought to look them up. Now, if you'll excuse me, gentlemen, I must see to other business." Sublette extended his hand to the reverend. "Sorry my time has to be so limited."

"On the contrary, we appreciate the time you've given us, and the good recommendations. Much obliged." They shook hands, and then Allen and Bannister stepped outside, squinting against the brightness of the morning.

Samuel Bannister didn't waste any time. He strode directly over to a man dressed in buckskins and asked if he knew where he might find the Limms. The man shook his head and grunted. Bannister looked for the next likely source of information.

"Excuse me. Any chance you might know the whereabouts of the Limms?"

"Yes, sir. Saw them over at the blacksmith just a bit ago," a bearded old-timer said before he walked away.

The blacksmith shop was nothing more than a shabby lean-to with a makeshift anvil and a campfire. The Limms had not been there, but the smith had seen them buying food supplies. He pointed in a vague direction.

"Allen, I hate wild-goose chases. Any idea how to track down this couple?"

"I think we just need to keep asking."

Bannister grumbled, then continued to ask passersby.

Allen rather enjoyed the task. He walked by stands with hanging meat and skins. Others had layer upon layer of blankets and bright-colored fabrics. He stopped to breathe in the smoking venison on a rack and then again where fresh biscuits were coming out of a Dutch oven.

After fruitlessly circling the area for two hours, Bannister headed back to camp. At least fifty people knew that an aggravated preacher was searching for the Limms. Hopefully, the couple would learn of this and find the missionary band.

Allen made conversation with some of the people he met, particularly the Indians. He learned that some were Oto, Sioux, or Ute, but he couldn't tell them apart like the mountain men could. People of many tribes and races passed through the fort trading for supplies. But supplies weren't the only items traded: news, weather, travel reports, the value of furs and goods, and any other information that made a profit or kept a man alive.

Allen shook his head when they rode into camp and spotted two red mules tied in the shade of a tree.

As the two men dismounted, Olive said, "Here they are now. Honey, come and meet Mr. and Mrs. Limm. They've been here for more than an hour waiting for you."

Allen chuckled at the irony.

Bannister said a few choice words under his breath, then greeted the folks as though they were long-lost relatives.

"So you're the Limms? Nice to meet you. Mr. Sublette said I should look you up to discuss hiring you as trail guides. We are on the way to Oregon and would like to get at least as far as Walla Walla—"

"Yes, dear, they already know that." Olive smiled.

"Oh. Well, we'd like to leave here as soon as we can get resupplied—"

"Dear, they know that also."

"Okay. Let me introduce you to everyone then. These are the Fosters and the—"

"Samuel, the Limms met everyone while we were waiting for you."

Everyone stared at the reverend.

"What don't they know then?"

Gwen Limm, a woman of medium build and height, brown hair, and big brown eyes, held a floppy-brimmed hat in her hands. Back in the States she'd be considered pretty. But here, hardened and tanned by wilderness life and dressed in men's clothing, she appeared rugged. Allen imagined she could turn as tough as a bobcat in a moment's notice.

Allen studied her husband, Humphrey. Quiet, just as Sublette had said, but Allen figured he wouldn't tolerate much nonsense.

"We'll get you over the mountain," Gwen said, "but we can't start until we get some other business done. We can pull out next week. I reckon it will take you folks that long to get ready anyway."

Bannister stared at Humphrey.

Allen knew Bannister well enough to know that discussing business with a woman was as foreign to the reverend as a woman behind the pulpit.

"We can be ready to go the day after tomorrow, or the following day at the latest," he said.

"No, sir." Gwen shook her head. "Your animals need rest, and so do the womenfolk. Besides, it will take that long to put your supplies together. This ain't Saint Louis. You'll have to make do with what's available."

Gwen was right, and Bannister had to know it. He probably didn't like the idea of having a woman make a command decision, but in the band's interest, Allen believed Bannister would respect her sound judgment about the health of the group and livestock.

To be sure, the men needed rest as much as the women. The group had been through a stressful and traumatic two weeks, not to mention the months of traveling. Mrs. Herbert still seemed frail after the frightful event with the Indians and Jacob's ordeal. Martha's death weighed heavily on everyone. Bannister would have to accept that his band was weary and that it would be foolish to push on too soon. He would have to be pastor for a few days rather than wagon-train master.

"Well, I guess the rest won't hurt us. Fine then. We will plan to leave one week from today." Bannister shook Gwen's hand and then Humphrey's. "Perhaps it would be helpful if you could assist us in making a list of the things we will need between here and Walla Walla."

"Dear, we already made a list while we were waiting for you," his wife said.

The reverend scowled. "Well. We shall see you in a week then."

The Limms nodded and mounted their matching mules. "You might want to pull that wagon around to this tree. Stack some boxes in front of it to make a wind break," Gwen said as they turned away. "Your cook fire will be easier to manage."

Evidently no one had considered that option, but it made sense. Jacob and Virgil set out making the adjustment. Bannister mumbled something and went into his tent. The rest of the band resumed their duties of cleaning, sorting, and repairing.

"The Limms are an interesting couple, don't you think?" Gloria said to Allen while unloading a box of utensils. "Gwen is not like some of the other frontier women I've seen. She seems tough, but she still looks like a lady. I expect she would be rather pretty in a dress."

"She sure looks like she can handle herself out here. Mr. Sublette said they've done some beaver trapping together. He rates her and Humphrey right along with the best of the mountain guides. Even mentioned Jack Burkett and Joaquin."

At the reference to the mountain men's names, Gloria's cheeks flushed. "Oh, are they here at Fort Laramie?" She tucked loose strands of hair behind her ear.

Allen smiled at her reaction to their names. "No. He said they might come back through when they finish their business with Jim Bridger. It's hard to say if they'll show up at all. That's why he suggested we look up the Limms. The reverend seemed caught off guard, didn't he?"

She grinned. "Yes, he did. I'm sure glad we get a week to rest and prepare for the next part of the journey. I wouldn't mind two weeks, for that matter. I can't seem to get enough sleep. And we all need to grieve for Martha."

That night after supper, Allen taught Joseph and Benny how to whittle miniature canoes they could float in the river. The boys didn't venture far from the camp and were prompt to obey their parents. Allen noticed the boys' somber expressions when they watched the Indians camped around them.

"Don't worry, boys. Just stay close to our camp and they won't bother you."

"Ma says we don't have to worry because we'll be going home soon," Joseph said.

Allen hid his surprise. Did Rachel mean a new home in Oregon, or did she intend to return to New York?

CHAPTER NINETEEN

FOR THE NEXT FEW DAYS, Allen went with the other men on rounds at the fort, checking new suppliers and travelers to find the essentials they would need. Each night they reported their trades, and Virgil surprised everyone by turning out to be effective at bartering. In three days he'd successfully filled more than half of their necessities. He traded his wife's furniture, clothing, and personal item to Indian women. Several mountain men traded with him so they would have nice lady's things with which to pursue the Indian gals.

One of Virgil's best trades was his ornamented Pennsylvania rifle for a Hawkins .50-caliber plains rifle.

Allen watched as Virgil traded with an old Oto man who had developed an overwhelming desire for whiskey. Virgil wouldn't give him whiskey but suggested that the Oto take a tortoiseshell comb and brush set to the whiskey seller, who was sure to give him a jug for it. The only thing the old Indian had to trade was a top-grade red fox pelt and a bear claw necklace.

Phineas scoffed at Virgil. "You're a fool to be doing business with the old man. What in the world are you going to do with a fox pelt?"

"Someone will see the value, and that will mean another trade and a profit."

Phineas just shook his head. Allen winked at Virgil.

The Oto fingered some silver coins that spilled out of a leather pouch onto Virgil's blanket. He seemed interested in the images on the coins, so Virgil displayed some copper pennies. The old Indian's eyes lit up as he examined them closer. He called to a young woman sitting next to another woman and child.

She picked up a buffalo blanket and brought it to Virgil. He seemed certain he was getting the better part of the bargain for the few coins he offered. The Indian told her to stand by Virgil's horse. The girl obeyed and kept her head down.

"Umm. Virgil?" Allen felt suddenly nervous.

Virgil studied the girl, then looked between her and the Oto. That was when it dawned on him that she came with the buffalo blanket. He looked at Allen. "I don't need a wife or a slave." He stroked his chin as he considered his options. He took a deep breath and nodded his agreement to the trade.

Mills stood by, his mouth agape.

Allen watched as Virgil wrapped up his belongings, as did the Oto, and prepared to leave. "Relax, Brother Mills. I don't intend to keep her."

"But what will you do? You can't possibly consider trading her to some mountain man who might treat her as cheaply as he would a bottle of liquor." Mills talked fast as he hurried behind Virgil.

"We shall see what the Lord provides in the next barter."

Mills continued to argue, but Virgil headed for a trading tent that was tied up against the outside of the fort wall.

Allen held the bundle of goods and leaned toward Phineas. "I believe we're witnessing the Lord's provision."

An elderly American woman sat there with a variety of goods on display around her. "What you looking for?"

Virgil read through his list of supplies, but she couldn't fill any of them. She did, however, have some things he knew they would need but weren't on the list: a small keg of gunpowder, bullet-making supplies, and a brick of cheese. He offered her cash money or some ladies' items. She wasn't interested in either.

Virgil pulled out and displayed the fox pelt. "What will you give me for this?"

"Why didn't you show me that in the first place? I can work with that." Stepping out of the tent, she called a man over. He took a quick look at the pelt and offered an axe, a hammer, and two tomahawks. The woman took the tools, then told Virgil he could have the gunpowder, bullet supplies, and cheese.

"Your wife can carry these for you," she said.

"She's not my wife. An Oto gave her to me for a few coins. I thought I was buying a buffalo blanket, but evidently she came with it." Virgil watched the woman's eyes.

"They'll both keep you warm come winter."

"I don't intend to keep her. I suppose I'll give her some money and let her go on her way. Free," Virgil said.

"I took you for a pilgrim right off. But I didn't take you for a foolish one," the trading woman said. "If you turn her loose, she'll either starve or get beaten to death. She don't have no family or anyone she belongs to now except you. She wouldn't know what to do with money. It would be a very cruel thing to turn her loose, mister."

"I don't understand the way of things here. You're correct. I am a pilgrim of sorts. What do you recommend I do with the woman?" Virgil lifted a tomahawk off the box and felt the weight of it.

"You can lose her at cards or trade her off. Happens all the time out here, fella. She ain't the first girl to be passed from man to man or to be traded like a blanket." The woman stroked her chin for a moment, and then her face lit up. "Take her into the fort kitchen and ask for Edna Beamer. She might take her from you." The woman turned her attention back to her new axe and hammer.

Allen pointed toward the fort's kitchen. "I guess doing business out here rubs the sympathy off a woman."

They found Edna Beamer in the kitchen. She was one of the cooks for Sublette's company. Edna listened to Virgil's story and asked if the girl could cook.

"I'm sorry, ma'am, but I can't speak to that, as I've only just acquired her." Virgil shook his head at his own words.

Edna spoke in an Indian language to the girl, who responded slowly.

"She said she was born to the Pawnee, but her father traded her for a Cheyenne pony. She thinks it's been three winters since she's seen her mother. I guess I can use her as a helper."

"Thank you very much. She can keep the blanket." Virgil sighed in relief.

"That's good of you. Wait here." Edna left but came right back, hoisting a large bag of flour. Two men followed her with more flour, sugar, coffee, and a sack of pipe tobacco.

"What's all this?"

"For the girl. Don't give anything away out here, pilgrim. I'll make sure she gets treated well." Edna hoisted the buffalo blanket.

"I'm much obliged, ma'am," Virgil said. "But I don't need the tobacco. None of us smoke."

Edna shook her head. "You take it. You always need tobacco for trades or gifts."

Virgil glanced at Reverend Mills and shrugged. "All right then, thank you."

Upon settling at camp, Allen made his report. "Virgil purchased all of the necessary items on the list for only a few cents."

The women clapped for him.

Virgil held his hat in his hands. "We need to be thanking the Lord. And I'll say that I have no regrets using my wife's belongings for the sake of the band. We'll just say it's her way of giving back now."

The afternoon before the band's departure, Allen rode from camp to camp in hopes of finding his own interesting trade. On the way back to the fort, he spotted a train of freight wagons and a few Conestogas. He rode by to take a look. In the lead wagon was one of the men Allen had seen in Sublette's office. When he reached the last two wagons, he jerked back the reins. The Mills and the Herberts were in line with the others heading east.

He pulled up next to the wagon Phineas Mills drove. "What's happening? Why are you here?"

Phineas wouldn't look Allen in the eye. Eva hid hers behind the brim of her bonnet. "We're heading back home, Allen," Phineas said.

Allen detected sadness tinged with shame in the man's voice.

"It's been too much for us to handle. Herberts too. Rachel can't go on. She's been weak with fear ever since Jacob got lost, and she can't shake the feeling that she's going to end up like Martha Jolifer, may she rest in peace. Jacob was reluctant but gave in for her sake. And you've seen how the boys have lost their spirit. It's no use trying to talk us out of it, Allen. We made the decision a few days ago. We were just waiting for the right time, and God answered our prayers when this train pulled out."

"Answered your prayer?" Allen frowned. "You've known for days this wagon train was leaving, and you planned on returning to New York without saying anything?"

"You know how hardheaded the reverend can be. He wouldn't understand that we're turning back."

"What about the mission and the commissioning? You said yourself that you were prepared to give your life for the mission."

Mills remained silent.

Allen looked beyond the Mills' wagon. He studied the Herberts' wagon and spotted the boys sitting behind their father. It was true—they had little spark left. Rachel's constant fear had gotten to them. The journey had been rougher than any had anticipated.

"Well, maybe it's for the best. It's only going to get harder down the trail."

Eva chanced a look at Allen, maybe because she heard sympathy in his voice.

Allen stroked his horse's neck. "Do you know what you're going to do yet?"

"No. We'll just get back to Buffalo and figure things out. The Lord will open a door for us somewhere," Mills said.

"Yes, I'm sure he will, and may he bless your journey." Allen extended his hand.

Mills shook it and nodded.

"God bless you, Allen," Eva said.

Allen smiled, to indicate it would all be fine. He turned his horse to the Herberts' wagon. Rachel appeared ashen and despondent. Not even the prospect of heading home seemed to have lifted her spirits.

Jacob swallowed hard. His large Adam's apple bobbed. "My Lord, Allen. I guess I'm glad you found us. I didn't like leaving without saying proper goodbyes, but it just seemed best to avoid any arguing. I hope you'll understand."

"Reverend Mills explained your decision. As much as I don't like saying goodbye to you all, I believe I can understand. I'm just going to miss you folks, especially the boys." He smiled at them, but they looked down and frowned.

The wagons moved forward.

Allen nudged Caleb to stay alongside. "Do you have all you need for the way back?"

"We sold some things and bought food. We'll be fine," Jacob said.

"I guess you'll be safe enough traveling with this train. Most of them look capable."

"Mr. Vandenberg, the master, said that Dark Wolf is off raiding to the west, so this is a good time to get out of his country."

Mrs. Herbert pressed into her husband's side.

"Then I'm sure you'll be fine. I hear Vandenberg is a good man." Allen felt awkward tagging along with the train. He'd best just say his goodbye and get it over with.

"God bless you, Jacob. I'm sure going to miss you." They shook hands.

Jacob's eyes welled. "God bless you, Allen."

"Now you boys keep an eye out for that big horned toad down the trail. He's waiting for you to give him a ride to New York. I'm sure he'll want to meet all your cousins. And maybe even go to church with you."

The boys smiled at Allen's challenge.

"Goodbye, now." Allen turned his horse, trotted away, and let the wind dry his tears.

When he returned to camp, Gloria was alone, preparing for the next day's departure. Without the Mills' and Herberts' wagons, the camp seemed empty.

"Oh, Allen. I'm so glad you're back. I didn't know what to do. The Mills and Herberts left, and I couldn't leave camp to go tell the Bannisters."

"I saw them with the freight wagons. They told me."

"Did you try to get them to stay with us? We're supposed to leave tomorrow. The reverend is going to be very upset."

Allen shook his head. "I made no attempt to convince them. In fact, I believe it's a wise decision. Mrs. Herbert wouldn't make it out here. And the Mills won't be persuaded. They can't be forced to stay against their will."

"But what is Reverend Bannister going to say?" Gloria's eyebrows furrowed, and the corners of her lips turned downward.

"We'll find out soon enough. How may I help you here?"

The Fosters came into camp first, with Olive. Allen could tell that they noticed right away that something wasn't right. Gloria and Allen explained what had happened.

A few minutes later, the reverend strolled into camp with Virgil.

"What?" Bannister boomed after hearing about the two families' departure. "You just let them ride off? How in the world can they quit on us the day before we leave?"

Allen remained quiet. The decision had been made. The reverend was shocked by the departure, but he'd get over it.

"If you want, I'll ride with you to go talk to them," Virgil said. "They can't be very far up the trail. But truth be known, I don't imagine they'll change their minds. I believe they're making the right choice."

"Making the right choice? There was no choice to be made." Bannister fumed. "They signed on to be a part of this band, and they were commissioned by the church to do the same. No, they have to buck up and be strong through the trials and tribulations that come our way. As it says in the book of James, we must 'count it all joy when ye fall into divers temptations, that worketh faith and patience.' They should have brought their concern before me. I would have pointed out the weakness of their faith and given them encouragement."

"Perhaps that is why they left without speaking to you, Reverend," Virgil said. "They knew you would convince them to stay, but it would have been against their will. And somewhere down the line, it would have turned into rebelliousness or contention at a time when it would be dangerous for all of us."

Everyone nodded in agreement except Bannister. "This can't be. My band is falling apart."

Olive suggested they have a bite to eat. "Then if you still feel it is the right thing to do, dear, you can ride up the trail and bring them back."

Bannister eyed the group. "I guess that's what I'll do." He was quiet as he helped load the last of their supplies onto the wagon while Gloria and Olive fixed supper.

After eating, the reverend asked Virgil to ride out with Foster to find the wagon train, not to bring the Mills and Herberts back but to say farewell.

"Samuel, dear," Olive said. "Don't you think you should be the one to go?"

"We can put everything in order here," Allen said as he coiled a rope.

Bannister seemed to ponder his wife's question. He sighed. "Very well then. Virgil, ride with me, will you? Reverend Foster, you can take charge of organizing the wagons and supplies. I'll go speak to the Mills and Herberts."

That night, Allen surveyed the rich blue twilight sky, the camp-fire, and the reduced fellowship. "Lord, this is a wondrous mystery."

Foster led the prayer for the safety of their trip and a blessing for the two families heading back East.

"Hello, the camp," someone called out of the darkness. Gwen and Humphrey Limm stepped into the glow of the campfire. "Looks like you're missing a couple of wagons," Gwen said right away. "So the Mills and Herberts did leave."

"You already know about it?" Bannister seemed surprised.

"Heard they left with Vandenberg. Figured you might go bring 'em back though," Gwen said.

"I rode out to bless their journey home—"

"Looks like you're ready otherwise. We'll be back shortly after daybreak." They turned to leave.

"Don't you want to go over the checklist to make sure we have all the provisions?" Bannister seemed eager to prove they were competent in traveling.

"No. Heard Mr. Jolifer did most of the trading for you, so I expect it's complete." They mounted and trotted into the darkness.

Earlier that day, Dark Wolf sat motionless with his back to a log. He made no attempt to hide. His elk-skin shirt did not blend with his surroundings. He watched the trappers' wagons roll by only forty paces in front of him. These white men were careless fools. They deserved to die. Dark Wolf would make all others fear his power.

One wagon driver and a rider looked in his direction and could easily have shot him, but they did not seem to even see him. When the fourth wagon passed, Dark Wolf stood—the signal for his men to attack.

Kicking Lion and eleven warriors raced shrieking out from the trees. They spread out and swooped down on the panicked trappers. As the first driver raised his gun, an arrow hit him in the chest. He fell to the ground.

A rider kicked his horse to run away and dropped the lead rope of his pack mule. A warrior chased him, leaped onto the back of his horse, clutched him around the neck, and stabbed him repeatedly in the chest and belly. The warrior shoved him to the ground, where he bounced and rolled. A second warrior jumped from his horse, and with a quick slice, scalped the fallen trapper.

The attack was over in minutes. Nine men lay dead. The Indians stripped the wagons of their cargo, then set them on fire. Dark Wolf stepped up to a fallen white man, raised both hands in the air, and shouted a victory cry. He bent over, sliced the man open, pulled out his liver, and dropped it into a leather bag. The warriors scalped and mutilated the other bodies in a bloody frenzy until Kicking Lion shouted for them to stop. They rode away into the trees and disappeared, leaving stillness and death behind.

CHAPTER TWENTY

THE MORNING DEW BROUGHT OUT the smell of the earth and a damp but comfortable chill in the air. The wagons stood at ease in formation, waiting for the Limms to arrive and march them westward. Standing around and chatting, Bannister tried to cover his anxiety. The Rocky Mountains and the Oregon Territory were ripe unto harvest, and he was the laborer who would bring in the sheaves. Oregon was where his vision would become reality and where his mission would surpass all others. Even Jason Lee and those Presbyterians would be impressed.

The Limms hadn't arrived, and the group was ready to leave. Bannister considered starting the journey without them. Let the Limms catch up to them. That would certainly show them that Bannister was a man of decision and drive. Yes, he would get them started on the trail.

Just as Bannister was about to get them moving, Humphrey Limm rode up, walking his red mule slowly past each wagon. He inspected the loads and the animals.

Humphrey was of medium height and build. His brown wavy

hair spilled out beneath a weather-worn leather hat with a wide brim. His hazel-green eyes didn't seem to miss a detail.

"Who's got the lead rig?"

"That would be mine," Bannister said. "Good morning, Mr. Limm. I was beginning to wonder if you were going to make it—"

"Your oxen won't make it very far the way that harness is set up. You'd better fix that right away." He inspected the rest of the wagons and seemed satisfied that all was in order.

Bannister groaned as he walked to reset the harness and the guiding reins beneath the yoke. He had to admit that he'd not harnessed the team well. Besides not having solid control, it would have rubbed a sore patch that would annoy even an ox.

"After you get that fixed, lead your wagons past the fort to the west. You'll see a trail leading off through the trees. Gwen will meet you there with the other wagons." Humphrey spoke evenly, yet the order carried authority.

"What other wagons? I know nothing of any other wagons." Bannister's frustration slipped out.

"Some freight wagons bound for Fort Hall and a couple more travelers like yourself," Humphrey replied. "I'll meet up with you before long." He trotted off.

Bannister climbed to the seat next to his wife. "Freighters? I don't want to travel with a group of foul-mouthed freighters. I hope they're not drunkards. The Limms must be trying to squeeze a few more dollars out of the trip."

"Dear, the Limms are good people. I think you should trust them." Olive patted his arm.

They passed the fort and made for the tree line. Bannister wished he'd saddled his riding horse so he could scout ahead for the trail and Gwen, but it was too late for that. The wagons skirted the edge of the trees until the trail became obvious.

"This must be the trail." Bannister turned his oxen down the lane through the willows and cottonwoods. "It looks like I am ahead of our scouts, so we'll have to wait. Let them catch up."

A half hour later, Gwen appeared from in front of them. "Reverend, we have been waiting for you up ahead. Follow me." She led them up the trail for a hundred yards. They joined up with five freight wagons and two more Conestogas, and then Humphrey rode up.

"I figured you'd be farther along than this," he said. "Reverend, we're going to need your cooperation in order to make good time traveling."

Bannister's ears burned.

The Limms didn't stop the wagons for a lunch break but continued pushing into the wilderness. The terrain was different from the wide-open spaces of the prairies. Mountains rose on all sides. The farther they rolled away from the river, the more ravines and gullies they crossed.

The wagons braked down a steep hill and finally came to a stop near a small stream. Scattered pine trees and sagebrush spotted the dry, grassy slopes. "Make your meals, clean up, and then put out your fires. There will be no campfires tonight," Gwen said.

"Is that for safety over comfort? Old Rag tried to get us to do that, but we seldom complied." Allen missed Old Rag and his knowledge of the plains, but he was gaining a similar respect for the Limms.

"This is Cold Springs," Gwen said. "It's not the best for protection, but we can make do. Reverend, one of the freight men has agreed to spell Allen in the supply wagon tomorrow so he can ride scout with us and help with some other tasks." She went on to line up the men for guard-duty assignments, urging each one to carry two rifles.

At about three thirty in the morning, Allen sat at his post close to a hundred yards from the camp. He recited psalms to himself to keep alert. He felt a movement at his side and turned to see Humphrey kneel next to him. Humphrey wore moccasins, and Allen wondered if that was the secret of walking silently. But it bothered him that he hadn't seen the guide approaching.

"I see you're staying awake. That's good." Humphrey spoke in a low tone.

"I don't feel sleepy at all, but I'm not as alert as I thought. I didn't see you coming. To be honest, my directions are all twisted around since driving through those ravines. I'm surprised I still know where north is. It's over there, correct?" He pointed.

"Yep, that's still north. We drive through the ravines to keep to low ground as much as we can. It's hard to hide those canvases from the Indians, but we sure ain't going to announce we're here."

"How often you get back to the States?" Allen studied the mountain man's rugged face.

"Ain't been back but once in the past five years. Don't care to go back."

"Gwen feel the same way?"

"She likes it back there even less than I do." He paused. "The mountains make you feel alive like nothing else." He sat back on his haunches. "I got to go check on the others. You keep alert now. A mountain man taught me years ago that you got to listen with your eyes and watch with your ears. That's how you stay alive."

Humphrey left as silently as he'd come. Allen watched him fade into the shadows.

The sky slowly brightened, and when Allen saw movement in the camp, he headed in for a cup of coffee. Within the hour, the wagon train was a half mile up the next wash. Allen rode Caleb, glad to be off the wagon seat. He took turns searching for routes that would keep the wagons clear of hazards.

They passed through the basin of Cottonwood Creek. When the last wagon lurched out of a shallow ravine, Allen caught up with Gwen about fifty yards ahead of the lead wagon. Her brow furrowed. Her mule's ears twitched, and its nostrils flared.

"Something's wrong up yonder. Come on!" She kicked the mule into a run.

Allen followed. They cleared another rise and ran until they could look into the valley below, only to pull up abruptly at the terrible sight of wagons on fire and people lying motionless on the ground. Allen checked his rifle.

Out of the corner of his eye, Allen noted Gwen straightening in her saddle and scanning the valley, up the sides of the hills, and around the horizon. She relaxed, evidently deciding the danger was past. She seemed to breathe more easily.

Allen spotted a rider off to the left who looked as if he was following tracks. He saw another man giving aid to someone stretched out on the ground. Humphrey stepped from behind a burning wagon.

"Let's ride in and see if we can help," she said. They heeled their animals to a canter.

Allen stared at one of the dead men with an arrow in his side and his head scalped. The dark blood made his stomach roil. Gwen rode straight for Humphrey, who had joined the other man kneeling on the ground. She dismounted and told Allen to tie his horse to a wagon wheel. She dropped the reins, and the mule stood still, not at all affected by the smell of blood or burned flesh. Allen's gelding fought the reins, stamped, and snorted, clearly wanting to run away from the bloody slaughter.

"Is he going to make it?" Gwen bent over with her hands on her knees.

"He's hurt bad," Humphrey said.

As Humphrey stepped away from the wounded man, Allen saw that the mountain man giving aid was Jack Burkett.

"Jack . . ." Allen said, then swallowed the lump in his throat. The man on the ground had been scalped and stabbed several times but still managed to fight for his life. His buckskin shirt was soaked in blood, and his bearded face was pasty. Jack had given him a drink of water and moved him to the shade.

"Guess it's a good thing we got a preacher on hand. We'll have a fine burial for these folks." Jack stood up. "This man's lost a lot of blood, Gwen, but see if you can help him."

Humphrey turned to Allen. "Gwen's a good field surgeon. She ain't never studied medicine, but she's patched together trappers after Indian fights, brawls, and accidents."

"Jack, I doubt I can do anything more than what you've already done." She glanced down at the man. "Do you know him?"

"No. I don't recognize any of them," Jack said. "They came through South Pass a couple of weeks ago with a load of furs they collected in the Bear River country. We came across their camp a couple miles back. Then we saw this smoke."

Jack looked past Allen, who turned to follow his gaze. The wagon train was coming over the rise.

"I don't see the Mills or the Herberts. They lagging behind?"

"No, they headed back East."

Jack wiped his bloody hands on a piece of canvas. "Even though you brought the choir, Reverend Hartman, I don't think we're going to have time for the whole funeral service."

"Certainly we will bury them!" Allen felt a sense of duty.

"Yes, we will. Let's tidy up the dead the best we can before the ladies get down here," Jack said, yanking a canvas off a wagon. "Let's drag them over there and cover them up. We'll get those freighters to help us dig graves. Humphrey, there are two bodies on the other side, if you don't mind."

Humphrey found two dead men who had evidently tried to run from their attackers. Allen worked with Jack. Nine graves would have to be dug, including one for the wounded man, who was not expected to last long. A few of the bodies had been so hideously mutilated that Allen lost his breakfast.

"The hearts and livers were removed for some devilish witchery," Jack said.

Just before the wagons approached, Joaquin Del Castillo rode up. "It was Dark Wolf and twelve men, about three hours ago. They started for the mountains but circled back to the north with the horses and mules loaded down with furs and food."

At the mention of Dark Wolf, bile rose in Allen's throat. He had to turn his head and spit. He gripped his gun and scanned the horizon.

"Let's stop those wagons right there and get these men buried. It shouldn't take long," Jack said.

Jack spoke to the freighters, who jumped into action. Some grabbed shovels, and others grabbed their guns and set up watch posts. Virgil worked with Allen to gather rocks they'd use to cover the shallow graves. Bannister and Foster kept their wives calm, and Gloria went to see if Gwen needed help. Because of the hard ground, it took an hour to get the nine graves dug to a depth of only about eighteen inches. The trappers would have Scripture read at their burial—a sight more formal than most mountain funerals.

Allen dropped a pile of rocks and watched as Jack tossed a shovel into the wagon.

"How badly is he hurt?" Gloria knelt beside the victim.

Gwen lifted the wounded man's shirt to expose the brutality that had been inflicted—several stab wounds and a slashing that had opened the man's torso. Gloria gasped but maintained her composure. His eyes were closed, the eyelids caked with dried blood from his scalp, and his breathing was short and quick.

"Why was he allowed to live?"

"Must be they thought he was already dead," Jack said.

Jack leaned close to the man's face. "You got some grit for sure. All the others are dead and buried. It was Dark Wolf that killed you and your friends. We'll do our best to get him for you and get your horses back. But you leave that to us. You go on now and find you some shining beaver plews." The man barely nodded his head, his breathing relaxed, and in a few moments he was gone.

"I hate to sound brash, Miss Shannon, but we have to get this man into the ground with his friends and be on our way. It's not safe to stay here any longer," Jack said.

"I understand."

Allen stepped beside Gloria and brushed his hands on his pants. "This is a terrible sight."

"It's hideous. I've never seen such evil work."

Bannister approached, Bible in hand. "I have a sermon for these freighters and will give an altar call. Allen, I want you to be ready to help."

"Sir. We won't have time for that. It was Dark Wolf's gang that did this killing."

Bannister gulped. He called the group together, quoted Psalm 23, and offered a prayer.

The freighters searched the damaged wagons and saw nothing significant they could salvage. When everyone was ready to pull out again, the lead wagons made a loop to turn back the way they'd come.

"What's this here?" boomed the reverend. "What is the point in turning back?"

"We're heading back to Fort Laramie as quickly as possible. We won't be safe until we get there," Jack said.

Bannister's jaw dropped. "But we are going west!"

"Not today," Jack said, "and probably not this week. Dark Wolf is on the warpath. He's been attacking all over the area. He claims this as his territory, and he won't tolerate trespassers, even kind-hearted ones. He and his warriors have attacked several camps and murdered trappers. They burned out Justin Tilly's cabin on Horse-shoe Creek just two days ago. That's about fifteen miles from here. They won't let anyone pass, Reverend. They're a murderous lot."

"But I say we push on. Certainly they would not be foolish enough to attack a party this size." Bannister sounded desperate.

"They just murdered nine experienced Indian fighters. They wouldn't hesitate to attack a wagon train with women and preachers. The fact is, you'd be a special prize for them." Jack rubbed the back of his neck. "We'll return to Fort Laramie until things settle down." His answer was firm.

Bannister was relentless. "What if we push on through the night? We'll keep to low ground. We can be out of Dark Wolf's territory in just a couple of days."

"Sir, it's likely we're being watched right now. Furthermore, I noticed that Virgil is traveling alone and that two other wagons are no longer with you. If you continue west, you'll have no one to help with your mission work." Jack turned and rode off.

Allen thought it was absurd for Bannister to argue with Jack in the midst of a violent scene.

Olive tugged on her husband's sleeve. "Dear, I think Mr. Burkett is right. We should wait until it's safe."

He gave in with a grunt, climbed onto his seat, and followed the freight wagons heading back to the fort.

Allen retrieved his horse and came alongside Gwen as Jack conferred with Joaquin, Humphrey, and the freight master about a plan to get back to Fort Laramie. "We'll take the quickest trail possible," Jack said. "I'm thinking Dark Wolf and his boys will hide the horses they stole or trade them for slaves. If we're lucky, that will take a couple of days."

Humphrey leaned in. "We can make the fort by late tomorrow."

"Sure appreciate you tagging along with us, Jack. I know you and Joaquin could make it to Fort Laramie by tonight," Gwen said.

"Don't mention it, Gwen. I hate to see that scoundrel take advantage of good people. No one deserves to die that way, not even an ornery old trapper."

They pushed on until almost dark and then made a dry camp. The animals needed rest because they would be pushed hard the next day.

They started at first light. Allen kept as close as he could to Gwen. After a couple of hours on the trail, Joaquin rode in from scouting with the disturbing news that they were being followed. "They're not Dark Wolf's men, but probably some young warriors out for blood."

Not even a half hour had passed when a rifle shot rang out. About a quarter mile away, Humphrey, who had also been out scouting, raced his red mule down a hill, heading for the wagons. A cluster of Indians appeared over the hill several seconds later. They were less than two hundred yards behind Humphrey.

Gwen moved first. She ran her red mule like its tail was on fire straight for Humphrey. Skidding to a stop on a small rise, she lifted her Hawkins .50 and fired.

Allen saw the puff of black smoke before he heard the bang. The lead Indian fell back off his horse. Gwen turned and raced alongside her husband. The red mules ran stride for stride until they stopped behind the first freight wagon.

Jack and Joaquin sprinted toward the Indians. Allen kicked his gelding after them, gun in hand. When they reached the rise from where Gwen had shot, they halted. No more shots were fired. The Indians disappeared into a draw.

"They're lighting out. We won't see any more of that bunch, not today anyway. Let's go hear what Humphrey has to say," Jack said and spun his horse around and saw Allen, gun ready. "Well, Parson, were you fixing to get into the scrap with us? You know it might have cost you your scalp."

"I don't know. I guess I didn't think about it. It just seemed like the right thing to do," Allen said.

Jack cocked an eyebrow. "It's fine by me, but you're going to have to explain yourself to Reverend Bannister."

Samuel Bannister waited by his wagon, his fists firmly planted on his hips. "Allen! What do you think you were doing, racing into a fight? You might have been killed. You are not here to fight with your gun. You should leave that to these experienced men and stay back in the protection of the wagons." Bannister's brows were knit together. The scowl twisted his face.

"Relax, Reverend Bannister," Jack said. "Allen went out to save those poor heathens. He was fixing to preach a sermon that would put them to sleep right in their tracks. But when he pulled out the offering plate, they just took off running." Jack winked at Allen, while the others standing around chuckled. "Now, let's hear what Humphrey has to report, and then we'll be on our way."

"I'd finished scouting the trail ahead, so I was returning to the wagons," Humphrey said. "I dropped into a gully and almost ran right into the midst of the Indians, who were painting themselves for the attack. All young bucks, except for one. He was a bit older, and scalps hung on his belt. As I think about it, I reckon he was from a different tribe. He was mean looking."

"Might be the one Gwen plugged. He was older than the rest," one of the freighters said, an old-timer with a sharp eye.

"I broke into a run, and they set to chasing me. I was sure glad to see the wagons when I came over that hill. Fired a warning shot, and then Gwen came out. Guess you-uns know the rest."

"That were fine shooting, mighty fine," said the old-timer. "A hunert and fifty paces at a fast movin' target. Derned if that weren't fine shooting."

The men looked at Gwen and nodded. Single handedly she had turned the raiders from their attack and likely saved many lives.

Gwen shifted and toed a stone, obviously uncomfortable with the attention.

"Well done, Gwen," Jack said.

She nodded to him.

"That's my wife. Ain't she a beauty?" Humphrey gave her a quick peck on the forehead.

"All right, folks, let's get rolling. I don't expect trouble from that bunch again, but we can't relax."

At Jack's command, everyone moved. They were on the trail within minutes, and every eye was alert and scanning the trees and gullies.

They rolled into the clearing at Fort Laramie as the sun was just about to drop below the western horizon. The Limms guided them to a campsite near the fort.

About an hour later, Bannister gathered the band around a campfire and led devotions of thanksgiving for their safety. "In the Lord's providence, we are safe. However, I believe he would have protected us had we continued west."

Allen shook his head. How could Bannister be so naïve?

Jack and Joaquin rode up, leading a lightly loaded packhorse. "Evening, folks," Jack said. "Glad to see you relaxing."

Olive welcomed them to the fire. "Please join us, Mr. Burkett and Mr. Del Castillo. We want to thank you so much for seeing us through this dreadful time. We felt secure in your care."

Bannister scowled at his wife. The rest of the group poured out praises on the two mountain men.

"Yes, thank you both," Bannister finally grumbled.

After a few minutes of recounting the adventure, Jack asked to speak to Bannister and Allen alone. The three men moved out of the hearing of those around the fire.

"Reverend, I talked with Sublette and some others. They're reporting many more attacks than even we knew about. They recommend sitting tight for a week to see if things settle down. They're putting together a posse of fighting men to track down Dark Wolf's band, but it's going to take a while to gather enough men and track the witch doctor. In the meantime, I'd like to take Allen hunting for a few days."

Allen's eyes widened. This sounded too good to be true.

"Will that be safe?" Bannister folded his arms.

"Yes, sir. We'll be heading north, away from the trouble area," Jack said.

"You'll be leaving first thing in the morning?"

"We'll be pulling out right now. We can ride up into the hills for a few miles before making camp."

"All right, then." Bannister put his hand on Allen's shoulder. "You be careful,"

"Thank you, sir." Allen looked to Jack, knowing his eyes must be sparkling.

Jack grinned. "You'll need only your gun, powder, and a bed-roll."

Allen saddled his horse and was ready in minutes. He couldn't believe his good fortune. He'd be hunting with two of the best mountain men who had ever crossed the "crick."

CHAPTER TWENTY-ONE

THE THREE HUNTERS RODE INTO the black night. Jack in front, followed by Allen, then Joaquin, who led the packhorse. Allen could discern the backside of Jack's horse only by the light-colored canvas bedroll tied behind the saddle. Neither Jack nor Joaquin appeared the least bit affected by the darkness. As they traveled up the river, then into a mountain canyon, Allen trusted the gelding's night vision. Heading northwest, they' rode for two hours before Jack claimed a camp spot.

"It's better to count ribs than tracks," Jack said after picketing the horses.

Allen lay on his blanket with his hands behind his head. The Big Dipper and other constellations were the same as at home, but that night he was on an adventure in the wilderness with skilled mountain men who slept a few feet away.

Yesterday he'd helped bury nine men, and that morning he'd seen an Indian attack thwarted. The sobering thoughts showed him just how vulnerable he was—they all were. He reflected until he dozed off.

His eyes flew open. "Count ribs?" The riddle provoked his mind. Ah . . . he got it. Picketed horses couldn't eat as much, and eventually their ribs would show. But that was better than following the tracks of a missing horse in the morning. Allen smiled and shifted to his bedroll.

At dawn, someone squeezed Allen's arm until he fully awakened. "Here, put these on." Jack handed Allen a roll of buckskins.

Allen stood and examined the buckskin shirt, pants, and moccasins with simple beaded decorations. "Thanks."

Jack and Joaquin were packed and ready to go. Joaquin ate something out of a leather pouch while watching the tree line. Allen stripped off his clothes and slipped on the Indian garments.

Jack winked. "Now you're looking like one of the boys. That's an old set, but they look to fit."

"Yes, they fit fine. Thanks again." Allen moved around to get accustomed to the new feel. The moccasins covered his ankles and tied with a leather strap. Tight rows of blue beads were sewn across the top. He rolled up his bedding, clothes, and boots and tucked them into his saddlebag. "If you don't mind my asking, what's this unique smell?" He sniffed the sleeve.

"Bear grease. Keeps the water off. You'll have to get used to that. Indians around here put bear grease on everything, even their hair," Jack said.

Joaquin handed the leather pouch to Allen. "Eat some. Sorry— no time for coffee."

Allen reached into the pouch and pulled out a pinch of dried, shredded meat with something else mixed into it. He put the pinch into his mouth. It tasted all right, smoked venison and something sweet. He nodded his approval.

"It's pemmican—dried meat and berries. Help yourself." Joaquin swung onto his horse.

Allen scanned their campsite. Except for the flattened grass, they left no sign that they'd been there. Allen munched on the pemmican while riding, then tied up the pouch and tucked it into his saddlebag.

As the sky brightened, Allen studied his buckskin outfit. The small blue and white beads formed little clusters of no particular shape across the upper chest and sleeves. It didn't have fringe like Jack's shirt, which helped drain water, but the bear grease that had been rubbed into the leather would keep the water from soaking in.

After climbing out of a valley, they emerged onto a wide plain, grassy like the prairie, but the hills and knolls looked like dozens of giant haystacks. Jack led them northwest toward another ridgeline about ten miles away.

Following dry creek beds and skirting low ridges, they rode for hours. Finally, Jack stopped at a spring that made a circle of green grass about six feet around and then trickled down a slope. The pool was deep enough to fill a canteen.

"That peak to the southwest I call Flattop, for obvious reasons." Jack pointed in the opposite direction. "To the north is Horse Tooth Mountain. We'll head west along Horse Tooth Creek."

Cedars and scrub pines dotted the western slope of Horse Tooth Mountain. Below, the green belt of brush and trees along the creek wound its way west to connect with the North Platte at a section that flowed north to south. They followed a long arroyo until they reached Horse Tooth Creek.

Jack took no measures to conceal their presence. They rode to a rise and waited sky-lined before descending into a low canyon. Minutes later a couple of Indian scouts rode out of the brush straight for them. They weren't painted for war, but they brandished weapons as if they were intent on using them. The Indians said something as they passed Jack. They looked Allen over, shouted something and laughed, then ran back through the brush.

About two hundred yards ahead, along the creek's bank, were about thirty tipis amidst a grove of elm and cottonwood trees. It was a picturesque setting, not pastoral like a New England village, but a wilderness community where scouts stood guard for protection.

Joaquin came alongside Allen. "Those braves were mocking you back there."

"Should I have said something?" Allen didn't appreciate being the Indians' object of scorn.

"No. You did just fine keeping quiet. They recognized us, but they're wary of everyone lately. Too many attacks. There's a bad spirit in the mountains, and it makes them nervous. When we enter the village, just keep calm. They'll look you over, but we won't be here long." Joaquin pulled back on his reins, letting Allen move ahead.

The Indians stayed back as they stared at the visitors, curious but ready to run. Allen looked around, taking in everything. The children, some dirty and some clean, gazed at him with big brown eyes.

Joaquin reined his horse alongside Allen. "We will go into the lodge of their holy man for information."

"The one with stars on it?"

"Each man paints symbols of their accomplishments. It identifies the family with pride."

There were deer and elk hides staked to the ground. Drying meat hung on pole racks. Women stopped working at the hides and baskets to stare at the strange men.

Jack raised his right arm and spoke fluent Arapaho to a man who listened and then entered a tipi. He came back out with an older man who acknowledged Jack and Joaquin but stared at Allen for a long time.

Allen grew uncomfortable under the man's gaze but remained calm.

Finally the older Indian said something, and the two mountain men dismounted.

Wait here, Joaquin mouthed to Allen.

Allen swallowed hard as his mentors ducked into the tipi, leaving him alone. He wasn't sure what to do, so he just sat on his horse and smiled.

The villagers continued to stare at him. Some teenage boys made comments, and others laughed. They said things to him as if they expected a response, but Allen had none to give. One young man with a scowl spoke. Nobody laughed. He spoke again with a harsh tone and tapped a club against his open palm while staring at Allen.

He whispered a prayer. "Lord, what shall I do?" The answer came quickly in the growl of his stomach, so he casually reached into his saddlebag and pulled out the pemmican pouch. He ate and tried to ignore his audience. Slowly they departed. Only a few children stood around, while others watched from a distance.

He hoped eating in front of them wasn't culturally inappropriate. After what seemed like an hour, but he knew was really only a few minutes, Jack and Joaquin emerged from the tipi and mounted their horses. The old man stared at Allen again.

Jack waited until the elder spoke, and then they rode off.

When well out of view of the camp, Allen could no longer contain his curiosity and caught up to Jack. "What happened back there?"

"We stopped to get some news about what's going on in these parts. We need to know if it's safe to travel and hunt. He told us the whereabouts of those murdering horse thieves."

"How would the chief know that already?" Allen was mystified.

"Word gets around by scouts, runners, or traders. And sometimes word gets around by spirits," Jack said.

"Spirits?"

"Yes, spirits. That old man was not a chief but a holy man, a medicine man. In a way, he's the Samuel Bannister of the tribe. But then that might not be the best comparison." Jack smiled.

"The chiefs and many of the warriors and their families have gone down to the big powwow on the Arkansas. Two Rivers is the elder in charge of the camp while they're away. That's why those people were so nervous. Dark Wolf is attacking Indian villages while the fighting men are away. They're camping here because it's easy to defend."

"How would he know where it's good to hunt?" Allen couldn't get enough information.

"He sings a spirit song, which is a kind of prayer, and the spirits tell him the location of deer that are acceptable for hunting. They speak to him through bones or a deer skull."

"You mean some kind of evil spirit talks to him or gives him a message of the whereabouts of deer? I've never heard of the Holy Spirit working in that fashion. It sounds like divination to me." Allen viewed the practice through his Christian perspective. "I've never met someone who practices animism and believes that spirits indwell objects."

"It's not for me to decide if they're evil spirits or not. But I can tell you that we'll find deer in the canyon, just as he said. I've not known him to be wrong. He also has power to cure rattlesnake bites. It's hard to say that feeding the tribe or healing a snake bite is evil, isn't it? But that's how they live."

Allen pulled his horse back into line and practiced observing the surroundings. He listened to sounds and breathed in the smells of the wilderness. Chirping birds meant peace. Ground squirrels occasionally scrambled into holes, which meant a hawk might be soaring overhead. Danger for the squirrel was a thing of beauty for Allen. He watched a hawk gliding on the current. He smelled sage, pine, dust, his horse, and, of course, bear grease.

They dropped down a narrow draw and onto the flats of the North Platte. The river came from the west and curved southward about a mile upstream. Jack stopped at a cut in the bank formed by years of erosion at flood level. The water flowed about twenty feet from the bank. "We'll rest here for a bit and have something to eat. I want to let the sun drop some more," Jack said.

They took the saddles off and unloaded the packhorse. Joaquin led the three horses to water, and Allen followed, holding Caleb. Jack started a small fire at the bottom of the bank. The smoke dissipated through the branches of a tree. Joaquin scanned the area. They watched a red-tailed hawk circle above and then soar beyond a ridge.

"My Apache uncle used to tell me that the hawk's strength and cunning as he soars inspires peace," Joaquin said.

"Yes, well-spoken words," Allen said. "I guess that's how I feel with you and Jack."

When the horses finished drinking, they were turned loose. The packhorse rolled in the sand, and the others wandered off in search of grass.

"Sit down, Parson. Have a cup of coffee."

Allen and Joaquin leaned against the bank, while Jack squatted by the fire. He handed each man a large chunk of meat on a roasting stick. Jack poured three cups of coffee and then sat back and joined the other two in holding his meat over the fire. As the meat cooked, fat dripped onto the fire, making it flare and hiss.

Once the elk meat was cooked, Allen bit off a piece. The rich flavor melted in his mouth. He hadn't tasted anything so good since Thomas had roasted the buffalo loin.

"This is delicious. Thank you, Jack." Out of habit, Allen patted his hip in search for a handkerchief. He wiped his mouth with his sleeve. "I can't take another bite. You gave me more than I can eat."

"Go ahead and force it down. We're going to ride for a bit longer before we make camp. Might not eat like this again until tomorrow afternoon or the next day." If Jack had a plan in mind, he wasn't sharing it.

Why does deer hunting have to be so complicated? Maybe it has something to do with what Two Rivers told Jack in the tipi.

Allen spotted a crow circling overhead. Shortly, it came to light on a dead tree across the river.

"Do you think there might be a spirit in that crow watching us?" Allen would never have asked missionaries, but he felt secure the mountain men would take his question seriously.

Jack glanced at the crow and then looked to Joaquin, as if deferring the question to him.

"No. That's not a witch-crow. He's just waiting for our scraps," Joaquin said, then took a bite of meat.

Allen learned about mountain men's eating habits. They ate heartily. They could consume several pounds of meat in a day. When hunting was good, they took only the choice parts. Occasionally, they would make jerky or pemmican. Going without food for days happened more often than any trapper or brave cared to admit.

Jack finished the last of the coffee, then buried the fire with sand. "Time to be going."

Allen offered to go look for the horses that had wandered out of sight. Joaquin shook his head and then whistled like a bird. A moment later his black mare trotted in, followed by the other horses and Caleb.

"I must learn that whistle," Allen said.

With the men leaving no significant trace of food behind, the crow would have slim pickings around the fire. Riding out, they crossed the river and climbed into a quarter-moon canyon that hooked to the north. At the head, they found a wide pocket a hundred yards across with enough scrub pines for a hidden camp.

Jack and Allen dismounted. Dropping the lead rope of the packhorse, Joaquin kept riding. Jack unloaded the packhorse.

"We're close to where the horse thieves are camped. Tomorrow morning we'll ride in and steal them back. There'll probably be a dozen extra cayuses running with us, so you'll need to have your kit tied down snug. Check your powder, and keep your guns close at hand. We don't know how many braves are still with them, but they won't be expecting us. Best get some sleep now."

"Sleep?" Allen dropped his saddle. "How do you expect me to sleep knowing that I'm going to be stealing horses in the morning? Good Lord! What am I supposed to do? I've never stolen horses before."

"Relax, Parson. We'll just be taking them back from the thieves. It's good stealing. More than likely they'll be sleeping off their liquor, so we can slip in, untie them, and walk right out. We won't have to fire a shot. But we do want to be ready." Jack spoke as casually as if they planned to load a hay wagon.

"What do you mean by 'good stealing'?" Allen struggled to calm his anxiety.

"It's just like when Jesus taught the disciples about binding a strong man so they could go into his house and take his possessions. I believe He was speaking of taking back what the strong man had already stolen from them." Jack's biblical explanation was as surprising as his scheme.

Allen paced. He was two thousand miles from home, about to steal horses from murdering Indians, and being told it was the righteous thing to do by a fur trapper who quoted the Bible. How would he ever explain this to Reverend Bannister, or his parents, when he couldn't understand it for himself?

Mid-July's twilight sky faded to a deep blue. The eastern stars appeared as vague lights. About fifty yards from camp, Allen stood beside a small pine. It occurred to him that he had sought out protective cover even for a time of meditation. He was reacting instinctually to the dangers he faced. He took a deep breath to settle his emotions, then knelt down to pray for Jack and Joaquin and the adventure on which they were about to embark.

He prayed for the missionary band, his parents, the church back home, and for Deacon Abraham, Sister Lydia, and the Negro church on the Ohio River. It dawned on him that he had forgotten to pray for Violet. He blessed her but did not miss her. Allen persevered until the familiar sense of peace came over him, which put his heart and mind in order. His thoughts came back to Jack Burkett and stealing horses.

"Lord, I can't help but believe that you brought me here to this very moment to learn something new about my faith. What Jack said about the strong man seems odd, but it's ringing true in my heart."

He recalled the verse: How can one enter into a strong man's house, and spoil his goods, except he first bind the strong man? And then he will spoil his house.

"Lord Jesus, I bind the strong man, in your holy name. Make him blind and deaf to our efforts. Protect us as we recover that which was stolen from innocent people. Bring your justice, Lord, to those who would do evil. And if it be possible, let them understand your power and your salvation. Guard us with godly armor to keep us from pride and anger. May we serve you faithfully tomorrow. I pray in Jesus's name. Amen."

Allen stood and rubbed his knees. The immense field of stars affirmed his intercession. A night owl hooted in the distance. He returned to join Jack. Minutes later, Joaquin led his horse into camp, coming through the trees as if it were daylight.

"They're less than two miles west in a narrow canyon," Joaquin reported. "The bottom of their canyon opens north toward the river, about five hundred yards off. The stolen horses are in a steep bowl that makes a natural corral. Above them, the canyon splits with one branch to the east, and the other widens to the south."

"How many men?" Jack asked.

"Nine, and they're not drinking."

Jack looked at Allen. "That's bad news. Drunken thieves would be distracted and hungover in the morning, a weakness for them, but sober thieves will be alert and dangerous."

"And they all wear feathers," Joaquin said.

Allen had learned that Jack and Joaquin never entered into any encounter lightly. The murdering horse thieves were all seasoned warriors with battle feathers to prove it. And they had the advantage of terrain that had two or three escape routes. The odds were stacked against them.

"Let's sleep now. We'll get the horses at first light," Jack said.

Allen nodded, then smirked. Tomorrow he would become a horse thief.

CHAPTER TWENTY-TWO

ALLEN AWAKENED TO A PREDAWN gray sky. Relieved that he hadn't overslept, he rubbed the sleep out of his eyes and sat up, listening. All was quiet—too quiet. Twisting in his bedroll, he looked around. He was alone. In fact, he saw no sign that Jack and Joaquin had ever been there. Allen quickly checked the horses. His gelding was staked where he'd left him, and the little bay packhorse was loaded and ready to travel.

Allen hurried to pack his bedroll and saddle Caleb. He checked his long rifle and pistol, chewed on some pemmican, and waited.

Once he had enough light to see by, he scanned the area. He identified Jack's and Joaquin's tracks and followed them for about fifty yards. He stopped when an inner voice cautioned him to stay by his horse.

Not three minutes later, Allen heard a rumbling sound that grew louder and more intense. He mounted his horse and held the packhorse's lead rope. Caleb shuffled, pawed the ground, and tossed his head up and down.

Allen searched the area, desperate to understand the cause and location of the pounding.

There! Coming fast around a rise were more than a dozen wild horses, charging in fierce unity down the wide draw.

Joaquin was the first to come into view, then Jack, who hollered, "Let's go, Parson!"

Allen fell into form with the thunderous lot. They didn't break stride even for crossing the North Platte River. Shouting, Joaquin raced forward, and the herd followed him, splashing through the shallow water to the other side.

After they'd covered five miles of rough ground, Joaquin slowed the pace to a trot. Not much later, they made visual contact with several village scouts watching the back trail from strategic vantage points. Several boys rode out to help lead the horses into camp.

Allen noticed that the villagers no longer made fun of him. Instead, they looked on him with respect, just as they did Jack and Joaquin. He figured he'd proven himself worthy of admiration by stealing horses from dangerous men and returning safely. The young men who had teased Allen before were quiet, and one offered to take his horse.

Old Rag had said back on the prairie that stealing horses was one way a man earned respect. Allen came into that truth.

Jack and Joaquin dismounted and started for Two Rivers's tipi. Jack glanced back at Allen. "You coming?"

From one day to the next, Allen had earned the right to sit with them in the medicine man's lodge. He jumped down and followed, ducking low to step into the dark tipi. A small fire burned in the middle of the floor. Dirt surrounded the fire for a couple of feet. Beyond lay a carpet of buffalo and elk hides. The three guests sat crossed-legged before the fire. Across from them sat Two Rivers and two other Indian braves, one older and one younger. Two women gathered some leather bags and left.

Jack and Two Rivers exchanged words, which Allen couldn't understand. Two Rivers then pulled out a long, flat pipe and lit it with a burning stick he pulled from the fire. He stood, lifted the pipe, and then turned to the north, east, south, and west. He puffed on it several times and waved the smoke over his head and shoulders. Then he passed the pipe to Jack. He puffed long and hard and passed the pipe to Joaquin, who smoked and passed it to Allen.

"I took a vow at ordination not to use tobacco," Allen whispered. He searched Joaquin's dark eyes for some sympathy.

Joaquin nodded slightly and whispered, "It's bad manners not to smoke."

Taking the pipe, Allen put it to his mouth and drew in. As calmly as he could, he passed it to the next brave, grimacing against his screaming lungs. Turning his head, a cough burst out, but he choked down the next one. Those in the circle ignored him and continued smoking. When Allen recovered from repressing the cough, he relaxed, only to see the pipe coming around again.

Joaquin passed him the pipe and leaned over. "Just suck a little. Don't breathe in."

The directive saved Allen from further mortification. He softly drew in and puffed. Finding that it worked, he puffed again before handing it on. Allen nodded slightly at Joaquin.

Joaquin translated as Jack told Two Rivers of the escapade. A few times he motioned toward Allen, and the old medicine man nodded approvingly. Allen finally learned what had happened in the early morning.

"We approached their camp before dawn," Jack said. "We found those murdering thieves sleeping with only two men on guard. The horses remained calm, and we led them away. We walked past a third guard, whom we hadn't seen before. He was awake but never looked at us. And he stood only as far away as the next tipi. I don't understand, Two Rivers, why they let us walk away with the horses.

They never chased us, and weapons were unnecessary. It was as if they were blind and deaf."

Allen listened with great interest. He recalled that he'd prayed that the thieves would be rendered blind and deaf. He hadn't expected such a dramatic answer.

The young brave next to Two Rivers was called Blue Otter. His face was round, and his heavy eyelids gave him the appearance of one with weak eyesight. He had a birthmark the size of a small pinecone on his right cheek. When he smiled, his face lit up with an ear-to-ear grin, revealing a wide gap in his teeth. His ribs protruded below bony shoulders and thin arms.

Blue Otter whispered into the medicine man's ear. Two Rivers peered at Allen with penetrating eyes and spoke. Then Jack, Joaquin, and the other man stared at Allen.

Though Allen did not know what Blue Otter said, it was apparent that it had something to do with him. Allen looked into the fire, then at Jack, and then back at Two Rivers. The dark eyes captured Allen. He felt that the medicine man was searching his soul. Allen didn't feel threatened. In fact, Two Rivers seemed to look on him with understanding and compassion.

In turn, Allen studied Two Rivers's lined face, which reflected a generation of war, mysteries, and hardship. Allen saw a man powerful enough to command that he be killed if deemed a threat to the tribe. But Allen's security did not rest in Jack and Joaquin to protect him. In that moment, Allen rested in the shadow of the Almighty.

The Arapaho respected Jack and Joaquin because they lived by the Indians' values—strength, cunning, and courage. They'd earned the tribe's trust. Allen had proven his courage, but he sensed something else aided his acceptance, something that Two Rivers evidently saw in him.

Two Rivers spoke and Jack translated. "This man has powerful medicine, even though he is young. A mighty spirit calls him to conquer the evil that is on his path. He corrects injustice, and he has no fear. He speaks the truth that is sharp and straight like the arrow. His medicine spirit shines bright like the sun."

Two Rivers pulled some kind of dried plant out of a leather pouch and sprinkled it on the fire. A whitish smoke filled the tipi with a fresh, pungent aroma. Two Rivers wafted the smoke over his body and sang softly, which Jack could not translate. After a few minutes, Two Rivers stopped singing. Then, as if on cue, the two women entered the tipi and set food before the men.

Allen bowed his head. He didn't know what the food was, but he thanked the Lord for it and added that he was grateful to be right there.

When they finished eating, Jack nodded, indicating that they would leave. Two Rivers lifted a buffalo blanket, pulled out a satchel, and dug through it.

Allen caught a glimpse of a deer skull and wondered if that was what spoke to him.

Two Rivers stretched his weathered hand toward Allen. He said through Jack, "This is a gift to you. It is a gift of friendship by which I welcome you to my lodge. It is a whistle carved from a piece of deer antler."

Allen received the token. "Thank you." Perplexed, he looked at Jack. "I have nothing to give him in return."

"Apparently you've given him something of value already. It's no small thing being welcomed to his lodge after your first visit," Jack said.

As they stepped into the daylight, Two Rivers tapped Jack on the arm. Jack translated. "Allen, you're invited to stay here in the village. You'll live with Blue Otter and learn the ways of the Blue Cloud People—the Arapaho."

"Truly?" Allen smiled and could hardly believe his good fortune. Then he sobered. "Please thank him for the offer, but I'm with a group of people who are traveling west. Otherwise, I would be most pleased to live with his people." He bowed his head in appreciation.

Upon understanding, Two Rivers shook his head. Jack translated. "He says that your group will not travel to the West. A storm is coming that will stop them. A stream will rise and will carry the weak ones back to the East. Others will not be carried away, but none will go to the western mountains. It is good for you to stay with us."

Allen frowned. He peered into the old man's eyes, grasping for understanding. "Ask him if he means there will be more attacks on the wagon train. Who is going to turn back? Does he mean the Mills and the Herberts?"

Joaquin put his hand on Allen's shoulder. "It's not right to challenge the prophecy. He's making a gracious offer to you, Allen."

"Tell him that I will need to speak with the chief of my people for permission to live with him. My chief is also a holy man, and he's determined to go west no matter what kind of storms we face."

After hearing the translation, Two Rivers nodded. "Asking permission of the elders is the right thing to do," Jack translated, and continued after Two Rivers concluded speaking. "I am told that your people will not go to the west. I am also told that you will return to your chief now with plenty of meat. You will find the deer in the Canyon of Red Rock, where the trail comes near the rock ledge. A male deer will walk out of the brush and stand before you. He will have four horns on one side and three horns on the other side. That is the deer you will kill and take to your people. There will be three deer, one for each hunter."

Allen longed to ask more questions, but several young men were already herding the horses, proud to be helping the courageous horse thieves.

With the extra hands driving the horses, they made good time toward Fort Laramie. When the sun hung low, Jack led Joaquin and Allen off the course of the horses. They followed another trail that led them over a ridge.

Jack reined in his horse when they came to a clearing. "Up ahead is another part of the river that runs through the Canyon of the Red Rock. We'll ride up quietly and see if we find those deer. You go ahead."

"I don't know if I should believe this or not." Allen rode ahead anyway and stopped where they could see much of the canyon. He was taking in the rugged expanse when Joaquin pointed to a cluster of several deer on a hillside about a quarter mile away.

"Should we go after them?" Allen was ready for action.

"No, let's stay on the trail and see what's up yonder," Jack said.

Allen stopped again a couple hundred yards up the trail, where they had another good view of the canyon and the wide plains beyond it to the southeast. They were looking in the direction of Fort Laramie, but it was out of sight.

He dismounted and watched the clouds glowing in a brilliant splash of orange, yellow, and pink. Caught up in the spectacular beauty of the canyon, Allen noticed the trail ran by a rock ledge. He recalled Two Rivers's words: You will find the deer in the Canyon of Red Rock, where the trail comes near the rock ledge. A male deer will walk out of the brush and stand before you. He scanned the tree line across the clearing to his left. About sixty yards away, a buck stepped out of the brush and stopped, broadside to Allen.

"O Lord, what do I do?" Allen raised his gun, cocked the hammer, aimed, and fired. The buck lunged forward and fell dead. The old Indian's prophecy had come true. Was it a strange coincidence? Was it sinful to follow the prophecy that came through divination? Was it a blessing from God or a deceitful trap of the devil?

Jack and Joaquin trotted past.

"Fine shot, Parson," Jack said.

Allen nudged his buckskin and joined his comrades where the deer lay—its eyes black and dull.

"Go ahead and start skinning him; we'll help in a bit." Jack said, and he and Joaquin held their rifles ready and watched the tree line carefully. "We need to get these three deer dressed out and loaded before dark."

"Three?"

"This one came out just like Two Rivers said it would. And he also said there would be three deer, one for each hunter," Jack said.

The two of them dropped out of sight over a small rise. Allen pulled out his long knife and cut open the deer from the rib cage down along its belly. He crinkled his nose, trying not to inhale. Mule deer smelled musty compared to the whitetail deer back home. He heard two shots. He looked around but couldn't see the mountain men.

Shaking his head, Allen cut up the sternum to clean out the chest cavity. He'd soon be done and could go help the other two skin out their deer. Allen glanced up. Both were coming over the rise, each hauling a dressed-out buck. How in the world had they done that so fast?

They were back on the trail with the deer loaded, one on Joaquin's horse while he walked, and the other two on the packhorse.

"That's another good reason to pack light on a hunting trip," Jack said.

Before long they caught up to the horse herd, and in a couple of hours they rode into the clearing of Fort Laramie. After locking up the recovered horses in a corral, they rode over to the missionary band's camp.

Lit up by lanterns and a campfire, the wagon circle looked somewhat like home. Allen was eager to share his adventures.

Virgil stood when the men rode into camp.

"Hello, Virgil."

"Hey, everyone, Allen's back," Virgil hollered over his shoulder.

Allen swung down from Caleb and walked into the light. He felt his smile fade when he saw the startled expressions on his friends' faces.

"What on earth are you wearing, Allen?" Foster laughed.

Allen looked down at himself. They'd never seen him in buckskins. "Jack Burkett loaned me these for the, er, hunting trip."

"Well, you look ridiculous. Go get cleaned up, put on decent clothing, and then join us here at the fire," Foster said.

Just then Jack and Joaquin stepped into the light, followed by six young braves dressed in buckskins, a couple of whom were shirtless. The women gasped, and Foster's face turned red.

"Good evening, folks," Jack said. "Sorry to barge in on you like this, but we've made quite a ride today, and we're ready to turn in."

"Good evening to you, Mr. Burkett. Would you and your friends like to join us for a cup of coffee? I am sure we can find something for you to eat," Olive said.

"Thank you, ma'am. It's a kind offer, but we must tend to the meat and the horses. We'll camp closer to the creek with these young men, and perhaps we'll see you in the morning." Jack spoke in Arapaho, and two braves left.

"Allen, we're going to hang two deer in the trees over there, and we'll give the last one to these young men in payment for their help."

"Thanks, Jack. They earned at least that much. Hope to see you in the morning." Allen dismissed Jack and Joaquin with a handshake. He wished he could go with them. How was he going to explain that the venison was provided by a medicine man's prophecy? There was also the issue of his helping rescue stolen horses. Allen took a deep breath. It would all work itself out in the Lord's good timing.

"Come and get something to eat, Allen," Olive insisted.

"Thank you, ma'am, but I think I'll pass. I need to get cleaned up and turn in. It's been an adventuresome day."

CHAPTER TWENTY-THREE

"**A**LLEN! I WANT YOU TO** explain to me what happened the past couple of days. I have been hearing some rather incredible stories. It makes me think these men have been hitting their whiskey earlier than usual." Evidently, Bannister had risen early and circulated Fort Laramie to hear any news about the trail west. Instead, the fort was buzzing about a young preacher who had rescued stolen horses from a band of cutthroat savages.

By the time Allen finished buttoning his shirt, the missionary band had gathered around to listen. "We might as well sit down. It's going to take a while."

Allen gave them a full account of what had happened. He left out nothing, even letting the group decide whether the venison was the Lord's provision or that of some lesser god.

"What were you thinking, lad?" Bannister pointed his finger with every word. "You are a minister of the gospel, not some reckless adventurer chasing after danger. You must not put God to the test like that. What must the Lord think of one of his servants gallivanting through the wilderness?"

"That he's a good man, and a brave one, Reverend." Jack Burkett leaned on a wagon. "Pardon me for listening in, folks. Just coming by to share some news. But it appears that I'm just in time to defend Allen from a misunderstanding."

"Mr. Burkett! Why don't you join us?" Bannister said. "It is precisely a misunderstanding that we are trying to avoid. We were told that you were going on a hunting trip. And now that you're back, I hear by way of the rumor mill that Allen was involved with the recovery of stolen horses from a band of hostile Indians. I am holding you responsible for your part of the misunderstanding."

"Fair enough, Reverend Bannister," Jack said. "We left with the intention of hunting, and as you can see, we were successful. Recovering the stolen horses was an outside possibility, but it was not our primary intent. Otherwise, I would have taken a posse of experienced fighters with me.

"It was not until we arrived at Two Rivers's camp that the whereabouts of the thieves was confirmed. And I assure you that Allen was not aware of the situation until it was too late for him to refuse. But we never put him in danger that he was not capable of handling, a fact that also is evident.

"To be honest, I believe it was due to Allen's presence that we were successful in recovering the horses and no blood was shed. The victims of the attack you saw were not avenged, but at least we cut short the glory of those murderers. And that, Reverend, is called counting coup, which is highly regarded among the Indians and us mountain men."

"I appreciate your candor, Mr. Burkett," Bannister said, "but I fail to see how Allen's presence made any difference. You could have taken some Indians who would have been more experienced in fighting and horse stealing."

"Sir, if I had attempted to recover the horses by my own planning, I certainly would have taken an overwhelming number of men with me. But the fact of the matter is, Allen had God's favor on him. A company of fighting men would not have. I observed that, as did Joaquin and Two Rivers. Allen will tell you that he spent a good piece of time in prayer over the matter."

"Are you telling us, Jack, that you discerned God's favor on Allen? And that an Indian medicine man did also?" Foster's tipped head, hands on hips, and haughty tone indicated that only the properly educated possessed spiritual discernment.

Foster's comment didn't seem to bother Jack. "You may see me as no more than a fur trapper, Reverend Foster, but I can tell when God is watching over a man. It's very different from luck or sharp wits. And yes, Two Rivers saw it on Allen immediately. That's the only reason he told us where the thieves were hiding and that we would be successful in bringing back the horses. He saw that Allen has 'strong medicine,' and because of it, none of us would be hurt."

"Strong medicine? Humph." Foster folded his arms across his chest. "That old man practices divination and fortune-telling through pagan rituals and superstitions. Consulting bones to determine where deer are—that is stepping over the line of clear reason."

"I understand your concern," Jack said. "I can't tell you that I understand these things, but I've lived among the Arapaho, the Shoshone, the Pawnee, and other tribes enough to know that they understand the spirit world more than you want to give them credit for. I can't be as quick to judge them as you can. Whether it's divination or prophecy, I can't say either. All I know is that he told us where we would find three deer, and they stepped out just like he said."

"It was mere coincidence." Foster waved his hand, as if dismissing the mountain man's words.

Jack rubbed his chin. "You can draw your own conclusion. Two Rivers is a highly respected spiritual leader, and his word is taken as gospel around these parts. Only a handful of white men have ever been invited into his lodge, and Allen was regarded as an honored guest. That's why those young men rode with us to bring in the horses—they wanted to observe the man with a mighty warrior's spirit. And that's why Two Rivers himself extended an invitation for Allen to live with them."

Bannister and Foster stared at Allen with wide eyes and open mouths.

Allen just nodded.

Bannister cleared his throat. "I'll have to take these things into consideration. As to the invitation, you'll have to express our regrets to the Indian chief, but we're heading for Oregon in a few days, and it will not be possible for Allen to live with them."

"That's the reason I came by in the first place," Jack said. "Your departure will be delayed even further. There have been strong rains and even some snow to the west. The rivers and creeks are too high to cross safely. Bad weather will probably hit us later today. It's likely that you'll be set back a week or more."

"Bad weather? I'd say we are in for another lovely day." Foster looked at the sky.

"No, we're in for a spell of bad weather. It's a queersome time for this much rain. I'd suggest you fill your water barrels before the streams turn muddy," Jack said. "Back East a hard rain might mean muddy streets. Here in the wilderness, it means flash floods, rising rivers, scarce game, rotting clothes, and moldy food.

"When you've been here long enough, you'll start to understand what mountain folk believe." Jack spoke like a wilderness professor. "The Rocky Mountains were put on earth to test the hardiest of men. If a man is determined enough to make a life in this beautiful and terrible land, he has to prove his worth in the face of the most malicious trials imaginable."

Bannister regretted heeding Foster's advice rather than Burkett's. Just as the experienced mountain man had said, the weather turned ugly by four o'clock that afternoon. Within a half hour, the deluge soaked everything. The wind blew the rain horizontally and seemed to pound from every direction. The canvases became saturated, drenching the group's belongings.

For two days the storm raged, after which it slowed enough that they could tidy the camp and check on the condition of the supplies. Virgil reported that the river was high and dirty. He filled a water barrel, but it would take hours for the grit to settle enough to use the water or boil it for drinking.

After another couple of days, the rain stopped and the sun broke through the clouds. While Allen led the livestock to graze, Bannister and Foster walked to the river to see how much it had flooded. The fierce brown water swept away their resolve.

"Everything about this country tries to kill you," Foster said.

Humphrey Limm rode up on his red mule. "Just coming by to see how you fared the storm."

"A bit soggy, but we're in good spirits. Thank you for asking, Mr. Limm," Bannister said. "It looks like we are going to have to wait a couple of extra days for the mud to dry before we can leave."

"Wish that were the case, Reverend, but the rain fell just as hard up the trail. The mud makes for hard work on the animals. What's more is that the storming ain't done. It'll be raining for a few more days. Likely to snow too."

"Snow?" Foster felt like there was a conspiracy against them. "How can it snow in July?"

"Might happen every once in a while," Limm drawled. "But this is queersome weather, mighty queersome.

"You'll want to see to your food stores and such. Flour and grain's probably spoiled now or will be soon. You might as well dump it and resupply after things dry up. Salvage what you can." Limm showed the missionaries how to stack and cover the goods, giving them a better chance of staying dry.

Allen almost laughed the next morning as he brushed two inches of snow off the table. The low clouds kept visibility to less than a half mile. Rising temperatures would melt the snow and leave a sloppy mess of cold mud.

Boredom became their enemy. Isolated in their tents and wagons, the missionaries had little to do but try to keep warm, something they hadn't anticipated as a need in summer. When they could, they sang hymns, but too often the wind and rain drowned out their choruses.

Allen passed the time writing in his journal, thanking God for every discovery and adventure. Each day and night his longing to live with the Arapaho swelled. But he was mindful to sift his motives and find direction in the Word.

"Lord, if I am just being selfish, remove this desire from my heart. But if it is your will, increase it and make it possible."

A few days later, Allen wrapped himself in a spare piece of canvas and tended to the livestock. He stopped at Bannister's wagon.

"Hello, Allen. Climb on up," Bannister said. "How are the animals?" But before Allen could answer, Bannister continued talking.

When the reverend paused in his monologue, Allen asked him to consider his living with Two Rivers's band for at least a few weeks.

"I'd learn how the primitive people live, as well as more sign language. It might prove a valuable asset in communicating with the Indians on the way to Oregon," Allen said.

"No, definitely not. I don't think you need to spend any more time with them."

"It makes sense, Samuel," Olive said. "And besides, we're stuck here for a few weeks anyway. Allen may learn some helpful things."

"Let me consider it for a couple more days then."

"Samuel. He's not going to learn anything around here."

"Very well, Allen," Bannister said. "When the storm ends you can go, at least until we have safe passage to Oregon. Is that understood?"

"Absolutely, sir! Thank you!" Allen hurried out of Bannister's wagon and visited the others' wagons. He couldn't hide his elation; it was as obvious as a daisy in a mud puddle.

Gloria and Virgil were happy for Allen.

Foster was straightforward with his cynicism. "They won't be converted if you go live with them. That is precisely what they have to come out of. Don't you see? We must establish a mission with a church and a school and educate them in a civilized way to live. They have to learn discipline and order. They will come to us, and we will show them the light."

"The Lord has put it in my heart to live among them and show his love on their terms," Allen said.

"Don't confuse God's direction with fascination for this savage way of life. I am afraid, Allen, that you are subtly being drawn away by Jack Burkett and his daring escapades with the Indians."

Allen's faith did not waver. In his heart, he knew the Lord would make the way clear.

Sometime in the night, the wind and rain ceased. Morning sunlight greeted the missionary band. They spent the day cleaning and drying out clothes and supplies. Reverend Foster brought word from the fort that travel in any direction was virtually impossible for wagons.

Bannister sent Allen, Gloria, and Virgil on the task of replacing lost goods. Few merchants were out, as they, too, were recovering from the storm. In the dimly lit trade store, Gloria asked for flour, salt, and bacon. Muddy tracks across the plank floor led to Vernon Meecer, the quartermaster, who could offer them no deals or favors.

"Sorry, folks. Supplies are in high demand right now. I don't expect a new load for another week, or whenever the derned rain quits. River's up so high, even the tall freighters can't get through."

The door flew open, and in walked a short, plump redheaded gal in a brown dress.

"Howdy, folks. Good morning, Mr. Meecer." The new arrival's blue eyes sparkled when she smiled, bringing sunshine into the room.

"Good morning, Polly. Glad to see you made it in today." Meecer turned his attention to the lady. "This here is Allen and Gloria and Virgil. They're missionaries bound for Oregon."

"Oregon? It strikes me that this rain has you bound up at Fort Laramie." Polly giggled.

Her lightheartedness infected Allen, and he and the others joined in laughter.

"Folks, this is Polly McMasters. She's been in these parts for several years now. Lost her husband last year but decided to stay on, and we are mighty glad for that."

"It's a pleasure to meet you, Polly," Gloria said. "I am sorry to hear about your husband."

"No need to be sorry. I'm glad for the years the good Lord gave me with Ben, but his time had come. He was a good man who lived well and died well."

"Yep, Old Ben got 'et by a bear," Meecer added.

"What?" Gloria and Allen exclaimed at the same time.

Virgil hadn't taken his eyes off Polly since she entered the room. He opened his mouth, but no words came out.

"Yes, that's the fact," Polly said, as if it was old news. "A grizzly bear came into their hunting camp and went after Ben's partner, Luke Simmons. Ben stepped in to fight off the bear, but the bear won. Luke survived and told us how Ben was a true hero. That's just like Ben, but it cost him his life."

"My goodness! And you decided to stay here instead of going back East?" Gloria covered her mouth with her hand.

"Ben built us a lovely cabin a couple miles away. It didn't seem right to leave it. Besides, I don't have anyone to go back to in Pennsylvania. I like it right here on the Laramie, isn't that right, Mr. Meecer?" She turned back to her bundle. "By the way, I have some extra flour and sugar I'd like to trade for some needles and fabric, and maybe some candles if I can get them."

"Flour?" Gloria's eyes lit up. "We can make a trade right now. What kind of fabric are you looking for?" Stepping away, the young women talked of dresses and designs.

Allen looked at Meecer, who just shrugged.

Allen turned to leave the trade store. When he neared the door, he noticed Virgil was still standing in the same spot, his attention wholly on Polly. "Virgil, let's go."

Virgil seemed not to hear.

Allen stepped back to the man and elbowed him in the ribs.

Virgil jumped.

"Come on, Virgil. We've got to load the mule and get back to camp."

On the way, Virgil finally broke his silence. "Did you see the way her eyes sparkled? Prettiest blue I've ever seen."

As they approached the camp, Allen saw movement in the trees behind the grazing horses and oxen. "Virgil, someone is sneaking in the trees by the horses."

"Indians!" Virgil broke into a run.

CHAPTER TWENTY-FOUR

RIDING AT FULL GALLOP, VIRGIL veered off toward the wagons to get his gun and the other men. Allen ran straight for the livestock. Swinging down from his horse with his rifle in hand, he watched the trees. A sudden movement caught his eye.

He raised the Hawkins. "Come on out to where I can see you."

A head appeared, then slowly the man stepped out from behind a cottonwood.

Allen lowered the gun and smiled. "Blue Otter, what in the world are you doing here?"

Blue Otter raised his hand and flashed his tooth-gapped smile. "Good day, Allen. Two Rivers send me to find you. You go to Two Rivers's lodge."

"Today? You mean go to your camp today?" Allen grinned. "Well, I'll be. You speak English! That's good! I'm delighted to have an interpreter."

Virgil and Foster ran up, carrying their loaded muskets.

"Trouble, Allen?" Virgil held his gun to his shoulder with the muzzle down but in the direction of the Indian.

"What's happening?" Foster panted.

"We're fine," Allen answered. "This is a friend I met at the Arapaho camp. Meet Blue Otter."

"How do you do?" Blue Otter said a bit roughly.

"Just fine, and you?" Virgil said and shook Blue Otter's hand, watching the Indian closely.

Foster held on to his rifle and scowled.

"Let's go and meet the others." Allen guided his friend into the circle of wagons.

"Oh my!" Beulah put her hand to her throat.

"I'd like to introduce my friend to everyone." Allen stood next to their visitor. "This is Blue Otter. He's one of the men I met when I smoked the pipe at Two Rivers's camp."

Blue Otter shook hands with Bannister. He nodded to the women. "I am happy to know you," he said, tipping his head. "I take him to Two Rivers's lodge. He live with Arapaho. He eat with our people."

Allen looked expectantly at Bannister, who stared at Blue Otter.

Foster narrowed his eyes. "Where did you learn to speak English?"

"I learned to speak English with trappers and traders who come to our camp. I speak French with the Canadas. I speak Sioux, Crow, Shoshone, Cheyenne, more."

Foster smirked. "Quite the linguist then, aren't you?"

"Reverend?" Allen said. "Blue Otter has come to take me to Two Rivers's camp today. If he made it safely across the river, then I'm sure we can return that way. With your permission, I'll pack my things."

"It's rather sudden, but I guess we'll get along without you here." Bannister surveyed the group, and everyone nodded approval, except Foster, who hadn't taken his eyes off Blue Otter. "You will return three weeks from today unless we send for you sooner. Is that understood?"

"Yes, sir."

Allen packed and saddled his horse, only to find Blue Otter

surrounded by the inquisitive missionaries. Another half hour passed before they could get away.

A few hours later they arrived at the village. The people who had once watched him with suspicion now smiled, welcoming him. Allen and Blue Otter dismounted in front of Two Rivers's tipi. Blue Otter stepped to the entrance to announce Allen's arrival. Two Rivers emerged and took Allen's right hand in both of his.

Blue Otter translated. "Come. You will live in my lodge. You will be as my son."

Allen sat in the familiar tipi. Two Rivers's wife served him a wooden bowl with elk stew and some type of root, stringier than a potato and mildly bitter, and a greasy dumpling. Allen, hungry from the trip, ate as much as Blue Otter, then set his plate aside.

Allen thanked Two Rivers for his hospitality and the chance to learn the ways of the Arapaho. "Blue Otter, please tell him that my leader, my chief, has allowed me to stay for twenty days. Then we will travel to the west."

Blue Otter translated the response from the medicine man. "You will stay for winter in Two Rivers's camp. You will not go west."

Allen swallowed hard. He wasn't sure what Two Rivers meant— if he would be held a sort of captive, or if the band would not travel west. "Please explain that I made a promise to Reverend Bannister that I would serve with him in Oregon. We'll be leaving when the rivers subside, uh, go down."

"Snow will keep your chief in camp. Fear is deep in his heart. Your chief will not go to the West. Before the snow is gone, he will go back to the fathers in the East." Two Rivers gazed at the fire.

Allen frowned. "But how can this be?"

"I did not hear from the bones of the deer or from aspen tea. No, I heard this from the Great Spirit. The Great Spirit speaks much to me in these days. On the wind he tells me many changes are coming to the People. The clouds say that many dark days are coming on our land. They will come like a flood that starts slowly and grows so powerful it can't be stopped. Our sons and grandsons will fight, and they will see the flood take away their lives. Beyond those days, I cannot see." Two Rivers paused.

"I asked the Great Spirit if we could be saved from this dark flood. He spoke to me in a vision and showed me a small seed. The seed will be planted in the land of the Arapaho. The flood will begin, but it will not kill the seed. The seed will grow and become a great tree that will grow higher than the flood. Our people who survive the flood will live in the tree as birds. The tree will be their home and will feed them, for it is a great tree."

The solemn words weighed heavily on Allen's mind. Was the Great Spirit the same as his God, the Father of the Lord Jesus Christ? Or was it another god? He had so much to learn and understand.

Two Rivers took out his pipe, lit it, and raised it to the cardinal points of an invisible compass. He blew smoke and wafted it with his hand toward his forehead. He softly chanted a prayer song and passed the pipe to Allen, who puffed and handed it to Blue Otter.

When the pipe was done, Allen gathered his belongings and situated them in the tipi. "Lord God, give me wisdom and revelation so that I may know you better. Thank you for this great opportunity. Amen."

The next three weeks became a school for learning to live off the land. Some days Allen accompanied Two Rivers and Blue Otter to gather plants and roots. Other days they searched for valuables in a dry creek bed. The Indian men evaluated flint and obsidian for potential arrowheads or tools. Any rock that had a particular color, or perhaps the shape of an animal, they placed into a leather bag that hung over their shoulders. The stones might be for personal use or for trading. Nothing escaped their attention.

They hunted mostly by random opportunity. If a grouse or rabbit appeared, they quickly killed it with bow and arrow or a throwing stick. Two Rivers, whom Allen guessed was about sixty years old, had an uncanny knack for killing small animals with stones, even out to forty or fifty yards. One time, the medicine man threw a rock that hit a rabbit square on the head. Two Rivers picked up the rabbit, looked it over, then patted its head. The little creature revived and hopped away. The stunned rabbit was not exactly what Two Rivers needed, so he let it live to grow and reproduce.

One day Blue Otter live-trapped a ground squirrel. Then with Two Rivers's help, they built a small blind out of sticks and grasses, big enough for the three of them to hide under. Blue Otter tied the squirrel to the top of the blind. They waited several hours until a red-tailed hawk swooped down on the bait. Two Rivers reached through a hole in the roof and clutched the raptor's legs. Blue Otter wrapped a piece of deer hide over its head and dispatched it. They would use the feathers for special arrows or headdresses, and the head would become an amulet.

Two Rivers's wife brought Allen a new elk-skin shirt, golden from tanning and with long fringe down the arms. She had applied symbols made from red, yellow, black, and white beads to the yoke. "Hohou," Allen said, the Arapaho word for thank you.

She covered her mouth with her hand, giggled, and hurried away.

He worried that he'd said the wrong thing.

Twenty sunrises came and went. The last night, Allen reminded Two Rivers and Blue Otter that he was supposed to be heading for Oregon. "Thank you for your hospitality and all that you have taught me."

"You will leave when the new sun comes. You return when three suns come," Blue Otter said. "Two Rivers say you live here for winter."

"But—"

"Two Rivers say."

"Well then, I'll see you soon," Allen felt as if he belonged here in this Arapaho village, but his assignment was to travel on to Oregon. He'd see what the reverend would say about this.

The early morning sky sparkled. A prairie falcon soared past about ten feet off the ground. Allen rode toward Fort Laramie, accompanied by three of his new friends. They stayed on the north side of the river rather than follow Allen into camp.

Approaching the circle of wagons, Allen spotted Bannister and Foster sitting on chairs, reading while the women prepared lunch. Things were pretty much as he had left them three weeks ago. It didn't look as if they were packing for the westward journey.

"Well, look at the lonesome wanderer. Finally decide to come in from your adventures?" Foster seemed annoyed.

"Oh good! Allen Hartman, look at you. You're just in time for lunch." Olive welcomed him with a smile.

During the meal, Allen recounted the highlights of his time spent with Two Rivers. Because he'd learned and experienced so much that was beyond description, he kept those things to himself. He didn't want to risk any disparaging remarks by Foster.

"Overall, it was a fascinating experience. I would very much like to return and learn more. However, I'm ready to make the journey to Oregon."

Their silence screamed at him. He glanced around the table. Everyone averted their eyes.

Finally Bannister spoke up. "We will not be traveling anymore this year. With the poor weather and the Indian attacks, we have decided that it will be best for us to stay through the winter here at Fort Laramie. Lord willing, we will continue our journey in the spring."

Two Rivers's prophecy was true then.

"We believe that God has a special purpose in all of this." Foster's eyes glistened. "We will continue to pray for guidance, but I believe he is leading us to start a mission right here on the Laramie River. We have chosen a worthy site to build cabins and a church that will also serve as a schoolhouse."

"Schoolhouse?" This made no sense to Allen. Why the deviation of the commission to Oregon? And, what children?

"Yes, a church and a school. It's just what is needed to civilize this place. Just think of the enormous potential right here. All the Indians and mountain people will have a reason to establish a decent town. Yes, what they need here is order, and that is just what we can provide." Foster still would not make eye contact with Allen.

"It sounds rather permanent." Allen couldn't help but think they weren't telling him everything.

"Permanent? Yes, of course. We will get a mission started here. Then move on to Fort Hall or Oregon or wherever the Lord shall lead us. It is a vision with endless possibilities. The Lord will provide the necessary personnel when the time comes. Do not worry, Allen. You will get to see Oregon unless, of course, God appoints you as the head of this mission. We must all be willing and obedient to God's divine purposes," Foster said.

Head of this mission? School? Allen felt his face heat. He stifled his feelings rather than provoke an argument with his leaders.

When the meal was finished, Allen offered to help Gloria with her chores. He wanted a chance to talk to her. "I'm shocked at this departure from our original intention. How long has this new plan been considered?"

"We got the news last week about more Indian attacks on Americans. And it's been raining off and on for days. Reverend Bannister just lost his ambition for Oregon. Reverend Foster announced his new vision to us a couple of days ago and said he's been praying about it most diligently. What else are we going to do?" Gloria had evidently resigned herself to the idea.

"Is Virgil in agreement?"

"He hasn't said much. Just seems to be compliant with the pastors' judgment."

"Reverend Bannister's not his usual self, and Reverend Foster seems to be the one with all the ideas. In fact it appears that he already knows the outcome. He'll build a mission school and move on, leaving me in charge," Allen said.

"Is that so bad?"

"Gloria, I don't want to be a schoolmaster. I want to be with the Indians in their villages, teaching them the gospel by living it for them. It's what God has called me to, not to some other vision. I don't think it's going to work anyway." Allen paced back and forth. "The Indians here at the fort are just looking for handouts. Many of them are waiting for the next load of whiskey. They're transients, like the trappers and traders. Not that many people live here. I don't understand what Foster is thinking."

"He believes that if we build the mission here, it will motivate people to establish a community. The Indians will bring their children to get an education and set up permanent trade stores. It sounds reasonable." Gloria sounded like she was trying to convince herself.

"Bring their children? Do you really think they're so interested in learning the white man's ways that they'll come to school? I guess Reverend Foster has more faith than I do, because it doesn't sound practical to me." Allen broke off the conversation rather than risk saying something disrespectful. If only they would spend a few days in Two Rivers's camp, they would change their minds.

"Gloria, I have to go back and live with Two Rivers. There's so much to learn. He told me one night that he had a vision—a prophecy—from the Great Spirit that we wouldn't be going west. Bad weather and fear of the hostile Indians would detain us. I have to know if their Great Spirit is our God or some other spirit. The other part of the prophecy is that I would live with them throughout the winter. And I hope to go back. In fact I'm going to talk to Reverend Bannister right now." He paused. "Gloria, I wish you could come up for even a few days. The Arapaho are such a beautiful people. I know you would be thrilled."

"I'm quite sure it would be just as you say, Allen. But I'm equally convinced that Reverend Bannister won't allow two of us to leave the camp. I won't even bother asking. Perhaps another opportunity will arise."

When Allen asked Bannister about returning to Two Rivers's

camp, he made certain that Olive was present but that Foster was nowhere near. "Sir, I'm disappointed that we won't be continuing on to Oregon, but I certainly see the wisdom in staying. However, with your permission, I'd like to return to the Arapaho village for the winter. There's much that I can learn up there. Perhaps I can encourage them to move down here to the mission and send some children to school."

"Allen, I was counting on you to help us with the construction of the mission buildings. We begin within a few days." Bannister sipped his cup of tea.

"Yes, sir. Do you think it would be beneficial to recruit some of the local men for the construction? There are a number of experienced men who might be glad for the work, and you could begin preaching among them to begin the new congregation," Allen said.

"Samuel, I think he's right. If we have a friendly ambassador to the Indians, they will be more likely to come to the school. After all, that was our reason for coming west," Olive said.

"Ambassador, hmmm, yes." Bannister rubbed his chin. "I can see some potential in that."

Allen spied Foster walking toward them. "Thank you, sir. I am sure you won't regret it." He rushed off, nodding at Foster.

Allen gathered his things and said his goodbyes. "Maybe it will work out for me to come back for Christmas, but for certain I'll return at the end of February or mid-March, in time for the spring thaw."

Stopping by the fort, hoping to get word on the whereabouts of Jack Burkett and Joaquin Del Castillo, Allen found Milt Sublette speaking with another buckskin-clad man who seemed to know Allen's business.

"Hello, Preacher. Heard you was living with Two Rivers these days. What brings you out of the hills?" Sublette leaned his elbow on a stack of deer hides.

"Hello, Mr. Sublette. I came back because we were supposed to leave for Oregon, but all that has changed. Reverend Bannister decided to stay here through the winter. So I'm going to head back up to Two Rivers's camp until spring," Allen said.

"There's still several weeks of good traveling time before the snow gets deep. The reverend say why they're staying back?" Sublette brushed at the top deer hide.

"The rains and the Indian attacks up the trail."

"Indian attacks? There hasn't been an attack for two weeks," the other man said in a thick French accent. His dark, penetrating eyes reflected the same self-assurance Allen had seen in Burkett and other trappers.

"Allen, this is Fontanelle. He just came down from the Yellowstone country," Sublette said.

"Fontanelle, the fur trader?" Allen had heard stories of this man. "Pleased to meet you."

"And you must be the missionary who stole horses from Dark Wolf's band. I've heard of you as well. There will be a supply train heading for Fort Hall within a couple of days. And Father DeSmet is traveling on the Yellowstone River as we speak. He, too, is a missionary. They're not waiting for the weather."

"I've heard of Father DeSmet, the Jesuit priest," Allen said. "Reverend Bannister and Reverend Foster are going to build a mission right here. They'll start with a church that will double as a school, and hopefully bring in some Indian children."

"School? That don't make much sense. Most of the people around here are just passing through," Sublette said.

"Well, that's the new plan," Allen said. "Anyone know where Jack Burkett might be these days?"

"I heard he was on his way to Fort Union, up north," Sublette said. "Hard to say when he might be back this way."

"I need to be leaving. It was good to see both of you. And do me a favor and not say anything to Reverend Bannister about Father DeSmet or the wagon train? He's likely to change his mind, and I'd rather spend the winter with Two Rivers."

CHAPTER TWENTY-FIVE

THE HEAT FADED AS THE sun dropped into its final stages of the day. The basin between Horse Tooth Mountain and the river, spotted with golden-brown grass and gray-green sagebrush, spread before Allen like a theater. He entered into a scene where life and death were bold, determined, and patient. Four seasons played out: life, giving, death, and rebirth. As long as the spirits were content, the people lived in peace. But it was almost impossible to keep the spirits content. Allen, the missionary, rode into the encampment as a recognized friend and stopped in front of Two Rivers's lodge.

The old man and Blue Otter sat on the ground by the cooking fire, knapping a stone hide scraper.

"Well, you were right," Allen said. "My leader changed the plans. We won't be moving on to Oregon until spring. I have permission to spend the winter here. Thank you very much for the invitation."

After Blue Otter translated, Two Rivers said that Allen would stay in Blue Otter's tipi. Then he returned to his project.

Allen waited for a moment, expecting more—smoking a peace

pipe or something—but then turned away with Blue Otter and unpacked his belongings in the tipi about ten yards away.

Allen knelt and sorted his bags. "I have many questions to ask Two Rivers. Is it proper to join him at his fire?" He turned, but the tipi was empty. Looking out through the open flap, he saw Blue Otter walking away with other young men.

Allen lay on his bedroll, thanking God for the opportunity to live in an Arapaho village in the western wilderness . . .

Something stirred. Allen opened his eyes and gasped. Two men wearing strange masks and carrying war clubs stood over him. The masks' grotesque features, with horsehair, deer horns, and other materials adorning them, frightened Allen in the dim light. One of the men leaned toward Allen and shouted while shaking his war club rattle. He then stepped back and spoke in quiet tones to the other masked man.

Allen's eyes widened.

What in the world is this?

The second man removed his mask. It was Blue Otter, grinning widely. "Come. It is time for the people to know you."

Relief washed over Allen. "You had me worried for a moment." He gave his rumpled shirt a once-over. "Should I wear a different shirt perhaps?"

"Shirt good. Come now." Blue Otter followed the other masked man out of the tipi.

Allen trotted to catch up. They crossed the camp, only to stand behind another tipi. A group of young men in costumes walked by and stared at Allen. One of them made a comment, and the others laughed.

Allen was perplexed. Why wouldn't Blue Otter speak to him?

Allen stepped around the tipi. Several people sat around a bonfire. He moved back into hiding, pacing and shuffling back and forth.

After waiting for what felt like an hour, Blue Otter came to him. "The people know you now. Follow me to the fire. The people will see your face. The old ones will see you are good."

Blue Otter guided Allen around the circle, allowing everyone to have a look at him. They paused before the elders. He nodded to them and smiled, but no one smiled back. Blue Otter led him around the circle until he faced the elders again. In the firelight, Allen took in his surroundings, figuring close to three hundred had gathered.

Blue Otter told him to speak.

Allen swallowed hard. "What am I supposed to say?"

"Speak your name and your father's, your blood."

Allen's thoughts raced. His blood? He prayed to God that he wouldn't make a fool of himself. He took a deep breath to calm his pounding heart and looked around at the Arapaho villagers. He felt like he did when he'd preached before his seminary class. If he made it through that, he could make it through anything.

"My name is Allen Hartman," he began, "son of Arthur Hartman of New York. I come from a land far to the east, where many Americans live."

He paused so Blue Otter could translate. Children giggled each time Allen spoke, but most stared at him without expression.

He cleared his throat. "I traveled here to your land with a group of missionaries, led by the Reverend Samuel Bannister." He chided himself. They'd never heard of the Methodist evangelist. "I am a minister of the gospel, as is my father."

Blue Otter grimaced with a puzzled expression.

"A preacher."

Still puzzled.

"A holy man to my people."

Blue Otter nodded and interpreted.

"I have come not to trap the beaver or to trade for furs and beads. I have come to tell stories of the Great Spirit and what he has done for my people and what he has done for you."

An elder sitting near Two Rivers stood up and spoke and gestured toward Allen. Blue Otter translated as the people listened respectfully and murmured words of approval at what the man said.

"He say you are good man. Spirits say to him you sing a song with strange words, but it is a song of true words. You come in peace. We let you live in peace with us and trade stories of the Great Spirit."

Another elder spoke. "The spirits showed me not all white men can be trusted. But this one can be trusted because he steals horses from our enemies. We shall let him live with us, and he will learn to speak as a man of the Blue Cloud People."

Two Rivers stood, and everyone grew quiet. "This man came to us with friends, Burkett and Del Castillo. It is true he stole the horses. It is true the spirits speak of his coming. The spirits have shown me we must listen to his songs of the Great Father, for they are new songs we have not heard. He comes from people with strange ways and strange talk. But we will take him into our lodges as a friend.

"There are many enemies that seek to hurt us. Our worst enemy is Dark Wolf and his pack of murderers because they are traitors of the Arapaho. Perhaps this white man will sing a song that will protect us. Perhaps the Great Spirit sent him as a warrior to kill our enemies and stop the kidnapping of our children. We will wait to see what the Great Spirit shall do."

Two Rivers received approval from the crowd. He then motioned for Allen to take a seat near the elders as an honored guest.

Allen sat down, confused. He had not come to kill anyone. On the contrary, he had come to bring a message of peace and hope. And what of the kidnapped children? What was he supposed to understand?

Women brought out carved wooden platters filled with chunks of buffalo meat. A woman handed Allen a platter. There were no utensils, so he waited for others to be served. Two Rivers and the chiefs ate the meat with their hands. Allen did the same. He picked up a piece and took a bite. Boiled buffalo meat. It could have used a touch of salt.

Allen jumped at the loud pounding of a drum. Costumed dancers entered the circle. The seven drummers sang loudly with unintelligible words that sounded like screaming. But they sang in unison, so it must have been a traditional song.

Allen determined that this was a special ceremony, perhaps in his honor. Over the next several hours, the people, women and children included, participated in many dances while wearing a variety of costumes.

Allen studied the details of the costumes and movements. Was this worship or just cultural celebration? Perhaps someday he'd understand. If only Foster were here to see this, he might begin to appreciate this different way of life.

He was content to observe, but two warriors grabbed Allen by the arms and pulled him into the dance line. At first awkward and clumsy, he moved his feet in rhythm. Someone handed him a spear. Seeing that no one was watching him, Allen felt free to dance and be one with them.

The next day he stayed at Blue Otter's side, asking practical questions about food and cooking, drinking water, and caring for his horse. Blue Otter patiently answered all his questions.

Over the next days and weeks, Blue Otter proved to be an invaluable resource to enlighten the missionary and keep him from making cultural blunders. Blue Otter explained about child-rearing and family responsibilities, sharing food with neighbors, the appropriate distance to stand from a woman, and how to greet elders. Allen thanked God every day for Blue Otter.

During the weeks after his arrival, Allen would often sit with

Two Rivers and watch his skills in making stone tools, leather pouches, arrows, and medicines. Most of the villagers at some point would stroll by to greet the shaman and steal a close look at the white man.

One time Two Rivers made a comment to Blue Otter, and they both burst out laughing.

"Honestly, what is the laughing about?" Allen looked from one to the other. "Even the Arapaho must realize it's not polite to laugh at another's expense."

"Two Rivers sees that many young women walk by to see the white man, but you do not see them," Blue Otter explained. "He laughs because now the young women see me also. He says maybe now I will get a wife."

As Allen thought about it, he had seen many people pass by, but he never paid particular attention to them. While learning to chip his own obsidian knife, he seldom looked up at the people, even the young women. After that comment, he did notice.

One afternoon Two Rivers was called away to visit an elderly woman. Blue Otter and Allen caught their horses. While Allen saddled the buckskin, a young woman walked by with a string of small children. They stopped to look at Allen and his saddle, which was different from the Arapaho riding blanket.

"I need this big leather saddle so I won't fall off," Allen said.

Blue Otter translated, and the children laughed. The young woman also giggled. She hid her pleasant smile behind her hand and diverted her eyes in the typical Arapaho manner.

"Blue Otter, are you going to introduce me to the teacher?" Allen squeezed his friend's arm.

Blue Otter at first seemed perplexed, then understood. "Her name is Moon Cloud. She is the third daughter of Long Spear, one of the chiefs. She teaches the children stories of our fathers and the Arapaho way."

Her eyes still smiled, even though her lips did not. Colorful beads were tied into the long braids that hung below her shoulders.

Her warm brown eyes, smooth skin, and straight white teeth captured his gaze. She wore a honey-tanned elk-skin dress that moved easily over her full figure. The beaded yoke mirrored the natural colors of her face.

Allen noted something different about Moon Cloud—was it some kind of inner beauty? Maybe because she was a servant of the people and didn't attempt to attract men by emphasizing her good looks.

Allen smiled and extended his hand. Moon Cloud looked at his hand, uncertain. Blue Otter explained that American men shake a woman's hand as a greeting. She hesitated, then reached out and took Allen's hand. She smiled a friendly, sparkly smile, but then blushed. The children laughed and seemed to tease Moon Cloud, who hustled the children away.

"What happened? What are the children saying?" Allen's eyes followed the girl.

"Usually a man does not touch a woman's hand until they are married. So they say Moon Cloud is now married to the big white man." Blue Otter flashed his mischievous grin.

"Oh no! That's not what I meant. You have to call her back and tell her I just wanted to meet her, that I respect the work she does with the children." Allen's cheeks felt on fire.

"Long Spear loves his daughter and will not give her hand to just any man," Blue Otter said.

"I'm not thinking about marriage. I mean she's pretty . . . and she teaches the kids, but I'm not looking for a wife." Then why did his heart flop about like a trout on the shore?

Blue Otter just smiled. They rode off to the east to explore Sheep Mountain and the grasslands beyond.

After a couple hours of riding in silence, Allen asked, "How old do you guess Moon Cloud is?"

Blue Otter laughed out loud. "You look at the hills, but your mind sees only the girl?"

The grassy slopes didn't offer much to distract Allen's thoughts.

Moon Cloud was on his mind, and he surprised himself that he had to concentrate to remember his feelings for Violet Chamberlain. His perspective on life in the West was not as he had imagined it to be when he'd held hands with Violet. Now he could not picture her even wanting to step into a tipi. Why hadn't she written?

The next day Allen and Two Rivers sat in front of the medicine man's lodge, crafting their tools. A man with his teenage son approached. The boy laid a bundle of arrows in front of Two Rivers and then handed him seven more. The shaman examined the construction of the arrows. He looked down the shaft, evidently checking for straightness. He tugged on the binding of the feathers. He touched the arrowhead lashing. Finally, he spoke a few words, and the boy smiled proudly.

Two Rivers reached into a leather bag and pulled out a small stuffed bird and another smaller pouch. From the pouch, he took a pinch of red powder and sprinkled it on the bundle of arrows. He shook the stuffed bird, which rattled, and chanted as he passed it over the arrows.

Allen later learned from Blue Otter that Two Rivers blessed the arrows to fly true in the hunt and in battle. The boy had made the arrows himself in preparation for his initiation into the Tomahawk Lodge. It was one of the first steps to manhood, which moved him toward new levels of spiritual understanding and participation in tribal leadership.

While the sky grew black, Allen and Blue Otter sat at the fire in their tipi. Blue Otter smoked his pipe, a smell that Allen had grown accustomed to, and explained about Arapaho manhood.

Boys in their early teens would seek out a man about ten years older to be an advisor and teach them the songs and dances of the Kit Fox ceremony. Afterward, the boys were bound together in an obligation to support one another for the rest of their lives. They were trained in the values of adult life by growing strong and skilled in running and horseback racing, mock battles, and even raiding meat racks.

Then in their late teens, the group prepared for the Star Ceremony, which led them into greater responsibilities in the camp. A
young man on his first buffalo hunt would first seek elders to pray
for him and then give the first kill to one of them in honor and
gratitude.

The Starman, in time, found an advisor to lead him in the
prayer songs and dances of the Tomahawk Lodge. In this society,
he would gain spiritual knowledge for success in hunting and restoration of health. With years of experience, success in battle, and
providing for the band, a man would be initiated into the Spear
Lodge, the Crazy Lodge, and then the Dog Lodge. Each level was
more sacred than the previous and bestowed greater supernatural
power in battle, hunting, or protecting the people as they traveled
across the plains and mountains. Leaders and chiefs were usually
selected from among the Dogmen.

"To which lodge do you belong?" Allen lay on his side and
propped his head in his hand.

"I am Tomahawk, and in the season of long days, I will dance
the Spear."

"You mean next summer?"

"Summer, yes." Blue Otter described the seven-day process, before the actual dance, of preparing regalia according to their honors
and achievements.

Allen kept an eye out for Moon Cloud but didn't see her for
days. He carefully strolled by her father's tipi, but she wasn't around.
He asked Blue Otter if he had seen her.

"Long Spear take wife and Moon Cloud to other camp for
trade. Come back when finish."

After a couple of weeks had passed and still no sign of Moon
Cloud, Allen tried to stop thinking about her but often caught
himself looking at other women, hoping it would be her.

Allen had become a popular novelty around the camp. He practiced Arapaho words by playing games with small children. He spent time mastering skills with a bow and lance along with teenage boys. Young women worked to get his attention one way or another.

One young woman, Allen guessed her to be between sixteen and nineteen years old, captivated Allen. She was one of the most strikingly beautiful women he'd ever seen. Her almond-shaped eyes, high cheekbones, and tall, slender figure stood out among the other Arapaho women. Allen learned from Blue Otter that her name was Crow Feather, which was suitable, since she had flowing, raven-black hair and a free, high-spirited nature. She could gaze at a man with a compelling gleam in her eyes, as if she would capture him. Blue Otter cautioned about giving her attention, since she was being sought after by Chases the Bear, a mighty warrior.

Midday, Allen walked along the river, seeking solitude with the Lord. He soaked in the brilliance of yellow fall leaves. A movement to his right caught his attention. He spotted Crow Feather quietly stepping past the brush and into the water about mid-calf deep. She bent over and cupped water with her hands and rubbed her arms.

Allen thought he should practice some Arapaho words with her and was about to approach her, when his mouth went dry and his mind went blank for anything intelligent to say. He could only stare at the beautiful girl. Then without his having announced himself in any way, she looked over her shoulder, straight into his eyes.

He had to say something. He started to stand and then stopped. She was removing her deerskin dress for bathing. Allen gasped. He spun around and walked away, not allowing his eyes to linger a moment longer. A nagging internal voice told him to look back to take in her form, but Allen pushed away the thought as he pushed his way through the brush. A shape caught his attention, and he glanced to his left. Chases the Bear stood, feet shoulder width apart, arms folded across his chest, and fire in his eyes.

The missionary nodded, turned, and hurried straight back to camp.

He thanked the Lord for saving his reputation . . . and maybe even his life. From then on, Allen vowed to be very careful about looking at the young women. After all, his purpose in being there was to share the gospel and to observe Indian customs before traveling on to Oregon.

Later that afternoon, Allen served up some stew from the ever-present kettle that contained buffalo or elk meat that cooked all day with bitterroot, wild onions, and bear fat. He'd traded some sewing needles and white thread for a pouch full of salt from a woman two tipis away. He sprinkled a few grains onto the stew and stirred it. The salt gave life to the bland stew.

The sun looked like a white ball, glowing through the overcast sky. Allen gazed across the grassy hills, overcome with a contentment he'd never experienced before. Blue Otter walked up and served himself some stew from the black pot hanging on a tripod. He pulled out a knife and stabbed a piece of meat and put it into his mouth.

Allen noticed the elk-horn handle. "Is that a new knife?"

"Yes. I traded medicine rattle to Long Spear."

"Long Spear? Has he returned from the other camp then?" Interesting.

The next morning, Allen went hunting by himself. He spent most of the day in the field and came back with four quail and a rabbit he had taken with his bow. Taking two of the quail, he walked to Long Spear's lodge. Just as he neared the tipi, Long Spear stepped out and pierced him with a stare.

"Hello, Long Spear. I just came in from hunting and thought I would share these quail with you." Allen held the quail out to him.

Long Spear stared at him.

Allen realized the man didn't understand a word he said. He glanced over his shoulder, hoping to spot his translator. Allen shifted his feet and smiled. He extended his hand farther, hoping the Indian would see it as a gesture of giving.

Long Spear stepped forward and received the quail. Just then Moon Cloud walked up with an armload of firewood. She paused. Long Spear looked at Moon Cloud and then back at Allen. Without a word, Long Spear dropped the birds by the fire and ducked into the tipi.

After a forever moment, Allen greeted Moon Cloud in Arapaho.

She replied.

He pointed at the quail and said the word for hunt. "Heeno-ah."

She corrected his pronunciation. "Hiinoo-ei."

For the next two hours, Allen sat on a log with Moon Cloud, the two exchanging words, learning sign language, and laughing.

When Allen returned to his lodge, he couldn't stand still. He moved firewood around, poked at the fire, and went in and out of the tipi. Then he noticed Two Rivers and Blue Otter watching him. "What?" Allen said, feeling his face flush.

They remained stoic.

"Why you are watching me?"

At that moment Long Spear walked up to Two Rivers. Allen could not catch what he was saying, but then Long Spear pointed his finger at him. Was he upset with Allen for keeping Moon Cloud from her work? He looked to Blue Otter, whose expressionless face held no sign of understanding.

Blue Otter finally spoke. "Long Spear hunt tomorrow. We go."

Relieved that he'd caused no offense, Allen prepared his hunting supplies.

Sitting at the fire, he asked Blue Otter about Arapaho courtship customs. "How do you go about courting a woman?"

Blue Otter stared at the fire for a long moment. "What is courting?"

"When you find a woman desirable and intend to pursue a

serious relationship." Allen kneaded his hands. "And you think you want to test the waters prior to tying the knot."

Blue Otter frowned. "Why would you tie a knot in the water?"

"What? No. That's not what I am saying. Listen. If you think you want to enter matrimony with a woman, how do you convince her that you are interested?"

"Marmony?"

"No. Matrimony. I am talking about marriage. How would you tell a woman you wanted to marry her?"

Blue Otter nodded and smiled, indicating that he finally understood. "I have no woman to make my wife."

"Not you. I'm speaking in general terms here." Allen rolled his eyes. "Fine. When you do find a woman you want for a wife, how will you tell her?"

Staring at the fire for another long moment, Blue Otter rubbed the back of his neck. "I am not sure. But I will do more than give her father a quail."

Allen stared into the stoic eyes of his mentor, then burst out laughing. "So you heard about the quail. Well, that explains a few things."

"All camp know about the quail."

"Time to hunt." Blue Otter ducked through the opening.

"I'll be right there." Allen pulled on a wool coat and bobcat-fur cap. He snatched up his long rifle, powder horn, and pouch and stepped outside into the dark morning. Two Rivers and Blue Otter were mounted up. Allen hustled to saddle his horse and climbed up. He nudged the gelding and fell in behind his companions.

They rode for an hour in silence. Allen wondered why Long Spear wasn't with them.

As the sun rose, casting light across the land, Allen recognized the terrain. They were riding over the mountain where weeks ago he had helped Jack and Joaquin steal the horses. Making their way down a long canyon to the north, they came to the river and found Long Spear sitting on a rock, holding the lead ropes for three horses. He wore a red three-point trade blanket coat. His beaked nose protruded from the coyote-pelt head covering that draped down his shoulders.

Two Rivers dismounted and stood next to his good friend. As he studied them, Allen guessed Long Spear was ten or fifteen years younger than Two Rivers. Allen was about to dismount, when he saw movement farther down the river. A young woman emerged from the brush. She wore a buffalo-hide cape, and her hair was black and scraggly. In an instant, Allen saw a resemblance to Moon Cloud, but this woman was heavier and rounder in the face.

"Cries Like Thunder," Blue Otter said. "Second daughter of Long Spear."

"How in the world did she get that—"

Allen smiled when he saw Moon Cloud push through the brush behind her sister.

Moon Cloud glanced at the hunters but averted her eyes and walked to her horse. She wore a white trade blanket capote with red and yellow stripes and a belt that snugged it to her waist. Her hair was combed and braided. Her features were finer and smoother than her sister's, and her eyes expressed joy in living. She stole a glance at Allen.

"My heart is flopping like a trout again," he said.

"What trout?" Blue Otter said.

Not realizing he had spoken out loud, Allen felt the heat smolder in his cheeks. "Pay me no nevermind."

Long Spear nimbly swung onto his horse and moved upstream. His daughters followed. Two Rivers mounted his black-and-white pinto and motioned to the west. "We cross river, hunt canyons. They go east. We make circle. Meet here."

They traversed one grassy canyon ridge after another for over an hour, looking for game of any kind. When they jumped a covey of quail, Two Rivers called Blue Otter to help follow them. Left alone, Allen made his way over the next small rise to look into the shallow draw beyond. As he scanned the brush, a covey of quail burst into flight to his left. Suddenly, an arrow rose from the brush and dropped a quail.

Allen searched the brush from where the arrow flew. He nudged Caleb forward a few steps, then halted. Moon Cloud stepped out from a cluster of sage and greasewood brush about twenty yards away. She paused and looked at Allen. With the bow in her left hand, her right hand held another arrow against the string. A quiver hung on her back, with a bulging leather bag hanging at her left hip. She nodded toward the downed bird and moved to retrieve it. Allen dropped to the ground, tied the horse, and followed her.

Moon Cloud picked up the bird and gently removed the arrow. She showed Allen. "Cenee," she said. "Cenee."

"Cenee," he repeated. "Quail. Cenee is quail."

"Kwell," she said.

Allen nodded. "Quail."

She smiled and put the bird in her bag. He reached over to hold the bag open and looked inside. "My goodness. You have one, two, three . . . six. You have six quail already." He held one up. "Cenee. Umm, neetoox. Six." He held up six fingers.

Moon Cloud giggled. "Niitootoxu."

"Niitootoxu."

Allen stared into Moon Cloud's brown eyes and long lashes. He wanted to sit down and learn more words, but she motioned toward the brush. "Kwell."

"Yeoh, hiinoo'ei," Allen said. "Yes, hunt."

Allen followed as they weaved through the brush to where they had last seen the covey. Moon Cloud stopped and examined the base of the greasewood bushes and the grass. She took a few more steps and stopped, scanning. Crouching, she moved forward.

Allen waited, watching, admiring her stalking prowess.

More steps. Stillness. Slowly Moon Cloud raised her bow and drew back the arrow. She held for a moment, then released. The string snapped. A sudden rush of fluttering as the rest of the covey broke cover. Before Allen was aware of what had happened, Moon Cloud released another arrow and struck down a second quail.

Quickly she followed her arrows, picked up the birds, and set them in her shoulder bag.

Allen joined her, smiling. "That makes eight. Fine shooting." He patted his pockets, revealing that they were empty. Holding up his gun, he shrugged and smiled sheepishly. He waved his hand palm down, in the sign for nothing.

She smiled and said words he did not catch, and then headed back the way they had come. They passed Allen's horse and continued up the draw for a half mile. She paused to check the wind and inspect the view. With only hand gestures, she told Allen to sit where he was and keep watch. Moon Cloud crept along, studying the ground, and finally picked up the broadest leaf she could find. She walked quietly down the slope into the draw and knelt between sage bushes.

Not sure what she was doing, Allen watched. A minute later an agonizing sound broke the silence. He stretched his neck to see Moon Cloud holding cupped hands to her mouth. A few minutes later she repeated the wavering squeal.

Allen caught a glimpse of movement a hundred yards away. He cocked back the hammer and shifted his weight onto his right leg. He leaned his left elbow on his left knee to steady the rifle. Seeing a flash of tan through the brush that was closer and moving toward Moon Cloud, he aimed down the barrel.

The head and shoulder of a coyote appeared in a gap. It stood on high alert, sniffing the wind, twenty-five yards from Moon Cloud and forty yards from Allen. He had a clear shot. Resting the front sight on the shoulder, he squeezed the trigger. The rifle bucked.

Allen lost sight of the coyote. He reloaded. Not detecting any movement, he rose and made his way to where he had shot. Moon Cloud moved forward. They met at the downed coyote.

Relieved that his shot was true, Allen leaned his rifle on a bush. Moon Cloud knelt beside the animal and rubbed her hand across its fur. A full-grown male with a healthy yellow-and-rust hide. She said words that Allen understood to mean good value. She quietly sprinkled sage leaves across the body and lifted more to the sky. She then pulled out a knife and began skinning the hide. Allen slipped out his knife and matched her cutting motions. Pulling back a bunch of fur, their hands touched. Allen beheld her eyes for a moment. Then they both looked down and continued their work.

I never thought skinning a coyote could be so pleasant.

CHAPTER TWENTY-SIX

ONE DAY RIDERS CAME IN from another village, reporting the deaths of some people. This news, along with the visions declared by the seeing elders, instantly instilled apprehension. Worried mothers held their children closer.

That night, Two Rivers called for Allen and Blue Otter.

When Allen stepped into the shaman's lodge, several elders, medicine men, and chiefs were already there. They were smoking pipes and talking softly, but all eyes went to the young missionary as he took a seat in the circle around the fire.

As Two Rivers spoke, Blue Otter translated. "For many days we have been making preparations for the Dance of Winter. We honor the spirits for the food that has been provided, and we ask the winter spirits to be gentle. Now Burning Stick and White Owl have come from their village"—he acknowledged them with his hand—"with news that the Death Cloud claimed the lives of five people. Two were kidnapped: a young girl and a medicine man.

"We believe that Dark Wolf, Kicking Lion, and their men rode in under the Death Cloud to murder and capture the medicine man and the girl." Two Rivers's eyes belied his worry and fatigue.

"Dark Wolf sent the Death Cloud," Burning Stick said, clutching his medicine pouch.

"We do not yet know that Dark Wolf has the power to send the Death Cloud," Two Rivers continued. "He is able to do much evil. He captures medicine men to steal their power and torment their souls. But the Death Cloud has always come and taken many lives."

Allen listened carefully to the talk of spiritual things. "What does he mean that the Death Cloud takes many lives?" he asked Blue Otter.

"The Death Cloud comes in the night, like a hand that presses down on us. In the morning, we find dead ones."

"Are they killed by a knife or poison?"

"No. They are just dead."

Allen studied the wizened men, their eyes dark and weary. The glow of the firelight deepened the lines on their faces. What could he tell them that would bring hope?

"Will the Death Cloud come tonight?" He probed for insight.

"It will come on the night of the full moon. Two more nights," Blue Otter said.

"Ask Two Rivers and the elders if the Great Spirit does not offer them hope. How has the Great Spirit rescued them in the past?"

Blue Otter translated. Two Rivers listened to the question, frowning. Finally he answered. "We call upon our spirit guides to protect us, but still some are taken."

"The Great Spirit has not given a song to rescue you? The song of a savior?"

The council, confused by the question, looked at one another.

"I'd like time to pray. I'll seek wisdom from the Savior, Jesus Christ, and his Spirit book. I believe there's an answer to this evil," Allen said.

He gleaned as much information as he could from Blue Otter, then spent the next day fasting, praying, and searching the Scriptures for faith and wisdom to offer Two Rivers. This would be an opportunity to share the gospel, only much differently than he'd expected.

In prayer, Allen's thoughts led him to read 1 Peter, as if a voice spoke to him. "Be sober, be vigilant; because your adversary the devil, as a roaring lion, walketh about, seeking whom he may devour." A lump rose in his throat as he recalled how a demon had manifested in a young girl back in Ohio. *How am I supposed to handle a demon that attacks an entire village?*

By late afternoon he found encouragement that God rescued the oppressed, from Psalm 22. Faith was forming. It wasn't his fight. The battle had already been won. He needed to allow his faith to be used by the Victor, just like Daniel or Mordecai.

When Allen returned to the village, he noted the oppressive fear growing within the hearts of the people, like birds in a basket trap with no hope of escape. Hunters were called in from the field, children were kept in camp, and horses were closely guarded. Fighting men organized shifts and teams to protect the band from raiders. By nightfall, the tension was palpable.

Allen heard singing and chanting throughout the camp. Protective symbols had been painted on tipis. Large fires burned in various places to ward off the darkness. Allen expected a fog to drift in, but the night stayed clear.

When boldness found Allen, he grabbed Blue Otter and led him to the center of the camp. "I'm not going to let the Father of Lies have a victory tonight. Translate what I say."

Shouting at the top of his lungs, Allen prayed, "Oh, Great Spirit, Heavenly Father, you are great beyond compare. There is no other god like you. Only you are holy, you are almighty, and your love is deeper than the great sea, higher than the tallest mountains. Your truth shines brighter than the sun and the moon. You sent your Son, Jesus Christ, to free us from the grip of darkness. He came to undo the work of the devil. It is in his holy name that I pray. Deliver us from the Death Cloud. Deliver us from evil men who scheme against your children. I declare that Death Cloud has no power over this camp. You must go back to where Jesus Christ commands you."

Blue Otter translated as best he could, shouting aloud with Allen. The songs in the tipis grew quiet as the people listened to the strange words of the white man.

Allen began singing "A Mighty Fortress Is Our God" as Blue Otter struggled with the words. "A mighty fortress is our God, a bulwark never failing—"

"What is barwol?" Blue Otter said.

"Bulwark. It means a strong fort that cannot be conquered," Allen said. "Just do the best you can. I'm just not sure these demons speak English." He continued singing, carrying the tune as if he were in church back home. Blue Otter screeched out of key, with no sense of the melody.

The two sang through the night until Allen's voice faded. He switched to reciting psalms of praise and victory, while Blue Otter stayed with Allen's focused determination to defeat the Death Cloud.

Around three o'clock in the morning, Allen sensed a break in the tension.

Allen and Blue Otter, in perfect unity, shouted with joy. Allen dropped to his knees in thanksgiving and didn't cease his praise until dawn.

When the sun sent streaks of light bright enough to see across camp, people drifted out of the tipis; the guards wandered in from their posts. A crowd gathered around as Two Rivers stepped to Allen's side.

"Have any been found dead?" the medicine man called to the people.

Young men ran through the camp, checking every lodge. Finally the report came back that all were alive. Not a single person had died in the night. No child had been kidnapped. No horse had been stolen. According to Blue Otter, for the first time in the elders' knowledge, the Death Cloud passed by empty handed.

The village stared in awe at Allen and Blue Otter. An elder from the Crazy Lodge shouted, as if announcing good news. Old women moved forward and touched Allen. Some women quietly wept.

The crowd eventually broke up, and with his throat hoarse and exhaustion setting in, Allen moved toward his tipi. He longed for sleep. But he couldn't refuse acknowledging the grateful people who came by with gifts of tobacco, food, tools, hides, and beautiful beadwork. Finally, to the sound of drumbeats, Blue Otter called him for a dance ceremony.

Allen was seated among the elders. During the ceremony, Two Rivers presented Allen with a long smoking pipe and gave a speech. Blue Otter wasn't nearby, so Allen didn't know what the medicine man said or what might be expected of him. All he could think to do was shake hands with Two Rivers, nod to the people, and raise the pipe to the sky, the earth, and the four compass points, and then he sat down. He hoped it was the acceptable thing to do. Then they danced into the night.

Afterward, Blue Otter held the ceremonial pipe with admiration. It was about forty inches long with a bronze ax and pipe bowl. "The falcon feathers mean courage," he explained. "The black-and-white feathers of the magpie signify wisdom. The hide of the black bear indicates strength and wisdom. This is good pipe."

Looking at the black bear hide that wrapped the stem, Allen asked, "I understand strength, but why wisdom?"

"When he is wounded, the black bear hunts for roots and leaves with healing power."

Allen carefully rolled up the pipe in an elk hide and put it among his belongings.

As weeks passed and frigid mountain winds swept into the prairie and dropped a thick blanket of snow, life in the village slowed. Hunters still ventured out for their preference of fresh meat, but most of their efforts focused on keeping the firewood supply stocked.

Some days when the temperatures were bearable, children played games and women visited. Allen often watched Moon Cloud as she told the children stories of history, legends, and myths. He admired her and the ease with which she kept the children's interest. Quite often, teenage boys lingered at the edge of the circle to listen to her stories.

Surely Moon Cloud would become a believer if he just had a chance to tell her about Jesus Christ. She'd also make a good missionary's wife. Allen groaned. He had no right to think about her in that way—he was promised to Violet. But after what he'd experienced, he was convinced she'd never make it out here. Violet had not replied to any of his letters.

His heart soared whenever he saw Moon Cloud. But the missionary band would leave for Oregon soon. No point in pursuing a deeper relationship with her unless the Lord opened the door for him to stay among the Arapaho. Perhaps he should just stay and say goodbye to the band. But no, the call was to Oregon, and he'd pledged, just like the others, to go all the way.

Through the months of December and January, Allen told gospel stories, usually in crowded tipis as an invited guest. At times, the crowd broke out laughing, as though the stories were too far-fetched, though brave warriors like David, Samson, and Gideon held their attention.

Two Rivers often requested to hear accounts of deliverance and healings by Jesus and the apostles. He was particularly fascinated with Allen's ability to speak meaning from the strange tracks on the leaves in his book.

"We learn the songs of many different spirits," Two Rivers said one night. "But you call to the Great Spirit in this name, Jesus Christ. You do not learn songs from the other spirits."

All of his theological training had not prepared the missionary to answer questions of spiritual power in an aboriginal setting.

"Creator made the world and everything in it. He made a valley for First Man and First Woman to live in that had fruit and berries and roots of many kinds. They lived in peace and spoke often with Creator. There were two trees in the valley. The fruit from the Tree of Life made them strong and gave them joy. The Tree of Knowledge of Good and Evil grew fruit of pride that gave them knowledge and strength, but no joy. The fruit tasted good, but it turned bitter in their stomachs.

"Creator told them to eat from the tree of joy and they would hear his voice. To eat from the tree of pride would turn their hearts away from Creator. They would always search for joy but never find it. They would grow bitter and hurt one another because there was no joy.

"The evil spirit, a trickster, told them to eat the fruit of pride and they would have the wisdom of Creator for themselves. First Man and First Woman ate the fruit of pride, and their hearts grew bitter toward Creator. They had many children, and the seeds of pride went into them, and they hurt one another. The children took pride in going to war. They took pride in stealing horses and killing their enemies. There was no joy. No peace. They tried to hear the voice of Creator, but many times listened to the voice of the trickster instead.

"Creator grew sad and weary because their hearts were bitter with lies. Creator sent his Son, Jesus Christ, to teach the children to eat again from the tree of joy. The bitter children killed Jesus Christ. They hung him on an ugly tree. But the Son came back to life because he loved the children. The eyes of the children were opened. They saw that the ugly tree became the tree of joy and life. It will feed the children from its fruit.

"I've eaten from the tree of life." Allen opened his Bible to an illustration of the crucifixion scene on Calvary. "This is the tree of life—the cross of Jesus. I do not call on the other spirits for help because I fear they would deceive me from the wisdom of Jesus Christ and his joy."

Two Rivers listened to the story. He didn't respond.

By the end of February, Allen heard reports that white trappers were traveling west. There was only snow in shady patches on the north slopes of rolling hills and mountaintops. It was time to return to his own people. His own people? To call them that seemed almost ironic. He'd grown so comfortable and purposeful among the Arapaho band. He'd adopted many of their ways . . . but Oregon awaited.

Two Rivers called out, then stepped into the tipi. He sat at the fire with Allen and Blue Otter and pulled out his pipe. "Let us share the pipe of friends one last time."

Allen sat cross-legged. "I am to leave soon. What do the spirits say to you, my father?"

"I see that it is time for you to leave the camp of the People. The spirits do not give me wisdom about your trail. I have asked the Great Spirit to have you live among us. But I only see that you ride away. Then there is darkness that blocks my sight. The Spirit does not want me to see the trail. My heart is at peace, though it is sad to see you ride out." Two Rivers's face appeared somber, but in his eyes glowed a small light of hope.

"My heart is at peace, Father," Allen said in Arapaho. "I will pray that our trails will cross again soon." He could only be grateful for the friendships and life lessons he'd learned. If God had blessed him so, it was for a reason, because nothing ever happened in vain.

Allen turned to his companion. "Blue Otter, my friend and brother, you have been my echo. My voice and my ears. God gave me a very special gift when he led us together. I will never forget you." Allen reached into his bag and pulled out a small bundle, which he handed to Blue Otter.

As he carefully unwrapped the deerskin bundle, Blue Otter's eyes widened upon seeing the silver object with small symbols carefully carved in it. Allen reached over and pulled the knob on top. The small door popped open, clearly amazing both Indians.

"This is a watch my father gave me when I completed seminary, the school for holy men. That is a tintype of me," he said. It was difficult to make out the image in the dim light of the lodge. "It was made by a man in Boston who came from Switzerland. The engraving is a noble huntsman. That is why I am giving it to you. You are a life hunter and have the noble name of a son of the Great Spirit. The clock works well if you remember to wind it."

Blue Otter remained quiet. After a few moments, he reached into his possibles bag and drew out a leather necklace on which hung a large, irregularly shaped nugget of gold. Allen's eyes widened. The nugget was as large as the end of his thumb, only flatter. It had been worn smooth by countless years in a stream, and a natural hole through one end made it ideal for a simple yet valuable necklace.

"I found this medicine stone many years ago. I wore it around my neck very proudly. One day a white trapper tried to kill me to take it. But I killed him. It gave me the strength of a man to kill him and much respect from the elders. It gave me new life. I give it to you because you give me new life."

Now it was Allen's turn to sit quiet and be amazed. Blue Otter gave him the beautiful raw gold necklace, and in the pouch were several other smaller nuggets. *This was too much . . . it's worth*—Allen's first thought was how much this gold could buy, but then he understood that to Blue Otter it had a different meaning—it was a symbol of strength.

The next day Allen loaded his belongings and gifts onto two packhorses. He led the buckskin around the camp as he said his goodbyes. Many women gave him beaded necklaces, and a few children gave him obsidian stones. Allen knelt by the children to do a final handclap game. His endearment to this village seemed as deep as when he'd left his congregation in New York. It was a sense of belonging, and he would cherish the opportunity to remain with them, but out of respect for Reverend Bannister, he must tear himself away.

Stopping by the lodge of Long Spear, Allen gave a wrap of tobacco to the subchief. Moon Cloud stepped out of the tipi. Her face lit up upon seeing Allen. Even without a word, her pretty, smiling eyes made his heart leap.

"I will greet you again someday, Long Spear," Allen said in Arapaho.

"You are welcome among our people," said the chief, who wore a woolen trade coat. Nodding toward his daughter, he added, "You are welcome to visit my lodge. I see that Moon Cloud smiles when she looks at you."

"I would cross the great mountains to see her smile," Allen said, looking at the girl.

She didn't blush or cover her smile with her hand. Instead, surprising everyone, she stepped forward and shook Allen's hand. Long Spear and his wife's eyes grew wide. Though Moon Cloud's bold move was unheard of between an unmarried couple, Allen recognized her expression as respect and friendship.

He could no longer deny that Moon Cloud had awoken a part of his heart he hadn't even known existed. She was a pretty woman, but her inner beauty drew him to her. Could she be a missionary's wife? Lord willing, he'd return someday. But for now, he had to leave her. His heart felt like it was tied to two horses running in opposite directions—tugging him to stay near Moon Cloud and wrenching him to fulfill his duty to the call. He quenched the flame by smiling and moving on through the camp.

Allen made his way back to Two Rivers's lodge. Mounting Caleb, he scanned the faces in the crowd watching him. He recalled their reaction to him the first time he'd ridden into camp, their suspicious and hostile eyes. Now they were familiar and connected by the bonds of sharing life, hardship, and laughter.

In a glance that lasted a single moment, he gave and received friendship with Blue Otter and Two Rivers. Then prodding Caleb, he rode out through the draw to the south. Before dark he would be back with the missionary band. He hoped they would be ready to hit the trail soon—he could not stay in this vicinity without yearning to be with Moon Cloud. Would she be excited to see him when he returned? Would his feelings still be this strong? Would he really ride across the mountains to see her again?

Allen rode dutifully away from where his heart desired to remain.

CHAPTER TWENTY-SEVEN

ALLEN TURNED HIS HORSE off the trail and out onto the point of a grassy knob overlooking the North Platte River Valley. The clear sky allowed him to see for forty miles or more. To the west, Laramie Peak stood high above the other mountains. Even the lower peaks and ridges still held snow, but the valley was a patchwork of various shades of tan and brown. To the east, the valley spread into flat prairie—the grassy sea that separated him from his life-long friends and congregation. They were a memory as distant as the horizon. To the west, Oregon was an unknown venture. How could it exceed the joy he was leaving in an Arapaho camp?

The line of the Laramie River wound out of the limestone bluffs to the south until its confluence with the North Platte. Beyond the intersection of the tree line was a wide-open pasture, the clearing of Fort Laramie. As he stood on this side of the trees, the fort remained hidden from view.

"Well, Caleb, before long we'll be with the missionaries. What are they going to think of me now?" At that moment the gelding looked behind them. Allen chuckled. "I'd like to go back too, boy."

Allen nudged Caleb and led the two pinto packhorses down the draw to the valley floor. A couple of does bounded out of the brush and ran about a hundred yards before stopping to look back. They were in range, but he had several pounds of dried venison in his pack, along with a good chunk of elk quarter. He would let the does run free today. He hoped to get a taste of bacon once he arrived back to the fort and the band.

Crossing the North Platte where it was only knee deep to the horses, Allen made his way through the brush and cottonwoods. Coming out on a bluff, he gazed down on Fort Laramie, a quarter mile away. Beyond, almost a mile upstream on the Laramie River, he noted another building under construction.

Allen rode into the courtyard and tied the horses in front of the quartermaster's store. There was no one around except two Oto men wearing American shirts and coats. They shared a large jar of rum.

Allen entered the store. Mr. Meecer, bent over a journal, was busy writing. He tilted his head up and squinted in the dim light, in which dust motes soared. "Well, I declare. Is that you, Preacher? I almost didn't recognize you."

Allen shook his hand. "I just came out of the mountains. I've been up at Two Rivers's camp. Now I'm back to prepare for the move to Oregon with Reverend Bannister and the others. Is their mission cabin close by? Please don't tell me it's that large adobe building that's going up across the clearing."

"No, the fort's being moved over there. This one's falling apart with rot. You'll see the mission school and cabin set up in the draw southwest of here," Meecer said. He changed the subject to freight wagons from the East that he expected any day now.

Allen traded some otter pelts for a few pounds of bacon, flour, sugar, and salt. "I'm anxious to taste bacon and biscuits. I'll get Mrs. Bannister to fix some up for me," he said.

Meecer was quiet.

Allen thanked him and rode toward the mission station. He glanced back at Meecer, who looked down at the pelts.

Dismounting in front of the log church, he tied the horses to an eight-foot-high pole. A flat piece of metal hanging from the pole served as the church bell. Gloria strolled around the corner of the second cabin. She stopped and stared.

"Allen!" She ran to hug him. "I'm so glad you're back."

"I'm most happy to see you too."

"Look at you. You look so rugged, like the mountain men." She held both of his hands.

"I hope that's good." His brown wavy hair had grown to his shoulders, and he hadn't shaved in a couple of weeks. "Where is everyone?"

She hesitated, then her eyes lit up as a man stepped out of the cabin. "Allen, I want you to meet John Lockwood." She paused. "He's my husband. We got married a month ago." Gloria tipped her head, bit her lower lip, and blushed a soft pink.

Allen's jaw dropped open, and he stared at Gloria, trying to grasp what she'd just said.

John stepped forward to shake hands. "Gloria has told me many things about you. It is indeed a pleasure to meet you."

Allen still could not speak. The world seemed to shift beneath his feet.

"Come into the house. We'll put on a pot of coffee and get supper cooking while I tell the rest of the news," Gloria said.

They stepped into the tidy cabin. The two men sat at the table while Gloria set the coffeepot on a metal hook over the fire. "Last October," she went on, "several weeks after you went to live with Two Rivers, John came with another Baptist missionary, Reverend Wendell Weymore. They came to Fort Laramie for supplies."

"We've built a mission on the South Platte River, about one hundred and forty miles to the southeast," John added. "I was immediately impressed with Miss Gloria Shannon. Not just because she's the prettiest lady on the frontier but because she's a godly woman."

Allen nodded and smiled at Gloria. His shock at the unexpected news was giving way to joy for the obviously happy couple.

"Reverend Bannister allowed them to make their camp nearby. We enjoyed their fellowship for about a week before they returned to their own mission." Gloria mixed the biscuit flour in a bowl.

"I promised to visit in the spring but couldn't wait. So I rode through a blizzard in order to see Gloria for Christmas," John said. "I spent another week and lent a hand with the building."

"I guess he swept me off my feet." She brushed hair from her eyes with the back of her wrist. "John and Wendell returned in February for more supplies—"

"And that's when I got down on my knee and proposed marriage," John said. "Reverend Weymore married us."

"I never imagined that a love could be so deep, Allen," she said. "It has to be a miracle of God to bring us together way out here."

"Reverend Bannister let someone else do the ceremony?" Allen cocked his head to the side.

Gloria stopped mixing. "Allen, he couldn't have. He'd already gone back East. The Bannisters and the Fosters returned to the States in January. They don't even know yet that I'm married."

Allen's jaw dropped open—again. "I can't believe . . . how . . . this is so confusing. What about Virgil Jolifer? Did he go back with them?"

"No. He's still here. But he's married too. He married Polly McMasters about a month before Christmas. They're living in her cabin about two miles from here. He's the happiest man in the world." Gloria resumed her mixing.

She set three cups on the table. "At first the reverend refused to do the wedding for them, since not enough grieving time for Martha had passed. But then he changed his mind when Virgil said he would find someone else to do it. Virgil is such a different man, so full of joy. I'm happy for him."

John nodded his agreement.

Gloria had placed the dough balls in a Dutch oven and leaned over to set it in the coals. "Reverend Bannister had been corresponding with the general secretary of the Foreign Missionary Society about establishing this mission on the Laramie. He received a reply letter in early January that said Reverend Bannister had been appointed to be the superintendent of the Maryland Conference. Foster was reassigned to Missouri as the administrator for the Mission of the Federated Tribes of the Cherokee Nation. The Indians are being relocated, and the mission needs someone to supervise the transition of schools and churches. They've witnessed a large number of converts and don't want to lose any while moving west.

"The Bannisters and the Fosters began packing their belongings the day after the letter came, and they were gone within a week," Gloria said. "The reverend has left you in charge of this mission, Allen. He said he trusts that you'll do an outstanding job taking up where they left off."

Overwhelmed, Allen finally found his voice. "But I'm not interested in being in charge of this mission. I thought we were going on to Oregon. What about the vision for evangelizing the Northwest?"

"Everything is so different now. I don't know what to say." Gloria rested her hand on Allen's shoulder. "It seems that both Reverend Bannister and Reverend Foster lost motivation for the original vision last summer when they chose to winter here. Perhaps it was the bad weather or the Indian raids, but after you left to live with Two Rivers, their enthusiasm quickly faded. Their vision shifted to building this outpost and school to start educating the nearby Indians."

"What about you two? Why don't you take charge here? I can keep working among the Arapaho in this area." So much was being thrown at him that Allen's thoughts dashed in several directions.

"Allen, we've already considered that, but we just can't do it. John already has a significant mission where he's needed, and there are children there that I can teach. We'll be leaving soon. Honestly, I've only stayed here in order to see you. It's good that you came out when you did. I would have felt terrible leaving without giving you the news, both good and bad. And I wanted you to meet John."

Allen sat quietly for a several minutes, staring at the table. Gloria went about preparing food while Lockwood tended the fire and the biscuits.

How could Bannister and Foster turn back after all the planning, the commissioning, and direction from God? How could the reverend even consider going back when there was so much to be done here and so few laborers? Disturbed that he was expected to tend a mission he didn't believe in, Allen shook his head, as though trying to dislodge the frustration that was settling in.

Regardless, he determined to set that problem aside for now and enjoy Gloria and John's good company—and maybe some bacon.

"I must say I'm quite stunned by the news," Allen said. "But we might as well enjoy supper and celebrate your wedding. I'm truly happy for you, Gloria, and for you as well, John. Congratulations!"

Gloria beamed. "Oh, Allen. I can't imagine how difficult this must be for you to come out of the mountains and learn about all the changes. You certainly are a true friend." She came around the table and hugged Allen's neck.

They ate their meal of bear steaks, bacon, potatoes with gravy, and biscuits. Allen amused the newlyweds with stories of living with the Indians and some of the unusual things he had eaten. Besides deer, elk, buffalo, and bear, the usual fare, he'd eaten cougar, dog, rattlesnake, hawk, and beaver. Horse meat was difficult to get used to at first, but then he developed a taste for the common meal.

John Lockwood invited Allen to stay the night in the cabin. They'd visit more in the morning. Allen agreed and offered to help with their packing for the coming move.

Before turning in for the night, Gloria handed Allen a letter from Reverend Bannister. He sat down on the floor by the fireplace and leaned against the stone hearth to read by the firelight.

Dear Allen,

May the blessings of Almighty God, the Father of our Lord Jesus Christ, abide with you richly. May his wisdom be your guide and the lamp unto your feet.

I rather imagine that the news brought forth in this letter will come as a surprise. And yet I trust you will acknowledge that God has opened a door none of us expected. The ways of God are a mystery to mere mortals such as ourselves.

By way of post, I received a letter of calling at the bishop's request, and with leave of the general secretary of the Foreign Missionary Society, to fill the position of superintendent of the Maryland Conference. My duties will commence upon my arrival in Baltimore, hopefully no later than the first of March.

Our brother in Christ, the Reverend Reginald Foster, likewise has been given the new assignment within the missionary society of administering the work with the Federation of Nations in Missouri. As you are well aware, we have many converts to Methodism among the Cherokee, who are in transition and need the proficient skills of Reverend Foster.

We both have the assurance of the Holy Ghost that these changes are necessary and in accordance with God's will. Therefore, we have resigned our commissions to the far West and, with regrets, leave the fledgling yet thriving mission at Fort Laramie.

However, we entrust the work of the mission, church, and school to your capable hands, recog-

nizing your profound interest in the natives of that region.

It is with sorrow that I say farewell through this impersonal letter, yet I pray God's richest blessing on you, as I am

Your Faithful Shepherd,
Rev. Samuel Bannister

Disappointment poured over Allen. His soul was heavy. Bannister's band had disintegrated, not lasting even a year. What should he make of a calling and commissioning that couldn't fulfill its primary purpose?

Bannister and Foster both had been genuinely determined in the goal and motivation of establishing missions among the Indians in the Oregon Territory. Thoughts flashed through Allen's mind like a wind-driven snow, so fast that before one could finish, another demanded his attention. He recalled both ministers arguing with Reverend Covington on the prairie. Bannister had tried impressing Ragsdale with assurances of his determination to take the gospel across the Rockies. Allen recalled the riverboats and canals, the planning, and organizing. Every memory streaked through his mind and left only confusion in its wake.

Allen stoked the remaining coals in the fireplace and put together a pot of coffee to start heating. He went outside to greet the morning. The sky was just dimly lit, still waiting for the sun to break the horizon. Finding the horses in fine condition, he walked up the low bluff behind the corral to look out over the Laramie Valley. The letter bound his thoughts.

Allen would have to live without an answer. He'd never know for sure if Bannister secretly asked for the superintendency just to escape the hardships of missionary life. Had he been frightened off by the deaths of Martha Jolifer and the freighters? Did he give in to fears of Dark Wolf or the unusual storms? Had Covington's argument broken his resolve? Bannister would never admit to fear or weakness but would merely testify, as he did in the letter, that God works in mysterious ways.

The introspection drew Allen deeper toward anger and despair. He struggled to escape the dark thoughts. Perhaps it was for the best to have learned of the band's demise by letter. Discussing their exodus face to face would have been worse. Speaking civilly to Foster would have been impossible. Any questions Allen voiced would have been considered insubordinate and ended in a sharp rebuke. Perhaps Foster's and Bannister's gifts and ministries would be more appropriate in these new situations, and quite possibly would have been misplaced or detrimental in the wildlands.

Allen felt certain that the men and their wives wouldn't have adapted to Two Rivers's village. Why then were they not directed to those positions before the journey began? God's wisdom should have been more efficient than this ill-fated venture. Could all of this have been God's provision just to get Allen to where he was supposed to be? *Would I have gotten here on my own?* Or was it solely because Samuel Bannister had come to him with the prospect of a mission in Oregon Territory? And what of Gloria and Virgil?

Allen interrupted his preoccupations when the sun climbed above the horizon line. He faced east and raised his arms and quoted from the book of Job. "'Where wast thou when I laid the foundations of the earth? Declare, if thou hast understanding. Who hath laid the measures thereof, if thou knowest? Or who hath stretched the line upon it?'

"Lord, you are great and mighty. Forgive me for being presumptuous. All things work together for the good of your servants. I leave the Bannisters and the Fosters in your wise care. And I commit myself again to you, Heavenly Father. Grant me your wisdom and revelation with regard to my place. Shall I stay here or go on to Oregon? Lord, I seek your counsel. May your will be done on earth, and in me, as it is in heaven. Amen."

Shortly after the couple had arisen to the new day, Allen strolled into the cabin and asked how he might make himself useful. Gloria fried griddlecakes and more bacon for breakfast.

"You seem cheerful this morning, Allen," Gloria said.

"I've come to peace with regard to the Bannisters and Fosters leaving. I'll admit it weighed heavy on my heart all night. But I believe now I can wait upon the Lord for my next step. In fact, I believe it will be revealed to me soon enough. So I don't need to worry."

"Allen, I'm thinking that we should be moving south and might as well leave today. I hope you don't feel that we're rushing away," John said.

"On the contrary, I believe it would be wise for you to leave as soon as we can load your wagon. And if it is not an imposition, I'd like to ride along, at least for a few days."

"Oh, do!" Gloria said. "That is a wonderful idea. I'd love to hear more of your stories about living with Two Rivers's people."

"Your company would be most welcome, Allen," John said.

"It's settled then," Allen said. "After breakfast we'll load the wagon."

Gloria placed a platter of griddlecakes on the table before the men. "It sure is strange how things have worked out. To think back over this past year is almost too much for my mind to fathom." She gave Allen a small smile. "Can you believe all that has come to pass since we left New York?"

"I think about it often." Allen accepted a cup of coffee from John. "I still can't make sense of it. When we're on the trail, remind me to tell you about someone special I've come to know. Her name is Moon Cloud."

Gloria almost dropped the pan of bacon.

CHAPTER TWENTY-EIGHT

ALLEN AND THE LOCKWOODS JOURNEYED southeast into the grassy rolling hills and ravines of the upper prairie. During the two weeks of travel, Gloria peppered Allen with questions about the Arapaho. She couldn't seem to satisfy her inquisitive nature.

"Moon Cloud sounds like a wonderful young woman, the way you describe her, Allen." Gloria sat in the wagon next to her husband. "But what are you going to do about Violet? Aren't you promised to her?"

Allen nodded his head as he rode the buckskin alongside the prairie schooner. "I'm not sure yet. I've written several letters to her but haven't received anything in reply. To be honest, so much has changed for me that I don't believe I have the same feelings for her I once had. It is difficult to imagine Violet Chamberlain out here or in an Arapaho camp."

"Can you imagine her skinning a coyote?" John leaned forward to look Allen in the eye.

Allen burst out laughing. Gloria poked John with her elbow. He responded with a grunt.

"No, I don't suppose I could," Allen said. "Violet was a good fit back in the city, but I don't expect I care to move back there. The wilderness is my home now."

After close to twenty miles, they made camp. Gloria brought out the remaining biscuits from the previous nights' dinner and fried bacon over the campfire while John arranged their bedding on a ground cloth under the wagon. Allen led the horses to water at a small spring and then hobbled them near the wagon.

"Come to the fire; food's ready." Gloria wiped her hands on a light-blue apron. "Allen, I am so glad you've spent these two weeks with us. It has made the travel so much more pleasant."

"Me too. I needed your company more than words can express." Allen savored the bite of bacon. It reminded him of his mother and the family farm.

"What are your plans from here?" John moved a box closer to the fire to sit on.

"I believe I will climb up Scott's Bluff for a time of fasting and prayer. I need to hear from the Lord about what my next steps shall be." Allen's eyes followed the sparks as they rose with the smoke.

"I won't want to say goodbye, my dear friend, but I know it has to be." Gloria's smiling lips quivered. "I hope someday you will find your way to our mission post."

"Lord willing, it will happen soon. But let's save the farewell for morning." Allen's heart felt as warm as the coals. It was a beautiful moment to cherish.

When the sun broke the horizon the next morning, Allen greeted the Lord with praises and petitions. "It's a new day, fit for a new revelation."

Breakfast and packing took only a few minutes. John and Gloria stood side by side as Allen tightened the cinch. He turned to his friends. "It's time. May God bless you richly."

"Oh, Allen." Gloria embraced him tightly. "And may God bless you with wonderful blessings and joy."

He shook hands with John and then swung effortlessly into the saddle. "Farewell."

Swinging Caleb around, he nudged him to a trot and was off to the northeast.

Anxious to hear from the Lord, Allen decided to begin the fast immediately. He'd ride to the top of Scott's Bluff, from where he could overlook the Platte River Valley, running east and west. He'd be above the trail the missionary band had traveled less than a year ago, not so far from where Martha Jolifer had died. Fort Laramie stood about forty miles west. Since time presented no immediate concerns, he believed a day or two of prayer would be appropriate. He could make it a vision quest until he heard from God.

By midafternoon, Allen arrived at the base of Scott's Bluff. Since the sandstone bluff lay several miles long and steep most of the way around, he chose a slope that would lead him to the top. The rugged walls seemed to fashion the mountain into a fortress. He could envision a cathedral with jagged spires.

Once on top, Allen made a campsite. He put Caleb on a stake line and laid out his bedroll. He built a small fire against some big rocks to keep the glow to a minimum. He'd let it burn for only a couple of hours.

The sun set behind clouds on the western horizon. The silver lining against the fair blue background reminded Allen of shining lace, which brought to mind the hope of the glorious riches of discovering God's will. He recited psalms and gave thanks before turning in for the night.

In the deepest part of the night, Allen snapped awake, jarred from a dream that was a whirl of confusion. Though he couldn't remember the actual dream, it left him with a feeling of fear and gloom. Fear of what, he couldn't say. Caleb snorted and stamped.

He moved in an uneasy circle, his ears flicking in every direction. Allen rose and went to check on the stake line and pat his faithful steed on the neck.

"You feel it, too, boy?" Allen said softly. "Do you smell something? Is there a wolf out there, or a cougar?" After waiting for several minutes, Allen couldn't shake the feeling that he was being watched or stalked. The eeriness reminded him of the demon-possessed girl back in Portsmouth.

With his rifle cradled in his arms, Allen circled the camp area, spreading wider and wider with each pass. He declared aloud, "Lord Jesus, you are the Living One, the Lamb that was slain and lives again. It is you whom I serve and whom I worship. I praise your holy name."

His voice grew louder as he circled, as if he were preaching to a large crowd. He prayed like this until a band of light seeped over the eastern horizon. He didn't know when, but the oppressive feeling was gone.

Leaning against a rock, he read from the gospel of Mark as the morning sun climbed higher in the sky. At times, Allen walked to the northern rim of the bluff to look across the valley at the green belt of trees along the river.

He meditated on the significance of "believing," as Saint Mark described the works of Jesus. He read the many accounts of healings and demonic deliverance brought about by faith, either that of the person being healed or of their friends. Jesus's many encounters with the Pharisees and teachers of the law were admonitions of their mistaken belief system. The Messiah stood right in front of them, but they refused to accept him or believe him.

How could Allen teach a new belief to the Arapaho or any other people? Would it require miracles and healings, or would they understand his teaching? *Why isn't God answering? What happens next?*

Even though the hunger pangs gnawed at him throughout the day, Allen resisted the temptation to take a bite of jerky and ease the discomfort. The point was self-denial and humility in order to hear a clear message from God. He ignored the temptations and continued praying.

When the sun settled below the western hills, he fell asleep, half expecting to be awakened again by the oppressive wave of fear. If it did come, he would arise and rebuke it again, even if it took a few hours. Sleep was not as important as the revelation he sought.

Allen snapped awake after a vivid dream. He'd been riding his horse through familiar country near Two Rivers's camp, when a black wolf charged him, snarling and snapping—out for blood. His horse bolted. Allen fell off, and the wolf lunged toward him but stopped and crouched a short distance from him. The black wolf's fangs dripped with saliva. With lips pulled back, revealing a set of large sharp teeth, it growled and continued to snap. The yellow eyes blazed with loathing, yet the wolf didn't advance.

Allen woke up, sweating and panting, scared yet feeling strangely safe in the knowledge that the wolf attack was hindered.

He rose and rebuked the spirit of fear and intimidation. When daylight came, he stood at the edge of the bluff with his arms raised high. He shouted praise to God and blessed the people of the land. The sun had reached its nine o'clock point when Allen's intercession faded. Kneeling down with his head bowed low to the ground, his mind quiet, his spirit still, he heard the word.

It didn't come as an audible voice, but a very clear impression that flowed up from his heart. The simple message was pregnant with meaning: "Go now."

He knew at once that he was to ride toward Fort Laramie, and he would discover his next step on the way. Allen thanked the Lord, broke his little camp, and rode down to the valley below.

It didn't even matter to Allen if he ended up staying at the mission at Laramie. He would be doing God's will, not his own or anyone else's. His desire was to be obedient, not selfish. He would go wherever God led him.

Allen rode down the south side of Scott's Bluff and worked his way over the breaks and rolling hills, angling toward the North Platte River, where he'd find the trail. He cleared one draw and dropped down into another, a more sharply sloped canyon that opened up to the north. Just as Allen cleared the high brush, he glanced toward the river and saw a wagon about three hundred yards away traveling east. He couldn't see the whole wagon, just the white canopy and the backs of the oxen. Seeing the travelers gave hope of news from the post.

As Allen approached, he saw two covered wagons, and not wanting to cause alarm, he slowed. He waved and moved forward when the driver waved back and pulled to a stop.

"Good morning, folks," he said. "I'm on my way to Fort Laramie and was wondering if you might have news."

"Well, we was through there about five days ago, but only stayed long enough to pick up supplies. Didn't find the folks too friendly. Maybe you'll be treated better," the man said. A scowl etched his face. Reddened by the sun except for where a full beard covered his round face, he slouched on the seat, clearly not interested in talking. His plump wife hunched next to him. Her eyes looked dull under a dirty sunbonnet.

Another man, the driver of the second wagon, walked forward. Tall and gaunt but willing to talk. "Morning. Pleasant day for traveling, don't you say?"

Before Allen could respond, he continued.

"Sure beats the rain. I get so tired of tracking in the mud. I like a nice clean camp, and the mud makes it messy. Name's Plumley, and this is Gast. We've been up north on the Powder River, but now we're heading back to St. Louis. Them redskins are too ornery. Couldn't get a cabin built or a farm started—they kept stealing from us. Lucky to get out of there with these oxen."

"You say you were setting up a farm, trying to settle up there?" Allen shifted in his saddle.

"We were going to farm there by Father DeSmet's mission. Them Crow Indians put up a fuss. They even killed our other partner, Vance. That's when we decided it was best to pull up and head back to the States."

"That's too bad. I'm sorry to hear about your friend," Allen said.

"He was young too. Sad thing is, he left a wife and child behind. They're both laying back in the other wagon. Sick with grief. I ain't never seen anything like it. They're so upset, they broke out with a fever and a rash. Both of 'em. Strangest thing I ever saw." Plumley kept talking, but Gast just sat, scowling. "I didn't get your name."

"I'm Allen Hartman. I'm heading for Fort Laramie right now to continue my work."

"Hartman? Ain't you that Methodist preacher we heard about? They said there was a Methodist preacher who captured stolen horses." Plumley recounted the story with animation.

Allen smiled.

"They said you snuck in and killed a dozen redskins single handed and then brought them horses back."

Allen's smile faded.

Gast glanced at Allen, then stared at his hands, grumbling.

"No. That's not the way it happened." Allen feared a terrible rumor was spreading.

"Yes, snuck right in there and killed them redskins an' took the horses back. I say I'd like to get my horse back. I'm tired of sitting all day long," Plumley said.

"Let me clarify for you that I did not kill any Indians, and there were two other men with me." This outrageous story had obviously gotten out of hand.

"How many horses was there? A hundred? That's what they told us up at Two Rivers's village. A hundred horses. That's good work, I'll say." Plumley beamed, as if he wanted to give Allen a medal.

Allen perked at hearing of his friend. "You were at Two Rivers's camp, up on Horse Tooth Creek?" Maybe this unusual character was God's instrument to give him a word of instruction.

"Yes, we was up there about two weeks ago. We stayed with him for a few days. They were good to us. Gave us food and blankets. They even took special care of Vance's woman and the girl," Plumley said.

"You must have arrived the same day I left. Did you meet Blue Otter?"

"Blue Otter. Yes, I think he's the one who spoke American. He's the one who told us about you. He was very helpful. He even knew Father DeSmet."

Allen doubted that Blue Otter would have told the story of the horse rescue with the added details. "How was Two Rivers?"

"That old man was real nice, but then he started to do some strange dancing and moaning over Vance's wife, shaking a rattle, and he wanted to give her a special tea or something. We decided that he was a witch doctor and didn't think it was right to let him go on, so we left the next morning."

Allen searched the man's face for some element of prudence. How could he explain this behavior to Two Rivers?

"Perhaps I could see Mrs. Vance and give her a word of encouragement," Allen said.

"Guess it won't hurt nothing." Plumley waved for Allen to follow him. "If it breaks her out of her grief, it will make this trip more pleasant."

Allen nodded to Gast and his wife and rode behind Plumley to the second wagon. Allen dismounted, then held back the canvas. The air was hot and smelled of sickness. The woman and girl were lying on a bed that had been made on top of a row of supply boxes. The pair looked uncomfortable, though the girl appeared to be asleep. The woman's eyes were open, but she stared vacantly at the canvas. They both looked miserable—their faces were covered with sweat and reddish spots. This wasn't grieving.

Smallpox.

"They've been like this since you were up on the Powder?"

"Yes, since Vance was killed. I told you they've been sick since he died. I guess they feel hopeless," the gaunt-faced Plumley said.

"This is smallpox," Allen said, trying to keep the exasperation from his voice. "The reason the Crows ran you off was because of smallpox. Vance probably had it. Now his wife and daughter do. The rest of you might be carrying the disease as well. That's why they didn't want you to stay at Laramie. How long did you say you were at Two Rivers's camp?"

"Two or three days. Why?"

"Smallpox is likely to sweep through an Indian village and kill a good number of people. It happened in Wisconsin and Missouri. It's likely that you've infected a lot of people. This woman and girl will probably not make it clear to St. Louis. If either one survives, they might go blind. They need medicine right away. I truly hope it goes well for you."

Moon Cloud! Two Rivers! Allen mounted and raced away, hoping and praying that the disease was not silently working its deadly way through the camp.

CHAPTER TWENTY-NINE

ALLEN RODE HARD. HE HAD no thought but to reach the village and make a difference, then reason slowed him to a moderate pace. He had to formulate a plan. He would ride to Fort Laramie, check on the mission and his packhorses, and then in the morning supply himself for Horse Tooth Creek. Surely there would be news at the trading post, and then hopefully he'd find Two Rivers, Blue Otter, Moon Cloud, and the others safe. But deep within his heart, he feared the worst.

Riding into the Laramie Valley a couple of hours before night-fall, he went straight to the post. News spread quickly over the frontier. One rider told another, one trader told another, and so on until word reached the post.

Meecer smiled when Allen entered the building, but when the subject of Plumley and Gast came up, he had nothing good to say. "Fools" was the kindest name he had for them.

"The word is that the pox killed some folks there in Two Rivers's village," Meecer said. "I don't know any names in particular, only that they moved the camp and left many to die."

Allen had heard reports that in the past ten years, smallpox had claimed the lives of millions of people and had decimated many tribes. The natives had no resistance to the disease. They lived under harsh conditions and ate food that most white folks would never touch. They took herbal medicine that would bleach the stain out of a white shirt. But they were devastated by diseases like measles and smallpox that some whites could survive. Allen had been vaccinated with the missionary band before they'd left New York.

Allen fought the twisting and churning in his belly. "I'm inclined to ride up there and find them. Where do you think Two Rivers will be camped?"

"Before you go riding into their camp," Meecer said, "remember that they've just been hurt bad by white men. Their friendliness was repaid with death. They just might try to kill you. They won't trust you now, not even Two Rivers. Best let things lie low for a while, until the vengeance anger is wore off."

"I don't know what to do. It wounds my heart deeply to lose their trust."

No one ran out to greet him as he approached the abandoned camp.

Caleb's ears laid back, and he fought the reins. The mule refused to go another step. Allen tied the animals and walked the rest of the way.

In another hundred yards, it became evident why the horses refused to come closer. The stench of death emanated through the trees.

No amount of warning or description could have prepared Allen for what he walked into. Coming into the clearing, a deathly stillness reached him. No people, animals, coyotes, or vultures. The place stood void of any smoke or breeze. A shroud of death and stark loneliness blanketed the area.

The Death Spirit had not just swept through as it would during a battle, but it lingered over the community that had once rejoiced in life.

Allen choked back bile that rose in his throat. He pulled out a handkerchief and crumbled sage and pine needles into it, then folded it and tied it around his nose and mouth. It proved a meager protection from the nauseating odor that hung in the air. As he trudged through the village's skeleton, Allen recognized the positions of the tipis still standing, and he could picture where others had been. Thirteen tipis remained, most standing, doorways closed. A few had collapsed.

Body remains left by scavengers lay to one side. He peered into the nearest tipi and saw what appeared to be a mother and two children. Vultures and crows had been at them. Repulsed, he moved on, trying to breathe fresh air but not finding any. He forced himself to think clearly, else he feared his mind would spin out of control. He checked each of the lodges and found bodies in every one. Some had been covered under buffalo robes and were more intact, yet still hideous and unrecognizable. Overwhelming pain consumed him. Allen's heart cried under the burden of sorrow, shame, guilt, and remorse.

He froze at the sight he feared most. A sealed tipi bore the familiar markings of Blue Otter's lodge, Allen's former home.

"No! No! Oh, Lord, it can't be."

He lingered at the buffalo-hide doorway and with shaking hands untied the rawhide thongs. Opening the flap, he hesitated before leaning in. He did not want to see the body of his friend, but he had to be sure. Three small bodies lay under a robe. None of them was Blue Otter. It was a small relief, but he would not be comforted until he saw his friends alive. These three children may have been nephews and nieces of Two Rivers or someone else's children. It didn't matter—it was utter sadness by any account.

Three lodges remained—one belonged to Long Spear's family. He slowly pulled back the flap. "No. No. Please, God." He dropped to his knees before the body of Moon Cloud. He recognized her by the design of the beads on her dress. Her face was so disfigured by disease and death that Allen closed his eyes so he would remember her pretty smile and charming laugh. Next to her lay both parents. They had died together.

Sadness and grief pierced deeply. He sat back in the dirt. His and Moon Cloud's paths would never cross again. Meeting Moon Cloud had been like discovering a new part of his heart, like a spring of clear cool water. His courtship with Violet Chamberlain had never produced such an emotion.

He forced himself to check all the tipis. In the last one, he found more dead bodies, mostly children. He staggered to the creek to drink and wash. But the stench of death did not wash away, nor did the shock. The cold water sharpened the horror of the grim scene. Allen vomited until his stomach, already empty from fasting, seized him with pain.

He emerged from the water and dry heaved on the rocks. "Oh, God . . . Oh, my Lord Jesus." He wept, his heart breaking.

No birds sang, no squirrels chattered, only the gurgling creek offered any sign of life. After Allen had no more tears, he washed again and drank slowly. Exhausted, he forced himself to move. He would set up a camp away from the smell and spend the rest of daylight gathering firewood.

Late into the night, Allen stared into the fire, watching but not seeing it die into glowing coals. Occasionally, he'd toss in a sprig of sage and let the smoke wash over him. The sounds of village laughter, chatting, and songs echoed in his head. While pounding a thick branch on the earth, he sang as best as he could the mournful chant of a death song. But it didn't satisfy his soul's need to grieve.

Rising early the next morning, Allen strolled along the creek, searching for a high cutaway bank. He found a section that would serve his purpose. The creek wound its way to the river with many sharp turns. He chose a point with a six-foot-high bank where the water no longer flowed. The curve formed a corner about forty-five-feet wide.

Allen led the mule to drag dry wood bundles and logs to the cut bank. For two days he tossed wood into the corner until it was full.

The third day, Allen dragged forty lodge poles from the forest several miles away, stacking them along the top of the bank.

On the fourth day, he fastened the poles to the firewood to form a support wall. Then he lashed horizontal poles as rails along the top.

The fifth day, Allen tied poles across the top of the firewood from the dirt bank to the support wall to make a rustic platform. He walked across to make certain it would bear the weight of many dead. The funeral pyre was complete.

On day six, weak and weary, Allen pleaded for strength to finish. He had to honor his friends who had been so unfairly victimized by the stupidity of travelers who didn't know they had devastated a village. He fought against a growing anger with Plumley and Gast by forgiving them over and over in his heart. Their ignorance was costly, but perhaps they were paying with their lives out on the prairie.

Again, covering his face with the handkerchief, Allen went through the village, from lodge to lodge, pulling out the swollen, decaying remains of a once joyful tribe. He cut out sections of hide from the sides of the tipis to cover each individual. He bound them with rawhide cord and strips of hide. The firewood travois rigged to the mule acted as a primitive hearse, carrying the deceased to the burial ground. One by one, sometimes two, and painfully, three small children, he moved the bodies and reverently laid them on the funeral platform. Allen didn't stop until all forty-seven were in place.

The last he brought was the body of Moon Cloud. Allen picked bundles of wildflowers and sage to set upon her buffalo-hide casket. He spread flowers on the three children found in Blue Otter's lodge.

During the final hours of the day, the grieving missionary pulled down the tipis, meat racks, and any remnants of the village. He dragged the contaminated skins and poles to one side of the firewood platform and scattered every rock pile and fire circle. When the camp was gone, Allen dragged himself to bed and surrendered to fatigue.

On the morning of the seventh day, the sun lit a still-overcast sky. The grayness reflected his soul.

Standing on the bank, the Reverend Allen Hartman presented the dead to their creator. They would return to the Great Father in the smoke of prayer—an offering of the meek and poor in spirit. He quoted Psalm 23. "Though I walk through valley of the shadow of death, I will fear no evil . . ."

Allen placed bundles of dry grass and leaves in several places at the base of the firewood altar. He twisted a wad of grass into a knot, poured gunpowder on it, and lit the rustic torch. Moving from one bundle of tinder to another, he set the wood to burning. The crackling soon turned to a rush and then to a roar as the flames worked their way up through the tangle of dry wood. Certain that the blaze would continue, Allen moved away.

"O Lord, forgive us for our sins and injustices against these people. Theirs was an undeserved death. Yet only you are wise and can redeem this land. Bring new life, Lord. Restore life to the Arapaho and to this land. Please, Lord, heal the land."

The flames reached thirty, then forty feet into the air. It was not a demon flame that mocked him but a cleansing fire that lifted the cherished offering in the smoke and sparks higher and higher into the sky.

The intense heat consumed wood, hides, flesh, and bone. By late afternoon it had run its course. All that remained was a great pile of ashes, charred rocks, and dirt.

On the eighth day, the day of new beginnings, Allen washed in the river. He would continue the fast, aware that his body was weakened by the lack of food and the days of labor. Believing that his mind was clear and his attitude hopeful, even optimistic, he returned his attention to discovering God's will.

The physical strain of the burial aided his grieving, bringing to his soul a measure of refreshing peace. His act of kindness, he sensed, was at the same time prophetic. God had used him as an intermediary, someone who stood in the gap for those lost through injustice. It had not been God's judgment of doom on Two Rivers's village but rather the consequence of sin and evil in the world. Allen had ministered unto the Lord as a priest bringing reconciliation of spirit and restoration of hope to the land. Much more, so much more, needed to be done to right the wrongs and heal the wounds.

A spirit of darkness suffocated the land because of the defilement of sinful men bound in snares of temptation. Men were given over to their lusts of the flesh and greed for the world's distractions. Blood had been shed on the land, yet there had been no one, no priest, to represent the sanctifying blood of the Savior. For God to heal the land, an intercessor was always required in the ministry of reconciliation.

Allen's heart quickened with the understanding that illuminated his spirit and mind. He wanted to spend time, holy time, with his heavenly Father, but he didn't feel clean. Washing with cold creek water had refreshed him momentarily and cleaned his skin, but the stains of death remained.

He stripped off his buckskin clothing, and wearing nothing more than a loincloth, Allen built a rough sweat lodge. He tied saplings and brush together and then lashed them to stakes in the ground to form the dome. Aligning the doorway to the east, Allen designed the hut as respectfully as he could. He didn't bother with other details but covered it with his buffalo robe and a blanket. Building a fire outside the small lodge, he heated stones, of which seven would go into the center ring. There he would pour water onto the stones, creating steam in which he would sit, breathe, and pray.

The thick air caused him to breathe slowly and carefully. This would have seemed strange to him a year ago. Allen rarely practiced the discipline of silence and stillness, but now he found it refreshing. Back in the hustling city, his devotional practice included daily Bible readings and prayers. But these present circumstances were far removed from his previous life and understanding. The desire for wisdom and revelation, to be in God's confidence, required a spiritual effort that was beyond intellectual knowledge of God's Word.

Sitting in a lumpy imitation of an Arapaho sweat lodge didn't bother Allen's sense of propriety or his yearning to listen to the Holy Ghost. There wasn't a church or cathedral within five hundred miles of Horse Tooth Creek. The sweat cleansed his body, the steam symbolized his rising prayers, and the dome represented the circle of the universe, but those were not his concerns. Allen sought the face of God with all his heart.

Peering out the small door flap, he saw his shadow stick, a crude sundial, and guessed that an hour had passed. He crawled out of the tiny hut and found a deep spot in the creek. Lying down, he allowed the frigid stream to sweep over his body for about five seconds. Then shouting and gasping for breath, he stumbled to shore. Allen squatted in a ball until he caught his breath. Then forcing himself to stand, lest he succumb to cramping, he reached toward the heavens and shouted, "Hallelujah!" After the full body spasms subsided to mere shivering, he wrapped a doe hide over his shoulders. Sitting on the grass, he read from the book of Isaiah. Every couple of hours, after reheating the seven stones, he entered the sweat lodge for an hour and then emerged for a cold rinse.

The next day he repeated the practice, only varying his pattern by reading from Jeremiah. In the afternoon, he caught the singing of a few birds—the first he'd heard in days.

On the third day, Allen entered the sweat lodge three times. While reading about Ezekiel's vision of the valley of dry bones, the young missionary was inspired with a new gift of faith.

"Yes, Lord. You alone can give life to the dry bones. You are the Life-Giving One. O Lord, I see now that you will indeed restore life to these people. You will raise up a holy remnant among the Arapaho. You will heal the land. Oh, thank you, Father. Thank you, Great Father."

Allen stood, and with his hands lifted toward heaven, he praised God.

He dismantled the sweat lodge. He burned the old garments he'd worn during the burial week—the ones Jack Burkett had given him many months before. He dressed in the elk skins Two Rivers's wife had made for him.

Walking through the site of the former village, Allen was pleased with the work he'd done. Even if Two Rivers's band didn't take him back soon, he'd done what needed to be done. In that peace, he looked forward to the day of reconciliation.

The wide black stain of scorched earth remained. "Lord, cannot the stain be washed away?" he prayed. He walked back to his little camp, restaked the horse and mule, and tied a canvas sheet between two cottonwood trees. He started a small fire, and for the first time in ten days, he ate. While waiting for his coffee to boil, Allen leaned back on a rock, chewed the savory venison jerky, and counted the stars as they poked through the broken clouds.

Scouts had seen Allen on the first day back in the valley. They alerted Two Rivers, who came with a few others to see what the missionary might do. They would not approach their former encampment because of the Spirit of Death, which still frightened them. They could not comprehend why the white man would return. Was he a fool? Could he not see that Death waited to take another? They watched as he attended to the dead, intent on every detail that demonstrated respect to these people. The Arapaho wondered at this act of caring for the dead of those who were not his people.

Two Rivers had loved Allen, but when the others came claiming to be missionaries of the same Christ, Two Rivers's people suffered a terrible fate. The running-face sickness had claimed many. Was it punishment from their tribal spirits for welcoming a white man into his village and even into his own lodge? Tribal law demanded blood vengeance. The scouts believed that it was right for this white man to die as a traitor. Two Rivers held them back. They watched.

Allen had come back, defying the Death Spirit and touching the bodies of their loved ones. The great fire freed the souls of the unfortunate who had died.

Joy crept back into Two Rivers's heart at the faithfulness of the one he called friend and son. This white missionary loved his Arapaho brothers and his God. Why else would he do such a noble thing? Why would he go so long without food and pray in a sweat lodge? Yes, Allen could be trusted.

As a tear rolled down the old man's cheek, he whispered a prayer to the Great Spirit. "Great One, this one says many strange things and acts in strange ways. He honors us as he honors you. Return him to favor among the spirits. Keep him strong on the path that will test him in greater darkness. Thank you for sending this one to my camp."

During the night, the clouds burst open, loosing a powerful rain. Grateful for the lean-to but unable to sleep, Allen waited out the night.

At daylight he checked the creek. It looked normal sized, but the debris and mud gave evidence that the water had risen during the unrelenting storm.

After a breakfast of pinion nuts and jerky, Allen walked to where the funeral platform had burned and left the deep black scar on the earth. He saw the indent, but the black stain had been washed away.

"Thank you, Lord. Thank you for this sign of your grace."

When his canvas and blankets had dried, Allen packed and rode along the river. "Well, Caleb. What do you say we go for an elk hunt down around Laramie Peak?"

When the scout told Dark Wolf that White Falcon had returned, fear leaped into his heart. He stomped into the cave and with a war club released his anger against his bound slaves.

The witch moved into the firelight. "What vexes you? The white man? You know what to do. Draw him by his ignorance, and you will capture him. Capture him, and you take his power."

Dark Wolf's lips curled into a snarling smile. The witch sat by him at the fire and began singing. Dark Wolf sent his spirit into the underworld.

"Send an elk to the hunter," the spirit guide said.

CHAPTER THIRTY

THE GAME TRAIL LED ALLEN to a canyon in the foothills northwest of Laramie Peak, a prime place for elk to bed down at midafternoon. Taking a moment to choose his way, Allen caught movement far across the grassy canyon, some four or five hundred yards away. A rider—no—two riders with packhorses were moving among the scrub pines along the far side. Upright in their saddles, he identified them as white men. In fact, something about these riders was familiar. Jack Burkett and Joaquin Del Castillo. Allen angled into the canyon to meet them.

When he came into view, the two mountain men paused. Upon recognizing a friend and not a threat, they urged their mounts forward.

Allen kicked his buckskin into a trot across the grassy field.

"Wagh! Out of wilderness rides a welcome stranger. The Reverend Allen Hartman," Jack shouted. "Once a tender pilgrim and now the shepherd of a wilderness flock. What say, Pastor Hartman? Have you tamed the mountain sheep?"

"I've tamed all but two." Allen smiled.

Jack laughed and Joaquin grinned from ear to ear. The three dismounted and greeted one another with bear hugs.

"I can see that you've come a fair piece, Allen. You have the look of the mountain in your eyes," Jack said.

"Well, I feel like I've crossed the mountain and then some."

"What's the news from Fort Laramie? How are those other missionaries holding out? And what about that fair lass, Miss Shannon?" Jack asked as he lit his pipe.

Allen recounted the winter's events and subsequent challenges. He hoped that sharing his feelings with Jack and Joaquin would free his heart from the burden of burying Moon Cloud and disappointing Two Rivers. It didn't.

"Guess I'm not entirely sure of where my next steps will take me." Allen's weary eyes sought an answer along the western horizon.

"That's an interesting turn of affairs, I'd say." Jack scratched the stubble of his angular jaw. "Sounds to me like you could use some inspiration. This is too fine a day to have your soul in a quandary." Turning to his quiet companion, he said, "Compadre, what say we lead Allen down to Shining Canyon?"

"Good idea." Joaquin mounted his horse.

"Shining Canyon?" Allen said. "I don't mean for you to go out of your way, but I do appreciate the company."

"Don't worry yourself, Parson. We can use the inspiration ourselves," Jack said.

Eight or nine miles to the south, after climbing a long grade, they came around the shoulder of the mountain. Breaking through a line of trees, they emerged onto a rocky slope. Boulders pushed through the grass. They rode down to a shelf where they could see into the basin. The canyon bowl was a mile and half across with granite spires jutting around the rim. A spring flowed in the bottom of the basin, surrounded by aspen trees with budding, green leaves and shining white trunks. The trunks of the Ponderosa pines glowed red as the afternoon sun shone right up the west-facing canyon.

Allen gasped at the beauty.

"La Catedral de Luz. The Cathedral of Light." That was all Joaquin said—it was all he needed to say. The name captured the brilliance of what their eyes beheld. The clouds shifted colors from puffy white to shades of pink, red, and orange on a field of royal blue.

Jack and Joaquin stepped onto a rock ledge. Jack stretched out his arms and recited Psalm 95. "O come, let us sing unto the LORD: let us make a joyful noise to the rock of our salvation."

Allen joined in the spontaneous worship. "Let us come before his presence with thanksgiving, and make a joyful noise unto him with psalms."

Joaquin smiled at Allen and joined in the chorus. "For the LORD is a great God, and a great King above all gods. In his hand are the deep places of the earth: the strength of the hills is his also. For he is our God; and we are the people of his pasture, and the sheep of his hand."

Jack sat next to Allen, and they watched the colors change and the shadows grow long.

"Thanks for bringing me here, Jack. You were right—I did need some inspiration."

"You need to feel small for the right reasons sometimes," Jack said. "Humility before God is inspirational, but feeling weak under a burden is a hardship to the soul."

Joaquin abruptly rose and moved into the cover of the trees.

"We best get over to the horses," Jack said.

Uncovering their rifles and checking the primers, they waited until Joaquin returned with a report. He trotted out of the trees and nodded, signaling that someone was coming, but they were safe.

"The Prophet comes." Joaquin's keen sense of hearing had picked out an unusual sound that Allen had yet to hear.

Jack sighed. "This will be interesting for you, Parson."

In another moment, Allen heard a sound that grew to a bellowing, deep voice, like rolling thunder. He knitted his brows.

"He's the Prophet Elijah. Trappers call him that because he wanders in the wilderness shouting prophecies and preaching, although I doubt he went to seminary. Knows the Bible even better than Old Jedediah Smith."

Allen could make out the words being shouted for all creation to hear even before he laid eyes on the eccentric mountain preacher.

"Hear ye, all creatures, the Lord your God, the Almighty Jehovah, is the Great God. Clap your hands, ye trees. Shout for joy, ye stones! Behold the glory of the Mighty One." He rode through the trees into the clearing, waving his hand in a sign of peace. The stout man's full beard reached his chest, and his silver hair hung below a raccoon-skin cap. His elk-skin clothes were dyed black. He dismounted from a tall, mottled Appaloosa and dropped the reins.

"Thank you, Lord, for making your will evident," he said. "Greetings, brothers. I come in the name of the Almighty God, Jehovah."

"Welcome you are, Elijah. Will you join us for an evening meal?" Jack extended his arm toward the fire.

"I shall," he boomed, "but only if you allow me to add to the coffers. I've some beaver tail taken fresh this morning. I'd be glad to share with the servants of the Lord." He pulled a leather bag off his small bay packhorse, handed it to Joaquin, and walked straight for Allen, looking him in the eye.

"This is the man of God. The Gospels teach that the Lord Jesus sent out his workers two by two to cast out demons, yet you stand alone. The Lord be praised, for his ways are not the ways of man. His thoughts are not our thoughts. His plans are not our plans. His wisdom is great and far beyond the understanding of mere man."

The gaze from Elijah's gray eyes penetrated deep into Allen's heart. It was not unlike the feeling he'd experienced around Two Rivers, but this mountain prophet spoke Scripture familiar to Allen. "Amen" was all he could muster.

"We're coming up from the Green River, bound for the post on the Laramie with some furs we cached," Jack broke in. "Where have your travels taken you, Elijah?"

Turning to the fire, which Jack was fanning to life, Elijah said, "I been up north, into Canada. Now I be traveling south along the Continental Divide, prophesying to the land. Troublesome times are coming to these parts. The good Lord is telling me to speak peace to the land where much warring and change are coming."

"You're a bit east of the Divide to be here with us," Jack said.

"The Lord has detoured me." He nodded at Allen. "Let's sing us a hymn whilst the tails are roasting." He stood and turned toward the last of the setting sun, and with a strong baritone voice, he sang in perfect key.

Allen knew the Methodist hymn "O For a Thousand Tongues to Sing." Singing aloud like this was common to Allen. He gave it his all but was astonished he barely heard his own strong voice because the curious old man's voice overshadowed his. Jack and Joaquin listened and minded the roasting meat.

"Hear him ye deaf, his praise ye dumb, your loosened tongues employ. Ye blind, behold your Savior come, and leap ye lame for joy!" Elijah's voice filled the basin with praise to God. Allen fell silent, inwardly rejoicing that God would send a ministering angel in the middle of the wilderness. His soul filled with wonder and peace.

After making a meal of the beaver tails and sun-dried huckleberries, Elijah went off alone.

Allen sat by the fire, comfortable against the growing chill of the spring night. "It's been a rather remarkable day, I'd say."

"I have a feeling it's not over for you, Allen," Joaquin said.

Allen looked at the chiseled face across the fire from him. When

Joaquin ventured to make a comment, it made sense to listen.

The prophet returned into the glow of the fire. Sitting on a rock near Allen, he stared at the flames. "The Lord saith, 'Be strong; take courage! For you will enter into the depths of the horrible pit. You will be caught in the miry clay, but he will set your foot on the solid rock. Be strong; take courage! You will enter the darkness, but behold, the light will come to you. You will win the victory if you do not give up.' Thus saith the Lord." With that he said no more.

Allen wanted to ask what the prophecy meant, but he sensed no answer would be given. Horrible pit? He had just been through one horrible pit when he buried the dead. Why did he have to face another? Enter the darkness? Allen felt his pulse quicken. He took a long, slow breath. The looming mystery made him weary. Maybe in a few days he would understand the grim words.

At daybreak, Allen was alone, though the fire still burned. The tracks told him that his comrades had left an hour ago. The basin that had been glorious the evening before remained in the shadow of the eastern rim. Allen packed up to continue his hunt and eventually make his way back to Fort Laramie. It still wasn't clear what he'd do next. The strange words of Prophet Elijah hung in his mind as he rode out of the basin.

A couple of hours later, Allen's stomach growled, pulling his thoughts to his surroundings. The wind picked up, carrying with it a prickling cold. He studied the sky. Gray clouds formed overhead. They weren't the clouds that held a soft spring shower; rather, they were more like dark winter clouds filled with heavy rains or even snow and sleet.

Allen thought it might be prudent to look for shelter. He doubted he'd find game in this foul wind.

Just then a spike bull elk broke out of a brushy creek bottom fifty yards away. It leaped over a bush and then stopped broadside, presenting an easy target. Allen quickly removed his musket cover, took aim, and fired. Certain of his shot, he saw the young elk stagger and then bolt forward. It dropped out of sight in a ravine where Allen expected to find it dead.

But then the elk came out the other side and ran around the shoulder of a ridge and beyond his sight. Allen reloaded as he rode and watched the ground, looking for the blood trail. He found splatters on brush in several places. The pinkish specks in the blood indicated a solid lung shot, so the elk would not run far.

When Allen rounded the shoulder, he could see into the next draw. There was the elk standing still and nibbling grass. This time he dismounted and tied Caleb to a tree. Carefully stalking to within thirty yards of the wounded elk, he saw a blood spot on its ribs—a perfect shot. He aimed again and fired. When the smoke cleared, he caught sight of the elk trotting deeper into the draw. What in the world? Two solid hits. *Why isn't that thing falling?* Allen found the elk's tracks and blood splashes. He followed on foot.

Stopping under a tree along the side of a creek, Allen wondered if he should go back to get his horse. The wind gusted and sent a shiver down his neck.

If he wanted the elk, he'd have to stay on the trail before the blood washed away. His eye caught the elk's white rump moving through some brush ahead. Allen hurried forward, but just then the coal-colored clouds released their fury. Buckets of icy rain fell.

The elk would have to wait. He followed the small creek toward a rock wall where the water pooled and seeped underground. Stepping around a low boulder, he discovered a cave opening. He sidestepped through the narrow, jagged crack to get out of the rain.

Allen moved into the cave and leaned against the rock wall. It looked deep, and he thought he might explore if he had a torch. He squatted to read the dirt but saw no bear or cougar tracks. Outside, a thick fog smothered the canyon. He watched the rain, discouraged the elk would be harder to find. Why hadn't it dropped right away?

After several minutes, it was evident that the downpour wasn't going to let up anytime soon. He peered into the dark cave and took a few steps deeper in, stopping to let his eyes adjust. The cave opened into a larger passageway that angled slightly downward and appeared to go far into the mountain. Allen stopped and glanced back at the opening. Still raining.

From behind Allen, deep within the darkness, came a whisper of sound. Straining, he heard it again. His heart pounded. He stood, holding his rifle at his hip, thumb on the hammer, ready to cock. Then he inched into the black passageway. The farther in he stepped, the more he sensed a presence in the darkness with him. Swallowing hard, he carefully placed each footstep. A sound, a soft murmur, steadily grew.

He distinguished a dim light ahead. The faint glow cast flickering shadows against the cave wall. With a few more steps forward, Allen came to a corner to his left. He peeked around it. A small fire burned in a wider space. No one was in sight, but the murmuring increased. It sounded like moaning and whimpering.

Curiosity overcame his yearning to flee. Allen stepped around the corner and past the fire into the shadowy chamber beyond. Another step forward and he bumped something, not hard like a rock, but soft. He squatted and strained his eyes. He reached out his left hand and touched a bare leg. Allen fell back. The firelight cast a glow on a skeletal head with sunken eyes and a gaping mouth. The starved being leaned forward. What hideous creature was this?

Allen pressed back against the cave wall, trying to put distance between him and the dark figure, whose shriveled arms stretched toward him.

Allen forced himself to look at the creature. He froze when he realized it was a person bound with heavy cords.

The captive uttered a grotesque, gagging chatter.

Another shadow person appeared and leaned toward Allen. Allen was unable to breathe, his blood rushed in his ears, and his stomach did somersaults. He stumbled back toward the fire—to something he could see and touch, some kind of familiar reality.

Gasping for air, he stared back at the dark hole, a hidden closet of revulsion. Allen clenched his fists—his hands were empty! His heart raced and his knees went weak. He'd dropped his rifle back there. He couldn't leave his rifle. He had no choice but to summon the courage and retrieve it.

Allen spun around at the noise behind him.

A small man moved into the fire's glow. With a quick motion, the Indian tossed something into the fire, which then flared. In the brightness Allen saw that the Indian wore only a loincloth. Black and white stripes marked his body. A dark-red streak that ran from his mouth down to his chest shone in the firelight. The man laughed and pointed toward the slaves of darkness. He moved around the fire as Allen backtracked toward his escape, back to the cave opening and the rain.

The Indian spoke, then reached behind a rock and pulled up a black wolfskin.

Dark Wolf!

Allen faced the cruel witch doctor, the archenemy of Two Rivers and the purveyor of death. His dark deeds were responsible for the deaths of many people, both Indian and white, including Martha Jolifer.

Knees trembling, Allen swallowed hard and forced his breathing to normal. He worked to keep his mind focused. Too late he realized he had been lured into the domain of terror.

Dark Wolf laughed as understanding came to his foe. He spat an invective that Allen couldn't comprehend. It wasn't Arapaho, but sounded otherworldly. The witch doctor reached behind his back and pulled out a large rattlesnake head to which several rattles were attached by a cord. He shook it, shouting more unintelligible words.

Allen took a few small steps backward; he would have to leave his gun.

Then as if in a surreal dream, the cave floor and walls began writhing.

Rattlesnakes slithered out of rocks and cracks in every part of the cavern. The fire flared again. Allen stared at Dark Wolf's display of power.

Allen forced a prayer. "Lord Jesus, help me."

Twenty or more rattling, hissing serpents cut off his way of escape. The memory of the snakes that had bitten Martha Jolifer flashed through his mind. He looked at the sorcerer surrounded by venomous reptiles whose rattles were silent as they slithered across his feet.

Dark Wolf spoke softly, and something moved beside Allen. Seeming to appear out of the air, a small woman shrouded in black stood before him. White, wiry hair scratched her shoulders. Black lips and eyes were stark against her ashen face. She held out a hand, palm up, and blew white powder into Allen's face. He gasped in surprise, breathing in the dust.

Allen twisted first one way then the next, searching for a way through the snakes to push past Dark Wolf and reach his gun.

The fire flared, reaching the cave ceiling. The flames turned blood red. The snakes undulated. The walls melted. Dark Wolf's face spun by, faster and faster. The witch's face joined the swirling illusion. Allen reached out to steady himself, but he clutched only air.

He felt the impact of the cavern floor, yet he registered no pain. Darkness overcame him.

His mind continued a dizzying fall deeper and deeper into a pit. He landed on a ledge. He was bound hand and foot. The pit was utter blackness, rendering him virtually blind. It weighed on him like a heavy buffalo blanket. Tormented screaming, like people in agony crying out for rescue, from somewhere beneath him echoed in his mind. The stench of burning sulfur stung his nose. Allen's chest heaved as he fought against his restraints. He tried shouting, but no sound emerged from his mouth. Fear soaked into his soul like cloth absorbing water. He strained against his bindings. *How did I get tied up?*

From out of the darkness, he heard a voice. "Allen, be strong. Take courage. I will see you through." He recognized the voice. Ceasing his struggle, he calmed his beating heart. Allen repeated the words in his mind until faith could cling to the thought. The fear faded as a small seed of reassuring peace planted deep in his heart.

Allen fought to regain consciousness. He became aware of jagged stones pressing into his face. He slowly opened his eyes and worked to get his bearings. He lifted his head slightly, but when dizziness threatened to return him to blackness, he closed his eyes and rested his head. He lay still. As his head cleared slightly and he became more aware of himself and his surroundings, he felt feverish and sickly. He blinked his eyes open and forced himself to focus on the firelight. Dark Wolf sat before the fire, uttering strange words and pouring sludge into a large gourd. His back was slightly toward Allen, and across from him sat the strange witch-woman.

Still cloudy headed, Allen couldn't trust his eyes entirely, but she seemed taller than the man. Was she seated on a rock? No. Allen blinked and concentrated. The woman floated more than a foot off the ground. He thought he was delirious, so he closed his eyes, then looked again. The witch was levitating. She slowly turned one way and then the other. What manner of evil power was this? Dizziness sent the cave and fire swirling. Unable to believe his own mind, Allen laid down his head and spun back to unconsciousness.

The heavy blackness returned. Allen seemed to rise above his motionless body lying on the cave floor. From the surrounding darkness, outlandish beings swooped forward and danced around his body. They were creatures with the bodies of men and heads of wolves, snakes, and crows. Their grotesque features and motions disgusted Allen. He sensed maliciousness and filth. The creatures set to strike. He tensed at the terror. "Lord Jesus, Lord Jesus, help me! Where are you, Lord Jesus?" Allen cried out, but the blackness swallowed the sound. Only agonizing silence filled his ears. "Lord Jesus . . . your blood."

CHAPTER THIRTY-ONE

IN A THREE-STORY VICTORIAN HOUSE in Baltimore, Reverend Samuel Bannister stirred in his bed. He had dreamed of a black wolf chasing Allen Hartman into a cave, and just as it leaped to strike, Bannister jolted upright, startling his wife awake.

"What's wrong, dear?"

After catching his breath and calming his nerves, he climbed out of bed. "I just had a bad dream about a black wolf chasing poor Allen Hartman." Bannister walked across the hardwood floor in his flannel nightgown and relieved himself in the chamber pot.

"Do you think we should pray for him?"

"Oh, I doubt if there is anything to worry about. We'll just trust him into the good Lord's care. Go back to sleep now."

Bannister let his body sink into the feather mattress and closed his eyes.

The darkness surrounding Allen in the cavern was so suffocating it awakened Reverend Arthur Hartman in Tonawanda, New York. In a cold sweat, he sat up in bed, breathing heavily. He looked over at his wife, Ruth, who raised her head off the pillow.

"What is it, Arthur?"

Not wanting her to worry, Reverend Hartman paused. "I'm not sure, but I had a frightening dream. It has disturbed me deep within. I can't shake the feeling, but I can't explain it."

"Did you hear something outside?"

"Not outside. Inside. In my heart. I believe it has something to do with Allen." He swallowed hard and breathed deeply. "I believe Allen is in some kind of trouble. Yes, I think he's in desperate trouble. And we must pray for him. Right now." Reverend Hartman stared at his wife.

Even in their darkened room, he saw her slight frown and pinched expression. "Come, dear, we must not delay. Put on your housecoat, and let's go to the front room. I want to have my Bible handy." He threw back the covers and wrapped himself in a robe.

Mrs. Hartman followed, wrapping herself in her blue housecoat.

"Do you think he's hurt?"

The reverend added a few pieces of wood to the smoldering coals in the fireplace and nurtured the flame back to life. "No, I think if we pray now, he'll be spared from harm."

Allen's father eased into a rocking chair, but immediately rose. His agitated spirit wouldn't allow him to sit still. He paced. "Come, let's pray."

"Yes, I'm ready." She sat with her head bowed and her hands folded. She began praying softly, thanking God for his far-reaching hands of mercy.

Reverend Hartman confidently entered the throne room of heaven, where he'd been so many times before. "Almighty God, our Father which art in heaven, may thy name always be kept holy.

May thy will be done now, Lord, on earth, in me, as it is in heaven. Thou alone art great and worthy of great praise. There is none other like thee who would bestow grace on those who deserve only thy wrath. But thou art merciful and the Father of mercy. Please, O Lord, we beg thee, we beseech thee, to extend thine arms of mercy and strength to our son—thy son, Allen.

"We know not his condition or his whereabouts as thou dost, O Lord. Thou dost see and know all things. Thou canst strengthen and encourage, heal and restore, when no one else can. O Father. O Father. Be with Allen now, I pray. His mother and I are indeed worried and are helpless except to call on thy strength. Thy Holy Ghost dost prompt us in this prayer, O God. Thy Holy Ghost dost move us and intercede within us. Father, be with Allen now. I pray in the name of thy holy Son, Jesus Christ, our Lord and Savior."

Arthur Hartman's chest heaved. "Lord, the grip upon my heart is so great. How can I endure?" He dropped to his knees and bowed his head to the floor. He could only allow the Holy Ghost to intercede with groanings that his human spirit could not produce alone.

Mrs. Hartman, still praying, also moved to her knees. The burden for her son intensified. He was in need, and she agonized at her helplessness. How could she reach across the miles into the wilderness to hold her son, except through faith in Jesus Christ? She knew now, just as she did when she released Allen to his missionary commissioning, that she could only set her son on a heavenly altar, trusting that God loved Allen even more than she did. God had always been faithful to keep his promises regarding her children, often with blessings much more abundant than she could ever imagine.

Now, her faith, the faith of a godly mother, was being put to the test. She didn't know where Allen was, nor did she know the nature of their call to prayer. It was a terrible test to feel that something was dreadfully wrong and be able only to relinquish her desire to help into the hands of an invisible God, whom she called Almighty.

A nagging thought intruded. Is he almighty or not?

She interceded silently as her thoughts battled with her soul. She didn't know how long she wrestled in her internal dilemma, but she finally willed herself to surrender her heart and Allen into the open, nail-scarred hands she saw in her mind's eye. Ruth Hartman spoke, "Oh, my blessed Savior," and she wept as the warmth of God's grace flowed over and through her.

Reverend Hartman had firmly established in his mind and heart that Allen was called to missionary service in a far-off and dangerous land. The fatherly instincts reflected a deep concern for his son's well-being, but the Holy Spirit prompted him to pray as a warrior.

As he shifted from kneeling to a prone position, he was silent except for an occasional utterance. "I praise the name of the Lord Jesus Christ."

Most of the time, he had no words to say, but merely allowed his heart to cry out to God. He pressed against the constant grip on his spirit. The fire in the fireplace had long since burned out; not even the embers glowed. Pastor Hartman fought intensely, motivated by the deep love for his son and his desire for victory in this battle.

As he interceded, he listened. With his eyes closed, he watched. The Holy Spirit revealed to his inner man the nature of the war in the spiritual realms. The images were not as clear as looking across the farm at midday. But he would catch a glimpse or have the slight impression of confronting malevolent beings too hideous to want to see in the light. Something looked like a wolf, only disfigured. Distorted figures that appeared even darker than the night sky darted before his mind's eye, as if silhouetted against a black cavern. Hordes of shadow creatures hovered over something, like flies swarming a carcass.

The cavern seemed a huge expanse of darkness, a thick blackness, as if it were the birthplace of hopelessness. He searched the images in his mind and saw a small light in the distance below. Not a real light, not even a candle, but more like a coal glowing yellow.

"What is the light, Lord?" The vision zoomed in. The light was Allen, lying still on a ledge, the only thing keeping him from falling into the endless pit.

Reverend Hartman strived to understand what the image meant. But as he considered different possibilities, the image faded.

Had Allen fallen to temptation? Was he injured and close to death? Reverend Hartman didn't want to lose the image, so he chose not to trust his own understanding but to wholly lean on the wisdom and revelation of God.

"Lord, forgive me. What do you want to show me? Please, let me see."

He waited until an image formed on the screen of his mind.

Someone was leaning over Allen. A man? No, it was like a man with a hideous wolf face who snarled at him. The creature was not content to kill him but desired to torture and enslave him, to control by holding him in bondage that would put his soul to death and barely keep his spirit alive within the body. What terrible evil had befallen Allen?

"Lord, save him. Rescue Allen from this monster." Reverend Hartman sensed himself withdrawing, moving a distance back from his son. In his vision he turned and saw hordes of demons waiting to devour Allen, to gnaw the vibrant life out of his soul. Something held them back though.

As Reverend Hartman watched the scene, he remained undetected. Still being drawn back and off to the side, watching from a different vantage point, he sensed he was not alone. An invisible presence that radiated peace and strength remained at his side. Reverend Harman knew that it was powerful enough to fight and conquer the wolf-man and all the demons, yet it withheld its indignation for some reason. It had to be one of God's warring angels. No, his spirit said. It is the Lord Jesus Christ Himself who stands at your side.

"Lord, will you save him?" He didn't hear an audible voice, but the impression in his spirit was clear.

I have given you authority. Do you have faith? What word would you speak?

"But, Lord—" Insecurity gripped him. "But wait. That is what I believe." Not only faith returned, but strength and boldness arose within him. His spirit reminded him of when David declared in bold faith, "When the lion came and stole one of my father's sheep, I pursued him and slayed him, and rescued the sheep from the mouth of the lion. And so will I slay this Philistine giant."

Reverend Arthur Hartman, man of God, husband, and father, fed up with the evil that threatened his son, declared his faith. "In the name of the Lord Jesus Christ, I rescue you, Allen, from the mouth of the lion. You are covered in the blood of the sacrificed Lamb that was shed on the cross of Calvary. The curse of witchcraft is broken, the oppressive chains removed, and you are restored to Him who has called you. The Lord rebuke the demons and send them off as far as the east is from the west. I declare your freedom in the name of Jesus Christ."

The burden of his heart was instantly removed, and peace flooded his soul. Reverend Hartman remained on the floor in humble thanksgiving to his Lord and Savior, to Almighty God, whose name is Faithful and True.

Finally rising, he rubbed his eyes and glanced at the grandfather clock in the corner. "Ten thirty!" He had prayed for nearly ten hours. Ruth was asleep on the couch, covered with a blanket.

Allen flinched when a creature with a wolf head swiped at him. Several demons loomed over him, as if waiting for a signal to attack. They stood just beyond arm's length.

"Be gone! In Jesus's name, I command you to go!" Allen shouted, but the words only echoed in his mind. The drooling horde did not move.

Then beyond them, three demons with heads like rattlesnakes tormented a woman. Two held her arms as the third yanked at her hair. Allen's eyes widened with recognition of Martha Jolifer. His mind told him to rescue her, but his body was numb. "Leave her alone!" His mouth was open, but no sound came out. Allen pushed against the jagged rock until his neck veins bulged. With a groan he slammed back down. He looked again to Martha. She fell to the ground and slowly vanished. Allen blinked several times. "I must be delirious."

Two dark figures with pale and pocked heads pulled another woman forward, each grasping an arm. She fought, twisting and digging in her heels. "No!" Allen cried. "Moon Cloud!" He lunged for her, straining at the invisible chains that bound him. "Aagh."

Allen crumpled. His body shook as he wept. "O Lord, why do you tarry?"

When he finally looked again, Moon Cloud was gone. The crowd of demons closed in, some hissing. Allen closed his eyes. "I give myself to you, Lord."

Be strong. Take courage.

Along the Ohio River, Sister Lydia bolted up in her bed. "Yes, Lord Jesus, I hear you. I'm a-getting up right now. Yes, Lord." She stood and wrapped her large body in a long wool sweater. It was tattered and worn and had seen many a long night in prayer. She tied the belt and slipped on oversized shoes she kept at the side of the bed for this very purpose. She picked up her Bible from the nightstand and crossed the room to her favorite rocking chair. Sister Lydia was ready for battle.

"Here I am, Lord. I love you, Lord Jesus, my Savior and my God. I praise your holy name tonight, Lord." She prayed for a time in thanksgiving, reciting portions of the Bible that were declarations of praise to God. Sister Lydia kept her heart humble before God. Her years of experience had taught her that there was no point going to the Lord with a high and mighty attitude.

All through the day, Lydia's heart had been troubled. Often she pleaded with great fervency for freedom of the slaves, and usually within a few days someone would show up at the church, seeking refuge after just having crossed the river. Her first thought in the early morning was that she'd been called to intercede for the protection of some poor runaway slave. Those that made it to her house testified of miracles that saved them from death.

Sister Lydia spent ample time giving praise to God in order to get her heart and mind in the appropriate place for listening and obeying. Missing sleep was not a worry—disobeying Jesus was. Then thoughts of Allen entered her mind.

"Well now, Lord, how would you like for me to pray for Allen? What does your Holy Ghost want me to know? Please show me, Lord Jesus." She sat quietly for just a moment, and then a picture formed in her mind: several snapping wolves surrounded Allen. One of them in particular growled and snarled at him, pacing before him. By experience and discernment, she knew that the wolves represented powerful witchcraft demons, and their aggressive behavior was more than just intimidation. These wolf-demons had enough power to destroy Allen. She stood and began pacing.

"Oh, Lord Jesus. You got to protect my boy right now. Save him from them devil-wolves. Oh, Lord, you got to save my boy, Allen. He's a good boy, and he's going to do you some fine work.

You save him now, Lord Jesus. Go on. I'll help you now. Just tell me what to do, and I'll do it."

A kerosene lantern cast a dim light around the room. She remained praying, speaking softly. "I take these thoughts captive to your authority, my Lord and my God. It is your peace that I seek." She rocked slowly, her left elbow on the arm of the chair, and rested her forehead on her fingertips. "Search my heart, O God, and see if there is any wicked way in me."

The rocker stopped. Sister Lydia grimaced and rubbed her face. "Lord, why you be showing me Allen and Gloria? They came into the church when we was singing."

Why were you suspicious?

"Well, Lord, you know how we hide runaway slaves, and sometimes the bounty hunters come looking for them. I was afraid that Allen and Gloria might be bounty hunters, but then I saw that they were good Christian folk, and I stopped worrying."

What was your fear?

"That's all, Lord. I wasn't afraid of them."

What was your fear?

"It wasn't really fear, Lord, it was worry that . . . Oh, Lord Jesus, I was afraid."

She leaned forward in the rocking chair, her hands clasped and elbows on the armrests. "Lord, I'm seeing Allen, but his face is changing to . . ." Gasping, Lydia fell back in the chair and covered her face with her hands. "No, dear Jesus, it can't be. Don't show me that. Please don't take me back there." Her arms went up to shield her head. "Why did he whip us? He whipped my mama. Oh, God, why did you let him whip us?" Startled, she dropped to her knees. "Sweet Jesus, forgive me. In my heart I been blaming you for that whipping. It was that man what didn't know no better. Forgive me, Lord. I see now that Allen looks like that man. He's got the same hair and blue eyes. You done used Allen's face to search my heart.

"I remember what Mama said, Lord. She told me so many times, 'It ain't right for him to whip us so, but you got to be strong,

Lydia. And strong don't mean you keep hate in your heart. No, girl, never let the hate stay in your heart.'

"Lord Jesus, I forgive the man that done the whipping. I forgive him for all the whippings and the cussing at Mama and me. I don't hate him, and I'm not afraid, because you are in me, and you are greater than that fear. I rebuke the fear in Jesus's name. And I set that man free so you can bring your justice, or mercy, on him as you see fit. I give him into your hands.

"Jesus, I forgive the other white men who have treated us poorly. Put a stop to the slavery, Lord God, and tell that Pharaoh-devil to 'let my people go.' Thank you, Jesus. I feel like chains have dropped off me. I'm free again. Thank you, Lord Jesus. Now, Lord, we have got to set poor Allen free. Tell me, Jesus, what's happening to my boy?"

She saw a cave in a mountain, and inside was a great battle in the darkness that sent a shiver up her spine. Allen's life was at stake. Lydia opened her eyes and stood up. She felt the evil presence right there in her house, as if she was being watched, and another shiver rattled her spine.

She stomped her foot hard on the floor. "Not in my house! You've been warned to never come into my house, and you may not touch or harass my children. You leave now, demon. I command you out in the name of Jesus Christ. Now!" She stomped her foot again.

The menacing presence vanished. Lydia walked around the room, praying and swinging her arms as if she were sweeping dirt out the door. Aware that she'd been loud, she went outside to continue praying. After making a circle around the house and requesting that God send more protecting angels, she walked to the edge of the yard where the cornfield started.

"Lord Jesus, you got to be with my boy Allen. You are great and mighty, and I praise your power. You are almighty and holy, and the angels sing of your great deeds. Lord, you set many captives free from chains of sin, from slavery of the soul, and from the voodoo witches. I know that wolf is a witch-man, and he's trying to make a slave out of Allen. But you are God Almighty, the Alpha and Omega, and you broke the power of the devil on the cross of Calvary.

"Thank you, Jesus, for spilling your precious blood to save us from our sins. Thank you for spilling your precious blood to save this poor slave girl. Now I'm free, Lord. I'm free because you set me free. And I'm free from the chains of fear because of your blood.

"You nailed fear and hate and witchcraft on the cross and made a public spectacle of it. You took that curse into the grave, and you left it there. You are so great and holy that you broke the very chains of death when you walked out of that grave. Yes, Jesus, you rolled back that big stone, and you walked right out of there as alive as you could be. O Glory! Glory to your holy name!"

In the upstairs loft, two young faces appeared at the window, and their eyes were big and bright. Lydia's children, Esther and Daniel, had been awakened by the shouting, and they watched their mama out in the field. Even though it was past midnight, there was enough light from the moon and stars for them to see her moving around.

Daniel tugged on his sister's nightgown. "What Mama shouting at?" He'd seen her pray like that in church, but not in the cornfield late at night.

"She's praying."

Daniel's eyebrows raised. "Is she shouting at Jesus?"

"She's shouting praises." They watched quietly.

"Why she shouting if Jesus be in her heart?"

"She's shouting so's the devil can hear her too."

"Don't that make the devil mad?"

"I guess Mama's fixing for a fight with him." Esther put a hand on her little brother's shoulder. "Don't worry. Jesus tells her what to do."

Sister Lydia raised her arms and shouted praise to heaven. She moved and danced and bowed and shouted for quite a while. She kept her intensity, sometimes standing, sometimes kneeling in the dirt.

She prayed against the work of the demons that were harassing Allen.

The Lord revealed to her the dark cave, the image of Indian warriors, and the ugly face of a witch. She saw the many snakes slithering around rocks in the cave. Startled and disgusted by this sight, she grabbed a hoe and began chopping at the ground, as if attacking and killing the snakes.

"With the sword of the Spirit, I fight back the demon snakes!" she declared with the ferocity of a mama bear protecting her cub. "Lord, your enemies form an alliance against you. Do to them as you did to Oreb and Zeeb, the wolf, when you destroyed them. May they perish in disgrace."

As she interceded for Allen, Lydia rebuked the devil with Psalm 83. "As fire blazes in the mountains, so consume them with your wrath. Let them know that you alone are the Most High God."

Esther and Daniel, still watching, saw their mother kneel down and lift her hands toward heaven. They could easily hear her when she shouted, but sometimes she was softer. Whatever she was saying, they knew it had to be important. Then something strange happened that made their eyes widen again.

"What that light there?" Daniel asked. A shining figure of light appeared hovering over the ground a few feet away from his mama.

"I've seen that before. It's an angel."

They watched as their mama continued praying with an angel by her side. Then something caused both children to turn and look behind them. Another angel stood beside their bed. They stared at the white shining light that touched the floor and ceiling. The unclear form within the glow seemed like a person. The angel's eyes were alert and watchful, like a soldier on guard duty.

"Look up there!" Esther pointed.

Daniel peered out the window again and saw hundreds, perhaps thousands, of angels in the sky above the cornfield. They were up higher than the tallest tree, just waiting, hovering. Neither child had seen so many people in one place before. There were more angels than all the people in Portsmouth.

"The devil be in big trouble now," Daniel said.

The children went back to bed, with the angel beside them.

Sister Lydia knelt and bowed low enough so her forehead touched the dirt. She'd kicked off her big shoes. There were angels about, but she didn't look to them. She was bowing in the presence of her Lord and King, Jesus Christ. Remaining there in silence, Lydia worshiped.

She finally stood and shook the kinks out of her knees. God's faithful warrior looked up and saw the angelic host flash away to the west. The rising sun had turned the sky blue. She dusted herself and went back toward the house, singing a hymn.

As Lydia reached the door, Deacon Abraham and Sister Savannah came around the corner of the house.

She called to her guests. "Good morning! Have you-uns had breakfast yet?" It didn't really matter if they'd eaten or not—Lydia would feed them.

An excitable woman, Sister Savannah had been in the church for only about two years. "Did you see them angels last night? I thought for sure Jesus was coming back. The glory of the Lord was upon us."

"Sister, why don't you go on inside and set the table for breakfast while I have a private word with Deacon Abraham." Lydia held open the door.

Sister Savannah looked between the two. "I'd be happy to."

Lydia closed the door behind her and invited the deacon to sit on a small bench. She sat on the only other chair. It creaked as she lowered herself onto it.

"I believe Brother Allen was saved from some powerful wickedness," Lydia said, hopeful that one day she would learn what it was all about.

"I was up at midnight and went over to the church to pray," Deacon Abraham said. "Sister Savannah and some others said they saw the church all lit up, so they came to pray too. Thing is, I had only two candles lit. I didn't see the angels like the sisters did, but I sure felt the glory come down. As I was praying, I seen Brother Allen, like he was hurt, and I had to pray for a long time before he got up."

"Well, hallelujah! I seen the same thing." Lydia raised her hands. "Praise the name of Jesus. I guess we is going to have to keep praying for my boy. I want to make sure he wins the whole victory."

"Amen, sister. Amen."

The smell of coffee and frying ham drifted out to the porch as they talked about what the prayers meant. "I'd sure like to give Allen a hug right now, make sure he's all right." Lydia clasped her hands together. "Thank you, Jesus. Thank you for taking care of my boy."

CHAPTER THIRTY-TWO

A BRIGHT SHAFT OF LIGHT STABBED through the black pit and engulfed the young missionary.

Allen!

Allen blinked, then opened his eyes. He took a quick mental inventory. The dizziness was gone. He no longer felt feverish, and his thinking was clear. Still in the cavern near the fire, Allen sat up. He looked around. Dark Wolf and the witch were gone. Reviving the fire, he found a torch and held it to the flame, then searched for his rifle where he'd dropped it. He grabbed it and held it at the ready. He lifted the torch forward, fearful of what he might see yet unable to ignore the need to know.

The dark shadows became forms. They were there. Seven people bound, naked, and withered, as if starved. The ghastly sight sickened Allen. The one closest to him reached out his hands, as if pleading for freedom. Allen knelt and pulled out his knife to carefully cut through the rawhide cords.

With a lunge as quick as a snake, the man reached out his clawlike hand to grip Allen's throat. Jolting back and twisting, Allen knocked the scrawny man to the ground. With strength that belied his skeletal frame, he lunged again. Allen struck the crazed man on the jaw with the butt of his rifle, knocking him lengthwise back onto the other slaves. Screeching, they beat and tore at the wounded man, like wolves turning on one of their own at the smell of blood. Had the wretched captives been driven insane by torture? Repulsed, Allen turned and sprinted out of the cave.

The daylight blinded him. He squinted against the brightness until his eyes adjusted. The sky was clear and the ground was dry. Allen had no idea how long he'd been in the cave. It didn't matter now. Only escape mattered. He ran out of the draw and across the field where he'd shot at the elk.

Thank God! His horse was still there.

"Sorry to leave you like that, old friend." Allen reached to untie the rein, but the buckskin flinched and thrashed his head. Stomping his feet, he drew back from his master.

"Whoa! Easy now, Caleb. It's me. It's me. I must smell like that evil cave. I don't blame you, boy. I was scared too, but we've got to be going." Allen grabbed the rein just as Caleb jerked, breaking the limb to which he was tied. Pulling the horse's head down, he made a quick step and swung into the saddle.

Allen steered the nervous gelding through an opening in the brush, and they galloped over the ridge. Forced into another narrow draw by a rocky ledge, Allen hurried to get as far from the cave as possible. Grateful to be out of there with his life and limbs intact, he breathed easier when he rode through some brushy trees into a clearing.

He started for the next rise but stopped short. Eight Indians raced straight for him. Allen wheeled his horse, but three more Indians cut off his retreat. Caleb reared and whinnied. He was surrounded by yelling renegades with bows drawn, war clubs and lances ready for any sign of fight.

Knowing his life would be prolonged only moment by moment, Allen chose a course of action the Indians might respect. He sat tall in his saddle and remained calm. He nudged the buckskin, looking each warrior in the eye. One of the warriors struck him on the back of the head, knocking him to the ground. Severe pain shot through him as well as a few flashes of light.

Immediately, the warriors let loose their war cries. They reached a feverish pitch. In an instant, several enraged fighters slid off their mounts and kicked and struck Allen. One drew a knife, ready to scalp him alive.

As the warrior brought the blade to Allen's scalp, a shout stayed the Indian's hand. All warriors fell silent. Allen rolled to his back and looked up. The faces glared down at him. Allen had never seen such passionate hatred. Any one of them would kill Allen in an instant. What had stopped them?

The same voice that had shouted now barked what Allen thought was a command. The vicious pack parted to allow two obvious leaders to pass through. Allen pushed himself to his knees, only to be swiftly kicked to the ground again.

He looked up into the eyes of Dark Wolf and Kicking Lion.

Dark Wolf spoke. The chieftain stared at him as if not understanding. Dark Wolf's voice quivered.

"We kill him?" Kicking Lion spoke in Arapaho, which Allen understood.

"Back to the cave," Dark Wolf instructed.

They tied Allen with a rawhide rope and yanked him up by his arms. They dragged him back over the rise to the cave's entrance.

They dumped Allen on the ground. He lay still, letting his body recover. *Lord God, if it is your will that I die now at the hands of these violent men, then so be it. May my death have the effect of a martyr. I surrender to you, Lord, not to them, and into your hands I do commend my spirit. May thine be the glory. In Jesus's name. Amen.*

Dark Wolf gripped his strap of rattlesnake skulls and paced near the gaping mouth of the cave. He shouted words that Allen assumed were a curse. The warriors stepped away from Allen. Kicking Lion moved forward, crouching, knife drawn.

One of the warriors cut away Allen's bindings and dropped the knife on the ground by him. Allen pushed himself up to his hands and knees.

Kicking Lion pointed to the knife with his own.

Allen was to fight the warrior. His death would mean little to them without a fight or torture.

Allen rose to his feet, but he refused to pick up the knife. He toed it a couple feet away from him, all the while locking gazes with his challenger.

Kicking Lion's eyes widened. The other men grunted, clearly wanting to see a fight to the death. He took one step forward, paused, then took another. He seemed to be taking Allen's measure.

Allen breathed deeply, trying to calm his pounding heart. Out of his peripheral vision he saw Dark Wolf clutching the medicine bag that hung around his neck. The shaman's hands trembled.

Looking into the eyes of a killer, Allen thought of how he'd just told God that he was willing to die for him. Dying would be easier than being taken hostage and thrown back in the cave. He swallowed. He couldn't go back to the cave. The knife blade glinted in the sunlight. The memory of facing down the thugs in Saint Louis dashed through his mind. God, forgive me for doubting. Increase my faith. In the span of a breath, he felt a renewing in his spirit.

The increasing tension in the air snapped. The circling warriors murmured. Without warning, the ground trembled. Dark Wolf cried out, as if pricked.

The chieftain looked from side to side. Gasping, he rushed at Allen, his eyes wide and his mouth open in a silent scream. He raised the knife, intent on plunging the weapon into Allen's chest.

Allen's hands moved as if being lifted by an invisible force. He grasped the warrior's wrists. He fell back with the momentum and lifted his right knee into the warrior's belly, flipping him overhead.

The assailant arched his back so he would land on his feet, but the ground sloped away and his back slammed against a jagged rock. He landed with a thudding crack and a huffing groan. Kicking Lion slumped to the ground, struggling to move his arms and legs.

Allen sprang to his feet and crouched, arms out. He stared at the other warriors. They looked from him to their powerful leader and back.

Dark Wolf scurried into the cave.

The pack of eleven turned and fled like coyotes running from a grizzly. The warriors continued through the brushy draw, up the slope, and over. Before they could reach the top of the ridge, a shot cracked, then another. Two warriors fell.

Jack Burkett, Joaquin Del Castillo, and about seventy Arapaho braves rode into view, releasing their war cries like a holy chorus. Some rode down on the nine remaining wolf warriors, ending their reign of terror. They died quickly under a hail of arrows and lances.

The two mountain men pulled up next to Allen, along with the rescuers, including Two Rivers. Seeing their enemy Kicking Lion at Allen's feet, many drew their bows.

Two Rivers raised his hand to stop them.

Kicking Lion stared at his captors with disdain.

Allen expected the Indian to rise and defend himself.

Jack leaned forward in his saddle. "What happened to him, Allen?"

"Not sure. He rushed me, and I tossed him overhead. He hit the rock and hasn't moved since."

Jack dismounted. He lifted Kicking Lion's arm and felt no resistance. "I do believe his back is broken" He looked back at Allen. "You all right, Parson?"

"I'll be fine." His head was spinning with shock and relief.

"Where is Dark Wolf?" Two Rivers scanned the tracks in the dirt.

Allen pointed to the cave opening.

The braves fidgeted and murmured between them.

Joaquin stepped beside Jack. "They say the cave is where devils live."

Two Rivers held up his hand. "Silence."

"What are you going to do about him?" Jack pointed to the wounded war chief.

"I don't want to kill him, Jack. Let's make a litter and carry him back." If God let Allen win the fight, it was for some greater purpose.

Jack didn't respond.

Joaquin ordered some braves to make the litter.

The braves voiced their desire that Allen should kill the chieftain and take his scalp.

"Do as Joaquin says," Two Rivers ordered.

The braves obeyed.

While several braves constructed the litter, others captured the dead warriors' horses. They brought Caleb back to Allen.

Kicking Lion groaned as they lifted him onto the litter of long branches and blankets. Paralyzed, he could do nothing but stare at his captors.

"You think we should go into that cave and hunt down Dark Wolf?" Jack pointed at the entrance.

"His power is broken. I guess we just leave him for God to deal with now," Allen said.

"We could smoke him out," Joaquin suggested, keeping the muzzle of his rifle pointed toward the cave.

"It's a deep cavern with many passages. I don't know if that would work." Allen turned and looked at Two Rivers, who seemed to be contemplating.

"His power is broken," the wise man said. "We go now."

Jack bit his lower lip. "I hate letting that rascal go."

The group at the cave rejoined the others on the slope, where they had dismembered the eleven evil warriors so that their spirits entered the next world unable to hunt or work, only to live in eternal torment. Upon seeing the wounded captive on the litter, they let out a victory cry. A few shouted claims of fighting prowess as they lifted scalps and bloody weapons.

Chases the Bear declared Allen's greatness as a warrior who had single handedly entered the underworld and broken Dark Wolf's power. Cheers of honor filled the mountainside.

Two Rivers raised his hand. "It is indeed a great victory that has been won today. Our white brother has counted coup against our enemies. He didn't fight against the Sioux or the Pawnee. He fought against Arapaho whose hearts had turned black with contempt. That is the worst of our enemies, when our own people follow the path of the Death Spirit. Their poison is more dangerous than the rattlesnake. Their poison is in the blood and has infected many. Now the power of the Death Spirit has been broken by a greater power. White Falcon has shown us a great power, a strong medicine. We must learn from him. We must learn to listen to Creator and walk in the new path.

"Now we return to our village with a captive. Do not hurt him or insult him. White Falcon claims this captive."

Shouts and whoops filled the air. Two Rivers raised his hand for silence.

In the distance a new but familiar shout was heard. Out of a draw trotted the Prophet Elijah.

Jack Burkett greeted the prophet, using his Arapaho name. "Welcome, Singing Thunder."

The warriors clearly regarded him as a spirit man, perhaps a bit crazy, but he had strong medicine.

He rode straight up to Allen. "Glory to God, brother, but I feel the mountain tremble. The hand of the Almighty has released the land from a dark curse."

Elijah climbed down from his horse. He dropped the reins and walked a few paces, raising his hands toward the cave. Allen, compelled to dismount, stood by the prophet and knelt on the ground, praying.

Jack, Joaquin, Two Rivers, and others dismounted.

Prophet Elijah began shouting. Allen recognized the words from Psalm 83 and bowed, agreeing with the words.

"'Keep not thou silence, O God. Hold not thy peace, and be not still, O God. For, lo, thine enemies make a tumult, and they that hate thee have lifted up the head. They have taken crafty counsel against thy people and consulted against thy hidden ones. For they have consulted together with one consent. They are confederate against thee. Do unto them as unto the Midianites. Make their nobles like Oreb and Zeeb. O my God, make them as stubble before the wind. As the fire burneth a wood, and as the flame setteth the mountains on fire, so persecute them with thy tempest, and make them afraid with thy storm. Fill their faces with shame, that they may seek thy name, O Lord. Let them be confounded and troubled forever. Yea, let them be put to shame, and perish. That men may know that thou, whose name alone is God, art the most high over all the earth.'" His voice echoed.

Allen bowed into the dust, exalting the Lord God Most High. Then compelled to stand, he declared the end of the curse and the power of the fearful cave. "You, O Lord, are great and mighty. You alone are God of heaven and earth. You manifested your power by sending your only Son, Jesus Christ, to take away the sins of the world. The power to conquer sin and death. Resurrection power that gives life to all who believe. You, O Lord, have won the victory today, as you won the victory when you nailed sin and death to the cross. Having spoiled principalities and powers, you made a spectacle of them publicly, triumphing over them. And in that triumph and by that blood and in the name of Jesus Christ, I say that the curse is broken and the power of fear and death is canceled."

"Praise the name of the Lord Most High!" Singing Thunder boomed.

The crowd of Arapaho warriors watched the two white men shout strange words at the cave. They did not sing. They did not dance at the fire. They merely shouted at the mountain.

Then a distant scream was heard. Dark Wolf bolted from the

cave. He screeched and ran back and forth, as if in blind confusion.

Jack and Joaquin raised their rifles, but before they could shoot, more strange creatures scuttled out of the cave—the captives Allen had encountered.

Blinded and tormented by the sunlight and evidently driven by a frenzy of bloodlust, they attacked Dark Wolf. He screeched in terror as they clawed and struck him. Some kicked and punched, while another choked him. The vicious fury raised a cloud of dust that surrounded the mob.

When Dark Wolf no longer struggled, they stopped and glared at their captor. Then as one entity, they screamed and pounded on his lifeless body with rocks.

Two Rivers watched the horror. "The Stolen Ones. They were medicine men who were poisoned by their greed. They fought one another for dominance. Yet Dark Wolf captured them all by stealing their power from the underworld. For years they have been under his control."

One of the wretched slaves shrieked when he spotted the audience across the draw. Together, the pitiful beings grabbed Dark Wolf's body and dragged it into the cave.

Allen gave the large group of warriors a long look. They were visibly disturbed by the vulgar scene. Pale creatures from the underworld had come into their world and carried back their enemy. There they would no doubt devour his flesh, or whatever demons did to stay alive.

Prophet Elijah raised his hands once again and bellowed, "May this portal be closed, in Jesus's name."

Slowly but steadily increasing in strength, the earth bucked and shifted. Allen and the prophet stepped back. The ground rumbled. Horses shifted and whinnied. Valiant warriors whimpered. The rumble became a trembling roar as the mountain before them shook. Dust blasted out of the passage.

They moved farther back from the cave as rocks tumbled down

the steep incline above the opening. The rocky cliff above shattered and collapsed, filling the corner of the draw that had just been the stage of Death Spirit's dance.

When the dust settled and peace returned, Prophet Elijah exclaimed, "We behold the marvels of God. Signs and wonders of his very hand. Blessed be the name of the Lord."

The warriors stood in stunned silence.

Allen looked at the prophet. Elijah threw his arms wide and let out a booming laugh. "We behold the mighty hand of God." They embraced as victorious warriors.

"I thank God for sending you, brother," Allen said. "Your words gave me strength."

"Not mine. It was the Lord's message for you." Elijah grinned. "Praise his name."

They turned toward the warriors, who watched them. Again Prophet Elijah raised his hands and bellowed a glory shout. "Hallelujah!"

The warriors whooped in triumph.

CHAPTER THIRTY-THREE

THE CEREMONIAL DRUMS JOYOUSLY THUNDERED beyond the row of trees at the river where dancers were silhouetted by the bonfire. Allen enjoyed the celebration and the honor bestowed on him. But after three nights, he needed quiet time. He built a small fire, sat on a log, and sipped coffee from a tin cup.

Elijah came over and squatted by the fire.

"Help yourself to the coffee, Brother Singing Thunder." Allen smiled.

"Don't mind if I do." Elijah poured himself coffee into a cup made from a gourd. "I don't think I'll ever eat again. I've had so much food the past three days. Lord, what a party! It's a celebration like I've never seen before."

"I, too, am worn out from feasting and dancing," Allen said.

"Dancing like King David, we were. Bless the Lord, O my soul. God must be up in heaven with tears of joy. He's just looking at his children singing and dancing their hearts out."

"It will be quite an interesting choir when we all get to heaven, don't you think, Elijah?"

"What a glorious day that will be."

They were quiet for a moment. "I've been out here for less than a year, but it feels like a lifetime. So many things have changed for me."

"I guess that's allowed, seeing as you've had an uncommon adventure." Elijah added a stick to the fire. "You had an encounter with the devil in the underworld. It appears to me that God has anointed you special. It's not every preacher, and it's not every prophet, that gets called to stand in the gap like that. God called you because you're faithful. He knew he could count on you."

"You don't believe that I stumbled into that cave on accident?" Allen swallowed the last drops of coffee from his cup.

Elijah shook his head. "It weren't no accident."

Allen didn't believe it was accidental either, but he tried to make sense of it all. How could he ever explain it to other pastors?

"Do you remember the word the Lord spoke that night we met, that night at Shining Canyon?" Elijah's piercing eyes met Allen's. "The Lord said you was going into the dark and horrible pit, but that the light would come. That was prophesied. It weren't no accident. You went into the dark pit, and the light brought you out."

"Yes, I remember. You said, 'Be strong; take courage,' and I clung to those words when I was in that cave. But I tell you, I didn't feel very courageous when all those snakes came out of the walls. However, I did have a quiet sort of peace. I guess it was faith that I would make it through. It's as if I wasn't alone, even in that dark pit. Someone must have been praying for me."

"Brother Allen, I left you at Shining Canyon, and the Lord told me to ride in a circle around the mountain to pray and prophesy. One of those nights he showed me a shining storm cloud coming in from the east. It was dazzling bright with Pentecost fire. It came to rest on the mountain, and the mountain shook. Indeed, some powerful prayers were going up to the Lord on your behalf that night. Lord Almighty, but it was strong." Elijah seemed awed by what God had revealed to him. "But I knew that them wolf Indians would still be dangerous until they was destroyed."

"My father is a man of prayer. It wouldn't surprise me to learn one day that he was involved in that effort. And it's likely that some friends in Ohio were praying also," Allen said.

"Glory to God," Elijah said.

"I'll say amen to that." A voice outside the fire's light interrupted them. "May we come in?"

"Please join us, Jack, Joaquin," Allen said. "Help yourself to the coffee."

"Thanks all the same. But I just ate half a buffalo and have to give my belly a rest." Jack patted his stomach. "So you're thanking the Almighty for his handiwork, I take it."

"I was just telling Elijah that I barely left home a year ago, and I surely had no idea that I was headed for all this." Allen fingered his beaded buckskin shirt.

"Do you have any regrets?" Jack packed tobacco into the bowl of a pipe.

"No. How can I regret seeing God work in such a powerful way? I just don't even feel like the same man who left New York. I can't go back to the way I used to think and believe. I trust the Lord so much more. I trust the Word, and I trust my prayers far more than ever before. I'm overwhelmed." Allen craned his neck to look up and behold the stars. "Do you understand what I mean?"

"I saw something happen that I can't explain." Jack puffed out smoke. "It had to be a miracle of God. And yes, I believe more deeply because of it. When I was a lad at the Jesuit mission school, they taught me to believe in God and that Jesus Christ suffered and died for our sins. All through my life, I've seen things that have convinced me it's the truth. Now that I've witnessed justice for Dark Wolf and his lot and experienced that mountain quaking, I'm overwhelmed. But I've never seen the love of Christ so clearly in a man as I've seen it in you, Allen Hartman. You are a man after God's own heart."

"Amen," Elijah said.

Joaquin grinned and patted Allen on the back. "Amen."

"Thank you," Allen said, deeply moved.

The four mountain men talked around the fire long into the night. They spoke of the mysterious death of Martha Jolifer, the Bannisters and Fosters abandoning the vision, and how the rest of the band had dissolved. Allen told them of his meeting Deacon Abraham and Sister Lydia and that they'd taught him how to cast out demons. He recounted his vision quest that led him to burying the dead of Two Rivers's village.

"Do you have any idea what's to become of Kicking Lion?" Elijah asked.

"I'm not sure yet," Allen said. "It's too soon to know if his back will heal properly. But we'll do the best we can to see him through. I'll have to keep praying for wisdom about him, because I don't know what will happen after that. I just know it's not right to put him to death."

A tipi had been set up for Kicking Lion out of respect for Allen. Their mortal enemy was allowed to live because his reign of terror had ended. Allen visited him in the mornings to pray and anoint him with oil, and then again in the afternoons. The chieftain must have been in great pain, but he covered it with his hardened demeanor.

"Well, may God grant you that wisdom," Jack said. "It's a tender predicament. We're likely to pull out in the morning. But you've earned my respect, no matter what happens to Kicking Lion."

Joaquin had been sitting quietly. "Don't worry about Kicking Lion. More has been broken in him than just his back. The miracles didn't stop at the closing of the cave. What you have done . . . what God has done through you has broken an ancient curse on the land. It's a new day for the Arapaho. It's a new day for you, Allen—and one for me as well. I must confess that I doubted we'd see you come out of the cave alive. I thought you went in there to suffer and die. But now I've seen the power of the resurrection. I believe because I've seen the story of Jesus Christ come to life in you."

"Thank you, Joaquin. That's good to hear." A blessed assurance swept over Allen upon hearing the testimonies of deepened faith in the two wilderness rangers. God had used them to be encouragers by their confidence and skill. And Joaquin's words had the ring of prophecy in them.

Suddenly, Joaquin turned his head to peer into the darkness. Then he relaxed and returned his gaze to the campfire. A moment later, Blue Otter and Two Rivers stepped into the light.

"Welcome, friends," Allen said in Arapaho. "Have a seat if you would like."

They remained standing in their full regalia. The tribal elder wore a headdress of eagle and magpie feathers tied into a horsehair roach-dyed red. Many colorful bead patterns and rows of porcupine quills adorned his elk-skin shirt. He held an ancient ceremonial rattle in his left hand. Blue Otter had painted his face and chest vermillion. Several necklaces of beads and fur strips hung around his neck. His headdress held feathers and symbols of his lodge.

Blue Otter waved his arm in the direction of the bonfire in the distance. "Two Rivers say that dance is good. Two Rivers say that it is good day for the Blue Cloud People. The stomachs of the people are filled with meat. The hearts of the people are filled with peace. Mothers do not fear the night of the full moon. Their enemies are gone."

There was a long pause.

Finally Two Rivers broke the awkward silence. Blue Otter translated. "For many years I have seen dreams of a flood coming that will wash away the buffalo and our lands. The first time I saw the white man's fort, I knew that the flood waters were starting to rise. But I also knew that there is no way to stop the flood. It will come.

"I began to seek from the Great Spirit wisdom that would at least save a few of our people from the flood. I feared that the souls of the Blue Cloud People would also be lost in the rising waters.

"One day while I was trading at the fort on the Laramie, I

saw two Indian men. I could not say what tribe they were from, because they wore white man's clothing and they drank much firewater. I was sad because their souls were lost; they did not know who they were.

"Another time at the fort I saw a white man in black clothes. With him were two Cherokee men who wore the same black clothing. They spoke of following the white man's religion, which was a religion of truth. They said that they no longer danced in the old ways but sang a new song. I didn't understand why my heart felt sad for them. Their eyes said that their words were true, but they seemed only to want to make the white man happy. My heart was confused by what I saw.

"I spent many days asking the Great Spirit for wisdom to understand the dreams of the flood and the other things I had seen. In the time of new leaves, a year ago I saw a dream of a white seed being planted that grew into a great tree where many birds and animals could live. I now see that the tree is a tree of life for the souls of the People.

"In a different dream, I saw a weeping White Falcon fly over the great tree. His tears gave strength to the tree to keep it from being swept away by the flood. He cried out to the Great Spirit for mercy, and it was given.

"I believe you are the White Falcon of the dreams. I believe you have wept over the tree of life. Now it is time to understand how to live so that the flood does not wash us away. Our people must protect their souls in the tree of life.

"When Jack Burkett told us that you had gone into the underworld, we came to fight. I did not believe I would see you again. I believed that Dark Wolf had won a great victory. Then I saw you with your enemy at your feet. He was broken, but you did not raise your hand against him. You brought him to your lodge, and you pray to restore his strength.

"I have heard in the white man's religion that one loves his enemies, but I have seen only revenge and killing in the way of the Arapaho and the Sioux. Now I have seen that a man can love his enemy. Only One Who Gives Life can give a man's soul true peace."

Allen regarded the revelation that had come to his friend. He heard the distant drums throbbing like a heartbeat. It seemed that two streams were about to become one.

"I desire to be the first of my people to walk on the trail of One Who Gives Life," Two Rivers continued.

Allen gasped and sighed at the same time. "Yes, yes, of course."

"Thank you, sweet Lord," Elijah whispered.

The missionary stepped before Two Rivers and looked into his eyes. Allen silently prayed for the Lord to guide the moment. Then he spoke to the elderly shaman as one brother to another. "My father, I will show you the trail of One Who Gives Life. I will walk on the trail with you. We will walk so that you do not forget who you are. We will ask every day for wisdom while we travel this trail."

Blue Otter translated. He paused, breathing rapidly and with eagerness in his eyes. "I too desire to walk this trail."

Two Rivers laid down his rattle and raised his hands toward heaven. Both men cried out for their souls to be saved by One Who Gives Life. Allen had supposed he would lead them in prayer as he would at an evangelistic rally, but they poured out their hearts in their own way. He perceived the presence of the Holy Ghost.

Two Rivers continued crying out as he removed his headdress, then his shirt and necklaces. He stripped down to his loincloth and bowed into the dirt. Blue Otter followed.

Allen turned to Joaquin, who quietly translated the meaning. "They are begging One Who Gives Life to receive them as they are, poor and naked, and to allow them to walk on the new trail. They say the name of Jesus Christ, who loves even enemies. They plead to walk the trail as White Falcon does. They thank the Great Spirit for the tree of life."

Prophet Elijah overheard the translation and stood behind the humble pair. Raising his hands toward heaven, he shouted his prayer. "Great and living God, the Father of our Lord Jesus Christ, receive these men into your kingdom. I declare forgiveness and peace, in your holy name."

When the praying ceased, Two Rivers stood, and Blue Otter translated his question. "What clothes do I put on now?"

The medicine man had surrendered his soul to the Lord. In his humility he would even dress as a white man if that meant knowing the ways of One Who Gives Life.

Allen stooped, picked up the ceremonial garments, and held them before Two Rivers. "My father, put on your shirt and headdress and wear them proudly, because you are Arapaho. One Who Gives Life has clothed your soul in a mantle of righteousness. That is what we shall wear now as we walk the trail together."

Allen picked up Blue Otter's garments and received him in the same manner. Then he said, "Lord Jesus, One Who Gives Life, I thank you for your victory on the cross and the victory here this night. You reign supreme, and we humbly seek to serve you with wisdom and faith. I praise your name. Amen."

Two Rivers replaced his clothing and headdress. Making a slow circle, he searched for anything he might have missed. Satisfied with his appearance, the shaman squared his shoulders but then walked another small circle. He smiled broadly and bounced on his feet, like a boy with his first horse. "I must go dance and sing my new song."

Blue Otter translated and added that he, too, must dance. They hurried back to the big fire. The mountain men laughed together.

Allen looked at Elijah, and the big bear of a man hugged him tightly. "Praise be to God," he boomed.

Allen wept for joy in his arms.

"The wonders will never cease," Jack said. "Once again I have been thrown off my horse. I can hardly believe what I just saw. Parson, I must say, we will stick around a few more days to see what else God will do."

"That's good news, Jack," Allen said. He turned and hugged him with a slap on the back. "And thank you, Joaquin." He embraced him in the same way. "You are both great and trusted friends."

"Shall we go on down and watch them dance?" Elijah shuffled his feet.

"I wouldn't miss it. And I might just eat the other half of that buffalo." Jack slapped the prophet's shoulder. "You coming with us, Allen?"

"I'll be along shortly, thanks."

As the three men strode off into the shadows, Allen stepped beyond the campfire glow to the edge of the darkness. Breathing in deeply, he let the cool air and rich aroma of sage fill his nose and lungs. Calculating that his commissioning service had been about one year ago to the day, Allen shook his head. He was a new man. Old things had passed away.

Just as he was about to release his thanksgiving, the snap of a twig caused Allen to jerk his head. Squinting against the firelight, he saw movement. A silhouette materialized and drifted toward the light. Details formed with each step. He squeezed his eyes shut and blinked as if smoke stung them.

"Allen."

The voice drew his unbelieving mind back into reality. He gasped.

"Moon Cloud?" He stepped carefully to her, afraid she might vanish. Touching her shoulders, he exhaled his relief. "It really is you."

Her beautiful smiling face shimmered in the firelight.

"I thought you had died. Back at the village." He mixed Arapaho and English. "I saw the dress and beads. I thought I had buried you." The recollection of that dreadful day gripped his insides. He swallowed the hard lump that hard formed in his throat.

"My sister." She blinked away tears. "I had given her my dress for the journey."

"You're alive. Thank God you're alive." He pulled her to him and wrapped his arms around her, holding her close to his heart.

When Moon Cloud stepped back, she kept her hand on Allen's right forearm. "I see Two Rivers and Blue Otter calling out to your God. I too want to walk in the path of One Who Gives Life. May a woman follow your God?"

Allen's face lit up. "Yes! Yes, of course. You may follow him. I can teach you many things about God. And I will learn from you as well."

"This will take a long time to teach me these things?" Her eyes twinkled.

He grinned. "Yes. This may take many years to teach you, many wonderful years."

"I want to dance." Moon Cloud took Allen's hand.

"Let's go dance." He smiled up at the bright moon and stars. "Hallelujah!"

ORDER INFORMATION

To order additional copies of this book, please visit
www.redemption-press.com or www.michaelwhenry.com.
Also available on Amazon.com and BarnesandNoble.com
or by calling toll-free 1-844-2REDEEM.